Box of Tricks

'A wonderful, extremely original novel that manages to be achingly funny and touchingly sad – as well as rather sinister. The atmosphere of New Brighton in the 1960s is extremely real – I know, I was there – and the characters are drawn with insight and warmth. I loved every minute'

Maureen Lee

'*Box of Tricks* is a colourful and authentic addition to the English Seaside Novel – as full of faded expectation, crushed ambition and whispering ghosts as any amusement arcade'

Robert Edric

'A gentle but sharply-observed evocation of the English seaside as it once was. In his spot-on portrayal of the crowded seaside boarding house and its inhabitants, Phelps beautifully catches the essential innocence of the time'

Gaynor Arnold

'With deceptive simplicity and skilful storytelling, Jeff Phelps takes us into the evocative world of the seaside of the early 1960s. Phelps's characters – the landlady, the lad with good intentions who turns to crime, the larger-than-life actors who are staying in the boarding house, the slightly sinister man who runs the joke shop – are always real people, their lives and motives opened up for our scrutiny with moving clarity'

Clare Morrall

Box of Tricks

Jeff Phelps

First published in July 2009
by Tindal Street Press Ltd
217 The Custard Factory, Gibb Street, Birmingham, B9 4AA
www.tindalstreet.co.uk

A CIP catalogue reference for this book is available
from the British Library

ISBN: 978 0 955647 69 7

Typeset by Country Setting, Kingsdown, Kent
Printed and bound in Great Britain by CPI Bookmarque, Croydon

Dedicated
to the memory of my parents,
Ron and Hilda,
sister Ann and brother-in-law Bob

Box of Tricks

I

The first thing we heard was laughter, then the slamming of taxi doors. So it was pretty obvious they'd finally arrived – the Rodney Cooper Light Opera Company. From inside Vi's boarding house I could tell it was like they *were* the opera, even if they weren't actually performing it at the time. You could hear the noise following them round. I wouldn't have been surprised if an orchestra had come out of the taxi with them.

My Auntie Vi, who was in the kitchen, walked down the hall when she heard them, trying to take her pinny off as she went. But somebody had already pushed the front door open and was standing in the hall singing 'Coo-ee' at the top of her voice. 'Coo-ee. Vi? Anyone at home?'

This was a pretty stupid question. Vi's boarding house was the first you came to from the seafront, so it was nearly always busy. Sometimes people just saw the Vacancies sign in the window and walked in and ended up staying. So there was nearly always someone at home at Vi's and the front door was open during the day. Now Vi was beetling down the hall and even my cousin Ray had crawled out of his pit and come to the top of the stairs rubbing his eyes. Quarter past eleven on his day off was early for him.

I stood in the hall like someone waiting to be overwhelmed by a giant wave. The Coo-ee woman had a fake fur coat and bangles that slid up and down one elegant, freckled arm when she talked. 'Oh my God, Vi, you look fantastic. What have you been doing with yourself?' She squeezed Vi and let her go again like she was a sponge.

This was hard to take because Vi was a little woman with a face tight and screwed up from years of scrubbing floors and shopping and cooking and looking after the place with only a bit of help from her mother, Nanny, and a lot of hindrance from Ray. To me she always looked the same. She still had that ingrained smell of disinfectant and spud peelings.

Then the rest of them were in the hall, filling it up. I counted five, not including Vi, and an increasing flow of luggage. It was as if they were on a stage that was too small for them, jostling for the middle in case they fell off. There were two youngish women called Maisie and Irene and, hovering near the door, a bloke with winkle-picker shoes and a pleasant face. He reached through and shook Vi's hand. 'Alastair,' he said and laughed a bit too loudly.

Charles was at the front, of course. Auntie Vi kept a framed photo of Charles on the sideboard in the kitchen. In the photo Charles was done up as Koko out of *The Mikado*. It was a real close-up of his face, which had been powdered white. His lips were dark and his eyes had been extended with slanted pencil lines. He had his hair pulled back under a little hat and wore a tunic with a Chinese collar. Handwritten in the bottom corner of the photo were the words 'To Vi with love as always' and a squiggle which was supposed to be his signature and three neat kisses, all in black ink. So I recognized Charles as soon as I saw him. Except for his hair. Now there was no hat to restrain it, it sprang up round his head like a halo, the colour of a baby orang-utan, contrasting with his bushy grey eyebrows.

Charles waited until the noise had died down before he held his arms out to Vi. She came and put her arms inside his coat which he had draped round his shoulders in a way that made me think he was just waiting for someone to take it off for him – some dresser or whatever they had in theatres. 'How are you, my Violet?' he asked in a voice as sharp as a gramophone needle.

'Glad to see you, Charles. At last. Just pleased to see you all.' She only came up to the purple handkerchief in the top pocket of his shirt.

Then Nanny bumbled out of her room, which was on the ground floor between the dining room and the kitchen. She was small, like Vi, but her shape had gone all to pot and she wore a dress of silky material so she looked like a miniature rippling waterfall. She shook everybody's hand, especially the ones she hadn't met before. 'And you are? And you are?' she said, like the Queen, to Irene and Maisie and Alastair.

The taxi drivers had been bringing the luggage in as we spoke and now the hall was full of suitcases and boxes. Nanny kept falling over them as she reached to shake hands. 'Well,' Charles said at last. 'This is wonderful,' which was meant to be a big hint. There was a silence.

'Oh. Let's show you to your rooms,' Vi said, finally understanding that they couldn't stand in the hall all day.

'My dear,' Charles said. 'Can we leave that? It'll wait, won't it? Our train was twenty minutes late. Sustenance please. We're desperate.' He made out as if he was dying of thirst, holding his throat. Brenda laughed – a bit too hard, I thought.

'Well, then, come in. My nephew Eddie will take your things up,' Vi said. 'He's staying for a while – helping out.' She meant me. I'd been standing by, waiting for this, my main duty of the day and now she was speaking as if I wasn't there.

I started to pick up the cases and bags and hat boxes. One of the young women, Maisie, looked back as if she felt sorry for me, but the rest of the Rodcoopers just trooped into the dining room. Vi went to the kitchen to make drinks. My cousin Ray was suddenly nowhere to be seen.

There was luggage everywhere, even a couple of cases in the space which Vi called the vestibule, between the front door and the glass inner door. I was about to pick them up so I could close the front door when I noticed this girl. She was standing outside, facing the road and I could tell even from the back, by the way she held her shoulders, that she didn't want to be here. She turned. She was older than me – seventeen perhaps – but her salmon pink dress and long legs gave her the look of someone at least twenty. Her dark hair was carefully flicked up in the latest style. She took off her sunglasses and looked at me as if I was a bellboy or a kitchen lackey.

'What are you staring at?' she said.

My mind emptied. Nothing I could say would be new or interesting to someone like her. 'You're Julia,' I said, suddenly making the connection.

'What if I am?'

'I'm Eddie.'

'Big deal,' she said and brushed past me into the hall with a breeze of flowery perfume. She turned and pointed to a huge, pastel green suitcase. 'That one is mine. And you can be careful with it if you don't mind.'

I struggled to lift it. 'What's in here? Crown jewels or something?' She gave me a look, raised her eyebrows in a way that implied I was beneath her contempt. 'The opera people are all in there if you want to go in,' I said, still struggling with her case.

She sighed and pulled out a compact mirror, examined herself in it and touched up her pink lipstick right there in front of me. 'I can hear their bloody racket, thank you very much.'

Then Brenda stuck her head out of the dining room.

'Oh, there you are, Julia. I was beginning to think we'd lost you. Do come in, for heaven's sake.' Julia sighed and went into the dining room without so much as a glance back. Open-mouthed, I watched her legs, her beige sling-backs disappearing.

Ray was at the top of the stairs towelling his hair dry. His hair was spiky and sharp and smelled of bedrooms even when he'd just washed it. It had an unruly tuft that stood up at the back and wouldn't be kept down no matter how much Tru-gel he used. Most of the Bartlett side of our family had it, me included. My mum was cursed with it and could never backcomb it out. On her most special evenings at the cinema or at a dinner dance it would spring from under her Twink perm when she least expected it and make her cry. The family hair-loom, Vi called it. Ha-ha.

When Vi talked about the Rodcoopers she became happy and animated, as if someone had switched a stage light on inside her face. But for Ray they were just an inconvenience – the same as the other guests, but a bigger and noisier one. 'The bloody theatricals are here, then?' he said as I got to the top of the stairs. He looked at the case I'd lugged up.

'Have you seen her?' I asked. I could tell by his eyes that he had. He'd been watching while I did all the work. He'd have stolen a look out of one of the bedroom windows.

But until then Julia must have slipped under Ray's radar. He never missed a chance with girls normally. He'd known Brenda's daughter was coming this year – Vi had talked about it and had made arrangements for their room – but he couldn't have known what she looked like, otherwise he'd have made plans and boasted about them to me. But he hadn't even mentioned Julia. He'd probably assumed she was about six years old. It was funny in a way. Here, under our own roof, was the most gorgeous girl imaginable and Ray had nearly missed her. He had a lot of ground to make up.

He flipped up the luggage tag on the pastel green case. 'Julia Vernon,' he read. 'I wonder what she's got in here. All her bits and pieces, all her underwear and bras and pants. Let's open it up and have a look.'

He started fiddling with the lock but I pushed his hand away. He wouldn't have done it, but you could never be sure with Ray. I picked the case up and struggled into the front bedroom which Julia and Brenda were to share. It was the best and biggest room in the house, with a little balcony onto the street, two beds – a double and a single – and a french window that Vi kept locked on account of the rotten woodwork.

I left the case by the door and turned. Ray was behind me, still with the towel in his hand. He rubbed his spiky hair again and smiled. 'Quite a looker,' he said. 'She's going to be a handful.'

2

The Rodcoopers settled in as if they'd never been anywhere else. By the next evening they'd practically taken over the house. If I went upstairs Brenda would be coming out of the bathroom wearing a silky kimono with huge sunflower patterns on it. There were unfamiliar umbrellas in Vi's vestibule.

In the dining room after dinner I came across Charles doing a crossword puzzle. He looked up when I went in, but didn't speak. That's how they went on, I imagined, making their home wherever they happened to be, claiming it just by being noisy and leaving their belongings about.

On my way out to the shop for Vi, I bumped into Alastair. 'I've been exploring,' he said. 'What's the night-life like here?'

'There's plenty of pubs,' I said.

'That's an understatement. There are pubs on every corner. What else?'

'Dancing, bingo, tenpin bowling, wrestling. That's just in New Brighton.' I didn't live in New Brighton but I knew it well enough and I'd heard Vi reciting the list to guests. 'There's the pier and the Floral Pavilion, lots going on at the Tower Ballroom if you like that sort of thing. The Beatles were there last year, Gerry and the Pacemakers, Rory Storm and the Hurricanes.'

'Sounds as if I'm going to enjoy myself,' Alastair said.

*

Irene and Maisie, the girls from the chorus, were sharing the big bedroom next to Ray and me, who were in the tank room. It was called that because it was behind the bathroom and next to the water tanks which gurgled and filled all night. You went up the first lot of stairs, then up two more and the bathroom was on the right with the tank room behind it. You'd hardly know there was a room there, sandwiched between the bathroom and Irene and Maisie's bedroom. Ray was used to it, of course, but I'd been staying at Vi's less than a week and was still learning to sleep through the endless drips and the locking and unlocking of doors. I could hear the girls chatting and giggling and when I looked out late that night, one of them had hung a joke notice on their door handle. 'Please disturb,' it said, with a cartoon of a girl in bed throwing back the covers. They must have bought it in one of the novelty shops that littered Vicky Road.

When I pointed it out to Ray that night he laughed. We sat on the top of the stairs. 'I hope they haven't been to the joke shop,' he said.

'Why's that?' The joke shop had once been what I liked best about New Brighton. It was tucked away in a back-street in a converted corner house with a shop window facing onto two pavements.

'It's not like it used to be, Ed. It's got a new owner. He calls himself the Great Montezuma. Something like that.'

Ray wore black jeans and a white T-shirt, thin from washing. Over them he wore a plastic jacket with cracks that showed lines of fabric underneath and baseball boots with the soles coming away from the uppers. He flicked at them with a fingertip.

'What's wrong with that?'

'He looks like Doctor bloody Crippen,' Ray said. 'I've

seen him walking round the amusements and he makes my flesh creep. Remember Ma Feeney?'

I did. She was the previous owner. Ray and me had got on all right with her.

'Well, she was his sister-in-law. Nobody's seen her since the night he knocked on her door. The day after, she just . . .' Ray clicked his fingers. 'Disappeared!'

'Blimey, Ray,' I said. I pictured the middle-aged woman sitting behind her counter.

'She was all right, Ma Feeney,' Ray said, meaning he could easily nick stuff when she was there. She'd always been too engrossed in her crossword puzzles. 'It's common knowledge what happened.'

'What?'

'He did away with her to get hold of the shop.'

'Honest?'

'Honest. Nobody's got proof, but everybody knows. Before he came here he'd been on the circuit – Sheffield, Manchester, Leeds – and after that he was on the cruise ships. Some kind of magician. They say he was good but, you know, a bit mad. Anything could happen. I bet he wasn't the sort you'd want to meet walking around a ship.'

'So he ended up here.'

'Yeah,' Ray said. 'He had to pack up the job in the end. A bloke got cut when a trick went wrong. His knives were too sharp – like bloody razors. Bad cut, too. Eighteen stitches.'

There was too much detail. 'I don't believe you,' I said.

'Please yourself.' He shrugged. 'But it's true as I'm standing here. And about Ma Feeney. Anyone'll tell you.' He slouched back on the top stair.

'Tell me what?'

'He sawed her into pieces, didn't he? Obvious. Threw her in Marine Lake. It's full of eels. Great big congers.'

I thought of Ma Feeney – her face smiling up at us over the counter – and the various, chopped up parts of her as food for eels. It was horrible.

'He's changed the name of the shop an' all,' Ray was saying. 'He calls it the Box of Tricks.'

'Box of Tricks,' I said. 'It sounds good, though. Shall we go up and see what it's like?'

'If you're brave enough,' Ray said.

'If you're brave enough to come with me,' I replied.

Ray had a job at Cadbury's biscuit factory. He'd been there three months and four days and hated every minute of it, and if it hadn't been for Vi constantly reminding him how lucky he was he'd have packed it in weeks ago – and he didn't mean the biscuits. Who else would put you on an apprenticeship and give you nine quid a week piecework? Vi wanted to know. Who else lets you buy reject biscuits by the bagful and much cheaper than you could get in the shops? But Ray only complained about how he had to get up early and how, if he missed the bus, he had a whole day's pay docked. He grumbled about the women charge-hands who kept him from his break and about how the linen hat he had to wear made his head itch.

On payday he'd come home with a packet of Munchies for Nanny, ten Embassy cigarettes for Vi and something for himself – usually an Airfix kit which he'd put together like an expert, never getting glue on the Perspex cockpit. His Spitfires and Hurricanes hung from the ceiling, gathering dust in whichever bedroom he happened to be at the time. He even bought the old-fashioned galleons with plastic sails and yards of black cotton which had to be cut up and fixed between the masts for rigging.

Apart from that he didn't buy much for himself. Money just ran through his fingers. He was a real soft touch, Vi said. He paid her some housekeeping and by the middle of the week his cash would be gone.

The next day, Saturday, was the Rodcoopers' rest day. I hadn't seen Julia again but I'd heard her going out with her mother. I was lying on the bed, flicking through a book – *Dream Dating* by Myron Bloomfield. I'd seen the advert for *Dream Dating: a Guide for the Modern Man* in *Tit-Bits* and had plucked up courage to send off for it. They promised to deliver it in a plain brown envelope so I sent off a postal order and waited. What arrived were ninety-six pages of greyish, pulpy paper with a red cover and the title in silver. It looked like a school textbook. I'd been expecting a racier read. I turned straight to the promising Chapter Eight on 'Sex' and the even more promising Chapter Nine, 'More Sex'. The diagrams looked like engineers' canal building instructions. Myron Bloomfield waxed lyrical about love. I turned back to Chapter Two – 'Rough Dater'.

Ray came in. I tried to hide the paperback, but it was too late. He snatched it out of my hand. 'What's this, Eddie? *Dream Dating*? Who are you trying to kid?' He opened it and started reading out loud – very slowly. "*An-tici-pation is the most exciting part of any new date.*" Really, Eddie? I never knew that. That's news to me, that is. I thought the most exciting part of any new date was feeling the girl up at the end of it, getting your hand inside her bra.' He threw the book across the room at me. 'You can't get it all from books. That's the trouble with you, Eddie. Just because it's written down somewhere you believe it's got to be true.' Reading had never been one of his strengths. He picked up a comb and laughed. 'Come on. Hands off cocks – on with socks. We're going out.'

'What? Now?'

'Why not? Have you got something better to do?'

I hadn't. 'What about the joke shop?' I asked.

'This is better.'

We went downstairs. 'Hang on there a sec, Eddie. Just gotta collect something.' He disappeared into the kitchen and I could hear him rearranging objects, rattling a tin. A cupboard door closed and he came back into the hall.

'Right. What we waiting for? Let's go,' he said, as if it was me who had kept him hanging around.

We went out of the back door, through the wooden yard gate and into the alley. Those sloping alleys with their drains and swill bins were secret passages only known to people who lived here. At the bottom of the alley was a long shed where Tommy Mann kept and painted his pleasure boats over winter. We turned onto the bombsite, littered with brick ends and glittering with broken glass even nineteen years after the war had finished.

Turning left would take us up to Vicky Road where the shops were – the banks and greengrocers at the town end and the cafés and arcades at the sea end where Vicky Road ran down to the pier and the buses terminated. This morning we went down the hill towards the seafront.

The summer Saturday whacked us in the face – the breeze off the river and a blast of sun. Kids clattered down towards the seafront with their buckets and spades at the ready. At the bottom we stopped at Noblett's, the corner shop. Ray had been getting his ciggies there since he was about six – first for Vi, then for himself. 'Twenty Embassy, love,' he said to the girl behind the counter. Usually he bought ten. At one time they'd even sell him a single ciggie in a white paper bag. He bundled a handful of notes and change out of his pocket and onto the counter. There was so much it filled his fist – at least three pound notes, a load of tanners and shillings – like treasure.

'Blimey, Ray,' I said when I saw it.

'It's OK. I got a bit of extra pay from work.'

'You sure?'

'Course,' he said. Outside he took the silver paper off the top of the ciggies and put the coupons in his back pocket. Vi was saving them for a new transistor for the kitchen. 'The Palace, then?' he said without looking at me.

'Yeah,' I said, but we were already on our way there as if we'd agreed on it. At the bottom of Vi's road, Marine Lake glittered like tinfoil just below the promenade, with the green-painted *Skylark* moored at one end. We walked past the little terrace of guest houses and Fairlane's, the new tenpin bowling alley. The *Royal Iris* chugged along full of holidaymakers.

Ray always said it was impossible to walk past the Palace Amusements – you had to go in. The wailing of the klaxon reminded you a ride was about to start and made you glance in, afraid you might be missing something. Then you'd see the rockets whizzing round, all coloured lights and you couldn't help yourself – you'd be inside, the whiff of doughnuts and frying onions, the floors scuffed and smelling of disinfectant, the cascade of coins rattling out of machines somewhere at the back. The next thing you knew you'd be standing by the dodgems, the attendants swinging on the backs of the cars, holding on to the poles, showered in orange sparks. By then it was too late. You were hooked and nothing about that summer day passing by outside mattered any more.

That's how it had always been with me and Ray. It made me jealous of him living here all year when I had to make do with occasional stays. Everyone knew Ray – the burger woman, Jean, who leaned over her counter, the attendants who stood round the edges of the rides in their maroon jackets with jangling keys and pockets full of change. 'All right, Raymondo?' they called out as we passed. 'How's it going?'

One of the attendants had ginger hair shaved into an

army crew cut, short on top and naked beneath. His neck looked like a piece of uncooked pork. Ray introduced us. 'You know my cousin Ed? He's staying at ours this summer – helping out, like. This is Codge.'

'Won't shake your hand,' Codge said, showing me the green-black stain of copper ingrained in his fingers. His jacket was frayed to nothing at the cuffs. There were letters tattooed pale blue across his knuckles. H-O-V-E.

Ray dug the mound of cash out of his jeans pocket and bought tickets. He unreeled them the way they measured cloth in the shops, and handed them to me. 'That should be enough to be going on with.' We went on the waltzers then had two goes on the rocket ships where Ray sat back and let me operate the handle that made the rockets rise and fall as we went round – low at first, then swooping up until I thought we were going to hit the roof girders. After that it was the ghost train – a ticket each so we could have separate cars. Holiday people wouldn't have done that. It made me feel as if I belonged here and wasn't just a visitor. I watched Ray in the car in front disappear into the darkness, but I couldn't see much after that – only the occasional cardboard gravestone, a luminous skeleton or two. There was lots of wailing, a spider that came down on a thread and at one point a jet of air in our faces. The carriages jolted to a stop and Ray was squeezing his hair back into place. 'That was good,' I said, but he just sneered and leaped out. He didn't want anyone to see him on a kids' ride like that.

We sat in the coffee bar and Ray told me about Codge, how he came every summer to work in the Palace and spent the rest of the year betting and collecting his dole. 'Does he come from Hove? Is that why he's got it tattooed on his knuckles?'

Ray laughed. 'No. He's from Bootle. He got drunk with his mates one time and they dared each other to get a tattoo. HATE was what he asked for – one letter on each knuckle. He was that drunk he didn't know what he was doing.'

'I'd have had an anchor or something,' I said.

'Yeah,' Ray said. 'Me too. Anyway the tattooing must have sobered him up. Once they started the needle he got to thinking about his mum and what she'd do to him if she saw HATE on his knuckles. She'd brought him up law-abiding and if she saw HATE she'd have beaten the living daylights out of him. So he told the woman he'd changed his mind and wanted LOVE instead. But it was too late. She'd already done the H and couldn't change it. Codge made her do the rest anyway. He'd paid for a letter on each finger and that's what he was having. That's how he got HOVE on his knuckles. Good, eh?'

I nodded. Ray spread coins on the table nonchalantly, put them in piles. 'Are you sure this is OK?' I asked. 'The money, I mean?'

'Course,' he said. 'I had a bonus from work.'

We went on the dodgems. Ray knew which were the best cars and made sure I got one, didn't even mind having a slow one himself as long as he could look cool, smoking and steering with one hand, his elbow over the side. When some smart lads bumped him he pretended not to be bothered and just jolted forward in his seat. He smiled and shook his head. But he was sure to catch them later with a good crack near the back of the car to send them spinning, facing the wrong way so they couldn't steer out.

Girls were different, of course. If they bumped him he'd treat it as if it was an accident. Then he'd follow them round with that smug smile on his face and nudge them from the back until they turned and started laughing. After that it was just a matter of hanging round until they got out of their car at the end of the ride and then saying something funny to them. Ray had met loads of girls that way.

I don't know how many rides we had. The tickets were endless. We could have ridden all day and all night if we'd wanted to. After a bit the tinny music started repeating itself. I'd heard 'Can't Buy Me Love' rattling off the ceiling at least three times, and Ray and me had worked our way up to the best two cars when suddenly Ray jumped out. He came across. 'Where you off to?' I asked.

'Bit of business to attend to. Won't be long.' He unreeled another yard of tickets and held them out to me.

'It's all right. I've got some left. Are you . . . ?' But before I could say anything else the cars were moving. I floored the pedal and jerked into the traffic. When I looked again he'd gone.

It was typical of Ray to start something and not finish, to leave with no explanation. Everyone was so used to Ray letting them down it was almost expected – the one reliable thing about him. Then I noticed a girl going round on her own. She had blond hair and drawn-on eyelashes, like a doll. She looked clear across the dodgems floor at me and smiled; something like a copper coin dropped heavy in my stomach and I was in love again. It was as simple as that. I tried to catch up with her as we went round, even took a short cut right across the floor, but she always seemed to avoid me at the last moment. I was sure I saw her laugh as she swerved away. An expert driver. Ray wouldn't have put up with this. He'd have been sharing her car, chatting to her by now, offering to teach her the best tricks, guiding her hands on the wheel. I resolved to do it. Next ride I'd walk over to her. Wanna share with me? You can steer? Few words, that's what Ray would recommend. After that, an ice cream perhaps. Juice on top?

Then the cars were losing power, as they always did in the end. I coasted to a stop. I was about to pull myself out. I was going to speak to the blond girl, was practising the words in my head when I saw something that stopped me dead. There, heading past the burger stall, was my Auntie Vi. She had her bamboo stick – the one she used to try and keep Ray in order. And she'd spotted me – half in and half out of the dodgem car.

Before I'd had chance to escape she was standing over me, whacking the air with her stick. It made an evil swishing noise. 'Where is he?' Her voice was tight as if she was struggling to keep it under control.

'Who?'

'You know who. Ray. Your ruddy cousin.' She was still wearing her pinny and slippers. She hadn't put her teeth in; her nose and chin were folding in on themselves like Popeye. The sight of her made me smile. 'Don't laugh at me.'

'I wasn't laughing,' I said. Music was coming from the other rides: 'Bits and Pieces', with that descending drum solo. But the dodgems had fallen silent and we were in the middle of the floor. I desperately pressed the foot pedal again, but there was no power. I was trapped. 'He was here a minute ago. He just went off.'

'Typical,' she said. 'That's ruddy typical.'

One of the attendants came across to see what was holding us up. 'Ticket, missus? Ride's about to start,' he said to Vi. It was Codge.

'Clear off, you,' she told him. Then she realized he probably knew Ray and she straightened herself up as far as she could and looked up at him. He was at least a foot taller than her and could have picked her up and carried her outside without breaking a sweat, but her fury was even stronger. Everyone was looking at us.

'Come on now, missus,' Codge said. 'If there's any disturbance I have to call the manager.'

'What? A big lad like you? What's the matter with you?'

'It's the rules,' Codge said.

'Well, here's another one: if you don't tell me where Ray is I'm going to stand here till closing time. How's that for a rule?'

'I don't know any Ray.'

She puckered her face and thrust it at him. 'Don't be funny. You know who I mean. Raymond Bartlett. He's a mate of yours.'

'Oh, him. I haven't seen him this morning. I've only just come on.' That was a lie as well, and all three of us knew it.

'I can check,' Vi said.

'Why, what's he done?' Codge asked.

'What's he done? The thieving little sod's only been in my telephone tin again, that's all. Took everything I've been saving for the phone bill. Nearly seven bloody quid.'

'Sod,' I said quietly, realizing where Ray's riches had come from. A bloke was hovering, waiting to get in my car.

'Are you riding?' he asked. I got out and stood next to Vi.

She turned on me. 'You're in this as well, Eddie. I suppose he was paying for you an' all.'

'I didn't know where he got the money from,' I said. 'I thought it was all right.'

'Listen, Eddie,' she said, thrusting her face up to mine. 'When it comes to Ray – nothing is ever "all right". Get it?' She swished the air with her stick. 'I'll kill him when I get my hands on him. I swear.'

Codge said, 'Sorry, missus, but if you haven't got a ticket you'll have to clear the floor. The ride's about to start.'

I thought Vi was going to lash out at him, but she stood there and folded her arms as if she wasn't going to move. There were cars all round us, full of people waiting to ride. A voice crackled across the loudspeaker. 'Clear the floor, please. Clear the floor.' Then the klaxon wailed and the voice said, a bit threatening, 'That means you, missus.'

The cars started, slowly at first then picking up speed. 'Come on, Auntie Vi,' I said, but she shrugged me off and started walking off the floor in a straight, determined line, as the dodgems rattled and sparked around her. 'Out the way, missus!' they yelled, swerving to avoid her.

'Ruddy things!' she shouted and swatted at them with her stick as they passed within inches of her slippers.

We found our way onto the steps of the dodgems. 'Sorry, Auntie Vi,' I said, but she was speechless with rage. She stalked off home, muttering about money and what she was going to do to Ray.

'Phew,' Codge said. 'Glad she's not my auntie.' I knew what he meant. But in a way I was proud of her, too, glad she was part of our family and not fighting on somebody else's side.

Then I remembered the girl with the blond hair. I looked for her but she'd gone. I couldn't blame her. Who'd want to go out with anyone whose auntie came looking for him at the dodgems wielding a stick and wearing slippers? I walked all round the amusements, then out into the blinding sun of the seafront. I thought I saw her in front of me in a crowd and I walked fast to get a look, but it wasn't her. And after a while I realized I mightn't even recognize her if I did see her again, which made me feel shallow. That's how random love was. Suddenly I had the idea that any girl could have emerged from the crowd that day and I would have loved her. The thought was like a ride on the waltzers – terrifying but at the same time dizzy and exciting.

I stayed out as long as I could, walked along the seafront to the posh end of town where we never usually went. There were detached sandstone houses where doctors and retired Liverpool businessmen lived, wide tree-lined avenues and modern blocks of flats with picture windows with views across the Mersey. But in the end there didn't seem much sense in staying out so I went back to Vi's.

*

The Rodcoopers were all either upstairs or out exploring New Brighton. There was a patch of sunlight in the hall, the heavy silence of strangers asleep in bedrooms.

Vi was in the kitchen, ironing. She stopped when I went in, looked me up and down, then returned to her iron with increased violence. I could feel her fury pressing onto the shirts and tea towels. 'I didn't know, Auntie Vi,' I said.

She stopped then, and the ironing board settled from its rattling. 'Did you think he'd suddenly come into a fortune? Is that it?'

'He said he'd had a bonus from work.'

'You're more gullible than I thought then, Eddie. God. A bonus. What did you think he'd got that for? Sleeping?' She laughed sourly. 'I wouldn't mind so much if he'd needed it, if he'd wanted to buy something useful – for his room or even for himself. Clothes or something. But no, he had to go and waste it on stupid rides at the amusements. My hard-earned cash. How pointless can you get?'

'He didn't spend it on stuff for himself, though. He could have done. He spent most of it on me,' I said, thinking it might make her feel better.

'Only to make himself feel good, the bloody fool. I know him, don't forget, Eddie – fancying himself like bloody Robin Hood, stealing off the rich to give to the poor. Only I'm not rich, am I?' She started ironing furiously again. Eventually she looked up, as if she expected me to have moved. 'Go and do something useful, Eddie, will you? You're starting to annoy me.'

There was no getting round Vi. She kept her fury bubbling along like a pot of stew and topped it up with whatever grievance came to hand. She knew Ray would turn up eventually and until he did she kept the lid on that pan and only let a little steam out at a time. Nanny didn't help. She had an unswerving knack of raising difficult subjects.

'Where is he tonight?' she asked Vi later while we were serving dinner. Vi swept past carrying plates of salad.

'Who?'

'Steven . . .' she tried. Vi looked puzzled. Steven was Vi's younger brother. Nanny hadn't seen him since he'd emigrated to America fourteen years earlier in 1950.

When Nanny wasn't taking her tablets she had trouble with names and objects. Sometimes she got really easy things mixed up like 'shoes' and 'carrots'. Ray teased her about it and would bring whatever she'd asked for even if he knew it was wrong. He liked the idea that one day she might put her best brogues in the oven or go to the shops wearing a bunch of carrots on her feet, but it only made her angry and frustrated with him. At least with names she had a kind of method, which was to work through the generations until she got to the right person. 'I mean *Eddie* . . .' she tried again, but Vi had gone to attend to the guests.

'I'm here,' I reminded her. 'It's me – Eddie.' Ray and me had some similarities – our hair, for instance, except mine wasn't as long as Ray's and I let it flop at the front to hide a rash of acne that wouldn't clear. Ray was taller than me, too, and bonier with a thin face.

'Ray,' she said finally, realizing she'd alighted on the right name. 'Where's Ray?'

Vi was on her way back through with another three plates. 'Ray's out.'

Nanny blundered on. 'Didn't he say where he was going?'

'No.'

'He's in trouble again, then?'

'Yes, Mother,' Vi snapped.

'What's he done this time?'

'He's been in the phone tin again, that's all. He and Eddie here decided they'd take themselves off to the fair on the proceeds of my phone tin.'

'But I didn't know,' I reminded her.

Nanny looked over her glasses at me. 'He's a bad influence, that Ray. Don't let him take you in, Eddie.' But it wasn't as simple as that. He was generous even if it was with someone else's money. He lived here and would let me chat with his mates as if I was one of them. He'd introduce me to real characters – people you'd never dare talk to if you were just visiting. Ray would take me to places that holiday people never went.

'When'll he get back?' Nanny wanted to know.

'We don't know,' Vi said. Her eye strayed to the bamboo stick, which had found its way back to the side of the fireplace. 'But just wait till he does. I'll give him such a . . .'

I did most of the washing-up on my own, including scraping over-boiled spuds out of the bottom of Vi's saucepans. Partly it was to pay Vi back for the money we'd wasted, and partly to keep out of her way.

After that the three of us sat in the kitchen. There was a wonky old settee and a table squeezed under the window so two could eat as long as nobody else wanted to get past. There was the sideboard with Charles's photo on it, Vi's chair and a twelve-inch black and white telly in a cabinet with doors. Above the settee was an aircr on pulleys that Vi was always hoisting up and down so the clothes landed on your head. It was pretty crowded in there. Not much room for people.

Nanny sat at the table and pulled out a battered presentation box. 'What do you think to these?' she asked, and tipped out a load of tarnished soup spoons with elaborate, decorated ends.

Vi glared at them. 'Where did they come from?'

'I went to the salerooms yesterday. I told you.' Along with the wrestling, the salerooms were Nanny's main weakness.

'God,' Vi said. 'If it's not Ray it's you. You're as bad as each other for wasting money.'

'This is not wasting money, Violet. We can use these – and I didn't steal to buy them, so there aren't any similarities at all.'

'Only that, as usual, I don't have any say in the matter. Only that I'm the one doing all the work round here, but I'm the last to know what's going on. Anyway, they're far too posh for us.' Vi counted through the spoons. 'Mother, there's only eleven. It's not even a full set.'

'What does that matter? They're from the Victoria Hotel,' Nanny said proudly. The Victoria had been full of notable people such as captains and pilots and ships' surgeons. In the old days they used to sit on the terrace bar, sip gin and tonic and look across to where the Mersey opened out and became the Irish Sea. Out there, beyond Ireland, it eventually became the Atlantic and there was nothing except cold, green water all the way to America. In those days the ships would be queuing up on the horizon as far as the eye could see – yachts and tankers and liners waiting to get into Liverpool, and closer in the dredgers keeping the channels clear and the tugs on their way back to port. It was all changing, Nanny said. People didn't want grand hotels these days. They were starting to go abroad, or taking day trips further afield in their new cars. It was the way of the world.

'And look,' Vi said, 'they've still got the initials on the handle. What use are they to us with VH all over them?'

'VH,' I said. 'It could be Vi's Hotel, couldn't it? No one would know.'

Nanny laughed and clicked the spoons back into place in the box. 'Good idea, Eddie. Vi's Hotel. Yes.'

'Don't encourage her, Eddie,' Vi said. I knew Nanny would sneak them into the drawer in the dining room when she thought Vi wasn't looking and that Vi would come across them in the washing-up. 'Vi's Hotel indeed,' she'd probably say as she rubbed them dry with the tea towel. Then she'd drop them in the kitchen drawer, making sure they were pushed behind the spud peelers.

After that, Nanny went to bed. Vi lit another ciggie and sighed. I could imagine what she was thinking about – all her phone money stolen, Ray disappearing without a word to God-knew-where and Nanny buying things we could do without. Vi turned the telly on and sat in her chair next to the fire. 'I'll just stay up and watch this for a bit,' she muttered. But I knew she was waiting for Ray to come back. In her own funny way she loved him; she just wanted him to be around more, and to be good occasionally.

I'd no idea what time she usually went to bed. I only knew it was after me and that often she didn't even bother going upstairs, but slept in her knackered-up armchair next to the Baxi, which was where she sat now with the bamboo stick propped in its usual corner so that, whatever time Ray got in, she could just lean forward, reach for it and lash out.

3

'About time,' Vi said when I appeared in the kitchen next morning. 'You can help serve the breakfasts if you want.' I'd been woken by the smell of frying bacon and the sound of a bucket being swilled in the yard below. Ray's bed hadn't been slept in.

Vi carefully didn't mention Ray, but she had on the same crossover pinny as the previous evening and a weary look about her, so I was sure she'd been in the chair all night, hoping to catch him sneaking home in the early hours. It was a battle of wills between two people who knew one another too well. Ray would be judging it – either to come back when Vi wasn't there or to wait until she'd gone past anger and would be relieved to see him. And Vi would be pacing herself, trying not to waste all her fury before she could vent it on him, trying to keep it stoked like the Baxi banked up for the night.

I took trays of bacon, sausages and fried bread to the Rodcoopers and the other guests, a family from Darlington. A nice young couple, Nanny said they were, with a pretty girl of about three. That was the problem with having the Rodcoopers for the whole season: it only left one room out of the six in the house for the ordinary holidaymakers. It was a pity because the ordinary holidaymakers weren't as demanding; they paid their rent up front and were easily pleased. They only came here to be happy, so they cheerfully put up with the rush for the bathroom in the morning and the odd blocked pepper pot.

The dining room smelled of warm HP sauce whatever time of day it was. I carried the breakfasts in, trying to remember who wanted what, and every time hoping to find Julia sitting next to her mother. Her place was set but she didn't show up. Charles, the star of *The Mikado*, was there, though. He'd already been out to buy his Sunday paper and seemed to be disembowelling it, spreading the pages across the table. I tried to find room for a rack of toast and he licked his fingers and moved the pages around. 'Curses!' he said loudly, getting greasy marks on the paper. He looked at the others over his little frameless glasses and raised his grey eyebrows in a way that gave him the look of a kid who had just been told off.

In between trips to the kitchen I told Vi about it. 'He's a real gent,' she said, sliding another piece of bread into the frying pan. 'He makes time for a morning stroll whatever the weather and he fetches his own paper – won't have it delivered. That's one of the things he likes about being here, he says – it's very clean and select and people don't stare.'

The real reason they didn't stare, I thought, was because people here didn't know him from Adam. They preferred to keep an eye out for pop singers or wrestlers in between bouts at the Tower. Besides, there were lots of strange people roaming the streets, from gypsies to donkey men and Irish navvies. But Vi would never have let me say Charles was ordinary. She liked to remind us how he'd studied in Milan under somebody with an Italian name, and had performed in theatres and opera houses all across Europe. Now his speciality was as a Gilbert and Sullivan patter baritone. Charles was even featured on LPs, which you could still buy in the record department at Lewis's.

But all the time that I was carrying plates I couldn't stop

thinking about Julia. I found myself looking out at the weather and wondering what she might wear on a day like this. In the end I asked her mother, trying to make it sound casual, 'Will your daughter be coming down to breakfast this morning?'

'Julia? Ha! She'll emerge at some time, no doubt – like a butterfly out of a chrysalis.'

'Should I leave her place setting?'

She looked at me carefully – a bit suspicious, I thought. 'No, you can take it away. She doesn't usually bother. There won't be time anyway – we've got to be out to the dress rehearsal in an hour.'

'Oh?'

'*The Pirates*,' Brenda said. 'Our season starts tomorrow – five and a half weeks of non-stop entertainment.'

I knew about *The Pirates of Penzance*. Vi never shut up about Gilbert and Sullivan and which operetta the Rodcoopers were going to do next and who would take which part and whether anyone could possibly be better than Charles. But my mind was on Julia. 'What pirates?'

She looked at me, shocked. 'Of Penzance, of course. What did you think I meant?'

'I was thinking about films. Captain Kidd and Bluebeard and –'

She interrupted me. 'There *are* no other pirates.'

'*I am the very model of a modern Major-General*,' Charles began singing from behind his paper, so quietly he could hardly be heard at first. Then he got louder and faster. '*I've information vegetable, animal and mineral, I know the kings of England, and I quote the fights historical from Marathon to Waterloo, in order categorical . . .*'

He moved his mouth, quick and careful, like jumping between stones so each word was clear. I couldn't say I understood them all, but anyone could tell by the way he sang them they were meant to be funny.

'Thank you, Charles,' Brenda said when he finally came to the end.

'I hate *The Pirates*,' Charles said mock-tragically. '*The Mikado*'s the one – such dignity and sadness.'

Vi liked to tell us that his voice was like a glass of vintage port, but it reminded me more of someone practising a tongue-twister, getting faster and faster and still not falling apart.

Then the two girls from the chorus, Maisie and Irene, broke into another song just for the sake of it. I didn't know which way to look, but I could see it was exciting to have people clapping every time you opened your mouth, as the couple from Darlington did now. They'd been quietly eating their toast in the corner. 'Bravo!' the nice young man cried, and clapped some more, and Maisie and Irene bowed in their seats and giggled.

I couldn't really understand why the Rodcoopers needed a dress rehearsal. They must have known everything already. Vi said that of course they would have practised before they got here, but they still had to know how to make their grand entrances in full costume and not trip over one another. I wondered how Julia fitted into all this, and my heart broke again just thinking about her – how she was older than me, worldly-wise and beautiful. Would I ever have the nerve to speak to someone like her, whose life of theatre and drama was so different from mine?

After breakfast my mum phoned from Grandad's house in Aberdeen where they were staying. Grandad had been getting steadily worse at answering his phone and when Dad asked him about how he was managing for food he gave evasive answers. After he hadn't answered his phone for two days Mum and Dad decided they ought to go and find out for themselves. They'd dropped me off at Vi's on their way up there.

Mum spoke to Vi for a while. 'It's OK,' I heard Vi saying. 'No, Eddie's fine.' Then she came and found me.

Vi kept the phone in a cupboard under the stairs as if she was afraid of it – like a mad dog or something. It was black and heavy and lived with the coats and the vacuum cleaner and shelves of dried peas and tinned peaches and bags of rags and polish. There were even holes in the door so it could breathe. Mum's voice sounded distant. She asked how I was doing. 'I'm fine,' I told her, which was the truth, because I'd rather have been here with Vi and Ray and all that was going on than in Scotland where I didn't know a soul. I'd only visited three times and I'd been bored and lonely. A weekend there seemed like a lifetime. 'How's Grandad?'

'Not so good. We think he might need to be looked after. He's not coping at all well these days.'

'Why not?' Grandad was Dad's father. He lived on his own in a place like a haunted house out of a Hammer Horror film.

'It turns out he'd fallen – and not for the first time. He hadn't told anyone and he hadn't been to the doctor. The house is a mess, Ed. He's such a stubborn old devil. We had no idea he was this bad.'

'I'm sorry,' I said. At least Grandad sent me birthday cards. And there was always a ten-bob note inside except when my mum forgot to remind him.

'That's what comes of living so far away, I suppose,' Mum said, dropping her voice to a whisper as if Grandad might be listening in. 'Luckily he hasn't broken any bones, but we think there might be something critically wrong with him. He's having tests done tomorrow.'

'Oh.' I must have sounded concerned.

'Don't get worrying about us, though. We're all right.'

I told her I wasn't worrying.

'Good. I've been trying to clean this place up all week.

It looked as though no one had touched it in months and it smelled like a stray cats' home. I thought there was meant to be a home help, but if there is she hadn't had her duster out.'

Mum said that was enough about them. What had I been up to? So I told her the bits that might make her laugh – about Charles and how he liked to be the centre of attention, and Maisie and Irene and the way they'd broken into song at the drop of a hat. I never mentioned the stolen phone money and being tangled up with Ray. I just hoped Vi wouldn't either.

'Don't be a nuisance there now, Ed, will you?' I told her I wouldn't. 'And do try to be useful.'

'All right.'

She told me she loved me, which surprised me so much I didn't know what to say in reply. Even when she'd left me at school for the first time she'd never told me that. I think she must have been feeling guilty now, as if she shouldn't have left me at Vi's.

Guests were the only people who knocked on the kitchen door. It was the boundary between their part of the house and our cramped, untidy quarters. Normally Vi would shout, 'Come in!' and a guest would stick their head round and say something like, 'Can I settle up with you, Vi, love?' or 'Have you got any, ahem, toilet paper for the little bathroom, please?' Vi liked to put those toilet rolls with a joke on every sheet in the bathrooms. They had slogans printed on them: 'Don't sit here and dream all day – £25,000 might come your way' or 'Psychiatrist has a silent P' with a picture of a weedy man standing up to his waist in water. She thought they'd cheer the guests up.

This time it was Charles. 'I wonder . . . can I have a word, Vi?'

'Come in, Charles,' she said. 'Sit down. Would you care for a cup of tea?' She wanted to make him feel like one of the family, not a guest. But as usual there was nowhere to sit. There were piles of ironing on every surface.

'Can't stay,' he said. 'I have a little paperwork to catch up with, then I'm off to the dress rehearsal. The others have gone already.' He prowled around, as if he was waiting for his cue.

'So,' Vi said, 'if you don't want a cup of tea . . .'

'Oh, yes. Thank you. It's about the room.'

'Oh?' Vi could see trouble coming. 'Is there something wrong with it?'

'No,' he said, 'of course not. The room's fine – tidy and clean as we've always come to expect, and the food's wonderful. The hospitality and the welcome are second to none.'

'Well, then?' Vi said.

'I'm sorry. I've become used to my little comforts, my indulgences. I'm old and spoiled and these days . . . a touch of angina. I have tablets.'

'Something you need?'

'Something – I could do without. Another person to be exact – in my bedroom.'

'Oh, you mean Alastair.'

'Well, yes. In past years you've always given me private accommodation and I thought it would be the same this year. Is there any reason? You didn't mention it, so I assumed arrangements as usual.'

'I thought it would be all right,' Vi said. 'Alastair's an addition to your party and it's his first year so I put him in with you. I didn't have anywhere else. I'm sorry, Charles.'

'I'm not sure that room is large enough for the two of us. We are practically tumbling over one another as we climb into our beds, and Alastair is – well, so energetic.' He smiled again. 'In fact, he's so wretchedly young and enthusiastic it makes me sick. Sometimes I think he'd be more suited to the variety stage. He insists on practising his songs and lines in front of the mirror – and in front of the mirror is, as you know, Violet, my rightful place.'

She laughed as if she wasn't sure whether he was trying to be funny.

'Last night he didn't turn in till about two o'clock in the morning. Goodness knows where he'd been. Talking with the girls downstairs, I think. Even then he was reading his newspaper in bed and laughing at the cartoons. It's been three nights now and I've hardly caught a wink. I need my beauty sleep, Violet.'

Charles was behaving as if he was on stage. He glanced around and talked in a pantomime whisper – as if he was making sure no one else could hear. Normally, of course, the whole audience would have been listening, but this morning it was only Vi and me, so we felt kind of privileged. 'I really am finding it difficult,' he whispered. 'I've borne it for three nights, but with the show starting tomorrow – well, Alastair's a grand fellow, but I don't know him too well and he needs his privacy. As a matter of fact, I need mine, too. I'm afraid I find myself becoming less tolerant as I grow older. I appear to have developed the habit of solitude.'

'Well, I don't know, I'm sure,' Vi said. 'We might be able to rearrange the accommodation. We could ask Alastair to move, I suppose.'

'No, no,' he insisted. 'That would be terrible. It's not fair on the boy. I'll move.'

'It'll be rather difficult, but let me see what I can do,' Vi said.

'I do hope you can,' Charles said. 'I hate to mention it, but if this were to affect my performance I . . .' He kind of stumbled over the words. He frowned as if he'd forgotten his lines. 'Well, I don't know what I'd do. I might have to ask Mrs Morris next door but one. I'm sure she'd put me up – I notice she's got a couple of vacancies.' I remembered he'd already been up to Vicky Road that morning to get his paper, so he'd probably checked the situation on his way past. The cunning old beggar.

'Oh, no,' Vi said in her poshest voice. 'That won't be necessary. We'll find some contingency.' She said 'contingency' the same way she said 'vestibule', like there was a stone in the middle of the word. And, of course, Charles was the main man – the show revolved around him. If he went the rest of the Rodcoopers would probably go with him and they might never come back.

'Thank you, Violet,' Charles said. 'I knew you'd understand.' He lifted his eyebrows, tilted his head to one side and put on a stupid grin without showing his teeth. I recognized it straight away from the photo on Vi's sideboard – that *Mikado* smile.

'Right,' Vi said as soon as Charles had gone. 'Let's get cracking.' There was nothing for it. We couldn't expect the guests to move so, as usual, we had to make the sacrifices ourselves. Ray and me were to go into the little bedroom at the top of the house, Vi and Nanny would have to share the tank room. Charles would get Nanny's old room on the ground floor. After the big front bedroom it was the best in the house. It was wide and light, had its own fireplace, a bell push that was once connected to the kitchen and a sealed-up french window onto the back yard with a view of the mangle and Ray's bike under a tarpaulin.

Nanny came bumbling out as we started shifting furniture and bedding. 'Are we on the move again? Can I help?'

'We'll do you in a minute, Mother,' Vi said. 'You and me are going in the tank room.'

'That'll be cosy,' she called from the bottom of the stairs.

'While we've got everything cleared you can do some dusting, Eddie, if you don't mind. Give the furniture a wipe-over.'

Piles of bedsheets appeared on the landings, drawers full of clothes moved from one room to another, clouds of dust spiralled above the stairs. The cupboard was emptied of Ray's old comics. 'I could do without all this,' Vi grumbled. 'I'll have to vacuum again. And there's the dinner to see to an' all.'

In the middle of the chaos Ray decided to come home. He'd probably been hoping to slip into the house without anyone noticing, and normally about this time he'd have got away with it because Vi would have been safely upstairs making the beds. He came through the back door while I was searching for a bucket under the sink, then stood there looking pleased with himself, but confused at the same time. 'Where did you get to?' I asked him.

'Just here and there.'

'Man, are you in trouble. She knows you took the money out of her phone tin.'

He shrugged. 'Tell me something I don't know.' So I told him about how Vi had spent the whole night in the chair so as to be able to grab the stick when he finally showed up. He shrugged as if he wasn't bothered, but he did go a bit thoughtful and quiet. Then he asked why everyone was moving around and I told him about how him and me were moving into the top room. Then I told him Nanny was moving out of her room so that Charles could move in. That's when he went mad.

He wasn't being selfish. He really looked out for Nanny. It was Ray who went with her to the salerooms or took her to the wrestling. It was Ray who put a bulb in her bedside lamp and popped up to the chemist for a prescription. He'd even buy embarrassing things for her, like stockings and Steradent. He started shouting, 'For God's sake, for God's sake. Why can't they just leave things alone?' Then he was slamming around in the back kitchen and kicking the wall. A saucepan I'd put on the floor went skittling in the air. 'Bloody nerve. Bloody Charles. Bloody . . . Every year they're the same – acting like they own the place, wanting this, wanting that, taking the bloody house over. God almighty!'

Nanny came shuffling in, looking for something. She was wearing her slippers and one of her best hats. 'Oh,' she said, as if it was the most normal thing in the world. 'Ray's back.' She shouted up to Vi, who was somewhere at the top of the house. 'Vi – Ray's back.'

We heard Vi coming down the stairs. It sounded as if she was taking them two at a time. Ray was panicking, looking round for the bamboo – hoping to get to it first. It wasn't by the fire where she usually kept it, so he started looking behind the settee, under the table. Everywhere.

But Vi came through the door like one of those samurai warriors and the bamboo was already in her hand because she'd had it with her all the time. Now she finally had the chance to use it and she didn't care who got in the way. Nanny and me were dodging, trying to keep clear of its ugly swish. Ray was trying to get behind the settee and Vi was shouting, 'You might be seventeen, Ray, but you're not too old for the stick.'

I wasn't sure she had it right because he was a good foot taller than her and pretty quick on his feet despite the smoking. It was only her being angry that gave her any advantage at all. 'You stole off me – then wasted it on fags and stupid rides at the fair. We needed that money for the phone, but no, you couldn't leave it alone, could you?' With every word she made a swipe at him. 'You're a lying . . . cheating . . . thieving . . . little bugger.' Ray covered his head and she whacked him on the legs. Then when he tried to protect his legs she went for his head. She was merciless, Vi.

In the end he grabbed the stick in his open hand. It must have hurt, because there was a splitting sound as it made contact with flesh. Ray gasped and muttered, 'Ouch, Mum!' But he'd managed to grab it. Then they were both twisting their ends, trying to wrestle the stick out of one another's hands.

Suddenly it was as if Ray remembered the reason he'd got so steamed up in the first place because his face went tight, and hers went like Popeye's again, and I could hear the bamboo splitting and splintering as they twisted it in different directions, but neither of them would let it go. Ray started on again. 'So tell me why the hell Nanny has to move out of her room? You know it suits her there, Mother. She's on the ground floor where she needs to be. Bloody Charles could have stayed where he was. They aren't the only people in this house, you know. I bloody hate them.'

'It's business, Ray,' shouted Vi. 'I wouldn't expect you to understand about business. You're too busy gallivanting about, wasting my money.'

'At least I wouldn't chuck my own mother out of her room.'

'How dare you! How dare you!'

Vi was nearly screaming and now Nanny was trying to get in between them. 'Stop it. Stop fighting, you two. Stop this minute!'

But Ray hadn't finished. 'Don't you think you ought to have asked her first?' He was dead fierce about it, looked Vi straight in the eyes across that useless bamboo.

'It isn't a case of asking, Ray. We all have to make sacrifices in this house sometimes. I wouldn't expect you to know about that either,' Vi shouted.

Nanny said, 'I don't mind, love. I'm used to it. It was the same during the air raids – every night out to the shelters.'

'The bloody war finished nearly twenty years ago, Nan,' Ray said.

'I know that. I only meant we had to make do with what we had. Not like now. Everything comes too easy now.'

She said it in such a sad way that Ray and Vi stopped twisting the stick and looked at her. She'd said it as if she missed the hard times, and maybe she did. She was always talking about how in the war everyone knew who they were fighting, except for spies. Now it could be anybody – the Russians, the sneaky politicians, the Cubans, even the police.

'Bloody hell,' Vi said, and she was nearly crying in frustration because this was one argument she didn't want to lose. She'd been thinking about it for twenty-four hours and now she could see it slipping away. It was because she loved Ray, I suppose, because he was all she had.

Ray reached across and patted her arm. 'Sorry, Mum,' he said. 'I love you. Honest.'

She never wanted to, but she forgave him every time. 'Look what you've done to my stick, Ray. It's all split and buggered. What am I going to do with you? I mean – I've tried everything with you. What am I going to do?'

'I dunno, Mum,' Ray said. 'I'll make it up to you.'

'You'll have to give me that money back out of your wages. I know how much you've had. I want half this week and the rest next.'

It was lucky Ray was still holding onto his end of the stick, because the next thing he said was, 'I might not be able to pay you back this week, Mum.'

'Why not?'

'Cos I've finished at the biscuit factory.'

Vi looked stunned. 'Finished? What do you mean? They sacked you?'

'Well, I didn't go in today, did I? They wanted me to work.'

'You can still phone in. Tell 'em you're sick. It's only a day.'

He shrugged. 'It's not the first time, though, Mum. I already tried phoning but they didn't believe me. They said it's happened once too often. So I told 'em where they could shove their job.'

'What?'

'You know I'm not cut out for that sort of work. It's the early mornings.'

'What sort of work are you cut out for, Ray? Tell me that.'

It was about to start all over again – Ray holding the bamboo stick with Vi trying to twist it out of his hand at the other end and Nanny trying to part them – when Charles put his head round the kitchen door for the second time. He'd probably been knocking, but with all the shouting nobody had heard him. He looked different again – shiny and enthusiastic. The light shone through his orang-utan halo. Ray and Vi stopped. They stared at him. 'Oh,' Charles said. 'So sorry. Have I got you at a bad moment?'

'No,' Vi said. 'We were just . . . discussing something.'

'Of course. Well, I'm off to dress rehearsal. Wish me luck.' So Nanny and Vi wished him luck. 'Big day,' Charles said. 'I just wanted to drop these in for you. Sorry to disturb . . .' Charles was embarrassed, but not half as much as Vi. He closed the door behind him, quick, before any of us could say anything.

Nanny was the first to recover. She toddled over to the sideboard and picked up what he'd left. She turned to us and her eyes were bright behind her ivory-coloured glasses. 'Four comp tickets to *The Pirates*,' she said.

Ray sighed. 'Bloody hell, Nan. I thought you were on my side. Is that all it takes to buy you off – four free tickets to a poxy show?'

Nanny thought for a moment, then she smiled. 'Two would have done it.'

*

Ray and me carried our stuff into the top room then finished helping Nanny. Ray wouldn't let her do anything even though she wanted to. 'Sit there,' he told her. 'You're too old.'

'I am not,' she said. 'This is typical of you, Ray. The work's already done and here you are at the last minute wanting all the glory.'

He laughed at her because he knew she couldn't resist him laughing. He picked a bundle of clothes off her bed. 'Sit there anyway till we've moved the heavy stuff.'

Ray and me took it in turns to carry her skirts, dresses and hats upstairs and pile them into the tiny wardrobe in the tank room. The rail sagged under their weight. The clothes smelled of mothballs. All the time Ray was grumbling about Charles and the rest of the Rodcoopers. He never talked about the normal holidaymakers like that. He accepted them and didn't mind their comings and goings, but something about the Rodcoopers upset him.

I said, 'They're only trying to make a living. What's the problem? They'll be gone by the end of the summer. Everything'll be back to normal then.'

'They're bloody highly strung – like a load of kids. And the old lady spoils them. What most of them need is a good smack round the head.'

'She likes them being here,' I said, 'and they bring in the money. They're reliable.'

'She lets them bully her. She always does it.' Ray's arms were full of ratty old furs from the salerooms and battered hats with no shape. His Airfix planes were still hanging from the ceiling – the last things to be moved. He stood on the bed and started taking them down carefully. 'Then she goes on at me. It's not fair.'

'Are you jealous of them or something?'

'Don't be stupid,' he said. 'What have I got to be jealous of? I'm going to be out most of the time anyway, so it won't bother me.'

'Do you think you'll be able to get another job?'

'Christ, don't you start. You're getting as bad as the old lady. As a matter of fact, they'd have me at the Palace Amusements any time. I practically work there already, so they might as well pay me. There's nothing I don't know about those machines and rides.' He had a point. That was probably at the back of his mind when he'd packed up his job at Cadbury's. 'I'll go and have a look later,' he said. 'I expect they can start me tomorrow. Someone's got to bring money into the house, haven't they?'

I wondered if he was trying to be funny, but there wasn't a trace of a smile on his face. He sneezed and dumped the clothes on the bed. 'Your turn,' he said. 'Go and get the next lot. I need a rest.'

Halfway down the stairs I met Nanny coming up. She was carrying an old Family Assortment biscuit tin. I stopped to let her past. 'What you got in there, Nan? Your life savings?'

'You don't think I'd keep money in the house with that Ray around, do you?'

I was shocked to hear her say that. 'He wouldn't take anything of yours, would he?'

'Why not?'

'He – just wouldn't, that's all.' I was going to say because he loved her, but it would have sounded sentimental and girly. Besides, he loved Vi but it didn't stop him helping himself to her phone money.

We took the last of Nan's clothes up to the tank room. She was sitting on one of the beds surrounded by coats. The other bed, which Vi would probably never get to use, was piled high as well. 'All right now, Nan?' Ray asked.

'Course. I stayed in worse places than this in the war. I'll manage.'

The biscuit tin was open. There was all sorts of junk in there – old photos, airmail letters, recipes and patterns with torn edges. She picked out a framed photo and put it on the bedside table.

'That's New Jersey,' she explained. I already knew. The photo showed three people in front of a bright green hedge, squinting at the camera – our Uncle Steve, his wife Marion and their son. 'Seven last autumn,' Nanny said. 'My own grandson and I've never set eyes on him. That's terrible.' It was, when you thought about it.

Even when he was young our Uncle Steve had the travelling bug. It was a family story how, before the war, he'd cycle off for days on end around north Wales – sometimes with a friend or two, but often alone. His sisters, Vi and my mum, never went. They'd stay at home and wonder how someone with such a taste for adventure could have been born into our family. It must have been a throwback, my mum said. It was to do with the sea. She'd always go on about how Steve camped out on the quiet hills in the days when those roads only had bikes and the occasional tractor on them and how on warm nights, he'd just sleep under a hedge or in an empty barn like a gypsy or something. She liked to add a bit of spicy detail to his adventures because he was a kind of hero in our family.

Three of Steve's war years were spent in the Desert Rats and he'd been mentioned in despatches by Montgomery for helping to capture a tank near El Alamein. Then, after he got demobbed in 1947, he was sorting out his belongings at home when he came across an old wallet he'd bought in Morocco. He emptied the corners of the wallet onto the kitchen table, hoping he might find the last of his army back pay. All that came out was a little mountain of greyish sand. He looked at it for ages and didn't say anything. But he wouldn't let anyone touch it. It reminded him of the desert, he said, and of his pals who hadn't made it home. In the end my mum put the sand in an envelope for him. It was probably still in the bottom of the sideboard even now.

Steve couldn't settle after the war. Vi said it happened to a lot of the armed forces. Something had changed in them. England was too ordinary after the excitement and companionship he'd known in Africa. After all those years spent yearning for home, England was a disappointment. I thought about Steve a lot, even though I didn't remember him because he left for America when I was two. Mum and Dad had moved to Derbyshire by then, where we'd lived ever since. I imagined I knew what it was like to have itchy feet, to always want to be somewhere else.

None of that explained why he chose New Jersey, though. 'There's opportunity there,' Vi said as if she was trying to make excuses for him. 'He was always impulsive.' One day he decided to emigrate and nothing anyone could say could make him change his mind. He went over on the *Queen Mary* – Liverpool to New York – to find his fortune.

'They call the boy Gary,' Nanny said. 'Can you imagine that? Like Gary Cooper. A real American kid – goes to school there and everything.'

'Fancy that,' Ray said. 'Do they have schools in America?'

In the photo Uncle Steve was wearing a short-sleeved shirt in blue and white checks. He looked happy. He'd just taken off a pair of sunglasses, which you could see in his right hand down by his side. His hair, which was sparse and almost white-blond, was swept back off his forehead so you could see his scalp through it.

Steve was the youngest of Nanny's children. My mum was the oldest, then came Vi, then Steve. So he was the favourite – in some ways the most painful for Nanny to lose.

It was strange to think he'd been here in this house after I was born but that I'd never met him properly and probably never would. In the photo his left arm rested easily on Marion's shoulder. She wore pink slacks, which Nanny didn't approve of. From this one detail Nanny had decided that at best Marion had no sense of the meaning of money and that at worst she was a bad housekeeper. But she looked perfect to me. I liked her cock-eyed smile and the way she put one foot slightly forward. It showed the shape of her hip, which provided a little harbour for the boy.

I asked if I could look at the other photos, but she wouldn't let me root around in her precious tin. She picked a selection and passed them across.

They smelled exotic, those photos – of buttermilk, I thought, which I'd read about in the American comics. There was something missing, though. After a while I realized what it was: the way Nanny talked I'd expected the photos to be of fields and gigantic trees and meadows. That's what it sounded like – New Jersey, fresh and milky. But they weren't. They were ordinary. They had ordinary backgrounds – gardens or scrubby parks. The houses were bigger – with overhanging eaves – and the colours were brighter, but apart from that it could have been anywhere. It could have been some suburb of Liverpool for all I knew. 'Why'd he go?' I asked.

Nanny sighed. 'He was bored. He was going to seek his fortune. It was the land of opportunity. That's what they used to say. Now he's married and they've got a son I haven't seen – not when he was born and not when he went to school for the first time or got christened or had Christmas or Thanksgiving or whatever it is they have over there.'

Ray said, 'Nan, you know you've been invited. Marion asked you last Christmas. She's always writing and asking you.'

'Yes, but I don't think she means it. She might be asking because she knows I'll never come.'

'Don't be daft, Nan,' Ray said. 'She likes you. She sends recipes.'

'We couldn't afford a trip like that, anyway. It'd cost hundreds.'

'If you're that bothered,' I said, 'why don't *you* emigrate?'

'They wouldn't have me. They check your teeth and if you haven't got your own they send you back.' Ray and me looked at one other and Ray shook his head. I handed the photos back and she put them carefully in the tin and closed the lid. 'Now clear off, the both of you. I'll finish the rest of the sorting out myself.'

The couple from Darlington came in as Ray and me went downstairs. They looked ruddy from the sun and wind. 'Busy day?' the man asked cheerfully. He'd seen the piles of sheets and furniture.

'You can say that again,' Ray told him and winked at me.

'We've just popped back for a rest,' the mother said, looking embarrassed.

'We popped back,' the little girl echoed. 'I've got a bucket.'

'Show us,' Ray said and she held it up for him. 'That's good, that is. You can keep crabs and things in that.'

'I've got a goldfish at home,' she said sadly.

After that I sat in the kitchen and read one of Ray's *Mad* magazines. I didn't understand half of it. I'd never heard of pizza pie and summer camp, but I liked the drawings and specially the adverts. If you lived in America you could send off for stuff: X-ray glasses that let you see a woman's underwear as she walked past, Tootsie rolls – toffee with chocolate in the middle – and Daisy guns that fired real pellets. You could even buy a device that let you throw your voice so people would think it was coming from inside a suitcase which a bloke was carrying on his back. There was a cartoon showing the man with a big question mark hanging over his head because he couldn't understand how someone could have got trapped inside the trunk. All you needed were dollars, which of course we didn't have. Dollars might as well have been gold. No wonder Steve had wanted to go to America.

I heard Ray go back into Charles's room to finish something off, then he made Nanny a cup of tea and carried it up with two Marie biscuits in the saucer. He must have sat talking to her for about half an hour because it went quiet after that. In the end he came back through the kitchen with the empty cup and washed it out, chuckling to himself and shaking his head.

4

It was past eight o'clock when the Rodcoopers finally burst through the front door that Sunday evening, their arms full of bottles of beer. Vi and me went into the dining room to find them all there and Brenda searching in the sideboard, rattling the shelves. Her face was flushed and happy. 'Do you have a bottle opener, Mrs B? Special night – hope you don't mind.'

I went and fetched an opener from the kitchen drawer. It had a Guinness toucan on the handle. 'Ooh,' Brenda said when I gave it to her. 'Will you just look at that?'

They'd brought bottles of Mackeson and pale ale. Brenda levered off the tops and started pouring into the glasses normally used for water. If it'd been any of the other guests Vi would have taken them to one side and had a quiet word in her most official voice: 'If you don't mind, we don't allow alcohol in the dining room or bedrooms.' But for the Rodcoopers she smiled and collected the empties and indulged them. She'd even cooked their meal hours late and kept it warm until they were ready. It was a miracle the way ten minutes of the Rodcoopers made her mellow for a whole evening. 'Supper's in the oven,' she said. 'Sit down and we'll bring it in.'

While we served up they were telling Vi about the dress rehearsal, filling their glasses over and over. Against all expectations, it had gone well. They'd only had to stop once and that was when Alastair, the Pirate King, had got his words mixed up. 'Wrong recitative,' Brenda warbled. 'Poor Alastair. Dress rehearsal nerves, I expect. You'll be fine tomorrow when it's the real thing.'

Alastair tucked into his lamb and potato. 'I hope so,' he said in between mouthfuls, pretending to grimace.

'You should learn to concentrate more,' Charles said.

'I *was* concentrating, Charles,' Alastair said. 'In fact, I might have been concentrating too hard. It's like walking a tightrope. If you think about it you fall off. I knew the words but –'

'Nerves,' Brenda said, 'that's all. We all get them from time to time. I recommend a stiff brandy before the performance. Never fails.'

'Knowing the words isn't enough,' Charles said. 'You have to live and breathe them. You have to love the words.'

'Oh, for heaven's sake,' Alastair replied. 'It's light opera not the Ten Commandments. People only come for a night out. They couldn't care less if the words are right or wrong as long as they rhyme.'

'Pah! It might be light opera to you, Alastair, but it's life and death to us. Being an entertainer is an important matter, and don't you ever forget it.'

Julia was there in a pale green trouser suit, sitting at the table near the bay window and looking bored. It was the first time I'd seen her since the day she'd arrived. She stirred the veg round in her gravy with her fork, a look of disgust on her face, and grimaced at offers of beer.

'It was perfect otherwise,' Brenda was saying.

'Yes, looks like we got away with it again,' Charles said a bit reluctantly.

'Hurrah for the Pirate King!' Irene sang, and they raised their glasses and drank to the success of *The Pirates*.

*

While Nanny served tinned fruit and ice cream, Vi and me cleared the plates and rushed through the washing-up. There were soapsuds up to her elbows. Then we could hear singing. 'Listen to that, Eddie,' Vi said. 'These are the times you remember long afterwards.' It sounded beautiful – three or four of them together, there in the dining room, as if it was just for us and not for an audience. It was nothing like the pop groups who stood on the stage at village halls because they wanted to be famous or to be mobbed by teenage girls. It had what Vi called 'a proper tune' – sad and strange at the same time. 'That's from *The Pirates*,' Vi said, drying her hands on a tea towel. 'Let's go in and listen. They won't mind.'

Brenda had moved the HP sauce bottles off the old piano and was playing. The two girls from the chorus, Irene and Maisie, were singing in harmony, their heads together. Irene had a broad face with dark curls that shook when she hit the high notes. Maisie had big eyes and a little, pursing mouth which gave her the look of a fish. But it was a lovely fish and if I'd ever caught her on the end of a line I wouldn't have thrown her back, but would have put her in a keep net like a mermaid and talked to her every day. '*Poor wandering one*,' they sang, '*though thou hast surely strayed, take heart of grace, thy steps retrace, poor wandering one*.' The words made no sense to me but it didn't matter, because sometimes, as Vi said, nothing made sense and then all you could do was laugh. The others watched, joining in the chorus. Nanny sat on a chair swaying gently from side to side, a couple of empty dishes in her hands. I supposed it was the Rodcoopers who were the poor wandering ones, with nowhere to call home all summer, except for Vi's cluttered bedrooms.

The drink must have gone to Alastair's head. He wasn't as experienced as the others and it made him reckless. 'Have at you, Charles!' he shouted once the music died down. He picked up the coal tongs from the fireplace and tried to fence like in *The Pirates*, but Charles was too dignified. 'Have at you! Come on. Are you a man or a mouse?' Alastair demanded, trying to thrust a poker into Charles's hand. 'Love the words – love the action!'

'Don't be ridiculous,' Charles said, refusing to get out of his seat.

'That's enough now. Please,' Vi said, not realizing Alastair meant it, laughing because she loved to see the house so alive. 'There's children in bed.' She went back to the kitchen, shaking her head and wiping her hands on her pinny.

'Are you a man or a mouse?' Alastair persisted. He was standing now, holding the fire tongs like a baton. 'Oh, God – it's a mouse!'

'Where?' Maisie leapt to her feet. Something was careering along the bare floor near the fireplace.

'There! There!' The two girls screamed in unison, just as if they'd rehearsed it.

That was the reaction I'd always hoped for with my practical jokes. It was obvious, of course – a tin wind-up thing, which bumped and whirred against the grate. Anybody who bothered to look would have known straight away. Alastair must have put it there when no one was looking. He laughed and picked it up and showed us the wheels underneath, the clockwork motor still going, then passed it to me for inspection.

'God, Alastair,' Irene said, her dark hair rippling as she laughed. 'Will you stop it? You'll give us all heart attacks.' She slapped him on the arm and he pretended to be wounded.

'It was a spider yesterday,' Maisie explained. 'He put it on the table in that pub and squeezed something and it jumped like a fish. Scared the living daylights out of me.'

'And tomorrow it'll be blood pouring out of my ears,'

Alastair said. He was a man after my own heart – though maybe not quite so mature.

'It had better not be,' Charles said sharply. 'Tomorrow is for performance. Perhaps if you concentrated on that instead of your absurd practical jokes you wouldn't be making elementary mistakes at this late stage in the production.'

Alastair looked shocked. Brenda said, 'That's rather harsh, Charles, don't you think?'

'Not at all,' Charles said. 'When I'm responsible for maintaining the standards in this company only the highest will do. Without standards we are lost. We need to remember that.' He stood up and wiped the corners of his mouth with a paper serviette.

'If you don't want me in the company . . .' Alastair started.

'Don't be melodramatic,' Charles said without meeting his eyes. 'Now I'm turning in. I have some work to do. I intend to go through my part again. Perhaps some of you would do well to do likewise.'

After he'd gone there was a brittle silence.

'Perhaps we should,' Alastair said.

'No,' Irene said. 'He's just getting overwrought. It happens sometimes at the start of the season. Come on. The night's still young. What shall we do? What about charades?' She opened more bottles of Mackeson.

But no one had the appetite for the physical effort of charades. The beer was making them sleepy. Maisie was knitting straight from a shopping bag on the floor by her feet. Pink and yellow wool overflowed the bag and she worked with such enthusiasm that one of the balls of wool bounced out and rolled across the carpet. She looked up. 'What about the Dictionary Game? The one where you have to invent words. We played that in Guildford last year, didn't we?'

Brenda put her hand up to her eyes. 'I haven't got the concentration tonight.'

'Or any night,' Julia added quietly and yawned. 'Not without a glass of whisky anyhow.'

'I know,' Irene said. 'Fortune telling.'

'Tea leaves and crystal balls?' Maisie asked.

'If you like. A woman told me once I had the eyes of a clairvoyant.'

'You should give them back to her, then,' Alastair said. He was suddenly lively again, Charles's reproach forgotten in the rush to enjoy himself.

Nanny was still sitting there with the dishes she'd forgotten to take into the kitchen. 'There used to be a fortune teller in the Tower Grounds, you know. She was there for years.'

Everybody looked at her in surprise. 'You never went to see her, did you, Mrs Bartlett?' Alastair asked.

'I did the once. But these people only tell you what you want to hear. Everyone knows that. They listen for clues and then give back what they've already heard.'

'Oh, I don't know,' Brenda said. 'I believe in it anyway.'

'Someone I knew had a séance,' Maisie said. 'They all sat round with the letters of the alphabet written on bits of paper. They turned down the lights and put their fingers on the glass in the middle and asked it questions.' She looked around, as if she was telling a ghost story, the pale yellow wool slack over her fingers. 'It was all right at first, but then it got scary. Someone asked what the future held for them and guess what . . . the glass started moving around the letters. It spelled out, D-E-A –'

'No!' Irene said.

'Yes,' Maisie went on, her voice rising. 'They tried to stop it – but the glass was out of control. It fell off the table and dashed to pieces.'

There was another silence and Alastair said, 'Perhaps it

was going to say, "D-e-a-r Joe, Don't forget to buy some milk on the way home . . ." '

'No,' Maisie went on. 'They were terrified. My friend couldn't sleep for a week after that. Then, less than a month later, the one who asked the question died.'

'Mind you,' Alastair said, 'she was eighty-six.'

'No,' Maisie said, missing the joke. 'She wasn't at all. She got run over by a taxi on her way home from the theatre.'

Nanny had finally taken the dishes into the kitchen while I sat on, taking it all in. 'Let's do the fortune telling, then,' Irene said. 'Mrs B's a good sport. We can have some fun with her.' Irene went and stuck her head round the kitchen door and brought Nanny back with her. 'We're going to do *tarot* cards, Mrs B. Are you up for it? We've already read Maisie's future and now it's your turn.'

It was a lie, of course, and she made the word rhyme with 'carrot'. Irene winked across at me and I winked back without understanding, not wanting to be excluded. 'I think you'll find they're tarr-ow cards,' Alastair said.

'Get you. Whatever they're called.'

'Oh, I don't think I want to do them, love,' Nanny said, coming back in. 'Odd things can happen when you start meddling with the supernatural.'

'But it's only a bit of fun, Mrs B.' Irene was encouraging everybody to join in. 'Just sit down here at the table. There – that's it.' Irene shuffled the cards and put them on the table in front of Nanny for her to cut.

'I don't want to, love . . .' Nanny started.

'It's all right,' Irene said. 'They won't turn up anything bad – and even if they do I won't tell you.'

'That's not much consolation,' Maisie said in her quiet, buttery voice.

'I've got a feeling about this,' Irene said. 'You know – a kind of sense. Go on, Mrs B. Please.'

'All right,' Nanny said. 'If you must.' She sighed and cut

the cards. Even Julia was watching. I felt her eyes on me, on the table.

'That wasn't too bad, was it? Now then.' Irene raised her eyebrows like she was on stage. She dealt cards on the table – one in the middle and twelve around the outside like a clock face. Then she went all dramatic again – staring into space and frowning just long enough to glance down at the instructions on her lap. I'd seen her take them out of the box so I guessed she didn't know as much about fortune-telling as she made out.

'Do get on with it,' Maisie said.

'Quiet now –' Irene said, staring across the room as if a ghost was hovering round the ceiling. 'I'm concentrating.' Finally she came out with, 'As in all our lives, Mrs B, there is good and bad.'

'That's obvious,' Nanny said. 'That's no secret. I wasn't born yesterday.'

'But look,' Irene said, pointing to one of the cards on the table. 'This card – the Chariot. It's connected to transporting or being transported, with links to trade and commerce or even political influence and power. And this one – the World – suggests your openness to the world's offerings. Does that mean anything, Mrs B?'

Nanny shook her head.

Irene went on. 'Drawn together these are definitely saying travel – possibly a great distance – a voyage which can be emotional but more often physical.'

'You're making that up, Irene,' Maisie said.

'I'm not. I've been practising and that's what it means – the Chariot and the World together.'

Nanny said, 'Well, I'm not going anywhere, so it just shows how wrong you can be.'

'Not today necessarily,' Irene persisted, 'but some time soon. I sense a great yearning. You never really know what the future might hold.'

Nanny sighed stubbornly, put her glasses on, took them off again.

'Wait,' Irene said. 'These cards are suggesting a place to me. Yes. It's this juxtaposition. Does America mean anything, Mrs B?' Nanny shook her head. 'Oh, it's New York. I can see it now, plain as day – not New York – New Jersey.'

'How did you know that?' Nanny snapped. 'You're just guessing.'

'No.' Irene was covering a smile with her hand.

'Someone told you, then. You couldn't have known it's somewhere I want to go. It's not fair. You shouldn't go raising up my hopes!'

I couldn't keep quiet any longer. 'But, Nan – you were only saying this morning how much you wanted to go to America to see Steven and Gary and Marion. The cards are right. You hadn't forgotten, had you?'

'Of course I hadn't forgotten, you stupid boy. But I'm not as gullible as you think either. That's not in the cards.'

'It must be,' I said. 'How else could Irene tell?' Then I looked round the room and they were all smiling, sharing the joke I'd missed.

Irene smiled sheepishly. 'Vi might have mentioned it. Some time today. I don't remember.'

'There,' Nanny said. 'You must think I'm a fool. You're taking advantage of me. It's bad manners. And I thought you were nice people.'

'Oh, Mrs B,' Maisie said. 'Nobody's poking fun. Irene didn't mean that.'

'Well, I'm sure I don't know what you mean by it. Of course I want to visit my son. I miss him. I've been missing him for years. But it won't happen. I've got to live with it. Do you know how far it is – to New York?'

Nobody seemed to know. Brenda shrugged helplessly. 'It's a long way,' she agreed. 'And we do understand, Mrs B.

We're actors, don't forget. We're separated from loved ones, too.'

Julia muttered, 'Not by far enough sometimes.'

'And you *could* go,' Maisie said in her gentle voice. 'If you set your heart on it. There are planes leaving London every day.'

'You wouldn't get me up in one of those things – being shut in a metal tube then shot into the sky at a hundred miles an hour. It's not natural.'

'There are still ships,' Maisie said. 'If your son went I don't see why you shouldn't, Mrs B. Folks go to America all the time these days.'

'You people don't know everything,' Nanny said angrily. 'We haven't got the money to go tramping halfway round the world. Vi wouldn't thank me for it and I'm not sure Steven wants me there really. What would he do with me all day?'

Nanny looked down at her hands. 'I'm just an old woman who misses her family. I'm used to it, and you've got no business lifting my hopes and making me sad again. I should never have let you talk me into this fortune telling. I was silly to let you.' She got up from the table and went out without another word.

We heard her creaking up the stairs towards the tank room with its boxes still waiting to be unpacked and its biscuit tin full of memories.

'Oh,' Alastair said. 'That's a downer.'

'I didn't mean anything by it,' Irene said. 'It was meant to be a laugh, that's all.'

'Course you didn't,' Maisie said. 'None of us wanted to upset her.'

But it was too late. Nanny had already been upset.

'I suppose that's it, then,' Irene said. But it wasn't. Suddenly, as if to round the evening off, there was an enormous crash from the next room. It could only have been connected to the Rodcoopers. Nobody else would have been worthy of it – the noise of metal hitting wood, jangling springs.

'Shit,' Irene said, probably thinking it was retribution for her fortune-telling lies. 'What was that?'

'Oomflah,' said a muffled voice with Charles's perfect enunciation. Brenda was first to react. She dashed out to help.

'What a bloody heroine,' Julia breathed. 'It's always her.'

And that was it. That moment which reverberated round the house like piano wires being hit with a lump hammer. We sat there in silence. Vi came in rubbing her eyes and asking what all the noise was about. She looked as though she'd been dozing in the chair.

'Whatever it is, it made me feel quite queasy,' Maisie said. 'I think someone just walked across my grave.'

Then Brenda came back in and Charles with her, looking dazed in a paisley dressing gown and leather slippers. 'If this is your idea of a joke . . .' he began, addressing the room in general, then stopped when Brenda gripped his hand.

'What happened?' Vi wanted to know.

'It was the bed,' Brenda explained. 'It – apparently – fell apart.'

'It collapsed. The moment I went to get into it.' There was a snigger, immediately stifled.

'But . . .' Vi said.

'It could have been an accident,' Maisie said lamely. 'Couldn't it?'

'Beds do not fall apart of their own volition,' Charles said. 'The legs had evidently been unbolted.'

'Someone could have forgotten to tighten them perhaps.'

'I don't think so, Maisie. The bed was perfectly all right when Mrs B slept in it last night. Why shouldn't it be now?' There was no answer. 'Luckily,' Charles said, 'I am unhurt. Thank you all for your concern.' And he went back to bed.

'I hope he doesn't think I've got anything to do with this,' Alastair said. We could hear Charles grunting, trying to bolt the bed frame back together.

Irene said, 'You could hardly blame him, could you? Look at the silly stuff you do. No wonder he wanted to change rooms.'

'That's got nothing to do with it. He moved because of the traffic noise.'

'Is that what he told you?' Brenda asked. 'You're more naive than I thought. He'd been all right in that room on his own in other years. The only difference this year is you, Alastair.'

'Me?' He looked shocked again. 'Well, I'm glad he moved. He snored like a pig all night.'

Julia stood up and stretched. 'Oh, dear,' she said. 'Bad omens for the opening night. And it was all going so well. You theatricals – so superstitious.'

Her mother said, 'Don't be silly, Julia. It's not a bad omen at all. Just a prank.'

'If that's a prank I'm Diana Dors.'

'Take no notice of her,' Brenda said. 'She doesn't want to be here.'

'Did Charles say anything else?' Alastair asked.

Brenda hesitated. 'He talks such rubbish at moments of stress. Pure Gilbert and Sullivan. Something about honour and principles. Something about it being war from now on.'

Alastair snorted. 'War? He's got a nerve.'

No one responded. The evening had fallen apart like Charles's bed. We sat for a moment, then Vi pulled the dining-room curtains open as she did every night in preparation for the morning.

'I wonder,' Maisie said in her buttery voice. 'Did he mean real war – or some other kind?'

5

Ray turned out to be right about the job at the Palace Amusements. They set him on with no questions and within a couple of days it was as if he'd always been there – which in a way he had. The only difference was that now he was getting paid for hanging round the rides and chatting to girls when previously he'd done it free of charge. 'Ideal job,' he said. 'Bloody perfect.' What's more, he didn't have to get out of bed until ten o'clock at the earliest and when he was on lates he could lie in until lunchtime, plus there was something like regular money coming in to the house. He was even keeping his fingers out of the phone tin.

I went down to talk to Ray at the Palace. He was easy to spot, hanging round by the ticket kiosk with the other attendants, joking and messing about. A girl was supposed to be selling the tickets, but she wasn't doing any business – just leaning over the counter and blowing pink bubble-gum bubbles.

Ray wore a maroon jacket now, the same as the others, and a chain of keys round his neck. When he saw me he flicked his ciggie end onto the concrete and swaggered across, a fully paid-up member of staff.

'All right, Ed?' he said in a funny way that I didn't recognize. This was a new Ray, with a job and important things to do. He knew exactly how hard to tilt the machines to make the coins come unjammed and what to do when the Nudge light went on. 'What you doing here?'

'I thought I'd come and see what you were up to. Nothing much going on back home.'

'I'm doing OK.' He half turned as if he was showing me how far his territory extended. 'As you can see.'

'Are you busy?'

'Yeah. Loads to do.' It was morning and some of the rides were still covered in green tarpaulin. A few people strolled around waiting for things to open. A pigeon strutted across the floor. 'Come on,' he said. 'I'll introduce you.'

'This is my little cousin, Eddie,' he said to the other attendants. 'Codge – you already know – Mickey, Bern and John.' They nodded. The girl's name was Rita. She popped another bubble then disentangled it from her lips. 'He's staying at our place,' Ray was saying. 'Helping out for the summer. We've got bloody theatricals in so we need a bit extra. They think they own the place. Eddie's the brains of the family.'

'Come off it, Ray,' I said. I'd just finished my O Levels. That was enough to make me stand out in our family.

'Brains like what?' Codge wanted to know.

'He's studying chemistry and stuff,' Ray said. 'French and Latin.' He was laying it on thick, making it up as he went along.

'Where do they speak Latin?' Codge asked.

'Latvia,' Ray replied confidently. 'And in books.'

I was sure I knew the reason why Ray was always making stuff up – it was because his own father was a whole part of his life that was just a story to him. He could transform it into anything he wanted. Ray's dad had been an engineer on the Atlantic merchant fleet. Vi had met him at a dance at the New Brighton Tower Ballroom during the last few weeks of the war. For a long time those were the only two facts Ray knew about him.

But as Ray grew older, and asked more questions, Vi reluctantly gave him a few more details: his name was Kamil and he was Polish. Apparently, Kamil could turn his hand to anything, and when the war finished he didn't go back to Poland but stayed on in New Brighton, went to college and learned plastering. My mum said he worked on some of the houses along the seafront that had been bomb-damaged. They probably had his plastered ceiling roses in them even now. Strange to think of Ray's dad catching the bus from his lodgings in Wallasey village every day, wearing his plasterer's overalls and carrying his plasterer's float in a bag.

Mum told me how Kamil and Vi loved to go out dancing most weekends. They were the best dancers in New Brighton and one night, when they did the veleta, everybody stopped and clapped. Eventually they got engaged. Then in the summer of 1946 Vi discovered she was pregnant. Within three weeks of that news, Kamil went back to Poland. He told Vi his mother had been taken ill and that she was asking for him. He'd be back within a month. But of course he wasn't. Vi wrote to him dozens of times in those first few months, but there was never any reply, not even when she wrote to tell him that he had a son who was going to be called Ray. That was when she knew she'd lost him. Anything could have happened in Poland in 1946. Finally Vi put him out of her mind and got on with the rest of her life. That's what my mum said.

Ray had asked if there were any photos of his father and Vi said no, there weren't – she'd got rid of them all. But Ray went on and on about it and in the end Vi remembered she'd kept one in the back of a drawer somewhere and she gave it to him. It was a little black and white photo of Vi and a thin man with bright eyes standing on the seafront. Vi looked younger in the photo of course, and dazzlingly in love, and the man wore a dark double-breasted uniform with silver buttons. There was a touch of Bernard Montgomery about him, as my mum described it, a sand-blown twinkly look. There were no letters, no souvenirs. That photo was Ray's only glimpse of his dad. He showed it to me once. He kept it in a transparent pocket in the front of his wallet.

I think that was why Vi didn't know how to deal with him – because she had to be his father as well as his mother, and she didn't have much idea about either. She wanted to beat the living daylights out of him one minute, but the next she was loving him to bits because he was her only precious reminder of a thin, bright-eyed bloke called Kamil.

'Besides,' Ray was saying, 'doctors use Latin in prescriptions. It's obvious.'

'The lad doesn't want to end up in a dead-end place like this anyway, does he?' Codge said, referring to me.

'It's OK here, isn't it?' I asked.

They laughed. Codge said, 'Yeah, if you want to spend the rest of your life chasing round after snotty kids and their gormless dads, pulling pennies out of knackered machines.'

The one called Bern took a pack of ciggies out of his jacket pocket and flashed them round. 'Want one?' I shook my head.

'You're a good lad.'

Codge said, 'It's OK here, but it's not a career. It's seasonal. I mean, there's no prospects. Look at me. I'll be back home on the dole by the end of September. You go and get yourself a proper job, lad. Be a professor or a teacher or something.'

Nobody from our family had ever been to university – not even my dad, who was a surveyor but had done it all through night school. I told them I'd get a proper job when the time came.

'Nice one,' Bern said and nodded his head. 'See you later, Eddie.'

Ray walked me to the door. 'Listen – me and the lads are going for a few drinks tonight. Do you wanna come?'

'Yeah,' I said. 'That'd be good.'

'Sorry I left you in the dodgems to face the old lady last Saturday. I didn't know she was gonna turn up.'

'Why'd you have to go, then? You just disappeared.'

'It was a kind of instinct.'

'Is that why you're asking me to come out with you – cos you feel guilty about dropping me in it?'

'Don't be so soft. It's cos you're my cousin – a mate.'

'It's OK anyway,' I said. 'Vi didn't tell me off too much. She knows who to blame.'

'Yeah.' He laughed. 'Me. But she doesn't know how to keep me in order. She thinks she does, but she doesn't.'

'What time, then?' I asked.

'What?' He was already looking around, afraid he might be missing some banter with Rita.

'Tonight – what time?'

'Oh. I'm finishing here at seven – so I'll come home, get changed and pick you up about half past.'

'Will they mind – your mates – me coming along?'

He laughed as if that was the most ludicrous thing he'd ever heard. 'Course not. Why should they? Whatever I say goes.'

After the amusements I went to the beach. It was full – families camping out, deckchairs and donkey rides and kiddies running backwards and forwards to the sea, paddling or scooping the muddy water out with their tin buckets. I hung about under the pier for a while. I liked it there. The sand was different – dampish and rippled. The pier supports were pocked with rust and ended in pools of saltwater, draped with clams. The air was cool and musty, but overhead thousands of holidaymakers clattered along in the sun.

I walked further along the beach, past the paddling pool

which filled with the tide. 'Hello,' I heard a voice say softly. I looked up and had to look again. 'It's Maisie,' she said. She sat on one of the reddish outcrops of flat sandstone with what looked like one of Vi's towels round her shoulders. She sniffed and rubbed her nose with it.

'I didn't recognize you without . . .'

'Without my knitting?' she said. 'Or without my clothes?'

'Either,' I said. 'Both.' I felt awkward standing over her. She had to shield her eyes against the sun. 'Is this where you come?'

She nodded. 'The water's not very nice sometimes – loads of slime and seaweed – but I like a swim. Just a dip.' She pulled the towel around her. She had the start of a fine curve of muscle on her upper arm.

'Are you a good swimmer?' I asked.

'Pretty good.'

'You'd fit in round here, then. Everybody swims. It's because of the river.'

Maisie said, 'I know. It's nice to get away from the rest of them sometimes. It can be a bit overpowering spending all day with them.'

'Don't they know where you are?'

'No. They'd think I was mad sitting on the beach like this all on my own, but I like it. Swimming's a treat even if the water's a bit grotty.'

She gestured along the beach. 'These are the sorts of folks who pay to come and see us, so it's advisable to keep in with them, too. You need to remember who your audience are and to understand them if you can. That's what I think. What about you? Have you come to get away from something?'

I laughed. 'Not really. It's a quiet part of the day and Vi doesn't need me and the weather was good, so –'

'I didn't mean that. I meant have you come to New Brighton to get away from something?'

'No. My mum and dad are in Scotland looking after my grandad. I think he's on his way out.'

'Sorry about that.'

'It's OK. I'm kind of dumped here until it's sorted out.'

'Like flotsam,' she said.

'What?'

'Flotsam and jetsam. The bits of wood and things that keep getting washed up. You must have seen it. Stuff from the ships – old salt cruets with tar on them, rope handles from crates, the wooden slats of bunk beds. That's what you're like.'

'Am I?'

'Yes. Anyway, I have brought my knitting – in case you were wondering,' she said, and she moved her towel to show the bag. She pulled out a few pieces that looked like the back and sides of a pale yellow baby jacket. 'My niece is expecting in September. What do you think?'

I didn't have any opinion about babywear. I shrugged. 'What's it going to be?'

'Matinée jacket. It's what all well-dressed babies wear these days.'

'It's nice. I hope it fits.'

She rolled it up, stuck the needles through and smiled at me. 'It should do. It's the fourth one I've done. I'm just going to keep knitting until the baby's born.' She smiled. 'You must think we're a strange lot, Eddie, mustn't you?'

'Why?'

'Just the way we carry on – with our silly arguments and jokes. We act like kids, I know, but we must all seem so old to you.'

She did seem old, but I wasn't sure what old meant. She looked about nineteen, but she had thoughts and ideas as if she was from my parents' generation. I told her it didn't matter much what I thought about her and the rest of the

Rodcoopers. Vi thought they were marvellous whatever they did. Nanny just loved to have the house full of activity.

'Nanny can be a bit strange sometimes,' I said. 'She has to take medicine for her memory, to stop her getting confused. But she enjoys it when people come to stay and she can make herself useful in the house.'

'That's good,' Maisie said.

'She feels life's worthwhile when she's helping.'

'We all need to feel like that,' Maisie said and then started telling me about the shows – how Charles could hold the audience with his silence, with a pause or just with his presence. From the moment he came on stage and looked around at the audience as if he was embracing each one of them, they fell in love with him. It was a gift, she said, like that part in the middle of the Modern Major-General song where he pretends he can't find anything to rhyme with 'strategy' and he holds the audience – keeps them waiting for what seems like minutes – while he searches in his head for the right word, his eyes cast heavenwards, and in the end he comes up with 'sat a gee' and everyone laughs even if they've heard it dozens of times before.

'Imagine that,' she said. 'He can capture them without saying a single word. That's what I aim for. I'd like to be able to do that.' She told me about Alastair and his practical jokes, how Brenda liked a drink to steady her nerves before she went on, but that her voice was as strong as it had always been.

I asked, 'What's Julia doing here?'

'Ah,' Maisie said. 'You've noticed her. She's gorgeous, isn't she? Stunning, really. What can a poor girl like me do against competition like that?'

'Don't be silly, Maisie,' I said. She was right, though. I didn't want to admit it, but the way Julia looked bypassed sense and logic, went straight to lust.

Maisie said, 'She doesn't want to be here. She's a bit like you in that way.'

'But I don't mind being here. I like it.'

'You're both stranded for a while, then. That's what I meant – like flotsam or something.'

'I suppose so,' I said. 'But most people here are stranded. It's this place. You should see it in the winter when the visitors go home and everything closes and the sea blows over the prom.'

'Maybe you're right,' she said. She smiled one of her sweet smiles and stood up, her big eyes shining. 'Now I need to get ready for the matinée. Would you care to accompany me home?'

She put a knitted sweater over her damp swimming costume and slipped on a pair of flat sandals and we walked along the seafront back to Vi's. I told her how I was going out with Ray and his mates later. She seemed impressed. 'Love you and leave you, Eddie,' she sang when we reached the front door. 'Enjoy yourself tonight. Don't do anything I wouldn't do.'

Of course Ray forgot he'd promised to collect me. I half expected it. Someone would have said to him, 'Coming for a drink, Raymondo?' and he'd have gone. He was everybody's friend, especially when there was money in his pocket.

I waited an hour in the house for him and when he didn't come I wandered outside. It was getting dark by now and someone was outside the front, sitting on the wall. It was Julia. She was smoking and at the same time pretending not to, cupping the lit end of the ciggie. She wasn't inhaling properly, just keeping the smoke in her mouth and letting it billow out. When she saw me she sighed in an irritated kind of way. 'What d'you want?'

'Nothing. I didn't know you were here, that's all. What're

you doing?' My stomach had lurched when I saw her alone. She was wearing lilac-coloured trousers and a matching top cut away to show her midriff. There were little fabric buttons down the side. The only place I'd ever seen clothes like that were in a copy of *Fabulous* I'd sneaked a look at in the newsagent's. I stared as she stretched dramatically to emphasize the gap between her top and her trousers.

'I'm bored,' she said. 'Isn't there anything to do in this place?'

'There's the bowling. That's OK.'

'Yeah, I've seen it. I wonder if there'll be any lads there.'

'Bound to be. I don't keep a lookout for lads myself.'

She looked at me lazily and stretched again. 'What do you keep a lookout for, then?'

I said I didn't know. Girls, I supposed and she mimicked me. 'Girls, I s'pose.' I hoped I didn't sound like she made me sound.

'How old are you?' she wanted to know.

'Sixteen,' I said. 'How old are you?'

'None of your business. I'm seventeen, as a matter of fact.'

'What's the problem, then?'

'It's her,' she complained, tossing her head vaguely towards the house. I assumed she meant her mother. 'The old trollop. She drags me here, then buggers off and leaves me.'

'They've been busy doing their shows, haven't they?'

'That's what she'd like you to believe. Half the time they're just sitting around on their arses. She only brought me to keep an eye on me, but I'm either hanging round here or in the bar of some pub while they go on endlessly about who sings what and who says what and who's letting the side down. They're worse than a load of kids. She buys me a port and lemon and thinks it'll shut me up.'

'Tell her you want to go home, then,' I said. In a way she irritated me. She was like itching powder that got between your shirt and your back. She had everything, but still she wasn't satisfied. Good-looking people could be like that – didn't know they were born. 'Isn't there someone else you could stay with?'

'There's only Dave,' she said. I sat on the other end of the wall – the end where her feet were. She was wearing strappy high heels that were so white they almost glowed in the dark.

'Who's Dave?'

'My boyfriend. He's twenty-four. That's why she's got me here. She doesn't trust me with him. Other years she's let me stay with my friend Samantha, but not this year. Not with Dave around. She pretends she's brought me for my education, or something, but really it's because of Dave.'

I wasn't sure what gave me the courage to speak to her in this way. Perhaps it was what Maisie had told me about us having something in common, about us both being stranded here.

'How'd you meet him?' I said into the darkness.

'Horse riding,' she said.

'You go horse riding?'

'Yeah. I had my own pony for a while. Dave was mucking out at the stables and one Saturday when I went for a lesson there he was. He just looked so – sexy. It was a hot day and he'd taken his shirt off. He must have known I was there. When I'd finished my lesson he came across and took the bridle. He was a natural with horses. He said he'd been watching me and that I was one of the most confident riders he'd seen for my age. That was it really. We just went on from there.'

This was a big disappointment to put it mildly, but the thing with girls was to get them talking, to show you were interested in them. It was in all the books. Even Myron Bloomfield agreed.

Julia was saying, 'I really fancied him. I mean, really. And now I miss him like mad. It's just cruel.'

'Oh,' I said. This conversation wasn't going the way it was meant to. I didn't want to hear about Dave. In *Dream Dating* there was a moment which Myron Bloomfield called 'the Clincher'. It was when your date made a kind of unspoken agreement with you. It was when your eyes met theirs in a certain way that could hardly be misinterpreted. Julia's eyes met mine, but in an impatient, teacherish kind of way. If I understood them properly they weren't saying, 'Yes, let's get to know one another a little better.' Instead they seemed to be saying, 'Keep up, will you? I haven't got all night.'

'So I'll be getting away from here as soon as I can. It's a complete dump.'

'It's not so bad,' I said.

'It is. When's the next train back to London?' I told her I didn't know. 'I'll hitch-hike if necessary. Mind you, I'd only have to give the word and Dave'd collect me before anyone knew what'd happened. He understands my needs.'

God, I thought. Now she had needs. She seemed so mature. Not a girl, a woman. My mouth went dry just thinking about her needs.

'If you don't know train times,' she said, 'what do you know?'

'I know where Fairlanes tenpin bowling is,' I said, 'and I know the café'll be open there.'

'Good,' she said, unravelling herself from the wall. 'Let's go then.'

So I walked with her down the rest of Waterloo Road and onto the seafront. 'You at school?' I asked.

'You keep asking questions.'

'I'm a curious person. Perhaps I'd like to get to know you a bit better.'

'Don't be getting any ideas,' she said. 'This is strictly platonic.'

'Yeah,' I said. I could tell by the way she said it that platonic wasn't good. It had that ring of some school or institution about it. Still, as we reached the corner, I managed to brush my arm against hers. It was a warm evening, but she shivered. 'Are you cold?' I asked.

'I told you. Don't be getting ideas.'

When we got to Fairlanes I realized I didn't have any money. It wasn't much better than being with Ray, except there was a chance someone might see us together and think I'd at least reached the point of 'the Clincher'. We sat on the side of the café opposite the glass wall that looked out onto the seafront. The lights were on now and the glass wall was like a mirror reflecting the rows of seats.

'Jesus,' she said when I told her I had no money. 'You know how to treat a girl.'

'You wanted to come here, not me.'

She looked across the table as if she'd only just noticed me and pulled out a white plastic purse and ordered a milky coffee from the waitress. 'What do you want?' she asked, and I ordered the same.

'If you must know,' she said, 'I've left school. I'm at tech now. Hairdressing. When I go.'

'Don't you like it?'

'It's all right. At least they treat you like an adult, but it's only temporary. I'm leaving as soon as I can. I'm gonna be a model.'

'What? Like a fashion model?'

'Well, not a bloody Airfix model, Eddie.'

I'd never thought about modelling before. 'How do you do that?'

'You just have to look gorgeous and pose for photos. It's easy. The girls at school never believed I really meant it.

They sniggered and said I was a trollop when I told them what I was going to do. That's why I hated it so much.'

'I hate school,' I volunteered.

'Bullshit you do. You love it. I can tell. I bet you're a teacher's pet.'

'I'm not. I had the cane once.'

'What for?'

'Well,' I said, 'I would have done. My best mates – the ones I always hang around with – got the cane for walking on the grass. I was off that day. But if I'd been there I'd have got it for certain.'

'Big deal,' she said. 'Can't you tell me a bloody lie for once?'

The coffee came in shallow cups with swirls of frothy milk. 'Do you know what?' she asked.

'What?'

'All the girls at school hated me. That's why I left.'

'Why did they hate you?'

'How should I know? They were all cows, that's why. They were OK at first. Like girls are. Then they saw how all the lads looked at me and chatted me up. They started saying I was stuck up, but that was only because the lads liked me more than them.'

She'd drunk most of her coffee. There was a film of milk on her upper lip like a pale moustache. The inside of her cup was draped with wrinkles of boiled milk and she prodded it with her teaspoon. 'I'd have done anything to be mates with them, but they'd already decided they were going to pick on me and make my life hell.'

'What did you do to make them hate you? I mean, you must have done something.'

'No,' she said. Her eyes went wide as she looked across the table at me. 'No, I never did. They couldn't stand the way the lads looked at me, that's all – different to the way they looked at the rest of them. It wasn't my fault they all fancied me, was it? The other girls didn't like it when I spent money on clothes and took time with my hair and makeup. Appearances are important. People don't think they are, but they are. These days, you know, it shouldn't be a sin to be attractive. Look at me. You think I'm attractive, don't you?'

I wasn't sure I understood what she was asking me. Everything was shifting. She was attractive. I'd known that from the moment I'd first seen her. But now she wanted me to say it to her face. Did that mean I actually had to do something? Perhaps put my hand on her knee? Perhaps she fancied me, after all? Where was Myron Bloomfield when I needed him?

'Yes, you're attractive,' I said unconvincingly.

Julia looked me in the eye from across the table. 'Really?'

'Yes, really. You're very attractive, Julia.' Was this 'the Clincher', finally? I tried to remember how I might recognize it, but Julia paused only for a second.

'Thanks,' she said.

I knew at once that I'd missed my opportunity. It was like the surfing I'd tried one summer holiday in Cornwall. You had to get from a straddled position to standing in a fraction of a second – otherwise the wave passed you by and you were left sitting there on the board looking stupid.

She went on, 'It's nothing to be ashamed of, is it? Being attractive. I'm ordinary in lots of ways, but if you've got good looks, Eddie, it would be absurd not to take advantage of them. For instance, some people can play a musical instrument. I can't.'

'I can a bit,' I said. 'I was in a group for about six months. Bass guitar.'

'Yeah,' she said. She seemed to be looking over my shoulder and when I turned there were two lads at the counter. They sported quiffs, leather jackets and motorcycle boots. Chains would be their weapons of choice.

'We should go,' I said.

'I'll be along in a bit.'

'I can't leave you here on your own.'

'Why not? I'm a big girl.'

'It's dark. Your mother'll be wondering where you've got to. You came here with me, don't forget.' But she pulled her ciggies out of her handbag again and put one in her mouth.

'Excuse me,' she called to the lads. 'Do you have a light?'

They came across and one of them leaned across the table and lit her up with a Zippo. So that was the way to do it. The lad with the cigarette lighter said, 'Mind if we sit here?'

'No,' Julia said, and they stood at the end of the bench seat and smiled in a menacing sort of way.

'You were just leaving, weren't you?' said one of the lads to me.

'No,' I said.

'I think you were. Didn't I hear you say you were afraid of the dark?'

'No.'

'It's OK. We'll see your sister gets home all right.'

'She's not my sister.' The other one had got himself behind me. I could feel his breath on the back of my neck. His leather jacket smelled of chip fat. Two extra cups of milky coffee had appeared on the table.

Julia said, 'Buzz off now, Eddie. Thanks for looking after me. I'll be all right.'

I couldn't stand it – I'd spent an hour listening to her go on about sexy Dave, and now this. But all I said was, 'I can't leave you on your own with two complete strangers.'

'These aren't strangers, Eddie.' She smiled up at them. 'What are your names, lads?' They told her. 'There. Now we've been introduced.'

Defeated, I slid out of the bench seat and walked to the

door, trying not to look behind me. I could feel a kind of restrained silence burning into me, as if they were all holding their breath. I walked past the café window trying not to look in.

I went down to the beach and stood on the rocks and looked towards Liverpool. I'd never understand how girls could be in love one moment, then want nothing but fun with somebody else the next; how they could say they wanted to know someone for their mind, but then go off with the first handsome lad they saw; how Julia could go from asking me to say how attractive and wonderful she was one minute to telling me to get lost the next. It made no sense.

A single green light moved through the darkness – a ship heading for the docks. I picked up a stone and hurled it, waiting for the splash in the dark water, somewhere out of sight. Then I picked up another and another and threw them, bending my arm back, hurling with all my fury and strength, each time waiting for the noise of the splash, each time throwing further into the blackness.

6

The following Tuesday, after the early August bank holiday, Vi asked me to take Nanny to the salerooms. The only person Nanny normally allowed with her was Ray, but he was working at the amusements and couldn't go. Vi had become almost optimistic since Ray started at Palace Amusements. He'd promised her a cut of his first wage packet and she'd soon only be fifteen bob short of forgiving him for stealing her phone money. I'd even heard her say that working there was the best thing that could have happened to him. He might not be a shipping clerk or a bank cashier or any of those, she said, but at least he was settled and getting paid regular. It was funny how she managed to believe the exact opposite of what she'd sworn was the truth less than a week earlier.

Vi had been worrying about Nanny recently, though, especially since she'd brought home the soup spoons. She thought Nanny wasn't taking her tablets. 'Don't let her buy anything stupid,' she instructed me. 'I don't want her filling the house with any more junk – no furniture or mangles or anything that needs delivering. And we've got enough plates and pans and cutlery, thank you very much.' Vi was ironing piles of handkerchiefs before starting on the sheets. A big brown scorch mark was working its way through the layers of her ironing board cover.

I'd never been to a saleroom in my life and had only the vaguest idea of how it worked. 'How am I going to stop her?' I asked. 'You know, if she gets it in her head to buy something?'

'You'll think of something. Go on – you'll miss the bus.'

Nanny was waiting in the hall, wearing her best hat and the hatpin with the thistle-shaped end.

There was a strong blow off the river and the spit of rain in the air; it was the kind of day when holidaymakers headed for the Floral Pavilion or the Troc or ventured inland to the ABC in Wallasey. Nanny knew I'd been strong-armed into looking after her and she didn't want me cramping her style. 'I don't know why you've bothered to come,' she kept saying. 'I'm all right on my own.'

'Just thought you might like some company.'

'Ha!' Nanny grumbled all the way up to the bus. Ray was better, she told me. He had a good eye for a bargain. Remember that time with the Timex? I didn't. Ray had got her to bid for a box full of stuff. No one else had noticed it there; no one else had bothered to root around the bottom of the box among the glasses and table mats. Four and six for the lot she'd paid. The watch was brand new, still in its presentation case and worth nearly seven quid on its own.

'Well, I'm not Ray,' I said, just in case there was any confusion. 'You'll have to make do with me today.'

At the bus stop she tried to lose me by sending me into Towneley's for cough sweets, but I wouldn't go. 'The bus'll be here in a minute,' I said, not budging.

'It won't. I'll make it wait for you. The conductors all know me.' As soon as she said it the bus appeared at the end of Vicky Road. Grudgingly she paid our bus fares. 'A half and a pensioner.' The bus conductor looked us up and down, but didn't say anything.

The bus went up Rowson Street and turned inland, past Stroud's Corner and on to a sprawl of shops and parks and houses. Without the sea to restrict them the roads ran in all directions. It was different from the seafront part of New Brighton – more permanent-looking and with shops that sold furniture or fabrics instead of rock and kiss-me-quick hats. Beyond were the docks, floats and bridges of Birkenhead.

The salerooms were better than I'd expected. You had to go up wooden stairs that took you above a row of shops – a long space piled high with leatherette armchairs and rolls of foam-backed carpet. In one corner there were unplugged fruit machines looking sorry for themselves, covered in grease and glass marks. There were windows in the roof and places where bits of ceiling hung down, with buckets underneath to catch the leaks. Rain rattled on the tin roof.

Holidaymakers didn't usually come this far – it was a couple of miles from the seafront – but one or two were hanging around in their anoraks and shorts to keep out of the rain. The rest of the customers seemed to be pensioners and fierce pub owners out for a bargain.

Nanny said our first job was to look around thoroughly and check the territory. It was important not to miss anything, but it was even more important not to be seen to be interested. If I did see something I was to pretend I hadn't. 'Do you want me to take secret photos?' I asked sarcastically, but Nanny didn't seem to notice. She was in her element.

'No need,' she said, 'just remember what you've seen. Memorize the lot number if you can – or jot it down when nobody's looking.' I was impressed. She seemed to know all the strategies.

After a while people began to drift to one end of the room and the auctioneer got up on a little stage where everybody could see him. He started auctioning off the lots. Antique horticultural implements were the first lot. That was another name for a load of old rakes and cracked plant pots. Then a catalogued record collection. That was a set of Mario Lanza LPs and a notebook. During the next bidding I noticed Nanny holding up her card. 'What are you doing, Nan? You're not bidding already, are you?'

She shook her head as if I was being daft, then shot her card up again. Before I could do anything about it the auctioneer had brought his hammer down and we'd bought a set of white damask tablecloths with an embroidered floral motif.

'How much has that set us back?' I wanted to know.

'Never mind, Ray,' she said. 'Leave it to me.'

Her voice was determined and oddly detached. 'It's not Ray,' I said, panicking. 'It's me – Eddie. You remember, don't you? It's Eddie.'

'Ssh,' she said. 'Mustn't let anyone know what you're thinking. Here – look at this and don't tell a soul.' She shoved her catalogue into my hands. She'd circled numbers and pencilled prices against almost every item.

'What?' I said. 'All these? Nan, we don't have this much money – and I'm supposed to be looking after you.'

'Don't be such a killjoy. You only live once.' Her card flew up again and before I knew it we'd acquired lot number 8 – a beautifully preserved 1928 fox tippet complete with glass eyes. It looked at me accusingly from across the saleroom.

'God, Nan. Stop. Please.' But it was no good. Her eyes had gone glazed behind her ivory-coloured specs. She started off again, flashing her card up and down. 'What are you after now?' I asked.

It was only when the crowd moved aside that I saw what it was – a full-size walnut wardrobe. She seemed to be bidding against one of the pub landlords, but she was in a world of her own. I saw her hand twitching at the wrist. That was how badly she wanted to put it up again.

'With the gentleman at the front,' the auctioneer said, looking around. 'Eleven pounds.'

Eleven pounds! What would Vi say? The wardrobe was enormous. It wouldn't fit in any of the bedrooms. I tried to imagine Vi's reaction as we struggled to get it upstairs. Nan opened her mouth to speak. Suddenly I snatched the card out of her hand and threw it on the floor. She looked at me, shocked, as if I'd appeared out of nowhere.

'Sold! To the gentleman in the maroon waistcoat.'

'I wanted that,' she shouted.

'Sold! Sorry, love, it's gone.' Her reply was drowned out by rain hammering on the tin roof, spreading in rivers across the skylights. There was a kind of mutter as the noise of the rain increased and people shuffled away from the walls. Others came in, shaking themselves like dogs. The drips into the buckets got heavier, became steady runnels. Then a little waterfall started over the auctioneer's platform. He moved sideways and slid a china pot under it with one foot, as if he hoped nobody would notice. But the noise was like someone piddling in a bottle. Old women started getting their rain hoods out of their handbags.

Then I realized Nanny had given me the slip. There she was on the other side of the room with her rescued auction card. What was she going for now? She seemed to be the only one raising her hand, but the price was still going up. Was it possible to bid against yourself? Four and six, I heard called. Five bob. I pushed my way through the crowds and grabbed her arm just as she was about to raise her own offer again. I managed to stop her, but it was too late – she'd already bought it. 'Sold. Card number 117 at the side there.' The hammer went down. Tap. That was it.

She seemed to recognize me then. 'Oh, hello, Eddie. Fancy seeing you here. I've bought us a vacuum cleaner.'

A big chunk of ceiling fell down in one corner of the room and rain started pouring over a dressing table. Someone shouted, 'Abandon ship!' The lights flickered, then came on again and it was strangely exciting because the salerooms really did feel like a ship sinking under the weight of all that junk.

'Come on, Nan. Let's get you out of here before you do any more damage.'

We had to go to a different place to collect our stuff. It was downstairs and slightly drier. The bloke wrapped the tablecloths and fox tippet in newspaper. 'Where's my vacuum cleaner?' Nanny demanded. 'I just bought a Goblin cleaner with hoses and brushes.'

He checked his list. 'You must have made a mistake. The vacuum was sold earlier.'

She wouldn't have it. She knew she'd bought the cleaner. She'd seen it and she'd bid for it. 'Sorry, missus,' the bloke said. 'This is what you bid for.' It was a china ornament – a pretty girl in an old-fashioned bonnet, a swirling pink dress and an expression on her face as if someone had slapped her and she was trying not to cry.

'God,' Nan said. 'I can't clean the stairs with that. Tell him, Ray.'

'It's Eddie,' I reminded her. 'I think that's what you bought, Nan. Maybe we ought to just take it.'

'That's right. Lot 23. Victorian china ornament.'

'Victorian, my Aunt Fanny,' Nanny said.

The bloke shook his head, wrapped it in newspaper and put it in a bag with the others. 'Be careful, missus. Sold as seen.'

Nanny scowled at him. 'I know that,' she said. 'I've been here enough times before.'

After a drink and a biscuit Nan's expression cleared and she began to recognize things again. Outside the rain had eased and there was a ragged bit of blue sky. The weather often changed when the tide turned. When you lived here or got to know the place you understood that kind of thing unconsciously, but you couldn't remember if anyone had ever told you. It was like you might have dreamed it.

'Oh, God, Eddie,' she chuckled when we were safely on the bus. 'I got a bit carried away, didn't I? I nearly bought the whole place today. You know, I could have done, too. I really liked that bike with "Family Butcher" on the cross-bar. We could have advertised Vi's place and you could have cycled along the prom with it. That would've been something, wouldn't it?'

We laughed. I said, 'There'd have been removal vans queuing up for a week if you'd had your way. And what about that wardrobe? What would Vi have said if you'd bought that?'

'Don't tell her, will you, Eddie? She'll stop me going again if she knows I nearly bought that wardrobe.' I said I wouldn't let her buy any furniture. 'You're all right you are. Nearly as good as Ray.'

'Thanks, Nan.' It was as much of a compliment as I was going to get. She took her stuff out of the bag to look at it. The tablecloths were crisp and white and didn't smell of mildew at all. They could almost have been new. She showed me the embroidered flowers round the edge, following the pattern with her bent fingers. The tippet had a fox's tail on one end and the head on the other, with vicious nippy teeth and glass eyes. Even the ornament wasn't so bad. Nan examined it carefully, peering into the china girl's eyes. 'She hasn't got an ounce of sense in her head. At least she's pretty, I suppose; all right to brighten up my new room.'

I said, 'Even Vi can't complain about that. We've been very restrained.'

She laughed and wrapped her booty back up in the newspaper. 'You restrained me, anyway. We've not done a bad job between us, have we, Ed?'

*

I hadn't seen Julia since that night at Fairlanes when I'd left her squeezed between the two sleazeball greasers. And in the few days since then she'd given the impression of being totally occupied. I thought she was avoiding me. I'd heard her voice in the evening and couldn't help noticing the hours she spent in the bathroom dolling herself up even if she was only going out to the shops. Once, she left remains at the dining table – some neat crumbs of bread around a plate, a crumpled paper serviette with a trace of pink lipstick – and I collected them up and took them into the kitchen.

One night I dreamed about her. She was a great distance down a field, riding a black horse, her hair jogging with the rhythm of its hooves. Later in the dream she swam in a pool as round and green as a pea and emerged dripping on a motorbike while I looked down from the lip of the pool. Then she was wearing a short skirt and a top patterned with bright diagonals knitted from Maisie's wool. She kissed me gently, touching the point of my chin. I woke up and Ray's bed was empty.

Until that dream I hadn't realized how much I was thinking about Julia. She was alive and staying under the same roof as me; she breathed and ate, that was all. She closed doors heavily, trod floorboards until they creaked, argued with her mother, with Irene and even with herself until she sulked. She sat alone where she could see the comings and goings of others and cut them dead when they approached her. Sometimes she smoked in secret parts of the house, christened them with fag ends – the floating butt in the toilet pan, in the street flattened by one strappy sandal or flicked fizzing into the gutter. I was dizzy with her presence and her absence.

*

Ray must have felt bad about forgetting to take me for a drink because on his first day off from the Palace he asked if I wanted to go to the joke shop, Box of Tricks.

In other years I'd wanted to try everything the joke shop had to offer – the fake boils you stuck on the side of your neck, the nail-through-finger complete with festering bandage, the vampire teeth and the Naughty Rover plastic dog turds that you put on the carpet to surprise your family.

I'd bought cellophane packets of itching powder and red hot sweets that looked like ordinary pastilles. The packets were decorated with cartoons of horrified fat women and bald men with astonished expressions. The ultimate reaction. I'd have spent every penny I owned to see Vi or my mum with that look on their faces.

One year Ray and me had bought a box of stink bombs. We let three off in the entrance to Woolies. We dropped them on the floor and casually ground them in with our heels. Then we walked away. We went back later, expecting to find the whole shop evacuated, people standing on the pavement with handkerchiefs to their mouths. But it was as if nothing had happened. A spotty lad was sweeping up fragments of glass with a dustpan and brush. There was hardly a trace of rotten egg in the air. I realized the world wasn't waiting for my humour. It was a big disappointment.

Vi had told us not to go there now. People were talking about comings and goings at all hours of the day and night. Ray said that was no different to a pub, then, or Vi's boarding house come to that. And Vi said just for once listen to what she had to say because just for once we might be surprised to find she was right. But that only made it more appealing – suddenly the joke shop had a new lease of life. It seemed as dangerous and unpredictable as the quicksand on the estuary.

But when we got there the joke shop was closed. From the outside it looked the same as always except it had a new sign with the new name: Box of Tricks. Ray looked at it and whistled. We looked at one another. It was our chance to chicken out. Ray said, 'We'll wait. He's probably having his dinner.'

So we hung around and talked about Uncle Steve and what it must be like in New Jersey. We were beginning to understand why Steve had gone. Ray and me had watched the flags and smoke of the liners setting off down the Mersey, and imagined ourselves on them, working our passage – maybe like the Great Montezuma or on the crew – throwing ropes ashore, calling to women hanging out of windows in Tangiers, getting drunk and nobody caring.

Eventually a bloke appeared at the end of the street. He was middle-aged – we could see that straight away – old enough to know better than to be selling kids' jokes and magic, you'd have thought. He was bald as a badger except for neat, dark hair over his ears. 'Is this him?' I whispered to Ray.

'I think so.'

'He doesn't look like the Great anything.'

'Good afternoon, gentlemen,' he said as he reached us. He took his little round glasses off and wiped them with his thumb. 'How may I assist?'

'We were hoping to examine the contents of your shop,' Ray said.

He looked at us suspiciously. 'Really? In that case would you care to enter the premises?'

'Why not? It'll keep us off the street,' Ray said.

He unlocked the shop door and pushed it open. It had been newly fixed to make a howling noise every time it opened. The Great Montezuma jumped, as if he'd never heard it before. 'Electric werewolf. I keep forgetting to turn it off.'

When we went in I looked up. What I saw made me jump much worse than the electric werewolf. It was like staring into the eyes of a crowd of zombies. Every mask you could think of was there – Elvis, Harold Wilson, Kennedy, the Queen and Winston Churchill. Between them were the most blood-soaked ghouls and monsters from the films with shrivelled flesh, shrunken heads from Borneo dangling on strings, Mickey Mouse, Yogi Bear, Mick Jagger, the Beatles in plastic, Cilla Black, Hughie Green.

'Looking for anything in particular?' he asked. Once we'd passed under the empty eyes the joke shop looked the same as it always had. The shelves of American paperbacks with their covers with half-naked women and rugged detectives were still there. The racks of plastic noses and moustaches hadn't moved. The shelves of pots and jugs with seaside captions were unchanged. Only Ma Feeney, sitting at the counter doing her crosswords, was missing.

'It's kind of a social call,' Ray said.

'You mean you've got no money.'

'Something like that.'

'Have a look round, then. Browsers welcome. No obligation to purchase. Lovely to look at, delightful to hold. If you should break it, consider it sold. And don't mess with anything. Got it?'

'Yeah,' Ray said. 'Ta.'

While Ray was browsing the owner called me over. 'What do you think to this, young man? Can I ask your name?' I told him. 'You're broad-minded, aren't you, Eddie?' I nodded in anticipation, my throat drying up. 'You can call me Pete, by the way.' There was no reference to the Great Montezuma or anyone else for that matter.

Pete pulled out a little box, put it on the counter and tipped out a biro, lifting it up so I could see it. There was a picture on the side – a girl in a black one-piece swimsuit. She had her hands behind her head and a sulky look on her face, like a 1950s pin-up. Pete gently tilted the end of the biro and the swimsuit slid away to reveal tiny flesh-coloured shoulders and perfectly drawn breasts with pink tips.

'Not bad, eh, Eddie? Better than in the magazines. Animation, this is called – like a cartoon, except you get to operate it yourself.' He carefully laid the pen back on the counter out of my reach. The swimsuit was frozen just above her crotch. 'Don't want to wear it out, though, do we?' he said.

'It's a bit tame,' I told him.

'You're hard to please, aren't you? What's up? Getting too much already?'

'Maybe.'

'Three and nine to you. Bargain.' But he could see it was out of my range and before I knew it the pen was in its box and back under the counter.

Then a bloke came in and I hung around while they talked. They were leaning on either side of the counter. Pete was demonstrating one of his tricks. He'd got a glass with some bright yellow liquid in it that was meant to be brandy. He pretended to take a swig, then he kind of dashed it in the bloke's face, as if he was chucking it over him. The bloke took a big step back and nearly fell over me, standing behind him. But nothing had come out. The bloke said, 'You had me goin' there a minute, Pete. I thought I was gonna have to give you a smack in the gob.'

'It's an illusion. Watch this,' Pete said, and he turned the glass upside down to show how the liquid was sealed in the bottom. 'I've got a different one somewhere – looks like an ordinary glass, but there are tiny holes in the side so when you drink it dribbles down your front.'

The bloke looked at him. He said, 'I think I do that anyway.' They both laughed, but I could tell Pete didn't think it was funny, then the bloke said, 'I'm not really into all that, like. Has my stuff come in yet?'

Pete acted surprised. 'Stuff? Whatever do you mean?' Then he stooped down behind his counter and popped up again with a magazine in his hands. His face was flushed. He reminded me of a frogman sticking his head out of the river, his glasses muddy with seaweed. 'Came in Friday.'

The bloke would have taken the magazine, but Pete dropped it into one of his brown paper bags and sealed it from the Sellotape dispenser all in one fluid movement.

He looked up at us as the man left. 'You still here?'

'We're customers,' Ray called from the back of the shop where he was browsing through *Mad* magazines and *Marvel* comics.

'Customers are people who buy things.'

'I might have bought that pen. You don't know,' I said.

'Yes, and pigs might have flown.' Then he said quietly, as if it was a secret between us. 'I bet you like tricks, don't you, Eddie?'

'Not the ones that come in plastic bags,' I said. 'I've grown out of those. I'm interested in proper magic, though.'

'That's what I'm talking about – conjuring.'

'What?' Ray called. 'Like the Indian rope trick?'

'I did that in Leeds once – the Alhambra. An Indian lad climbed up into thin air and I packed that rope back into my basket and went home. Never saw the little bugger again.'

'How do you do it?' I asked, but it was Magic Circle, he said. He wasn't allowed to show how magic like that was done. He could show me other stuff if I wanted. Three-card Monte, Find the Lady. I laughed. Chance would be a fine thing.

'How about this? Simple sleight of hand,' he said.

He took a sixpenny bit out of his pocket and passed it from one hand to the other. It should have been in his left, but when he opened it, it was empty. He smiled and opened the other. It was empty too. He shrugged and reached across to me very slowly, then pulled the coin out from behind my ear. It made me shiver, him touching my ear with his fingertips. He showed me the coin.

'I need to go,' I told him. Ray was still looking at comics.

'I thought you wanted to know how to do it,' he said. 'Stay and watch again. Look. Watch very carefully this time. You've got to keep an eye on my hands.' They were thin, with long, strong fingers.

He passed the sixpence from one hand to the other again. Then he gave it to me. 'Put it on the counter, Eddie.' So I did, and he took a handkerchief from the pocket of his tweed jacket and dropped it over the coin. 'Watch now,' he said. 'Are you watching?' He pulled the handkerchief away. The coin was gone.

'Good,' I said. 'That's good.' But he didn't reply, just opened his mouth slowly and stuck out his tongue a long way. It was a mottled greyish pink. The coin was there, balancing on the tip. He waggled it back and forth.

'Take it,' he tried to say, but it came out as, 'Aykit.'

'What?'

He made it waggle again, stuck his pointy tongue out even further. I shook my head. 'Now!' he managed, and nodded so I couldn't refuse. I picked the tanner off, dropped it on the counter as if it was red hot. It lay in a slick of spit.

'That wasn't so bad, was it?' he asked. But it was. 'Do you want me to show you how?' What would Ray think if I could make coins disappear like that? How powerful would it make me – if I could make money appear from every pocket and orifice? Such mysteries. Pete was about to show me more, but I saw his eyes shift behind his glasses, just a darting movement into the back of his shop. Behind me, I could hear Ray leaving.

Pete might have been middle-aged, but he was leery and quick. Probably his conjuring demanded it. He leaped round from behind the counter and dashed up the shop before Ray had chance to get out the door. He grabbed Ray by the wrist.

'Get off me,' Ray shouted, gasping as Pete pulled him into a neat arm grip. Where had he learned that? At the wrestling? On board ship? Ray was shouting in pain, helpless, getting close to kneeling on the floor.

Pete applied a little more pressure, his voice calm, light glinting on his glasses as he dragged Ray back down the shop. 'Now then, I believe you have something of mine in your possession.'

'I dunno what you're on about,' Ray said. 'Leave me alone. Ed, call the police. I'm being assaulted here.'

'I don't think that will be necessary. Let's see what we can find.' Ladies and gentlemen, he almost said, as he reached into the pocket of Ray's windcheater to produce with a flourish – 'A-ha' – an ashtray shaped like a skull with 'Poor old Fred smoked in bed' written on it. Very calmly, Pete put it on the counter without letting go of Ray's wrist. 'And more, I suspect,' he said and gave Ray a shake until he cried out again. A magazine fell to the floor.

It lay there, a spread-eagled centrefold of a sultry woman wearing nothing but a big hat, her long-gloved hands on her thighs. All three of us stood looking down at her. She had that look of pleasure – eyes half-closed, mouth half-open and moist. I wondered how she created that look.

Pete let go of Ray's wrist. 'Shit,' Ray said, rubbing his forearm.

'Don't ever expect people to fall for it – especially not an old pro like me. You must think I was born yesterday,' Pete told him. 'Using the kid as a decoy. It's the oldest trick in the book. You're dealing with a professional here. Don't forget that.'

'I wasn't a decoy,' I said angrily. 'I had nothing to do with it.'

'That's what you think, son,' Pete said. He exchanged a glance with Ray as if they had something in common, which in a way they did, because they both knew exactly how to deceive people.

'Come on, mate,' Ray said. 'Don't take it personal. You know how it works.'

'I'm not taking anything personally,' Pete said. 'I just don't want you in my shop ever again. If I see you here again it'll be me that calls the police. Do you understand?'

He brushed down the front of his jacket with his hands, adjusted his glasses. Ray shrugged, but I could tell he'd been shaken almost as much as I had. 'If that's the way you want it.' He walked to the door with as much dignity as he could muster. 'Come on, Eddie. We're taking our custom elsewhere.'

7

Having girls hanging around was a perk of the job at the Palace. Some blokes got luncheon vouchers or a clothing allowance, but Ray got 'chatting up'. 'On the amount they pay us,' he said, 'we deserve all the extras we can get.'

As part of his chatting up allowance Ray found out from this girl called Denise that she was having a party. He got her to write her address down and then he told me about the party and how good it was going to be. 'There'll be loads of ace judies there,' he promised and he described them to me, even the ones he'd never met. I must have sounded a bit uncertain because he said, 'You want to end up with a judy, don't you? That's what it's all about.'

'Maybe. I mean – not just any old bint. I have to fancy her a bit. If that's all right!'

'God, nobody's asking you to marry them. It's just for a night. You've got to get some experience, Ed, while you're young. You want some experience, don't you?'

Of course I did. I wasn't sure if it was another of Ray's fantasies, like the friends he had in the business world or the fishing tackle shop he was going to open or the outing to the pub he'd promised me. But this time he'd got the night off work and he'd had a bath so it looked genuine enough. He stood in our shared bedroom with a skimpy white towel round his waist and said, 'What you waiting for, then?' So I nipped down to the bathroom while Irene and Maisie weren't using it. I got washed all over, then collected the bottle of Old Spice aftershave from under my shirts in the bottom drawer and peppered it around my face and under my arms. It made me feel conspicuous, as if the smell went out in front of me as a warning I was on my way.

After that we had to get past Vi. 'No problems,' Ray told me. 'It's the *Alfred Hitchcock Hour*. She'll be too busy telly-viewing. Watch this.' And he stuck his head round the kitchen door like one of the guests and said, 'We're off now, Mother. See you later.'

'OK,' I heard her say and we were in the hall ready to go. Ray winked at me. But he hadn't shut the kitchen door quickly enough. 'Ray!' she called. We stopped in our tracks at the sound of her voice.

'What?'

'Come back in here.'

'But we're gonna be late,' he called.

'Never mind that. Get in here. Let's have a look at you.' So he opened the door again and stuck his head into the kitchen.

'What's the matter, Mother?' he asked. I couldn't see his face, but would have bet it had a pretend-innocent smile on it.

'I want to see you,' she said.

'I'm here, aren't I?'

'Not just your mug – all of you. And is Eddie with you?'

So we had to go back and stand in line, like in the headmaster's office. Ray had Tru-gelled his hair and combed it back and he was wearing a pair of tight blue jeans, his favourite baseball boots and a narrow tie with blue horizontal stripes. I was going for my best casual look. I'd only brought one set of going-out clothes with me – a sleeveless pullover and a bottle-green shirt which I wore now without a tie. My hair flopped carefully over my right eye.

She looked us up and down. 'So where are you two going, done up like Joe Brown and one of his ruddy Bruvvers?'

'Just to see a friend.' Ray was a confident liar. That's what made Vi suspicious straight away.

'Do I know him, this friend?' She said the word as if it had inverted commas around it.

'No.'

'What's his name, then?'

Ray sighed. 'Mother, I'm seventeen. I don't have to tell you everything I do.'

'You do as long as you live in my house. Anyway, Eddie isn't as old as you. You gotta look after him.'

Luckily for us the Alfred Hitchcock music started getting loud and insistent, which usually meant someone was about to be murdered. It meant violence. Vi just *had* to look at the telly then, and suddenly she'd lost her hold over us. It wasn't her fault. That's the way it was meant to work with Alfred Hitchcock. 'Get off with the both of you,' she said in an impatient voice, her eyes glued to the screen. Something sharp glinted in the air. 'And don't be late back.'

She started to speak, but we were already out through the door into the hall and Ray had shut it before he got to hear something else he'd prefer not to.

On the bus Ray started telling me about the party. He pulled a scrap of paper out of his pocket. It looked like the torn-off corner of a sweet bag and it had an address written in neat red biro. Definitely a girl's writing – there were little circles instead of dots over the 'i's. 'Denise's address,' he explained and made out as if to kiss it.

We got off the bus near the Birkenhead ferry and then walked through a maze of lanes and streets into a housing estate. It seemed as if we were walking away from the river, but there were so many turns that I lost my sense of direction. We stopped at an offy and Ray went in while I waited outside. Eventually he came out with a party can of beer in a plastic bag. He held it up. 'Our passport to international partying pleasure,' he said.

We found the house eventually and a girl came to the door with a glass in her hand. She seemed pleased to see Ray and put her arm through his and led us into the kitchen. She was wearing a tiny minidress. 'Me mam and dad are away,' she explained. 'They said no parties.'

'That's all right,' Ray said. 'So this isn't a party?'

'Not really. It's just a few friends getting together.'

'Oh, yeah,' Ray said. It looked and sounded like a party to me all right. There was a record player full blast in the living room and a transistor in the kitchen tuned to Luxembourg. The reception was terrible as usual, the music fading into adverts and snatches of foreign stations. There were people squeezed into the hall and sitting on the stairs. Ray punctured his can and poured beer into mugs. One of them had 'Liverpool FC' on it. He handed it to me. 'This is me cousin, Eddie, by the way.'

Denise glanced at me, but she didn't say anything. She was more interested in Ray, which was all right by me, except she was really obvious about it. She bumped her hips into him as they talked. Then she put one arm round his neck the way people in gangs used to do in the Junior playground to show they were mates. When she pretended to be looking across the room her cheek accidentally touched his.

At least she didn't ask any questions about what I was doing there. Apparently it was enough to know Ray. So I wandered into the front room and left them to it. Denise's front room was the length of two settees and after a while I started dancing with a girl who said her name was Lulu. I didn't believe her, so I told her I was a used car salesman. I wasn't sure why I said it. It was just the most reckless thing I could think of and happened to be the job I knew least about. It made her start on about Cortinas and Corsairs and for a minute I thought I might be in trouble. Her dad was thinking of getting one or the other and she wanted the advice of someone in the know. 'Cortina,' I said, 'definitely. Better suspension and more reliable.'

She looked impressed and I thought how easy it was when you didn't take life too seriously. I could see her again and make up more stories about cars until I got found out. I kept going into the kitchen to fill up with drinks and at least twice I took Lulu's glass, too. She said she wanted vodka, but I couldn't find any, so filled her glass up with Blue Nun instead. She didn't seem to notice. In the kitchen Ray and Denise had found their way onto a chair. They were wedged between a kitchen unit and the back door. Once when I went in for a refill, Ray was on top and another two times it was Denise. The second time Ray had his hand on her leg and the third time I couldn't see where his hand was because by now someone had turned the fluorescent off and the only light left in the kitchen was the glow from the transistor, flickering between stations.

I was losing track of time. I was losing count of drinks. I kept putting my Liverpool FC mug down and forgetting where I'd left it. At one point I was drinking with a bloke who said his name was Terry. We were standing in the hall and he pulled a hip flask from his back pocket and poured something into my mug. 'Rum,' he explained. 'You can decide for yourself what you want with it.' He rocked gently from one leg to the other, but I didn't think he was drunk. I realized he was wearing leg irons. 'The girls find the callipers appealing, believe it or not,' he said. 'They like someone to look after. A man like me – who's a bit squidgy.'

I must have looked shocked.

'They're real,' he said. 'I had a touch of polio.'

'I didn't know you could have a touch of polio.'

'Well, I did.'

My time with Ray, Julia and the Rodcoopers had shown me how many people preferred make-believe and lies to their real lives. With Terry I couldn't tell. Surely nobody would make that sort of thing up. Then I remembered Mr Charnock our history teacher telling us how, after the Napoleonic Wars, beggars used to pretend to be injured soldiers to get more sympathy. They made wounds out of layers of soap and bloody bandages. And that got me thinking about the masks hanging from the ceiling of the joke shop, about the joy people got from masquerading as someone else. I remembered Alastair pretending to be a pirate and challenging Charles to a sword fight. Then I thought about Julia, who one moment acted like a sophisticated woman-about-town and the next like a bored child.

Then Julia went out of my head because I was dancing with Lulu again.

She was wearing perfume that smelled like something I recognized, but I couldn't remember what. I asked her about it. 'Midnight in Moscow,' she told me and in that moment the music changed. The person sitting by the record player had put on something slow. I didn't know the song, but I was absorbed by Lulu's dark hair. 'Is that your real name?' I whispered into it.

I must have been slurring because Lulu asked, 'What?' I repeated the question.

'What does it matter?' she said.

I wasn't sure whether it mattered any more. I tried to remember how many drinks I'd had, but that was meaningless, too, because it was measured in mugs or glasses of different sizes. The next time I went into the kitchen Ray and Denise were gone and the back door was open. I looked at their empty chair.

And now I wanted to tell Lulu I loved her, but only

because the words would sound wonderful together. I thought that wasn't a good enough reason but I tried to tell her anyway and found I couldn't because the words were sounding like a bath being emptied. I started to laugh. *I love you, Lulu. Lulu, I love you. Truly, Lulu.*

'You're mad, you are, Eddie, honest,' she said, and she took me by the hand. I thought we might be about to go upstairs. Perhaps we could lie among the coats on someone's bed. I thought this very clearly and coolly. Not at all like I'd imagined. It felt inevitable, as if Lulu and me had never needed to talk about it, but both knew from the beginning what would happen.

'Let's go and find somewhere,' I said and we went out into the hall.

Then, right in front of me, the front door opened by itself. A man came into the hall and stood there in the half-light. He blinked at us. 'What in God's name's going on here?' he said.

'What d'you mean?' I said, more boldly than I'd intended.

'Who the hell are you?'

I had to think about this one carefully. 'I'm just a friend,' I said, which seemed diplomatic for a minute.

'Who are all these people?'

'We're all friends,' I said.

'Wait till I get hold of our Denise. I'll give her "friends". Where is she?'

I wasn't sure whether he expected me to know the answer, but he said it again louder. 'Where the hell is she?' In fact, he was shouting. His nose looked like it had been chewed up and thrown into the middle of his face. His eyebrows were starting to disappear into a furrow in the middle of his forehead.

A woman appeared behind him. She said, 'Bloody hell!'

'Bloody hell's right,' the husband started shouting. 'And that's putting it mildly.'

'Oh, God,' she said. 'Our house has turned into a squat. We'll have to let them stay here. We'll have to go and live in a hotel.'

'Don't be so bloody ridiculous. Denise'll be behind this.'

But nobody seemed to actually know Denise. 'We go away for a holiday and when we come back someone else is living in our house,' the woman wailed.

But the bloke wasn't having any of it. 'Who's in charge? I'll have the bloody police on yer. Who let you all in?'

Someone turned the record player off and a light went on in the kitchen. It went quiet. 'Oh, hello,' someone said cheerily. 'It's Denise's mum and dad. Did you have a nice holiday?'

'I told you she'd be behind it,' Denise's dad said, blundering round looking for her. But she was off somewhere with Ray. Then, when he couldn't find her, he started driving the partygoers out through the front door. 'Get out!' he was shouting. 'Get out of my house. Go home – and don't bloody come back.' Denise's mum started clearing the rubbish, putting on all the lights and mopping up.

'Out!' the dad kept shouting every time he found someone in a chair or under a table. He poked them with one foot like they were animals. Partly dressed people were stumbling out of rooms looking shocked. So suddenly me and Lulu were running through the front door instead of a bedroom door. It wasn't tragic. It was funny. By this time there were about ten of us on the pavement, standing in the dark, not sure what to do. I realized I didn't have a clue how to get home. I also realized that I didn't care.

Lulu said, 'Can you give us a lift home, Eddie?'

'Haven't got a car,' I said. 'Sorry. I'll walk you home, though.'

She said, 'I've never heard of a car salesman without a car before.'

'Oh – the car I was supposed to have, got like a puncture thing.'

'And they couldn't fix it?'

'Not in time, no.'

'Wasn't there a spare tyre then?'

'Well, it wasn't so much a puncture. More something to do with the cylinder head gasket or the big end.'

The bloke called Terry was leaning against the wall. He said, 'I can give you a lift if you want – or I can drop you off. Where you heading?' He knew where there was another party, he said. 'I'll just go and get the motor. Hang on there a minute.'

After a long while Terry appeared round the corner. He was driving a blue, three-wheeled invalid carriage. It was about the size of a large pram. And I looked at Lulu. She was laughing and suddenly I realized she was beautiful. Why hadn't I noticed before? It must have been the cold night air that made her face look so lovely. She laughed until her mascara ran. Her lips were full of colour. Her hands gripped the handle on her bag.

'Lulu,' I muttered. 'Look, Lulu. Is that your real name?'

The pavement was almost empty. Most of the crowd must have decided to walk home. The invalid carriage pulled up in front of us with a clatter and the blue door slid open.

Lulu said, 'You've got to be joking, haven't you? Where're we supposed to sit?'

'Who said anything about sitting?' Terry said. He had to climb out again to let us in. It looked as if there'd be room for one passenger lying on the floor, feet stretched under the dashboard. 'I've had three in here loads of times. It's dead cosy.'

So I scrambled in past the steering bar and Lulu climbed on top of me, legs and arms and Midnight in Moscow everywhere, her hair in my eyes. I felt the bony structure of her bum in my lap. 'I'll be sick,' she said. 'I've had fourteen vodkas.'

My head was about level with the steering wheel and if I craned my neck I could just see out of the side window. 'Is this legal?' I asked.

'Course not.' Terry climbed back into the driver's side. He was enjoying it. He was enjoying having her legs in his car and I didn't begrudge him. 'Bet you never thought you'd be driven home in style like this. Here, hold these.' And he gave us two walking sticks to look after. 'Now keep your heads down – specially if we see any blue lights! You ready?'

Terry's legs stretched into the nose of the carriage. He steered using the bar, rocking it round corners and roundabouts. All I could see were orange streetlights whizzing overhead, melting together. The taste of Lulu's hair was in my mouth. At traffic lights we were the last to pull away – the slowest thing on the road. I was sure Ray wouldn't believe any of this when I told him about it.

Finally we stopped at the end of Waterloo Road. 'I'll drop you off first,' Terry said to me, and we all had to unfold ourselves onto the pavement so I could get out.

Then Lulu was supposed to get back in, but instead she sat on a low wall. She was moaning gently. She put her head in her hands. 'Are you all right, love?' Terry asked and put a hand on her shoulder. She nodded, but the colour had gone from her face. Even in the streetlight I could see that. 'Are you going to be sick?' Terry asked.

She shook her head. 'I'll be all right in a bit.' So we stood around till she got to her feet shakily, then she started to climb back into the carriage. 'See you, Eddie,' she said and turned and kissed me on the mouth, quick and unforgettable.

The funny thing was she was still lovely even then, even with the colour drained from her face and something unspeakable at the back of her throat. 'Lulu, could we . . . ?' I began, but words were too clumsy for what I wanted to say. 'Do you think I . . . ?'

Terry was telling her about the next party. Maybe she just wanted to go home now. She nodded. She lay back on the cold floor of the carriage and Terry slid the door shut with a slam. Then he started the engine and they wobbled off into the night. I thought I saw her hand waving. I knew I'd never see her again.

Vi's house was only about twenty-five yards from where Terry dropped me so I walked down the road. I was feeling empty and sad thinking about Lulu and I turned into Vi's gate without looking. That was when I came face to face with her. Julia. She was carrying a duffle bag and had a guilty look on her face. 'Shit!' she said. 'Where'd you spring from?'

'I've been to a party,' I said, 'and I got a lift back from a bloke in an invalid carriage.'

She looked at me carefully. 'You don't have to tell me a load of lies.'

'I thought you wanted me to tell lies,' I said. 'Cos of it being more interesting.'

'Not now. Not in the middle of the night.'

I said, 'Well, make your mind up. And it's the truth, as a matter of fact.'

'Stop bloody confusing me, then.' Her eyes were darting up and down the road. I wasn't sure of the time but it had to be past one o'clock in the morning.

I said, 'What are you doing here anyway, Julia?'

'None of your business.'

'It looks like you're going somewhere. That's what it looks like to me.'

'What gave you that idea?' She smiled sarcastically. 'Anyway, isn't it past your bedtime?' A car turned into the road, and she stopped, made as if to step forward, but the car sped past without stopping. She said, 'I'm going for a night out if you must know. Dave's coming up from Sussex.'

'All the way from there, just to take you out?'

'I'm worth it,' she said. 'Look, stop going on, will you? You're starting to sound like my mother.'

I sat down pretty sharp on the stone wall between Vi's house and the bombsite next door. 'Everybody takes things so personal,' she said. 'Look – it's nothing to do with you. Just don't tell anyone you saw me, right?'

I shrugged.

She went on, 'If you must know, Dave's coming to collect me.'

'You already told me that.'

'I mean, we're going away.'

'What? Like running away?'

'Not so much running away – more like escaping.'

'How long for?'

'I dunno. A few days – for keeps maybe. We'll have to see. I can't stand it here any more.'

'Where'll you go?'

She glanced up the road again. 'How should I know? It doesn't matter anyway, does it? What matters is that we're going somewhere – together. He treats me like an adult, Dave does. He understands me.'

'You mean he does what you want?' She gave me a theatrical withering look, but it didn't scare me. I asked, 'Does Brenda – I mean your mother – know?'

'What do you think?'

'She'll go mad.'

'It's about time she sat up and took notice. She just carries on day after day with all her operatic types and doesn't give a damn about me. Anyway, I don't care what she thinks.' Julia seemed nervous despite her big words.

She kept walking to the edge of the pavement. A car turned into the road.

'Here he is. At last!' She turned to me. 'Not a bloody word. Do you understand? You never saw me. Right?'

Dave's car was a sporty red number with chrome fins. Dave was hunched down in the seat and he looked at us, then leaned across and opened the passenger door for Julia. She threw her bag in and got in without a word. The car screeched into the road and sped off in a cloud of exhaust fumes.

I couldn't help smiling to myself. Perhaps I'd never seen any of this. It could have been the result of too much canned beer, rum and cider. The road was completely silent, as if Julia had never existed, or Lulu for that matter. Then a dog barked somewhere in the distance and the wind got up and made me shiver and I knew it had been real. Tomorrow there'd be hell to pay.

8

It was about three o'clock in the morning when I heard Ray come in. He pulled his feet out of his baseball boots and struggled out of his clothes. 'What happened to you?' I asked.

'Had to walk home. Bloody long way.'

'Denise's mum and dad didn't catch you, then?'

'We were in their garden. They've got a very comfy greenhouse if you know what I mean – sunbeds and things.' He yawned. 'We were going to go back to the party, but we saw her mum and dad in the kitchen. They didn't look too happy – weren't supposed to be home till tomorrow.'

'Did you go in?'

'You joking? We went for a walk round till we thought they'd gonc to bed and then Denise sneaked in the back door.' I heard the springs rattle as Ray tumbled into his bed. 'You get back all right?'

'Yeah,' I said. 'Got a lift.'

'I told you you'd have a good time,' Ray mumbled.

'I met a girl called Lulu,' I said.

'Lulu.' He laughed. 'Lulu. That's good.' He was falling asleep as he spoke. 'Gotta work in a few hours . . .'

'. . . and Ray,' I said.

'What?' he muttered.

'I think Julia's run away.' But he was already snoring.

*

In the morning the Rodcoopers were in turmoil. There was a note from Julia:

Mother. I'm going away for a while. Please don't come looking for me. I'll be fine. Your daughter, Julia. PS Please don't worry. I know what I'm doing.

'Not even loving daughter, just daughter.' Brenda was in the dining room, her hands shaking as she read out the note. 'Why would she do this to me? She only wants to see me suffer. Why?' She was starting to wind up like an air-raid siren. I sat at an empty place and watched them.

Charles hadn't had chance to get his hair tamed this morning. It stood up like a flickering halo of flames. 'Please, Brenda, my darling. Don't let this affect you. It could just be a plea for attention.'

She tried to compose herself. I could see her rearranging the parts of her body one by one while chaos was breaking loose in her mind. 'You're right, Charles, of course,' she said finally. 'Excuse me. She's gone, I know, but I mustn't panic. She could be anywhere – with friends. I'll telephone them first. Oh, God!' Her voice was breaking away at the edges, crumbling like a piece of cliff falling into the sea. 'She's done this before. She's unstable. One summer she slept in a chicken house. Another time, oh God, there was a boy involved. She's so strong-willed.'

'We have to keep our heads, dear Brenda,' Charles went on. 'You know we can support one another at times like this.'

Then Alastair came downstairs. 'What's happened? Has World War Three broken out?'

'Brenda's distraught,' Charles said. 'Even you can detect that, surely? It's Julia.' Brenda shivered at the sound of her name.

Alastair poured himself a big bowl of cornflakes. 'Always

something going on round here. Worse than in ruddy Gilbert and Sullivan. What's she done?'

'She's run away,' Charles said. 'Or gone away. Whatever. Show some concern, man.'

'Sorry,' said Alastair. It was like *Play of the Week* and Julia got to be the star of it without even being here. Being absent was how some people found the limelight.

'She's probably gone to meet a friend, that's all,' Alastair said through a mouthful of flakes. 'Isn't anybody else eating?'

'There'll be a boy behind it,' Brenda said. 'She's been seeing a boy. She thinks I don't know, but he's old enough to be . . . to be her older brother. Someone must have seen something. People don't just disappear into thin air in the middle of the . . . oh, God . . . do they?'

And she looked at me and a picture of Julia passed through my head like a flash: Julia's long legs disappearing, not too elegantly, into Dave's car, Julia's lips with her best pearl-pink lipstick, and the knot on Julia's duffle bag.

'It'll be him. That Dave.' She spat his name out. 'I begged her. I instructed her not to see him, but she wouldn't listen.'

'Now,' Charles said, 'don't jump to conclusions. You don't know that yet, darling.'

'She'll be having a good time.' Alastair scooped up the last of the milk, clink, slurp. 'Mark my words. She'll have gone to Blackpool or Skeggy.'

'Why on earth would she want to do that?'

'Because she's a teenager. I don't know.'

Charles was trying to keep the situation in perspective, to keep control of it even though it was already spiralling. 'We'll phone the police if she's not back directly.'

Vi came in with a tray of cooked breakfasts. 'Police?' she said. 'What's going on?' As if it was a big shock even to hear the word in this house. The countless visits by friendly beat bobbies to discuss Ray's conduct had obviously gone out of her mind.

Part of me wanted to say, 'It's bloody Julia. What did you expect from her? She's gone off with a bloke. Not even a boy. He's twenty-four. Dave. I saw her. So what? What do you expect from someone so self-centred and disruptive?'

Knowing secrets was more dangerous than not knowing them. Charles shooed Vi's bacon and eggs away. 'We're not hungry this morning, Violet.'

'I'll have one of them,' Alastair said. 'Put it down here, Mrs B. And you can leave the others just in case.'

I was thinking about exactly what I'd got caught up in and I was close to saying what I'd seen, but I didn't. It was because Julia asked me not to. The secret was what we had in common and if I kept it maybe she'd fall in love with me.

Brenda went to use the phone to check with Julia's friends back home, promising to put the money in Vi's phone tin. None of the friends had seen her, so Charles went to phone the police.

'I tell you what,' Alastair said while he was out. 'We'll go and have a look for her after, if you like.'

'Thank you, Alastair,' Brenda said. 'That is kind.' An untouched breakfast egg on her plate was turning into a plastic joke egg, a piece of seaside confectionery.

'I bet Eddie here'll come with us. He knows places.'

'No. I don't know anywhere.'

Charles returned looking smarter. He'd evidently found time to quiff his hair into shape, maybe even to dab a bit more colour into it. 'The police will be here later. They asked a number of questions. They'll want to talk to anyone who might have seen her.'

'Oh, God,' Brenda said. 'This makes it real.'

'It might be on the wireless,' Alastair said. 'You know – last heard of in the Liverpool area.'

'It's not the Liverpool area,' Vi said sharply. 'It's Cheshire – the Wirral. We're over the water.' She turned to me. 'Eddie, help me clear these breakfasts, for Pete's sake. Don't just sit there.'

In the kitchen I started telling Vi about the message Julia had left. 'Girls always leave notes,' she said in disgust. 'You can rely on girls to make a scene of it.'

But the room was starting to spin. Too much frying, the swill of last night, dancing with someone who said her name was Lulu. 'Are you all right?' Vi asked. The police. *No Hiding Place*. One question from Inspector Lockhart and I'd crumble: yes I saw her leave. Then I'd be as guilty as Julia, aiding and abetting. I felt sick.

'Sorry, Auntie Vi. I don't feel too good. I think I'd better lie down.'

At the bottom of the stairs I had to give way to Irene and Maisie skeltering down. 'What's happened? We thought we heard Brenda. She sounded hysterical.'

'It's Julia,' I said.

'As if there's not enough drama,' Irene said. 'What's happened now?'

'Run away. Absconded. Eloped. I don't know,' I said. Maisie and Irene rushed off to breakfast, babbling like schoolgirls.

I lay on the bed and stared at Ray's Airfix planes on their bits of cotton. The way they floated and circled made me feel sick again. I was thinking about Julia, remembering Lulu and wondering whether the feeling in my stomach was to do with the model planes or the party or with girls like Lulu that I almost got to know, then disappeared.

There was a knock on the door. Alastair's face appeared round it. 'Oh,' he said when he saw me lying there. 'Sorry. Maisie and me are getting a search party together. I know you said you couldn't come, but are you up for it?' I shook my head. 'What's the matter? Are you ill or something?'

'I think I've got a hangover.'

'At your age? Come on – the fresh air'll do you good.'

'There's no point. She won't be in New Brighton.'

'How do you know that?'

'I don't know.' I could hear myself struggling with the deception. 'She left a note, didn't she? If you run off it means you've gone away.'

'You seem very sure. Anyway, I'm not staying in watching Brenda work herself into a frenzy. I can do that on stage any night of the week. Come on, Ed. You can be a kind of scout for us.'

'I'm past being a scout, thank you.'

Then Maisie put her face round the door, gave her sweet, fishy smile. 'Are you two ready? Come on, let's go.'

'He says he's not well.'

Maisie said, 'Oh, come on, Eddie. I just want to do something useful for once. I'm not hanging round to talk to the police. They give me the heebie-jeebies.'

'Police?' I'd forgotten about them. The thought of fresh air was suddenly very attractive. My head was clearing. 'I'll just put my shoes on.'

'Where to, Eddie?' Alastair asked as soon as we got out of the house. He was wearing sunglasses and a pork pie hat. He was supposed to be the leader of this expedition, but he was as bad as the rest of them – doing anything to make people notice him, then letting everyone else do the work.

'I dunno. How about the outdoor baths? They're nearly at one end of the seafront and we can work our way along.'

'That's what I was thinking,' Alastair said.

Maisie wore a pale blue cardigan and sandals with white ankle socks. There was no point in searching. Julia would be with Dave – having breakfast in a three-star hotel, planning their day while I stayed and stitched together their lies.

The seafront heaved with groups of girls, laughing and posing and tossing their heads. 'She could be anywhere,' Alastair said. 'Stupid girl.'

'She is stupid,' Maisie said. 'She's only done this to draw attention to herself.'

'And to inconvenience as many people as possible. Surely she knows what a turmoil she's causing.'

We stood outside the outdoor swimming pool and scanned the queues – families with shopping bags and sandwiches, lads my age with rolled-up towels under their arms – but no Julia. 'Do you think she'll be here?' Alastair asked doubtfully. 'It's not the sort of place you'd come on your own.'

'She might not be on her own,' Maisie said. 'She could have met someone.'

We stood by the exit turnstiles and gazed into the shimmering heat of the pool. It was dense with bathers.

'Shall we go in?' Alastair asked.

'Go in the café and see if you can see her from there,' I suggested. 'It's got a window onto the pool on the other side.'

But there were too many people – thousands of heads moving and merging on the endless decks. Alastair spent a long time trying to catch sight of her, or maybe he was just admiring the girls in their bikinis and swimming costumes. At least when he came out he was smiling and carrying three Eldorado cornets – oblong ones with ice cream dribbling down the sides. 'Waste of time,' he said.

So we drifted along the causeway between Marine Lake and the sea wall where the lake filled with saltwater at high tide and overflowed afterwards, pouring onto the beach below.

'From the seafront,' Maisie said in her buttery, ice-cream voice, 'it looks as though you're walking on water when you walk along here. Have you noticed?'

Alastair hadn't. A row of boys sat with lines dipped in Marine Lake, their bodies sandy and salted. Maisie stopped and looked in one of the toy buckets. 'A few angry crabs,' she said, 'that's all. I feel sorry for them. What did they do to deserve being put in a bucket?'

The causeway skirted the lake and dropped us by Fort Perch Rock with its massive sandstone walls rising sheer from the beach. Beyond the pier and in front of the Tower Grounds the beach was solid with people. I ignored them all as we picked our way between the towels and deck-chairs. 'You aren't looking, Ed,' Maisie said.

'She's not here, is she? It's a waste of time.'

Maisie stopped and stood in front of me, her toes in the sand. 'Come on, Ed. You can tell us. Where is she?'

'There's nothing to tell, Maisie.' The sun was beating on the sand and the flat rocks.

'Nothing to tell?' Alastair said. 'Only that he fancies Julia like crazy.' He took off his hat and sunglasses and mopped his brow with a hanky.

'Stop it, Alastair. Leave him alone,' Maisie said. 'Be serious for once.'

'I've seen the way he looks at her, and who could blame him? Poor Eddie. A gorgeous girl like that? I'd fancy her myself if she wasn't such a harridan.'

I didn't need to be there with them. I could have stayed in bed. 'I'll go and look further along the beach,' I said. 'I'll see you later.'

'No, stay, Eddie. He doesn't mean anything by it. He's teasing. You'll get used to him.'

Alastair said, 'Come on, Ed. She's gone off with a fella, hasn't she? We've seen you talking to her so you must know something. She's gone home – she's run off to London or

Paris. Has she met someone here? Your cousin – what's his name? Ray. She's mad enough.'

He danced around in the sand like a chimp. 'Leave me alone,' I said, though I couldn't help laughing.

'We just like the gossip,' Maisie said. 'It's in our blood.'

Alastair said, 'She's entered a nunnery. I know! She'll have gone off to be a beatnik in New York. She's pregnant – that's it, isn't it? – she's expecting the child of a high-up churchman and this is just a subterfuge.'

'A subterfuge?'

'A diversion,' Maisie explained. 'A trick.'

'It's not much of a joke, is it?' I said. 'Anyway, I can't tell you.'

Maisie was still walking alongside me. 'Oh, so you do know something. Come on, Eddie, come on. Here's a reward – a kiss from me.' She pouted. 'Boys like you are only thinking of one thing. How would it be if I got you introduced to one of these lovely girls here? I could do it.'

It would have been easier to say what I knew. It was only a few fragments after all – Dave and his car, Julia disappearing into the night. What did I owe her? Nothing. So why this ridiculous honour? I was in awe of her – that's why. I hated being so easily manipulated. 'No, Maisie,' I said, more angrily than I'd intended. 'I'll help you look, but that's all.'

'OK, keep your hair on,' Alastair said and kicked the sand, as if a toy had been taken away from him. 'I was only having a laugh. Why does everybody take it the wrong way?'

The beach seemed hopeless, so we meandered up through the sunny, sandstone banks of Vale Park, past the white-domed bandstand with names of composers on the cornice. Perhaps they hoped to come across her sitting on a bench like someone's lost handbag waiting to be found. We went out through a side gate and into the backstreets.

Alastair started telling Maisie about Charles's attempts at practical joking in revenge for the bed incident. He'd unscrewed the handle on Alastair's bedroom door so it came off in his hand and trapped Alastair inside. He was in there for twenty minutes before the man from Darlington heard him shouting and let him out. Maisie giggled. 'That's funny.'

'Not particularly.' Alastair pretended he wasn't amused, but he could see the funny side. 'Ever since that incident with the bed he's been pursuing me. Joking me to death. I wouldn't mind, but he's terrible at it. A rank amateur, in fact.'

We'd wandered off the beaten track. Maisie's feminine intuition had told her that Julia might prefer these quiet places if she was feeling low.

'After that it was pepper in my soup at dinnertime,' Alastair went on. 'Charles got the stuff up his nose and couldn't stop sneezing so I knew he was up to no good.'

'Oh, Alastair, don't . . .' Maisie said. He made her laugh so much it was almost an embarrassment. People would be looking.

I said, 'I bet you've done pranks on him in return. I would if it was me.'

'Of course I have, but it's in my nature – I plead guilty.' We'd emerged out of a back alley. 'What I wouldn't give for some decent jokes. Even I am running out of ideas. Isn't there anywhere in this town that sells snappy chewing gum, exploding cigarettes, black face soap? Oh, I long for them.'

Almost before I realized it I said, 'There's a good joke shop – the Box of Tricks – near here. I know the owner – kind of.'

'Oh, yes,' Alastair said. 'Just what I want. Show us where this Box of Tricks is, Eddie.'

I wanted to impress them with my knowledge of the

town, its best-kept secrets. The joke shop was only a road away so we walked there. Alastair's eyes lit up when he saw it. 'Ooh, fancy that. What a find. Thanks, Ed. Can you get us a discount?'

'No.'

'You must be able to. You said they knew you. Come on.'

But I shook my head. It was fear – from Pete forbidding us to go into his shop again and what he might do if we did. Who knew what he'd think up – a box with a trap-door in the bottom, a stage sword through the ribs, death by the Chinese finger trap?

'I'm not going in.'

'Oh, Eddie,' Maisie put her arm round me. 'Come on. What are you afraid of? It's only an old joke shop.'

I told her what had happened the last time me and Ray went in. 'But you didn't do anything, Ed,' Maisie said. 'The fellow won't mind, specially if you're with us. I'll put in a good word for you.'

But I refused, sat myself down on the edge of the pavement, my feet in the gutter. 'You go if you want. I'll wait here,' I said, feeling wretched and still slightly sick.

'All right then, Eddie,' Maisie said, following Alastair to the door. 'We won't be long.'

I called across, 'You have to mind the –' but it was too late. Alastair's enthusiasm had got the better of him. He'd already opened the door and let loose the howl of the electric werewolf.

The road was quiet in the late morning; nobody was about. I sat and waited, watching the sun glint off the shop windows. A mongrel made its way up the pavement, pausing at every tree, tongue lolling in the heat.

After an age they came back out, Alastair carrying a big paper bag, Maisie trailing behind. Pete was with them. I stood up in horror. What had they brought him out for?

Pete looked around, squinting in the sunlight. Then they were crossing the road towards me. Alastair said to Pete, 'This is the young man who told us about your shop.'

'Pleased to meet you,' Pete said. Then he recognized me. 'Oh, it's you – the disappearing ashtray trick.'

'I had nothing to do with it,' I said.

'Where've I heard that before?'

Alastair said, 'I've bought a bag full of stuff. Look. There's some great things in here. I can hardly wait to try them out. Charles won't know what's hit him! Boy, oh boy.'

'I never knew you were as bad as this, Alastair,' Maisie said. 'You should have seen him, Eddie – like a kid in a sweet shop.'

'Mr McCluggage used to be on the stage,' Alastair said. 'A fellow entertainer.'

Maisie said, 'We explained how you'd showed us where his shop was. That's why he came out.'

'To thank you for bringing such good custom,' Pete said. 'Perhaps we can be friends after all.' He held out a hand. It could have been a false one for all I knew, or one that gave an electric shock. I took it carefully.

'Thanks,' I said.

'Anything I can do to help – you know that.'

'You were going to show me how to make that tanner coin disappear,' I reminded him.

He laughed the way he might have done on stage when a child messes up an illusion by accident. 'You don't miss a trick, do you? I'm sure there's something I can show a young man like you. There's so much to learn.'

Alastair chipped in. 'Humour is very important to us theatrical types, Mr McCluggage. I'll definitely be telling my colleagues about your wonderful shop.' He wouldn't include Charles in that, of course.

'Call me Pete,' he said and shook hands with Alastair

and Maisie, then stood outside his shop until we'd turned the corner.

'That place gives me the creeps,' Maisie said as soon as we were out of sight. 'No wonder you didn't want to go in there, Eddie, with those masks like stripped-off faces. And that bloke, Pete – ugh.'

But I was too excited thinking about how I'd be able to go there again now and that I could almost count myself as one of Pete's friends. I'd thought I'd grown out of the place when Ma Feeney'd been there, but it had changed into something more alluring and dangerous now. Pete wasn't comforting like her; he was unpredictable. He could teach me how to deceive people with the slightest flick of the wrist, make coins disappear. If he could grab Ray and shake him until he yelled, what else was he capable of?

'I hope no one wonders where we've got to,' Maisie said, back to thinking about other people.

'Course they won't,' Alastair said. 'We've been on a special mission, haven't we?' His bag full of new tricks from the joke shop had cheered him up.

Maisie said, 'She doesn't deserve us, does she – that girl? She's spoiled rotten. Gets the best of everything and doesn't appreciate any of it. Horse riding, nice clothes and all the rest.'

'Oh,' Alastair said. 'Julia. I'd almost forgotten about her.'

Back at the house Brenda was sitting opposite Charles at one of the dining-room tables. They looked up when we came in. 'Any luck?' Brenda asked.

Alastair shook his head and put the paper bag behind his back. 'We searched everywhere we could think of – and some more.'

Brenda's mood had over-corrected itself. Now she was in a melodramatic passion. 'Julia's so wicked to put me through this pain. I can't believe what a thoughtless girl she's become. What did I do to deserve this?'

'Nothing, darling,' Charles said. He stroked her hand gently. 'She'll come back; they always do. It's nothing more than an escapade, you'll see.'

'But she might be dead by now and I wouldn't know. I feel so guilty . . .'

'Have the police been?' Maisie asked.

'Yes,' Charles said. 'They say they'll put notices out – that sort of thing.'

I breathed a sigh of relief. At least I'd missed them. How had I got myself into this position? None of it had anything to do with me. As usual I'd been a bystander, a watcher caught up in other people's action. The afternoon sun came white through the net curtains, reminding me that my head was still throbbing from the night before.

Brenda didn't appear for the early evening meal. Vi said, 'Go and ask her if she'd like something in her room, Ed, would you? I can get it sent up – some fish? Or a boiled egg?' Vi didn't often get the opportunity to make a fuss of her guests. She had a gentle side after all and it was made of soft, comforting food.

I knocked on Brenda's door. At first she didn't reply, but when I knocked a second time she appeared with an unfocused look in her eyes. She'd been drinking. I said, 'Vi wants to know if you'd like something to eat. She can send it up – fish or a boiled egg. Anything you want, really.'

'No thank you,' she said bleakly. Then she looked at me again. 'Do you know where Julia is?'

I was speechless. 'Me?'

'Somebody must know where she is. She can't have just disappeared off the face of the earth – and I've seen her talking to you. Didn't she tell you anything?' I shook my head. 'I'm sorry. I'm becoming desperate. I didn't mean to accuse.' She started crying. I felt sorry for her then. Even she didn't deserve the uncertainty. I hated Julia, but I hated myself more for letting her get under my skin.

So there were two empty places – Brenda's and Julia's, though Julia had never been much of a one for meals. Maisie and Irene came and sat on either side of Alastair. Irene, who'd been making herself scarce all day, tried to make light of it. Then, after the fruit salad, Brenda came in.

'I'm sorry I'm so late,' she said. 'I'm just distraught. I'm broken.'

'Oh, Brenda,' Maisie said. 'Come and sit down.'

'Why didn't she discuss this with me? That's what I don't understand.'

'That's girls for you,' Irene said brightly. 'They expect you to know.'

'But she's a child. Only seventeen. She's so innocent.'

Brenda sat on a vacant chair and stared out of the window. It was down to Charles to smooth it over. 'We must try and pull together in these difficult times,' he announced. 'We're all shocked but the tradition of our business requires us to carry on. It's what an audience would expect and it's for Brenda's sake – and Julia's, and for the show.'

'Hear, hear!' Irene said as if she was about to lead them in a cheer. But it came to nothing.

'Now, Brenda, if you prefer to withdraw from the show we'll understand. One of the girls can understudy tonight and you can return when you're ready. The Rodcoopers will pull through.'

It was amazing the way Brenda changed. She sat up straighter. 'Of course I'll appear. Where would we be if we gave in every time a personal inconvenience occurred? What happens in our lives has nothing to do with the stage, Charles. You know that. They are two separate – though interrelated – worlds.'

'Bravo,' Charles cried. 'All the world's a stage.'

Nanny came in, collecting the plates. She stopped with her hands full, as if she'd caught a whiff of something. 'You know,' she said, 'I haven't heard you singing so much. Not like in other years. I don't know what's the matter this year.' Perhaps she hadn't heard about Julia or, more likely, had dismissed her disappearance as a girlish adventure of the sort she'd seen before.

Charles began, quite suddenly, with no introduction. He stood up in his place and started singing very gently. I think it was meant to make Brenda feel better – a melancholy song with no sense. It was something about a bird sitting on a tree by a river. *Though I probably shall not exclaim as I die, 'Oh, willow, tit willow, tit willow!'* Vi said Gilbert and Sullivan was full of songs that made no sense. That's what she liked about them. They were just an escape into verse and music you couldn't put out of your mind, and nothing had to add up.

'Thank you, Charles,' Brenda said when he'd finished and she clapped her hands and everybody joined in. Charles's singing had made her calm and optimistic again. I could see it in her eyes. Music could have that effect if it was done right.

9

Ray and me took Nanny to the pictures the next evening. Julia still hadn't come back. Because of all the holiday people who needed something to do if it rained, which it often did, there were three cinemas to choose from.

Ray decided we were going to the Court. The support film was *Swinging UK*, with Brian Poole and the Tremeloes and the Merseybeats, and with backdrops of famous places in London. Nobody took much notice of it. There was a lot of laughing. A girl in the back row had seen a mate and called out, 'Eh, Sandra, is that you – down there in the front?'

'Shurrup, will you?' a woman shouted back.

Then someone dropped an ice cream from the balcony into the stalls and there was a big fuss about that. Eventually it all settled down and kids at the back started lighting up ciggies in the safety of the darkness and slipping their arms round their girlfriends' shoulders. Smoke spiralled blue across the screen.

Nanny said, 'I hope *West Side Story*'s better than this. Natalie Wood's in it.' I looked across at Ray, because I knew *West Side Story* wasn't on. He didn't say anything. He'd distracted her in the foyer with a story about wrestling matches and she'd been too preoccupied to read the placards.

In the interval after *Swinging UK* Ray bought three ice-cream tubs out of his own money. He had to help Nanny get the little wooden spoon out of the paper. He was kind with it and spread her hanky on her lap for her and didn't seem to mind. We threw the lids on the floor under our seats.

Then the main film started. It was *The Alamo*, with John Wayne and a cast of thousands. Straight away Nanny said loudly, 'Ray, I thought it was *West Side Story*. That's what you told me. Why did you say that?'

'I never,' he said.

'You damn well did, Ray, and you know it.'

'No, I said it was a western. You didn't hear me properly.'

'You never said that. You told me it was *West Side Story*. We talked about Natalie Wood.'

'I might have said it was like *West Side Story*, that's all. I must have thought it was a musical.'

'Since when has *The Alamo* sounded like a musical, Ray, tell me that? You're lying to me again.'

He put his hand on her arm, dead gentle. 'Stay now, Nan,' he said. 'Come on, you might like it.'

But she went on grumbling. 'You treat me like a damn kid. I haven't lost my marbles yet, though, Ray. I could give you a run for your money any day.'

'I know, Nan.'

'I wouldn't have come. If I'd known it was going to be cowboys again I wouldn't have come.'

'It does you good to get out occasionally.'

'Not to see this sort of thing – people shooting one another. It's noisy and it's bad for my blood pressure. You got me here under false pretences.'

The man in front turned round and told us to shut up and Nanny finally crossed her arms and settled down. She seemed to be watching, but I noticed her covering her eyes a couple of times when the horses galloped towards the camera and crashed to the ground in a shower of desert dust. ‘Those poor animals,’ Nanny said under her breath. ‘Why’s it always them that get hurt?’

‘Cos they’re an easy target I suppose,’ Ray said. He sat with his knees up on the seat in front. The wooden spoon from his ice cream was in his mouth. Every time something exciting happened he chewed it and spat out a few more splinters.

But I couldn’t concentrate. When, near the end, the whole cinema fell silent and seemed united in willing Davy Crockett and his gallant band to survive against all the odds I was still thinking about Julia and how I’d never wanted to know about her and Dave. She’d just told me about him. That’s the way she was. I happened to be in the wrong place at the wrong time when she left and didn’t get any choice in my own fate – not like poor Jim Bowie who had to be carried over the line in the sand because he had pneumonia and was too sick to walk. Going over that line meant he was willing to stay and would surely die, but at least he got to decide for himself. Things looked mighty bad at the Alamo but they looked even worse for me.

At the end, with nothing but gun smoke hanging over the remains of the Alamo, we stumbled up the carpet like stunned survivors. The front doors were flung open and we could smell rain. It was hard to imagine, but while we’d been inside the world had been carrying on as normal – families had been browsing in the late-night novelty shops, couples had been drinking in the pubs on Vicky Road – and it had gone properly dark. Lights were on in the amusements and the bingo arcades. The pavements were covered in a fine layer of wet – just enough to make the smell of dust rise up.

Nanny seemed quiet and a bit slow and Ray linked his arm under hers to help her along. He was good that way, and didn’t care who saw him do it, even though she was a sight in her hat like an old lampshade. She sighed and Ray said, 'What's the matter, Nan?'

'Nothing, love.'

'Look, I'm sorry it wasn't *West Side Story*.'

'It's all right. You can take me to see that another time. That film made me think of America, that's all.'

We nodded, Ray and me. Like it was some great secret nobody wanted to say out loud. America.

By now we'd reached the seafront and I realized I was hungry. Suddenly Nanny said, 'Look. There.' We went over to the railings and in the darkness saw what looked like a dance hall, floating in the distance. There were lines of coloured lights and below that another row of white ones and the whole thing reflected in the dark, oily water.

'A liner,' Ray said. 'Cunarder probably.' We watched in silence as the ship drew level with us, then turned out into the channel. It was the most beautiful thing I'd ever seen.

'Can you hear that?' Nanny asked.

'What?'

'Music. I'm sure I can hear music. An orchestra or something.' We listened again, leaning there on the railings, but Ray and me could only hear the lapping of the tide.

'She's imagining it,' Ray whispered. He shook his head like she was a bit barmy. But I knew it was wishful thinking on her part. Sometimes that happened if you wanted something badly enough. You imagined you could hear what you wanted or could really see what was only in your mind.

'Going to America,' Nanny said.

'Yeah.'

'I don't suppose I'll ever go to America now.'

'Why not?' I asked.

'Too old, love. I'm seventy-five next birthday, and there's your Uncle Steven on the other side of the world and a grandson I've never seen.'

'You can go, Nan,' I said. 'You're not too old.'

'We haven't got the money for that sort of thing. I'm resigned to it now.' She wasn't being dramatic, like some people I could have mentioned. She was just telling the truth. The liner shifted direction into one of the deeper channels and then I thought I caught a snatch of the music. But I couldn't have. It was too far away, gone at once, carried away on a breeze. The ship changed into a blur of yellowish light as it turned out to sea, then eventually became nothing more than a glimmer.

'Come on, Nan,' Ray said and tucked his hand under her arm again.

But she wouldn't budge. She went all stiff and stubborn. 'I'll stay here a while, thank you very much,' she said.

'It's getting cold, though.'

'I'll be all right.'

Ray moved his head sideways, which was his way of telling me to buzz off. 'I'll stay with you for a bit,' I heard him say.

'You don't have to,' Nanny said, but I could tell she was pleased. He put his arms on the railings next to her and dropped his head into his coat and looked into the darkness. He pulled a ciggie from the bottom of his coat pocket and lit it as casually as he could, knowing Nanny would have something to say about it.

'I don't know why I bother with you,' she said at last, still looking into the dark.

'Cos you love me,' he said. She tutted loudly and shook her head. 'We can't go on like this, can we, Nan?'

'What do you mean?'

'All this America stuff.'

'There's nothing we can do about it, is there? I'll get over it, love,' she said.

'You shouldn't say that,' Ray said. 'It's not right. You could go if you wanted. You know you could.'

I stood a distance off, but nothing changed. I could see the glow of Ray's fag as he drew on it. Then he flicked it into the sea in a spiral of orange sparks.

'I'm going to the chip shop,' I called.

'Right-o,' Ray said. I left them to it, walked along the prom, past the turning to Vi's boarding house and back up Vicky Road to the Rialto fish bar.

The Rialto had big mirrors with sailing ships etched on them. I bought six penn'orth of chips and doused them with the salt and vinegar shakers on the counter, letting it soak down to the bottom of the bag and into the newspaper.

I didn't open the chips straight away, but took them back to the seafront where I ate them hot from the paper in the shelter by the entrance to the Tower Grounds, blowing them in my fingers one by one.

That's when I heard a sound. It was somebody snivelling, then gulping and coughing. The tide was almost in, so I went back to the railings because that's where the sound was coming from. There was a dark shape hunched up near the bottom of the slipway. It stopped crying and its white face looked up at me. 'Are you all right?' I called down.

'What the bloody hell are you doing here?' a girl's voice replied. I looked around, wondering if she was talking to me.

There was nobody else, so I said, 'I was just standing there eating my chips – and I thought I heard something and –'

'Well, you can bugger off now, can't you?'

There was a familiar posh sound about her voice, as if someone had given her elocution lessons in swearing. 'Julia?'

She didn't reply, so I knew it was her. I walked to the top of the slipway and then down it to where she was leaning against the sandstone wall, just before the slope got its green covering of slime.

She didn't say anything or move, so I leaned next to her to see what would happen. She'd still got her duffle bag with her. She wiped her eyes with the palms of her hands. In the end she said, 'Have you got chips?'

'Where the hell have you been, Julia? Everyone's been worried sick about you. Is that all you're thinking about – food?'

She didn't reply so we shared what was left. I let her have more than me because she seemed to want them. I could tell because her fingers were digging in the scraps, even the ones in the bottom corners of the bag. 'Finish them off if you want,' I told her. So she did. Then she sucked her fingers to make sure she'd got all the salt and balled up the bag and the newspaper and threw it towards the sea at the bottom of the slipway. She tried to throw it dead angrily, only she'd got a girly throw. The rubbish didn't even reach the water.

'You were hungry,' I said.

'Bloody ravenous. I haven't eaten since last night.'

'They've called the police,' I said.

'Shit. Scotland Yard and MI5 probably.'

'Yeah, everybody. They're looking for you. Why the hell didn't you call or something?'

She shrugged. 'Didn't want to. They don't care about me. Not really.'

'They do,' I said. 'Your mother's been terrible – crying and everything.'

'Bloody crocodile tears,' she said.

Now my eyes were getting used to the dark I could see her face properly. It was streaked with makeup. Her lilac trouser suit was crumpled and her coat was grubby. Her usually carefully groomed hair was a mess. I said, 'So are you coming back?'

'No.'

'What are you doing then?'

She said, 'I was kind of just passing through. Eddie, do you know where there's a modelling agency?'

'No. I thought you had to go to London for that.'

'There must be some in Liverpool, mustn't there?'

'I s'pose so. Why?'

'I need to know, that's all. It's my next move. Dave and me had a terrible row. Obviously I'm never going to let him near me again.'

'Obviously,' I said. I didn't mean to sound as though I was happy about it, but somehow it came out like that. She didn't seem to notice.

'Never. It's finished between us.' The chips had revived her. 'I tell you, it was OK while it lasted, though. We drove over to Manchester – stayed at the Piccadilly. Dave did the works – a club, full English breakfast. We had to pretend to be Mr and Mrs Tomkins. He was so romantic.'

'You can spare me the details,' I said.

'Don't you want to know what happened?'

'Not really.'

She told me anyway. 'He's a lovely man, Dave. But he was so predictable. I mean, he took me out to a Berni's last night and told me he loved me. Can you imagine that? He'd bought me a ring. He only wanted to bloody marry me.'

I was shocked. Is that how quickly and unexpectedly it could happen? 'Didn't you want that? I thought women wanted to get married.'

'It's all right if you're about twenty and you want to live on some new estate and have three kids. It's all right if you want to spend the rest of your life looking after Dave like his mum's done since he was a baby.' She paused mid-flow. 'Have you got anything to drink?'

'No, sorry.'

'Those chips were a bit greasy.' She wiped her mouth with her sleeve.

'Sorry. You did mop up all the grease in the bottom of the bag with your finger.'

'Yeah, well, I was hungry. Now I'm thirsty.'

'I can go and get some pop. The chip shop'll still be open.'

'No thank you,' she said. 'I've been thinking about what I've got to do and I know I'm going to have to look after myself from now on. I've got to find my own way in life. That's what I've learned. I'm going to go travelling, get a career, have some fun before I settle down. Kids can come later.' She went on, 'Don't get me wrong. Dave was lovely. I really loved him. I still do.'

'Yeah,' I said. 'Course you do.'

'But do you know what? He was jealous. He was so possessive. When we were in that hotel bar I noticed it. We sat by a big window that looked out onto the street and there were all these girls going past. Fashionable Manchester types, straight from the boutiques. His eyes followed them – every one.'

I said, 'That's what lads are like, Julia. We can't help it.'

'I suppose so. But then when a bloke at another table kept looking across at me he didn't like it. The bloke was with his wife. Dave and him nearly got in a fight. We had to drink up and leave. I felt as if he couldn't stand anyone except him looking at me.'

'Doesn't that kind of show he loves you, then?'

'It didn't feel like that, I can tell you. It felt more as if he owned me. The bloke was only looking at me, that's all, and I don't mind that. I'm an attractive girl. You think so, Ed, don't you?'

She put her leg behind her on the lumpy sandstone of the wall so her knee stuck out towards me, but I didn't need to look. I already knew. 'Yeah.'

'But Dave – he was just incredibly jealous. He always knew I wanted to be a model. I've never hidden that from him, but he must have thought it was just a whim because he had my life all planned out for me. Once we were married he said he was going to set up his own stables and I could help him run it – you know, buying stock and doing the books and probably mucking out as well. He had it all worked out. It was frightening. Then, when I reminded him I was going to be a model, he said, "No bloody chance. No woman of mine's going to show her knickers in public." I mean that's the sort of thing his dad probably says. It's bloody prehistoric. Then he found out I was only seventeen. That's when he got really mad. Or maybe he was scared. Either way, he couldn't drop me fast enough.' She laughed bitterly. 'It's not my fault I look twenty-one, is it?'

The tide had gone out a few feet and left the usual junk at the bottom of the slipway – some planks from the ships, a couple of plastic bottles and a stink of tar.

Julia said, 'So that was the end of it. I caught a bus back – took me all bloody day. I need to get a few things before I go off again, that's all. I'm glad I saw you, though, Ed.' Her voice had gone deeper as if she wanted it to be mysterious.

'Why?'

'Can you go in and pick up my things from the house? Just the suitcase and a few clothes?'

The thought of creeping into her room and ferreting around among her clothes and belongings, then sneaking out again without anyone seeing made me shudder. 'I can't do that,' I told her. 'I'm in enough trouble already. They already think I helped you to escape or that I'm keeping you a prisoner somewhere.'

'But it's nothing to do with you. I'm just asking you to do this one favour for me.'

'No. I'm fed up of being involved in your lies, Julia. Look – why don't you just come home? Then you can think about it.'

'Oh,' she said, 'think about it. I don't want to bloody think about it any more. That's the last thing I want. I want to do something for once. I've done enough thinking since I've been in this bloody place.' She sighed and I wondered if she was going to start snivelling again. Instead she said, 'This is my big chance, Ed.'

'You'll have other big chances, won't you?'

'My heart's beating so fast. Here. Feel,' she said, and reached out for my hand. She put it under her coat where it was warm. 'Just do this for me, Ed. Please.'

She pressed my hand into a place where I could feel her ribs. I could smell her perfume and the vinegar on her fingers. 'Be adventurous for once,' she said.

A bubble of sound escaped my lips, like a little exclamation. 'God!' it said. She dropped her hand from over mine and I kept mine in the same place.

'You can feel it, can't you?' she asked. 'Come on, Ed.'

'What is it you need?' I whispered.

She told me she'd wait in the shelter on the seafront until I got back. At least there she'd be inconspicuous and out of the weather. 'What if Brenda's in your room?' I asked.

'She won't be. If they're back from the show they'll be in the dining room playing cards or gossiping as usual.'

'You don't know that . . .'

'And if anyone says anything you can make up some excuse, can't you? You're a bright kid.' I resented the use of the word 'kid'. 'Look,' she went on, 'don't worry. Most of my stuff's still in the suitcase under my bed. Just pick it up and get straight back here. That's all you need to do.'

'You could do that yourself, couldn't you?'

'If they see me anywhere near the place I'll have had it, won't I? My life's over.'

She knew how to be an actress when it suited her, fluttering her damp lashes as if she might cry all over again.

I said, 'Your life's not over, Julia. What are you talking about?'

'Not literally. Just go, will you. For God's sake,' she said, raising her voice a bit. Just enough. 'Oh, and Eddie . . .'

'What?'

'If you can pick up any ciggies on the way through, bring 'em, will you?'

For a moment I thought she was going to say 'thanks', like thanks for trudging round after her and risking going into her room and bringing her stuff back for her. Thanks for taking a chance and believing in her. But it wasn't her style.

She happened to be right about Brenda – she was in the dining room with the rest of the Rodcoopers. They must have come back straight after their performance in case there was any news about Julia. I stopped at the bottom of the stairs and listened until I could hear her voice. Charles replied and someone else, probably Irene, laughed too loudly. They almost sounded cheerful. Probably the show had gone well. Someone was playing cards. I could hear the flapping noise as they hit the table. I went upstairs as quietly as I could.

I stood outside Julia's door trying to pluck up courage to go in. What would I do if someone was in the room after all? I'd have to say something about coming to empty the bins or change the towels. That might do it, though it was an unlikely reason to be there at that time of evening.

Someone was coming downstairs from the second floor, feet creaking on the stairs. Two dockers from Cammell Lairds had moved into the room next to ours. They only seemed to be interested in getting drunk and had kept me awake with their arguing and snoring. The footsteps came nearer. I turned the handle and went in.

With the door closed behind me, the room was completely dark. The curtains were drawn. I'd never even thought about that. I began to feel around for the light switch, but it wasn't where I expected it to be. My hand explored further and further away from the obvious places. Nothing was as I'd seen it in my mind. There was a smell that only women could mix – expensive soap and a minty hint of toothpaste. I put my hands out in front of me and took a couple of blind steps into the room. I caught my shin on the bed edge and moved away from it too quickly, kicking something small and hard as I went. It sounded like a bottle. It fell over with a clatter.

Someone must have heard. I stood there, rubbing my leg, cursing myself. I could feel my heart thumping up into my throat. Then I listened. There was no change in the sounds coming from the rest of the house.

Eventually I felt able to move again. I remembered a pull switch over the bed and managed to reach across to it. The room was suddenly illuminated and I blinked in the yellow light. It wasn't as untidy as I'd expected. There were a couple of Brenda's dresses and some necklaces on the beds and there were copies of *Tatler* and *Variety* on almost every surface. But there was no sign of the suitcase Julia had promised. Brenda must have tidied up.

The bottle I'd kicked over lay in the middle of the floor. Then I saw the edge of a suitcase sticking out from under the single bed. It was the pastel green one Julia had had with her on the day she'd arrived, so I pulled it out and put it on the bed. Most of her stuff seemed to be in it, like she'd said. I glanced inside, thinking of how jealous Ray would be if he could see me now. She must have already taken some items when she'd gone off with Dave, but now she wanted stuff like clean socks and underwear and it made me smile to think she'd had all the fancy things with her – the perfume and makeup and the hair slides shaped like butterflies – but now, left to fend for herself, it was the essentials she asked for. She wanted shoes and a towel and soap.

I didn't look in any of the cupboards or in the wardrobe, but clicked the suitcase shut and picked it up. Then I walked across the room and went to pull the light off. At that moment the door opened and I came face to face with Brenda.

It was odd, that moment – the two of us, both confused, looking into one another's eyes. Hers were dark with lack of sleep, her jaw sagged. She looked shocked and old. For a second I thought I might have been able to get away with it. My mouth started making up excuses. 'I just came to . . . empty the bin . . .'

But she'd seen the suitcase in my hand. She put her hands over her mouth and within a moment she was babbling and screaming like she'd forgotten how to talk. Then she found the words. 'How could you?' she was burbling. 'My daughter's things – from under our noses. How could you? And you must have known, too . . .'

'It's not like that,' I said.

'And we're all so vulnerable. I should have locked the door, but we've never had to do that here. There's *never* been any dishonesty in this house until this year.'

She was winding herself up, getting more and more agitated. 'No,' I began again. 'You see . . .'

She started calling for help in between telling me to stay where I was. 'Alastair! Charles! Come quickly. We'll need to call the police again. There's a thief in the house.'

And they were clattering up the stairs, piling up one after the other and I could hear Alastair calling, 'What's happening? Brenda? Are you all right?' and Irene looked over their shoulders. 'You little sod,' she said. 'Who'd have thought it?' Then Maisie appeared with her knitting still in her hands. She just smiled and shook her head as if to say, 'I told you so.' I think she guessed Julia would be involved somewhere.

In the end it was me or her. Me or Julia. All along I'd been thinking perhaps I should be heroic. I should invent a story and stick by it, like they did on *Spycatcher*, even if it meant I'd be shot as a spy. I could have said I was moving stuff into another bedroom, or that I was looking for a clue to her whereabouts, or perhaps admitted that I was a thieving little sod. But none of these things came into my mind at the right time and anyway my nerve had gone.

So when Vi came up the stairs and said, 'Would someone mind telling me what's going on?' I was grateful to see her and to hear her being so strong. My voice had turned all shaky.

I said, 'I know where she is. Julia asked me to come and collect her stuff.'

There was a stunned silence, and Maisie made a humphing noise.

'Thank God,' Brenda said. 'Is she all right?' She was so fickle. She'd already forgotten about the indignity of me being in their room. I told her she was. 'Thank God,' she kept repeating.

So we had to go and find her – Brenda and Alastair and me. Alastair said we should take the suitcase with us, because she'd be suspicious if I didn't have it and might try to run off. They walked twenty yards behind me like a couple of shadowy secret agents, and when I looked back they pretended they didn't know me. Brenda gestured with one hand, shooing me along faster.

When I got near where I'd left her in the shelter they stopped at one of the gift shops and pretended to be looking in the window even though it was dark and the shop was shuttered up. The plan was for me to go up to Julia with the suitcase and they would come down directly behind me. So I walked slowly across that dark open space between where the shops ended and the shelter. She looked up at me and I put the case down in front of her. 'You got it. Well done, Ed,' she said and started laughing.

'I'm sorry,' I told her. 'Julia, look, I'm really sorry.'

'What're you talking about?' She was already reaching down to undo the lock on the case. Then she looked up and saw her mother and Alastair coming across. Brenda broke into a canter when she knew she'd seen her.

'Oh, for God's sake,' Julia said. 'I should have known. You stupid little –' and then she was overwhelmed by Brenda hugging her and checking her over and asking questions about what she'd been thinking of, to run away like that.

Alastair and me followed them along the seafront – me still carrying the case. In front I could hear Julia telling lies about where she'd been. Not a word about Dave. 'I needed time on my own, Mother,' she was saying. 'You understand that, don't you? Of all people?'

'Yes, poppet, of course I understand. But why didn't you tell me? We could have discussed it before you left. I would have listened. I thought I'd never see you again.'

'I'm sorry, Mother. I was confused.'

'But why did you take your clothes? And where've you been staying?'

'With some friends. I met them while you were rehearsing.'

'I thought you might have gone off with . . . you know, with him.'

'Mother. How could you think that?' Julia appeared shocked.

'I know how unhappy you've been here, and I thought . . .'

'Well, you shouldn't jump to conclusions, Mother.' At one point Julia turned and glanced back at me. I was awed by the ease with which she lied. It was an art, easy as conversation. It was reckless and breathtaking.

'How's that for escapology?' Alastair whispered and shook his head.

When we got back to the house I passed her on the steps. She smiled at me and breathed, 'One word from you about what you know and you're dead – understand?'

I nodded.

10

I had to keep out of the Rodcoopers' way after that. Vi cornered me in the kitchen, as mad as I'd ever seen her, her little eyes glittering and her mouth screwed up, demanding to know what the hell I thought I was doing. Didn't I realize how unprofessional it was even being in guests' rooms, let alone taking their possessions? Something like that could cost her her reputation – her whole business – if word got round. It was lucky it was the Rodcoopers, whom she'd known for years and years, and who were almost family.

Vi made me tell her the whole story – how I'd met Julia on the slipway after we'd taken Nanny to the pictures, how she'd told me where she'd been for two days and what had happened between her and Dave. 'I knew that girl'd be trouble,' she said. 'You shouldn't get mixing with people like her. They're not like us, Ed. They do things different.'

Vi said I had to keep away from the Rodcoopers for my own good. 'Stay in the kitchen and don't serve in the dining room unless I tell you to. Got it?' I nodded. She'd try and patch things up with Brenda. 'I'm disappointed in you,' Vi said. 'What were you thinking of, Eddie?'

I didn't know what I was thinking of or if I was thinking of anything. Julia told me a story; then she took my hand and put it inside her coat. 'She asked me, so I did,' I said.

'And if she'd told you to put your hand in the fire, would you?'

Difficult question. Probably, I thought.

I spent my time in the bedroom, flicking through Ray's magazines and war comics, stealing a look at *Dream Dating* and wondering why, although Myron Bloomfield had answers to everything, the answers never quite applied to me. He had plenty to say about how to behave on your first date – don't eat with your mouth open, don't get drunk, be sure to wash carefully first – but nothing about how to stop your brain turning to mush when a girl asks you to do something indefensible.

I wanted to go home, but Mum and Dad were still in Scotland looking after Grandad. Even Ray said I was a fool. 'Women always try to twist you round their little fingers,' he said. 'And this is what happens when you let them. You get into trouble. You get the blame for everything. I tell you, Eddie, you have to show them who's boss.'

He lay on his bed and blew smoke rings. 'Look at me and Denise,' he boasted. 'She's not the only fish in the sea and she knows it. Maybe I'll see her again, maybe I won't. Girls respect you for that.' He tongued out another couple of impressive smoke rings. 'Then there's the rest of the idiots . . .'

'Which idiots?'

'Alastair. Charles. That lot.' Ray hated the way they took over, as if they were the only people in the house. He especially resented the way Charles had wangled himself into the best bedroom and left Nan to share the little one with Vi, and the way Vi had let him do it. 'I mightn't even go to their show this year,' Ray said. We were due to go over to Liverpool to see *The Pirates* in two days' time. 'That's the way I feel.'

'Nan'll want you to,' I said. 'I don't know why, but she

thinks you're ace.' I wanted him to go, too, but I wasn't going to say that. I'd never been to one of the shows before. He'd make me laugh; explain things in a way I could understand.

'Well, I might not.'

'Ray, come on. I'm not going on my own.'

'I dunno. And what'd they say at the Palace if they knew I'd been to the flippin' opera? I'd be a laughing stock.'

'You wouldn't have to tell them. They wouldn't understand anyway. If you mentioned Gilbert and Sullivan to Codge he'd think it was a brand of ciggies.'

Ray laughed at that. He loved the shows in a grudging kind of way. They'd marked his summers out for the last ten years and he knew more about them than he cared to admit. Last time it had been *The Mikado*. I asked him about it.

'It was about China or somewhere,' he said. 'The music's old-fashioned as hell, Eddie. But there are always loads of women in it. Dead gorgeous some of them. Not much of a story, mind you. Not one that makes sense anyway.' It sounded strange to me. 'At least it was funny,' he conceded.

'Funny ha-ha?' I asked. 'Or funny peculiar?'

'Dunno,' he said, and took another drag on his ciggie and eased out a smoke ring. It drifted towards the ceiling where it hung for a few seconds by an Airfix of an ME-109. 'Both, I think.'

'The Rodcoopers aren't as bad as you're making out, Ray. I've spoken to Maisie lots of times. I went looking for Julia with her and Alastair. Guess where we went.'

'Where?' He was trying not to show interest.

'The joke shop.'

His head shot up. 'Well, don't blame me if they get cut into bits, Ed. That new owner's a psycho. I don't know why you went anywhere near it after what happened last time.'

'Alastair thought it was good anyway. He bought a load of jokes and things, spent a fortune. Pete said I could go back any time I wanted.'

'Oh, it's "Pete" now, is it?' Ray said. 'You better watch him, Ed. Don't be going up there on your own.' One minute he was advising me to be tough with women, the next he was treating me like a kid brother. There was a silence, then he started laughing. He had one hand behind his head on the pillow and it was as if he hadn't wanted the laugh to escape. First his chest started shaking, then the laugh crept to his mouth, which turned up. Then it was bubbling out of him, making the whole bed shake.

'What's so funny?'

'I was thinking about Alastair spending all his money on those pathetic jokes. Tit for tat.' He made a machine-gun noise. 'Da-da-da-da. Charles unscrews the handle on Alastair's bedroom door, Alastair puts black face soap by his sink and Charlie comes downstairs with his face black as the hobs of hell. So Charlie puts pepper in Alastair's soup, and Alastair buys a kipper, wraps it up in paper and leaves it to rot in Charlie's coat pocket. And so it goes on.'

'Vi says it's all getting out of hand. She'll be having words with them soon.'

'And I'm just sitting back and watching what's going to happen next. Like setting a fire and watching it get bigger and bigger until the next thing you know – *wham!* – everything's alight.'

I said, 'Well, Alastair shouldn't have done that thing with Charles's bed in the first place. That's what started it all off.'

Ray sat up slowly, stretched his arms and shoulders as if he was trying to reach across the room. 'Who said it was Alastair?'

'Who else could it be? I mean, nobody else is that stupid.' Then I saw the look on his face. 'You?' He smiled. 'What for?'

'Because I hate him.' Ray got off the bed and came over and thumped me casually on the thigh. Dead leg. Then, before I had chance to react, he put his arm round my neck from behind and pulled me backwards onto the carpet. 'Finally you get it,' he said, taking a step back to admire his handiwork. 'Just my idea of a joke, Eddie. Not a bad one, though, is it?'

My mum phoned again. I asked about Grandad's tests, but she said they hadn't shown anything. Apparently he hadn't been eating properly and was undernourished. That hadn't helped. Mum and Dad had decided to look for a place for him to live. 'Do you mean an old people's home?' I asked.

'Oh, don't be like that, Eddie,' she said. 'They've got nicer names nowadays: they're called rest homes and retirement homes.'

'Oh.'

'We need to find somewhere we know will look after him properly and where he's happy, whatever it's called.'

She told me they'd looked at five places the previous week and I could hear in her voice how unpleasant that was. She said, 'We've seen some terrible ones. Your dad doesn't want him in a place full of old women who sleep all day. He's not that bad – yet. But we haven't found anywhere.'

I didn't know what to say. Something about the long silences suggested she wasn't telling me all the details. I could imagine the smell of old people and stale dinners. The silences weren't exactly a lie – not like one of Julia's anyway – but they were a way of not saying something. Grandad was old. He could only get more and more poorly, less able to cope. We both knew that and neither of us said it.

Likewise, I wasn't telling her about Julia and how I'd been caught in her room, or about how Vi couldn't keep control of us, not really – she tried but she couldn't do it.

These small lies, these silences are how people drift apart, I thought, but I didn't want all the details either. Grandad lived hundreds of miles away. I didn't even know him that well.

Mum said, 'We'll be a bit longer sorting this out. I've spoken to Vi and she doesn't mind you staying on. She says you're a great help.'

'Good,' I said. 'I'm glad.'

'Your dad's sending her a bit of money for your keep, and I'll ask him to send some for you as well.'

'Is he OK – Dad? He doesn't much like it when people are sick, does he?'

'He's all right,' she said. 'There's so much to do – sorting through all Grandad's belongings, making money arrangements. It's like a full-time job. There's no time to worry about things. Except . . . perhaps in the evenings, that's all. You know, when it's quiet. But your dad's fine. He sends his love.'

I sent my love back to him.

'We'll finish before you have to go back to school whatever happens,' she said. 'Dad can't stay off work for ever either.'

The pips went on the phone she was using. 'I've no more change,' she said. 'Bye, Ed. Be –' and she was cut off before I could find out what it was she wanted me to be.

I went back to the Box of Tricks. I was getting used to thc electric werewolf on the door but the masks hanging from the ceiling still made me shiver worse than any ghost train with its pretend spiders and cobwebs.

Pete looked up from the counter and hastily put a magazine away. He was wearing a tweed jacket with leather arm-patches. 'Your amusing friend's been back again.'

'Who? Alastair?'

'Alastair. Yes. He seems to be stocking up for a war.'

'That's what my cousin Ray says.' I instantly regretted

mentioning Ray's name because Pete's expression shifted and he looked at me with his old suspicion. 'You said you'd show me some magic,' I reminded him. 'In return for bringing the custom in.'

'You're trying it on. I never said that at all.' But he stood over his counter and produced a pack of cards. 'Watch carefully,' he said, and he made me choose one, memorize it and then put it back into the pack. He shuffled and cut and spread them out on the counter. Each one had a picture of a naked woman on the back. He pulled one out and held it up between his slim, strong fingers. 'Six of hearts. Is this it?' But it wasn't. 'Would you mind checking your pockets?' I searched in my jeans. At first I couldn't find it. Then I looked in my back pocket and that's where I found the one I'd chosen. Jack of spades. I shuddered to think he could have put it there without me realizing, that nude woman on the reverse looking at me enticingly. He smiled as if waiting for applause.

'Show me how to do it?' I asked, but he wouldn't. Trade secret. 'Come on, you've got to show me a proper trick. Have you ever done the one where you stick swords through a cabinet with someone in it?'

'Of course. Regularly. But it needs preparation and lots of practice. That's the main thing – practice. It's a stage act. Couldn't be done here in the shop.'

A man with a kid came in. The boy was fascinated, browsing through the cheap jokes. I sat on a stool, feeling superior, like I was Pete's mate, while Pete engaged the man in conversation. I could see him trying to assess how broad-minded the man was. He tried him with rude postcards and cranked it up from there and before long he was ducking down to show him the magazines reserved for regular customers.

'Thought this might interest you,' he said, and slid it across the counter. The man flicked through, nodded approvingly, then opened a thick wallet. Pete winked at me as he slipped the magazine into a brown paper bag. 'Anything else I can get you today? Stud poker's very popular with the married men. Works every time. How about a special gift for the little lady?'

The bloke shook his head. A box had attracted his son's attention. 'You can't have that,' he said.

'Why not?'

'You're too young. It's not a doll. It's for grown-ups.' In the box a plastic couple were making love – wind them up and they were going at it like dogs, back and forth. 'Here. You can have this instead. Look.' He wound up a plastic set of false teeth and they clattered away on the counter-top long enough to distract the boy.

'Kids, eh?' Pete said and threw in a joke rubber pencil buckshee.

'That's the way to do business,' he said after they'd left. 'I've been making money all my life. One sort or another. Would you believe it? On ships, all around the world? The thing is to diversify, Eddie. That means to do different things in case one of them fails. So, for example, I'm not just selling jokes because if I did I'd be bankrupt. You think this is a joke shop, but it's more than that.'

I realized that the joke shop was a magic trick in its own right. It was like one of those seamless handkerchiefs that looked red but which, when you pulled it through your fingers, turned out to be yellow with green spots. Then, just when you thought nothing more amazing could happen, doves and burning candles would appear from inside its folds.

He started telling me about famous people he'd met on his travels. 'The Queen of Norway,' he said. 'Brian Epstein, Bernard Delfont, Lew Grade. Impresarios, in case you didn't know. I have an acquaintance with Christian Dior – introduced models to the catwalks in Paris and Rome.'

'Honest?' It seemed far away and exotic. Who could imagine such links with this little shop?

'Indeed. I showed Liz Taylor round Cairo when she had a few hours to kill. She was very interested in the market-place there. How do you think she got that part in *Cleopatra*?'

'Wow.'

'And Princess Grace. I cut her up once. But I managed to put her back together. Here – if you don't believe me – I've got something for you. Stay here a mo.' He went into the back. For a long while the shop was silent. Then, just as I was about to give up and go home, he came back carrying a mini-guillotine – about a foot high, complete with blade and heavy block.

'Have you seen one of these before?' I nodded. He launched into his patter, slid the guillotine onto the counter. 'It can cut an apple clean in half. Watch.' He searched for an apple, but there wasn't one. He looked at me, but of course I didn't have one either. 'I told you preparation and practice were essential.' He chuckled nervously. 'Here – this'll do. We'll try it with this. Not quite the same but you get the idea.' He took a cheap plastic doll off a shelf. He pulled the blade up again, put the doll's arm on the block. 'Are you ready?' I nodded and he let it go. It slid heavily, sliced through the plastic with a crunch. An arm, severed at the elbow, rolled onto the counter. 'So you can see it's sharp. Feel the blade.' I ran my finger across it. 'Careful. Now.' He wound the heavy blade back up. 'You trust me, don't you, Eddie?'

Of course I didn't. But you have to believe in the magician. 'Just put your hand in there, Eddie. This is the best bit. Is that comfortable enough? Would you like to count your fingers – just so you can check them again afterwards?'

Perhaps he'd hypnotized me without me realizing it. My hand felt distant and strangely weighted. I wasn't sure I could move it. 'Are you ready, Eddie? Don't close your eyes now, will you?' What would Vi say? Pete and me were alone in the shop. 'Any last requests?'

Then he released the blade. It hit the block with a whack. It sounded heavy and final. 'Oh,' I heard myself say. Cut in half. No pain. No sound of falling fingers. I looked down and my hand seemed to be intact. Maybe the blade was holding it together.

'Can you wiggle your fingers, Eddie?' I moved them. 'There. That wasn't so bad now, was it? Say thank you.'

'Thanks,' I breathed. But he kept the contraption in the same place, my hand trapped by the blade. 'Let me out now.'

He looked at me across the guillotine as if to let me know who was in charge, a crease of a smile, a glint of fluorescent light from his glasses. He leaned gently on the blade.

'You can let me out now, please.'

'Are you sure that's what you want?'

'Yes.'

He lifted the blade again. I took my hand out and rubbed my wrist. 'That wasn't so bad,' he said again. 'Practice. That's what it takes. Practice and trust.'

The next evening, a Wednesday, four of us – me and Ray, Vi and Nanny – piled into a posh black car that Charles had organized for us to go to the Rodcoopers' show. Charles wouldn't hear of us struggling across to Liverpool on the ferry. As his guests at the theatre we had to arrive properly and not wash up with the rest of the hoi polloi. Ray had decided to come, but he was wearing his baseball boots in protest. Vi hadn't noticed. He got in the front with the driver. I was in the back between Vi and Nanny. There was a drinks cabinet between the seats, with a button to open it. I had to sit on my hands to stop myself pressing it. There was the smell of leather seats and the static warmth of Nanny squirming in her best nylon dress.

We cruised into the long, steady dip of the Mersey tunnel. Its lights made everything inside the car look orange. At the deepest part Ray turned round. 'We've got the whole weight of the Mersey on top of us, Eddie,' he said. 'Watch out, there's water dripping. It's sprung a leak! Driver – get a move on.'

I'd heard that one before and ignored him. Vi said, 'Shut up, Ray. You're making me want to go to the lav.'

Vi and Nanny had had their hair done specially. Nanny wore layers of jewellery – a black and violet necklace, the fox tippet with the glass eyes, a green hat with a silver-topped hatpin. 'Where'd the fox come from, Mother?' Vi asked. 'I don't remember seeing that before.'

'Oh, I've had it ages,' Nanny said, and looked across at me. I was getting fed up of being included in other people's lies and inventions – even little ones like this. But there was no point in spoiling the evening so I didn't mention the salerooms.

Vi had dolled herself up in a dark blue suit and matching shoes. Her lips were so thin that she'd managed to mostly miss them with her bright red lipstick. She looked as if she had someone else's lips on.

The car dropped us outside the front door of the theatre. As we got out Vi noticed Ray's baseball boots for the first time. 'What are those on your feet?' she shrieked.

He put a finger under the loose sole of one boot and flicked it.

'What are you thinking of, Ray? Are you trying to insult me on purpose? Is that it? You get yourself all dressed up, then you put those on. You'll have to go back and change, Ray. I'm sorry. I'm not going in with you looking like that. You look like a tramp.'

The white sides of Ray's baseball boots contrasted

dangerously with his dark trousers. Nanny said, 'It'll be all right. No one'll notice.'

'I'll notice, Mother. Look at the state of them. He's trying to show me up. It's typical. Ray – you'll have to walk behind us. You're not with me.'

The impact of the boots seemed to cheer him up. Still, we felt like royalty, walking from the taxi straight into the theatre. All that was missing was the red carpet. Charles had managed to get us tickets for an evening performance this year and when the doorman saw them he showed us to our seats, which were practically the best in the house according to Vi – near the front and right in the middle. I could see the whole stage.

After a while the lights went dim. The orchestra filed in and started tuning up and mostly the audience stopped rustling its sweet wrappers and went quiet, which was nothing like the fleapits I was used to. The musicians had little lights over their music and there was even a conductor in a dinner suit who tapped the stand with his stick. Then the show started in earnest. The curtain went up and everybody was standing on the stage, which was meant to be the seaside at Penzance. The scenery behind them made it look like a real world, but with much brighter colours. The girls were prettier and happier too. I caught sight of Maisie and Irene – familiar and unfamiliar at the same time.

Alastair had a good part right from the beginning. He was the Pirate King and had a fantastic swirly moustache and boots with buckles. In the choruses he pulled a cutlass from his belt and swung it round his head, just like that time he'd tried to fight with Charles in the dining room on the day of the dress rehearsal. Maybe that was more real than I'd realized.

When Charles finally came swaggering on there was a cheer because everyone knew him. He was Charles Wilton – the celebrity – the wittiest and cleverest person on stage, like a favourite uncle who was always interesting to be with. He was Major-General Stanley. Even the rest of the cast were pleased to see him and were suddenly even brighter, as if nothing could go wrong now. Then the audience joined in, clapping and singing the chorus. Vi loved it. I think she'd have climbed out of her seat if they'd allowed it. She kept bouncing up and down like a school kid.

Brenda had the part of Mabel, which was far-fetched because she was supposed to be one of Charles's daughters, but she did look lovely in a white dress with her dark eyes that reminded me of Julia. I suddenly realized how Julia understood about appearances – she only had to see her own mother in a place like this to know that appearance was everything.

But most noticeable was that they all seemed utterly at home – alive and invigorated, not pretending at all. It was as if all the trivial things they worried about – telling stories or swapping rooms or searching for Julia – were only a distraction from this, which was real. The pirate costumes with their vivid red sashes and silver swords, the wigs and curly moustaches and the girls' dresses, pink or green and luminous in the footlights made me realize: This is why they are really here. This is the reason. I could see that when the stage lights went off, the Rodcoopers would remove their dazzling clothes and stage makeup and go back to waiting.

After the interval the comic policemen came on. Ray laughed when they marched and pretended to dance and he nearly joined in the chorus, moving his lips in time with the words. He approved of anything that made the police look stupid. He put his knees up on the seat in front until Vi whispered across to him to take them down because of his baseball boots. 'I thought I wasn't with you,' he whispered back.

'Just do as you're told.'

At the end there was a big chorus – one of those songs that the whole company joined in with and made you want to sway in time in your seat. It was 'Poor Wandering One', ending with '*Take any heart . . . take mine*' and there wasn't a single member of the company who didn't end up with a partner happily waltzing round the stage. Lots of the audience were singing along, too, and even Ray was clapping. When he saw me looking he stopped even though it was dark and everyone else was doing it. He was here under protest, after all; he didn't want to seem too enthusiastic.

The final curtain came down, then it went up again and everybody was on stage. The orchestra started up the chorus again and we were all clapping and stamping along. Charles was last on, of course, and took off his feathered hat and bowed to the audience. Then he sent a kiss out with his hand. Vi thought it was just for her. He did look in our direction at that moment, but I'm sure it was just coincidence.

I could see why it meant so much to Vi, though, that Charles made it look as if nobody mattered but us. The lights came up and she had this enchanted look on her face. 'That was lovely, wasn't it?' she said, and we all agreed, but our speaking broke the spell.

'He's invited us backstage, don't forget,' Nanny said, as if any of us could forget. That was the part I'd been looking forward to. We were friends of the Rodcoopers. Not everybody could say that. We were special. They were staying at our house.

'I'm not going,' Ray said sulkily, remembering he wasn't supposed to be enjoying himself. 'I'll wait for you here. I've seen it all before.'

'Oh, don't be like that, Ray,' Nanny said and held onto his arm so he couldn't escape.

Vi asked one of the theatre people and he checked with someone, then led us through a door marked 'Private' and we were into secret corridors which led off from the stage. The walls were painted cream and the ceilings a dark green.

There were dozens of people milling around – chorus and backstage staff we didn't know – talking and laughing. Maisie whizzed past and I hardly recognized her. 'Hello Eddie,' she chimed. She blew us a fleeting kiss.

Eventually we stopped outside a door and there was Charles's name on it – 'Mr Charles Wilton'. The man knocked and we heard Charles's voice. 'Yes?'

'Visitors for you, Mr Wilton.'

'Come!' The man opened the door and we went inside – Vi first.

'Vi!' Charles sang as if he hadn't seen her for years. 'My dear Vi. Thank you for coming.'

His dressing room wasn't as big as I'd expected. There was space for a seat under a makeup mirror with bare bulbs all round it, just like on the films. But clothes didn't seem to have anywhere to go. Charles's frock coat and his other costumes were on coat hangers hooked over wooden rails. There was a little table with bottles on it and that was about all in the way of furniture.

'Thank you for inviting us,' Vi said.

Nanny, Ray and me hovered, half in and half out of the room. 'Come on in. Do close the door, there's such a draught in this old place,' said Charles. 'Make yourselves at home.' That was easier said than done. Once we'd managed to close the door behind us we still had to stand up because there was nowhere to sit or settle.

'Tell me – how did you enjoy the show?'

Was he looking at me? I wasn't sure. I hoped it wasn't going to be like at school where they asked questions to make sure you'd been concentrating or sometimes just to embarrass you. I'd enjoyed the show, but had been so occupied with the music and the colour and the comedy that I'd missed the story. All I knew for sure was that it ended happily, but that was only because everybody paired up conveniently and the music sounded jaunty and optimistic. 'It was good, thank you,' I said.

Ray put one foot high on a ledge to tie his bootlace. 'Feet, Ray,' Vi said. He ignored her and tied the other one with a double bow.

'Tell me – what other Gilbert and Sullivans have you seen?' Charles asked me.

'I haven't seen any.'

'Your first time,' Charles boomed, running a brush through his hair to make it stand up more. 'Splendid! And which part did you enjoy most?'

'All of it. I liked the policemen.'

'*A policeman's lot is not a happy one – happy one!*' he sang, sinking down nearly to his knees on the last note, keeping his eye on Vi as he did.

Ray chipped in. 'I liked the end.'

Charles wasn't sure how to take this. 'I always enjoy the cheering and clapping, too. I love those finales.'

'But the beginning was better – before you came on,' Ray said, giving Charles his most insolent look.

'Ray!' Vi said sharply. 'Not another word out of you.'

There was a silence then.

The best thing about the dressing room was the smell. It was the smell of acting – sweat and costumes that weren't made of the sort of cloth you got in the shops, wigs with lining that looked like sacking. I picked up one of the makeup crayons and put it to my nose. There was a huge tub of cold cream with a label in French. Charles dipped his fingers in and massaged it into his face and neck. When he'd wiped it off I could see a line of orange colour near his hair that the cold cream had left behind. There were still smudges in the corners of his eyes and dark lines in the creases. Anyone who saw him would know he was an actor. Even hours later, in a restaurant or in the street, people would know.

Among the makeup on the little table was a wrapped bunch of roses. Charles picked it up and presented it to Vi with such a flourish that she gasped, which made Nanny clap again. That was how things happened in the theatre. Here it was as if that little gesture of a bunch of flowers completed the story and made sure everyone was going to live happily ever after. You felt obliged to cheer them on.

Then Charles was pouring fizzy wine for all of us, even Ray and me. We drank ours from glasses he'd fetched from the bathroom, Ray slugging it back like water.

'Is there anything you lads'd like to see?' Charles asked. Ray shrugged. 'Behind the scenes?' he went on. 'The stage, the flies. There must be something? The scenery? Speak now, for later Violet and I will be hitting the town.'

'Oh, no, Charles, there's no need for that,' Vi said.

'But yes. Of course. Dinner after the show. Nothing else will do – and I'm ravenous this evening. As always.'

'I'd like to see backstage,' I said.

'Bravo!'

'You creep,' Ray whispered.

Charles showed us the stage with the place he had to stand – a small circle of paper stuck on the wooden floor. It felt really ordinary standing there and I realized quite suddenly it had been the Rodcoopers themselves who'd made us see *The Pirates* the way we did. From where we'd been sitting we had believed in the whole thing, but now looking at the dusty wooden floor and empty theatre I could see that it was just an effect – something we all agreed on and which everybody had to believe in for it to hold together. It wasn't exactly a lie – nobody was deceiving anyone else – but it wasn't true either. The Rodcoopers had told us a story and we'd taken it in because we'd wanted to be taken in.

By now the theatre was empty except for a couple of women cleaning between the seats. I imagined it full again. 'Doesn't it make you nervous coming onto the stage in front of all those people?' I asked.

'Nervous,' he said. 'Yes. And terrified and fascinated and exhilarated all at the same time. It's indescribable.' He rolled the *r*s in the words like he did in the songs so they were clear and funny. Then he stood and sang a bit of a *Pirates* song to the empty theatre and the cleaners stopped, looked up and laughed.

Backstage there was a long metal sheet with a handle on the bottom and he shook it to show us how they made the sound of thunder. It was so loud I had to cover my ears, but Ray didn't. I knew he wanted to but wouldn't give Charles the satisfaction. Then Charles showed us how to tie and untie the ropes that let the scenery down from the fly tower. Above us I could see the huge flying backdrops shiver and move. Charles said they had to come down in the right order, one in front of the other.

'Be careful, boy!' he boomed at another point when we crossed the stage. 'Don't stand there.' I moved away quickly. 'Trapdoor! The good fairy goes down that one and the devil comes up. Beelzebub in a puff of smoke!' He laughed like he was the devil and the cleaners looked up again.

At the end of the stage he stopped and looked at his watch. 'That's it,' he said. 'End of tour. I must get you a car home. Violet and I have a supper appointment.' It was as if he'd suddenly got fed up of us.

Back in his dressing room Nanny wouldn't hear of us going home in a car. 'Still plenty of time to catch the last ferry,' she said. 'You two go off and enjoy yourselves.'

So we walked to the Pier Head, where we caught the ferry. It was a warm evening and Nanny and me sat out on deck, deserted except for a sleeping drunk and a courting couple near the front. We could see the lights of the other ships coming and going.

'What's up with him tonight?' Nanny asked when Ray went and sat on his own on the lower deck.

'He's fed up of the Rodcoopers taking over the house. Specially Charles. I don't think he wanted to come tonight, but I persuaded him.'

'Well done, Eddie. It wouldn't have been the same without Ray.'

In the dark the ferrymen in their navy sweaters slid the gates closed, wound ropes as thick as my wrist. Their faces were old and weathered. 'I always look forward to watching them do that,' Nanny said, smiling into the breeze from the river.

On the other side they threw the ropes ashore and slid the gangplanks across. The three of us walked up the floating pier and onto dry land. It was only after we'd walked nearly all the way home that Ray spoke. 'I don't know what she thinks she's gonna get out of all this,' he said suddenly.

'Who?' Nanny asked. 'Get out of what?'

'Her and Charles. She thinks she's gonna end up going down to London with him, I suppose – live in his big house in Chelsea or wherever.' Ray was walking along with his hands in his pockets and not really talking to us, more mumbling angrily to himself.

'She could do worse,' Nanny said.

'I don't see how.'

'She could stay here for the rest of her life for a start. Cooking for a load of holidaymakers who don't appreciate it, looking after me and you . . .'

'It'd only be the same in his house,' Ray said. 'She'd be slaving away in the kitchen just the same, only we wouldn't be around.'

'You've got a good imagination, Ray. Do you think she's going to end up as some kind of skivvy?'

He shrugged. 'Yeah, I do, as a matter of fact.'

'Don't you think she skivvies here for you?'

'Not really. I look after myself these days.' That was another lie. Vi had always cooked him anything he wanted, even fried egg or chips in the middle of the night. She still washed his clothes and ironed them along with everything else.

'Anyway, what's wrong with going to supper with Charles?' I said. 'She doesn't go out very often.'

'She goes to Bingo every Thursday,' Ray said. 'But that's not the point. The point is *him*. He's the problem.'

'Who? Charles? He's OK, isn't he?' I asked.

'No. He's the same as all the others. They only think of themselves, nobody else. They say things they don't mean.'

'You say things you don't mean,' I said.

'That's different. When I say stuff I mean it at the time. I know sometimes things happen and I have to change my story, but that's not my fault.'

'Whose fault is it, then?' Nanny asked.

Ray ignored her. 'But that lot don't even mean what they say when they say it. Look at Brenda when Julia disappeared. She was acting the whole time. They're actors. Not one of them means a damn thing they say. And Charles is the worst of the lot. He says stuff and makes promises he won't keep. I don't want Mum getting hurt.'

We'd stopped by this time. Nanny said, 'Well, I think this has got more to do with you than with her, Ray. I think you're being selfish. Don't forget what your mother does for you every day. She never goes anywhere. No holidays. What's wrong with her enjoying herself once in a while? She deserves to go out with someone special.'

'I don't see what's special about him.'

'I wouldn't expect you to understand, Ray, but people need a bit of cherishing now and again.'

'I understand that,' Ray said in an unexpectedly soft voice.

We fell silent and walked along a little further, Ray's baseball boots flashing dirty white in the dark. Nanny said, 'It was the same in the war when the Yanks came. They brightened our lives up. Everything seemed different when the Yanks were around.'

'Yeah. I know. Nylons, chewing gum, Hershey bars . . . I don't want her to go, that's all.' It was a good job it was dark because I didn't want to see Ray cry and his voice sounded like he was about to.

Then Nanny became all mellow as well. 'I'm sorry, Ray, I didn't mean to be hard on you. Just because Charles has got a big house doesn't mean your mum's got to live there. They've been friends for years.'

'And anyway,' I said, 'if he was going to marry someone he'd have done it by now, wouldn't he?'

'Maybe. What's it matter? No one takes any notice of what I say,' Ray said, and walked off in front of us.

At about half past one in the morning I heard them come in. Ray was snoring and I crept to the top of the stairs and listened. Vi sounded tipsy. Her words were slurred. I was glad Ray couldn't hear. It sounded sad, to tell the truth. A bit funny, but mostly sad.

Vi said, 'Wonderful evening, Charles.' She was repeating things over and over. 'Wonderful.' It wasn't a word I'd heard her say even once before. 'Come into the kitchen, let's . . . and I'll put the kettle on. Do you want a sandwich or something?'

'No,' he said, a bit shocked. 'Thank you. I've eaten sufficient.'

'Of course. Me, too. Cuppa tea, then?'

'Tea – would be good.'

'I loved that singing, Charles. I loved it when you sang tonight.'

He laughed. 'It's what I do, dear Violet. It's what they pay me for. And I'm glad you like it.'

'God, I do. Better than anything.'

They went into the kitchen and shut the door. When I went back into the bedroom Ray stirred. 'Where you been?'

'The bog, that's all.'

'I thought I heard them come back.'

'Yeah,' I said. 'It's OK.'

Ray turned to face the wall and soon he was snoring again.

That wasn't the end of it, though. In the morning Ray was up and fighting again. He never let his thoughts fester for long. Vi was already starting on lunch when he came down. He poured Shreddies into a bowl, right up to the rim then milk on top so the Shreddies were like a floating mountain in the middle. He shovelled a spoonful into his mouth. 'Mother, I don't know what you're thinking of . . .' he said as if he was continuing a conversation from a few moments before.

She came in from the kitchen, wiping her hands on a tea towel. 'What are you talking about, Ray?'

'You know what I'm talking about.' Ray made sure his mouth was full, took another spoonful. 'With him – Charles.'

'What's wrong with him?' she said.

'He'll never marry you, Mother. You know that, don't you?'

'Who ever mentioned getting married?'

'I saw the way you were with him yesterday. I can tell what you're thinking.'

'Well, that's where you're wrong. You don't know what I'm thinking, Ray. Besides, why do you begrudge me a bit of happiness?'

'I don't. I don't want you going off with him, that's all. You'll end up getting hurt.'

'Honestly, Ray. It's just a little dream of ours, you know – that I'll go down to London with him. He'd look after me and take me to the West End and I'd cook him the meals he likes. He's such good company, Ray. Nobody makes me laugh like he does.'

'He wouldn't take you back to London, though, would he?'

'He might. He's talked about it more than once.'

'He's bloody joking. He says that sort of thing all the time. He's just a windbag.'

'Don't talk about him like that. He's a lovely man – fun to be with and reliable.'

'Mother, he'd never marry you. He likes men, doesn't he?'

There was silence. Vi threw the tea towel onto the table. 'You selfish little sod. Do you think I don't know that? Do you think I was born yesterday? I've known him long enough. That's not the point. What I'm talking about is good company. I'm talking about wanting to be with someone. I don't expect you to understand how sometimes I need someone to talk to, to say sweet things to me, to treat me nice. Just look at me.'

She put her hands down by her sides and we both looked at her. Her face was the colour of pale tobacco, her hands red from too much scalding water. She tucked a strand of hair back under her knotted headscarf. There was a smudge of lipstick around her lips from the previous night. 'I'm worn out with looking after people,' she said. 'Don't I deserve something decent once in a while?'

'Course you do,' Ray said. 'I didn't mean that.'

'That's what it sounded like to me, Ray. Anyway, I've lived here all my life. What makes you think I'd throw it all away? You're here. Nan needs me. You both do.'

'Sorry, Mum,' Ray said.

'Just leave me alone to have a few dreams,' she said. 'That won't hurt you, will it?'

She was right. Her words seemed to make Ray ashamed for once. He went over and gave her a hug from behind – a suffocating bear hug, really, hanging over her shoulders. He dug his chin into her neck. 'Stop it – I can't breathe,' she started.

'Just promise us you won't go down to London to live, that's all.'

But she wouldn't promise him anything. 'I don't know, Ray,' she said. 'I might.'

'Please, Mum.'

'I'm thinking about it.' That was all the comfort she was willing to give him.

11

Julia had come up smelling of roses as usual. She made out that running away was a cry for help.

'Would you believe that? She ends up as the victim,' Maisie said. 'Butter wouldn't melt. Why do people always believe beautiful girls? It's not fair.'

So now Julia was allowed to do what she wanted during the day on condition she was home every night. She no longer had to trail around with the Rodcoopers to their shows or their occasional guest appearances along the north-west coast. Maisie said it was a relief not to have her with them on those days. Brenda had made Julia promise to stick to the agreement. 'It's dependent on trust,' Maisie said, mimicking Brenda. 'I wouldn't trust that girl as far as I could throw her.'

A couple of times I'd seen Julia in one of the greasy tea rooms on Vicky Road, sitting on her own looking out of the window. Once she was with a lad in a leather jacket. Another time I caught sight of her in the Palace Amusements in a shocking pink pinafore dress and her hair tied in a scarf, sitting on the steps of the waltzers talking to Ray. She touched him on the arm and on the shoulder and looked fascinated by what he had to say even though I imagined they were just Ray's usual stories. Even Myron Bloomfield agreed that touches of that kind were an unmistakable sign that a girl fancied you.

I didn't expect her to want to talk to me again. I thought that by keeping away from her I'd missed the opportunity to get closer. A moment's inattention and she was lost.

Then, on the Friday after we went to see *The Pirates*, Julia ran up to me on the seafront. 'Eddie, Eddie. I've been looking for you. Where've you been?' I tried not to show it, but my heart started racing, pounding the moment she appeared.

'I've been around. Keeping quiet like you asked.'

'I know. Thanks, Eddie. I mean, thanks for not saying anything about Dave.'

'I wouldn't have anyway.' She wore pale blue ski pants and a skinny woollen sweater that showed off her figure. She looked like a film star – too glamorous for this flat seafront. She smelled of something that might have been roses or lilies of the valley.

'Listen . . . I was going to ask.'

'What?' An invitation, perhaps. She'd been thinking of me, after all. Maybe she was going to find a way of repaying me for the trouble she'd got me into with her suitcase.

'Will you do me a favour?'

'A favour? You've got a nerve,' I said.

'Just a little one.'

'Listen, Julia, when I went into your room to get your bag that night I was doing you a big favour, or perhaps you've forgotten that. You might not have noticed, but I'm not the sort of person who goes creeping into other people's rooms in the middle of the night.'

'I know you're not.'

'Then when your mother came in and caught me red-handed . . . that was the worst thing. Worse than anything at school. I thought she was going to throttle me with her bare hands.'

'Didn't you say anything?'

'What was I supposed to say? That I was just borrowing a few pairs of your knickers?'

'You could have thought of something,' she said. 'I thought you had imagination. You were too bloody honest again.'

'Having an imagination's not the same as being dishonest,' I said.

'You twist things round. I never meant that.'

'I suppose you blame me for getting caught in your room?' I said.

'Of course I don't, Ed. It's just that when I saw them that night my heart just sank. I felt as if my life was over.'

'Julia,' I said, 'I don't really care. It's your life.'

We'd walked a little way along the front, almost without meaning to, like it was a coincidence we just happened to be going in the same direction. We stopped. She stood with her hands on her hips, a model's pose that made me laugh. She said, 'Come on, Eddie. Life's too short. Let's go for a walk.'

'Is that the favour you wanted?'

'No. Walk first. It'll wait.'

The sea wall was massive here – tall as a person, with seats set in. When the tide was high it was a good place for fishing. In storms it was perfect for dodging the waves that crashed over. The rest of the time this was a lonely, empty part of New Brighton. There were gaps in the wall with steps leading to the estuary.

'Let's go down to the beach,' Julia said.

'It's not a beach here. Just mud.'

'Don't be so bloody literal. We can just go and see what there is. Let's have an adventure.'

The steps had iron handrails knotted with rust. Fixed to the sea wall were warning signs about the dangers of incoming tides and treacherous sands.

It was silent down there, like a different country, with the town hidden by the sea defences. The tide was out –

the line of the sea visible in front of us across the grey mud and patches of sandstone. Flocks of seabirds took off, twisted in the air and landed further away in the stones.

'Oystercatchers,' she said. I didn't know she knew the names of birds and I found myself not believing her. It wasn't worth asking her, though. She lived in a make-believe world half the time and that could be dangerous if you couldn't tell it from reality.

'Where d'you wanna go?' I asked.

She shrugged. 'Dunno. Let's walk across to the lighthouse.'

It looked close enough – white and dazzling. The mud glistened all around. So we started out with Julia in front. She had on a pair of canvas shoes and soon they were being sucked into the mud. I looked back at the land. Already it was a long way off, as if we were on a raft. The lighthouse looked closer, but not much. The mud was making sucking and crackling sounds that I'd never noticed before.

Julia was a few paces ahead of me and I was following her footprints into the middle of nowhere. How easily she'd forgotten how she'd used me – first to keep her secret about Dave, then to run the risk of fetching her suitcase. She just expected it, never asked. I shouted ahead to her. 'Why do you keep doing crazy stuff, Julia? You can't go round using everybody.'

She whirled round. 'I don't intend to. Shit, it's the way I am. This place just suffocates me, drives me mad. I've got to be out of it. I don't know how you can live here.'

'I don't,' I said.

'Oh?'

'I'm just passing through. Like you.'

For a moment I thought she'd looked at me differently, as if I was worth more than a passing glance, but she said, 'Doesn't look like it to me. I thought you were part of the furniture.'

I started telling her about my mum and dad and how they'd left me here while they went up to Aberdeen to sort my grandad out. I never thought I'd get to the point where my mum and dad were a source of credibility, but I made them sound funny and slightly mad. I even managed to tell her about Grandad's house. 'There are always storms at night,' I said. 'Thunder and lightning – and all the doors and windows rattle. Like in *Frankenstein*.'

We kept on walking. At least we were side by side now, but she was concentrating on where to walk. Her foot slipped on a sheen of grey, went in past the uppers.

'Blasted mud. Whose idea was this?'

'Yours.'

She laughed. 'Look, I know you're a kid . . .' She waited for me to reply so I intentionally didn't. I wasn't that many years younger than her. We could still have things in common. '. . . but you're OK.'

'I'm OK for a kid?'

'What I mean is I don't expect you to understand me.'

'Sod off, Julia. What don't you expect me to understand? You've got fantasies of being some kind of model. You don't want to be here. What's so hard to understand about that?'

She stopped and we looked back. Our footprints were crooked dotted lines between the stones. In places they crossed and went apart. The bottoms of her ski pants were soaked. There were splashes of mud up her legs and on her face so she looked like a grimy kid, too.

'I'm sorry, Eddie,' she said. 'It's how it gets me just here.' Her hand went to her stomach. 'Like something I've got to do. You know, I'm just a big exhibitionist. Sometimes it feels as if I'm ill with it.'

As if to demonstrate, she began jigging up and down in the mud and singing one of the latest bouncy pop songs. 'Come on, Eddie. You know this, don't you? The Searchers?'

Nobody could hear us, which was just as well because her voice was getting louder and louder. Then she was singing to the land and the ships. She shouted, 'No one can hear us out here. No one!' A couple of gulls flew up from the rocks and landed again. She held her hair up on her head with one hand and started singing. This time it was 'Fever' by Peggy Lee. She had a good voice, quivering on the right notes. '*Fever!*' she was shouting.

'Eddie,' she said, suddenly back to normal. 'Eddie. It's about that favour. You've got to help me.'

'Help you how?'

'Look – I've decided now. I'm gonna be a model. I've been thinking about it. All you've got to do is ask around. You know people here, don't you? You can ask them for me. Once I'm started I know I'll be fine. Don't you think it's a brilliant idea?'

'I don't know people,' I said. 'I don't know anyone here. Why don't you ask Ray?'

She stopped. 'I've already asked him.'

'And I've already helped you,' I said, 'and look where it got me.'

'That was a mistake, that's all. It could've happened to any of us, Eddie. Come on – you're my last chance.'

'That's nice.'

'I didn't mean it like that. You know I didn't.'

'There's nothing I can do anyway, Julia, even if I wanted,' I said.

'You know people. You're sensible. People like you.'

For a moment, just for a fraction of a second, I could imagine exactly how she felt – breakable like glass – but after that she was back to how she was before: standing in the mud and looking at me. I said, 'What's the good of being liked? It doesn't do you any good in the end, does it? People say nice things about you, but they forget you as soon as you're no use to them. They've got their own lives to lead.'

'Please,' she begged, 'think about it, Eddie. There's got to be someone who can help me. Just think about it. That's all I'm asking.'

'I'll think about it. All right?' The truth was I'd have done anything for her. I'd never met a girl like her before, one who knew exactly what she wanted. Even through her makeup I could see her face starting to colour, touched by the sea air. Her hair was losing its shape, matting with salt. It made her look wild.

'Listen,' she said suddenly.

'What?'

'It sounds different. Has the wind changed or something?'

I realized I already knew. 'Tide's turning.'

'I can hear it,' she said. 'It's scary.'

I listened and heard the sound of the river meeting the sea, a faint stir of wind and the gurgle of water filling endless underground gullies.

I looked across to the lighthouse and already where there'd been sand was a sheen of saltwater. The river was closing in. It was the easiest thing to forget, that this was a river full of ships with a life of its own and no conscience.

'We can make it to the lighthouse,' she said. 'It doesn't look too deep – then we can wait till the tide goes out again.'

'What? Spend the night on the rocks? Look at it.' Seagulls were riding the tide, sweeping in towards the shore faster than we could walk.

'I can do that. A night at the lighthouse. They'd have to let us stay there in a big round room with a big round bed.'

'Don't be stupid,' I said. 'There's nobody there.'

'Course there is. They'd let us in. Who lights the lamps?'

'The light comes on automatically. We could knock on the door for ever and no one'd let us in.'

'Trust me, Ed. It'll be an adventure.'

I couldn't believe the way she refused to accept what was happening. 'The tide isn't pretending, Julia. We're not in a play now.'

'I'll go on my own if you haven't got the nerve. You go back and tell them where I am. I'll see you in the morning.'

'You'll be bloody dead in the morning,' I said, turning round. 'Look – we're cut off already.' The tide had swept between us and the seafront. I could feel the pressure of water squeezing through the sand under our feet.

'Come on, then,' she said, not wanting to admit that I was right. 'If you're so bloody certain. Quick.' We started back the way we'd come, hurrying towards the faint line of the sea wall.

'I bet people have drowned out here,' Julia said. She sounded cheerful about it.

'Of course they have. What else did you think happens?'

'If someone's spotted us – maybe one of the fishermen – they'd have to call the lifeboat out, wouldn't they?' she asked.

I didn't tell her I'd been listening for the sound of the lifeboat maroon for the last ten minutes. I said, 'Why would anyone be fishing off the sea wall if the tide's all the way out here?'

'They might be. I don't know. We'll be heroes if we get rescued. We'll be on TV.' She wanted to see the lifeboat come out full of men with yellow jackets, like she was a damsel in distress and they were knights in armour. As if they'd drag her onto the lifeboat and she'd faint into their brawny arms. But more likely they'd just give us a bollocking for being stupid and wasting their time. Getting caught on the sands with the tide coming in was the sort of brainless thing visitors did. People who lived here knew better.

We reached the bank of a channel. 'Oh my God,' she said when she saw it. On the way out it had been a hardly noticeable dip in the sand. Now it was a salty river – fast-flowing, twenty foot wide and getting deeper by the second.

'We'll have to get across here,' I said.

'Hold my hand,' she said. I could feel the gritty sand in her fingers. 'What if we get swept away?'

'Dunno. What if we do?' I didn't want to think about it.

'I've always wanted to get carried away with you.'

I looked across at her. She was shivering. '*Now* you tell me,' I said. With her hair damp, she'd lost the glamour. She looked almost ordinary, like any girl with mud and the smell of the sea on her.

She said, 'If we do get swept away, Eddie, will you hold onto me?'

'If you want. Why?'

'I don't want to be on my own. I'd like to think of us being found – you know in one another's embrace. It'd be romantic, wouldn't it? That's how I'd like to be remembered.'

'Nothing's going to happen to us,' I said, bluffing. 'Anyway, I can't think of anyone I'd less like to be found dead with.' That was a lie, too. I don't know why I said it.

Julia tried to let go of my fingers then, but I held them tight as we waded into the water.

'Holy shit, it's cold,' she said. She tried to laugh but her shivering got the better of it. I could hear her teeth chattering. The water was above our knees. Then it got deeper still and it was difficult to keep our footing on the shifting pebbles and sinking mud. From every direction there was the sound of water; a gentle, terrible noise.

'We're going to drown,' Julia screamed. She was vulnerable, even more terrified than me. I liked her for that confession at last, that chink of weakness that soon closed up again.

'I was only joking about not wanting to be found dead with you,' I said.

'That's a relief, I'm sure.'

The water was swirling around our thighs now. If the current got any stronger we wouldn't be able to keep walking. We'd be swept into the river and out to sea, to Ireland, the Isle of Man.

'Can you swim?' I asked.

'A bit,' she said.

Suddenly her feet slipped on one of the hundreds of mossy, slime-covered rocks. She floundered, chest-deep in rushing water.

'Help me, Ed,' she cried, splashing and trying to regain her footing. 'Help!'

I managed to get to her, pulled her up, half by the arms, half by the shoulders. Her woollen sweater was heavy with water.

'Come on,' I said. 'Keep going.'

'I can't, Eddie. Help me. I'm too cold and wet to move.'

'You can do it. We're nearly there. Come on.'

I persuaded and pulled her through endless knee-deep sea. Gradually it became ankle-deep. We dragged ourselves, gasping, onto the cold mud. Julia wanted to sit down. Anywhere would do. But I could see we were still a long way from the seafront. We could get cut off again. That was the way the tide worked – deceiving you into thinking you were safe. So we carried on. She was still holding my hand. My feet and legs were numb with cold.

At last we got to more solid ground – pebbly, shaly rocks with strands of seaweed. Between the rocks were chunks of timber lost from ships. Julia lowered herself down on the stones and I sat down beside her. 'I've never been so pleased to get onto dry land,' she said. 'Ta, Eddie. I'd have drowned if it hadn't been for you.'

I looked back to where we'd been. It was already part of the sea, with shallow breakers coming from both sides, folding over one another. They reminded me of Maisie's knitting, knit and purl, the way I'd seen her stitch a sleeve onto the body of a little coat with perfect overlap.

'I'm frozen stiff,' Julia said. 'Put your arms round me, Eddie.'

So I did and she held onto me, too. Her lips were almost blue. If any of my clothes had been dry I would have given her them to stay warm, but they weren't. They were gritty and soaked with saltwater, so we shared the coldness of our bodies.

I was so close to her I could feel her breath – closer than that time in the dark on the slipway when she'd been hurt and remote. 'You can kiss me if you want,' she said and put her face up, just a fraction. I could feel the gravity of her skin. I kissed her. Her lips were soft and icy cold and behind them was the vibration of her teeth still chattering. I wanted to warm her. Her hand came up to my neck and pulled me to her.

Was this for survival? I couldn't help asking myself. Kissing to stay alive. Even now I knew that Julia might be using me. Sometimes lies were easier than the truth. But this felt different. It was too good to be untrue, too sweet to be a deception, and it was far away from anything I'd read in my books, which never mentioned muddy sand or seaweedy rocks. The kiss had come up like the tide and taken me by surprise.

12

'Promise you won't tell anyone?' Ray said.

We were in the kitchen; Ray sprawled across the settee browsing through *The Victor*. He only read the strip cartoons – the ones where the hero took the enemy bunker armed with nothing but a Bren gun and ten hand grenades. He skipped the stories. They were dense with print and only had one black and white drawing at the top of the page.

Nanny was sitting at the table wearing her beige hat with silver hatpins, as if she was on her way somewhere – shopping perhaps. But she wasn't. She was staring at two little white tablets and a pink one in front of her on a saucer.

Vi had taken Nanny to the doctor's when she caught her putting jam on her cornflakes. To tell the truth I'd seen her do that, too, but I'd assumed it was a trick she'd learned in the war. Something to do with survival rather than confusion. Vi told me how the doctor wanted to know if Nanny had ever become lost or disorientated. 'Only a couple of times,' Vi told him and he asked her if Nanny ever forgot things or got people mixed up and Vi said all the time. Nanny said it wasn't all the time at all and Vi said it was quite often, if you wanted to be precise about it. The doctor said it wasn't unusual at her age and that was when Nanny told him about her only son, Steven, and how even though she sometimes got his name mixed up she was crystal clear about who he was and could remember exactly what he'd looked like when she saw him onto the *Queen Mary* in 1950, which was the last time she'd seen him. He'd been wearing a light brown tweed jacket and pale brown trousers and a Frank Sinatra trilby. The doctor said, 'A-ha, I'd wondered if there was some underlying cause.' Vi sighed and said there was nothing 'underlying' about it.

'But there might be,' Nanny said.

'The doctor doesn't want to hear about it, Mother. He's a busy man,' Vi said.

The doctor smiled and said, 'No – tell me. I've got a cousin in Wisconsin.'

'You'll regret it,' Vi told the doctor, and Nanny told him the full story of Steve and Marion and little Gary.

The doctor listened carefully while scribbling a prescription and said, 'It sounds like you've got a lovely family in America. I hope you get together soon.' He cheered Nanny up no end.

'Won't tell anyone what?' I asked Ray.

'Promise first,' he said, 'and not so loud.'

'I can hear you, anyway,' Nanny said as much to the tablets as to us.

Vi whizzed through on her way to put clean towels in the bedrooms. 'Just take them, Mother, will you?' she said. 'They're not going to disappear of their own free will.'

'That's what you think,' I heard Nanny say under her breath. She had a determined look on her face. 'Wilful' was what Vi called that look.

Nanny picked up her cup and put her hand to her mouth. She swallowed a mouthful of tea and made a face at the taste of the tablets. But she still had them in her hand. From where I was sitting I saw her drop them into the silky folds of her dress. She winked at Ray and me.

'There are too many secrets in this house already,' she said menacingly.

'I'm with you, Nan,' I said. 'I don't want any more.'

'In that case,' Ray said, 'I'm not going to tell you.'

'Don't then.'

He flicked at the pages of *The Victor*, then said quietly, just to me, 'I won't tell you I've got a new job. I won't tell you I've left the Palace.'

He glanced up to see if the news had sunk in. No more visits to the Amusements, I thought; no more being able to call in any time, knowing he'd be there. It felt as if the lights on all the rides had suddenly dimmed. I'd miss having a laugh with the attendants and the woman on the burger stand. It wouldn't be the same without Ray. Even Vi had got used to him being at the amusements. At least she knew where to find him. 'Why, Ray?' I said.

'Wanted a change.'

'But you like it there. What about your mates? What about the girls and the parties?'

'They're good, but I can do without them. Sometimes you have to move on, Ed. I need something, you know – steady.' I knew he wasn't telling the whole story. He'd been happy at the Palace, thriving almost. Steady work had never been one of Ray's needs.

'What's the new job, then?'

He pretended to be engrossed in *The Victor* again. 'The post,' he said at last. 'I've got a job on the post if you must know.'

Nanny had heard this part of the conversation. 'The post? Are you in the sorting office, Ray?'

'No,' Ray said. 'On the rounds.'

Nanny sputtered her drink. 'You couldn't even get out of bed for your job at Cadbury's and they started at eight. What time do postmen start?'

He shrugged. 'They want me there at five on Monday.'

'In the morning?' I shouted.

'No, in the bloody afternoon – of course in the morning.' It was impossible to imagine Ray on the streets at that hour. He'd be sleepwalking, kicking dogs in his dreams, delivering letters in his pyjamas. He'd never do it. 'What's so bloody funny? I've done a paper round, don't forget, and I helped on the milk.'

Nanny said, 'Yes, and most days your mother had to haul you out of bed by your hair.'

'You shouldn't discourage me. I'm trying to do something respectable for once. You lot are always telling me to get a proper job, so that's what I've done. I thought you'd be pleased as a matter of fact.'

He seemed genuinely offended. He thought he could make a go of it. Nanny got up and ruffled his hair like he was about seven. 'You're right, Ray. It's a good steady job on the post. Better than those old slots. I never liked you working there.'

'Thanks, Nan,' Ray said. 'There's a couple of days before I start, so I've got some free time. What would you like to do? I'll take you somewhere for a treat.'

'We can go to the wrestling. Does your mother know you've packed up another job?'

'No. That's the point. I want to get her in the right mood before I tell her. I don't want it spread about either. That's why I'm saying it quiet.'

'But . . .' Nanny started.

'Remember I saw what you did with them tablets.'

'Oh,' she said. 'Did you? All right, then. My lips are sealed.'

In that weekend between jobs Ray was as good as his word. On Saturday morning he took Nanny to have her feet done and waited forty-five minutes in the waiting room. In the evening they went to the wrestling at the

Tower Theatre. The Blue Angel v. Dirty Dick Swales was the main contest. Before they went Ray pretended he was Dirty Dick and pinned me against the dining-room door. Half nelson, body slam, full nelson. Submit? I refused. Eventually he walked off checking his biceps.

'That wrestling's just a big fix,' Vi said once they were safely out.

'How?'

Vi had read about it in the *News of the World* – how it was decided who was going to be the villain, who'd make a miraculous recovery and go on to win the bout. I was amazed.

'Are you sure?'

'They've worked out who's going to win before they even set foot in the ring. They agree on it between them. I tell you, Eddie, the folks who go are just as bad for letting them get away with it. It's criminal if you ask me.'

I could see she was right. I'd never been to the Tower but I'd seen wrestling on television and, yes, now she mentioned it there'd been times when it hadn't looked convincing. It was like one of our pretend fights. Why didn't he get up off the mat before that body came slamming down on top of him? Why didn't he bother to untangle himself from the ropes when he must surely know the arm slam was coming? He just hung there, shaking his head as if he was trying to regain his senses, and let it happen. I felt gullible and stupid again.

When Ray and Nanny came back they were laughing, reliving the absurd wrestling match.

'He got the Angel like this – in an armlock. Did you see? That was never legal,' Ray said.

'The ref didn't want to see it, that's why. He had his back turned.'

'What about that flying headbutt in the last round? I never thought Dirty Dick would get up after that.'

'That was when he lost his temper. That was when the ref got thrown out of the ring, wasn't it? He didn't know what day of the week it was.'

'The Angel should never have won anyway,' Ray went on.

'But I didn't want Dirty Dick to win. He's an ugly so-and-so.'

At least justice had been done and they'd enjoyed themselves into the bargain. The shouting out and booing at the wrestling had made them drunk.

It was at times like this that Ray told Nanny things he wouldn't tell anyone else, not even me. Vi said Ray only told Nanny his stories because he was pretty sure she'd forget them. But you could never tell what she'd keep in her mind. Suddenly, when you didn't expect it, she'd say something about Ray that nobody else knew – how he'd pulled a kid off the waltzers when she'd got frightened, or some titbit about one of his girlfriends. She'd talk about the girls, as if she'd been out with them and Ray and not just imagined it all through his conversations. Nan's stories would be full of detail about Denise's latest outfit or Vanessa's long auburn hair. That's how you knew she'd been talking to Ray again.

The evening before he was due to start on the post Ray and me were going tenpin bowling at Fairlanes. On our way downstairs we stopped off at Nanny's room. Ray said he wanted to make sure she was OK and that she wasn't worrying about him.

I hadn't been in the tank room since we'd moved out. Nanny had made it homely, with fresh flowers and a few ornaments. But she hadn't found a place for all her clothes.

Some of them were still in piles on the floor or on Vi's bed, which looked as though it hadn't been slept in. The photos of Steve and his family were still on the bedside table.

At first she was pleased to see us, but Ray was edgy. 'What's the matter with you, Ray? You're like a cat on a hot tin roof.'

'I'm all right.'

'Are you worried about the new job? Is that it?'

'No. I just came to make sure you were OK,' Ray said.

She looked at him suspiciously. 'Well, I am. As you can see.'

'We're on our way to Fairlanes,' I said. I was impatient because the bowling was popular in the evenings and we might not get a lane if we left it too late. I was trying to drop the hint to Ray, but he only understood what you were on about when you told him directly. He didn't do subtlety, which meant he hardly ever got offended, either. I liked that about him.

Nanny said, 'If it's money you're after I haven't got any.'

'What a thing to say,' Ray said. 'I wanted to make sure you had everything you needed, that's all. I mightn't see so much of you after I start my new job tomorrow. I dunno.'

'Very kind of you, I'm sure,' Nanny said. I was standing by the window and Ray did seem nervy – fiddling with things for the sake of it. 'Put that down,' Nanny snapped when he picked up her alarm clock.

'I'm only looking,' Ray said.

'Look with your eyes, then, and not your fingers.'

Next he picked an ornament off the shelf and turned it over in his hands. It was the one we'd got at the saleroom – the girl in the swirling pink dress. Nanny stood up slowly, went across and tried to take it off him. 'Leave things alone,' she said. 'You're a ruddy meddler!' But he pulled it back. 'Stop it now, Ray,' she said.

The ornament slipped out of his hands. I watched it drop. They grabbed for it together, but it fell against the tiled surround of the old fireplace and smashed.

'Ray!' she shouted. 'You clumsy so-and-so. Why couldn't you leave things alone?'

'It wasn't me,' he said.

'Of course it was you. You're in here messing about. It wouldn't have broken otherwise.'

'I'm sorry, Nan,' he said.

'It was the best bit of colour in the room,' Nan said, 'and now you've broken it, you great clumsy beggar. I was just getting to like her . . .'

Ray started to collect the pieces. 'I'll buy you a new one. Sorry, Nan. Honest.'

'Don't bother. You couldn't get another one like her anyway. She's genuine Victorian. Here – let me do it.' She didn't want him touching anything else. He was being so gangly and clumsy. So she pushed him aside and bent down. That was when she saw it. 'What on earth?' she said, and picked up something from among the broken bits.

'What the hell's that?' Ray said.

She held the little package up. It had an elastic band round it. 'I dunno,' she said, breathless. Ray and me gathered round to have a better look. 'Looks like money!' Nanny said, 'And you mind your language, Ray.'

'Blimey, Nan,' Ray said. 'How much is there?'

'I dunno.'

'Count it,' Ray said. 'Count it! There could be hundreds.' Trust Ray to be practical.

'Course there couldn't,' Nanny said. 'Could there?'

So she took the elastic band off. Ten-pound notes opened like a fan, and nearly filled both her hands. 'Blimey!' she said, suddenly realizing what it was.

'There's hundreds! We're rich.'

We called Vi upstairs while Nan was counting.

'Bloody hell,' Vi said when she saw it. 'How much is there?'

By now Nanny had counted it. 'Two hundred and eighty quid,' she said quietly. 'I can't keep it, of course.'

We all started protesting at once. We never got to even see that much money, let alone have the chance to keep it. Ray said, 'You've got to, though, Nan.'

'It wouldn't be right,' she said. 'I know it's nice to have a windfall, but someone'll be missing that money. Some poor old dear might have put all her savings there for safe-keeping.'

Vi said, 'Mother, you've had that ornament ages. They'll think you've gone mad if you take it back – and in pieces.'

'That's not the point, Vi. I've got to live with it on my conscience haven't I? Enjoying someone else's money – I've never done that in my whole life. We could take it to the police if the saleroom won't have it back.'

Ray was getting agitated, listening to this. He was walking around the tiny room and looking at the wedge of notes as if it might disappear at any moment. The idea of returning money went against all his principles. 'Yeah,' he said, 'and the old dear who stashed it away might be dead an' all, so no one'll even know it's missing.'

Vi said, 'If you take it back, Mother, d'you really think they'll try and find out who owned it? Course they won't. It'll go straight into the saleroom till – or the police benevolent fund.'

'It's yours, Nan,' Ray said. 'They're a bunch of scallies at the saleroom – I know. Please. Please.' I'd never heard him beg like that before.

'But it's taking someone's money. It's dishonest, isn't it?'

'I don't think so, Nan,' I said, trying to be rational. 'We bought it at an auction, didn't we? You paid for it – and don't you remember the man saying "Sold as seen"? That means if it'd been damaged or something you wouldn't have been able to take it back.'

'I know,' she said.

'So why should you take it back now?'

'That's right, Eddie,' Ray cried.

Nanny sighed. 'I suppose so . . .'

'Of course he's right,' Ray said. 'Good ol' Eddie – brains of the family.'

'And you said I was no good at finding bargains! How about that for a bargain?' I couldn't resist getting that one in while I had the chance.

'It was me who found it, as a matter of fact,' she said. 'Even if I did think I was buying a vacuum. You just happened to be there at the time, Eddie.' It felt like a little victory all the same – being there. She flicked through the notes again. 'If we're keeping it I'd like to buy you all a present – something you really want.'

'Don't be silly, Mother,' Vi said, though I imagined she was at least thinking about a new coat or a stair carpet or a set of sheets.

Ray chimed in, 'Not us, Nan. It's not what we want. It's your money. Like I keep telling you.'

'But I've already got everything, Ray – enough clothes to keep me happy, a bit of furniture. I know I like to go to the wrestling and have a few trips out, but that's just a bit of fun. What would I do with two hundred and eighty quid?'

For a moment I thought she was going to start on about the war again. Then I noticed we were all looking at her as if there was something we knew but weren't saying. It was obvious, so I said it. 'New Jersey, that's what.'

'America?'

'Course,' Ray said.

'Oh, no,' she said. 'It's something I've always wanted to do before I die, but it's just a dream. I never expected it –

not really, and now I'm not ready for it. I don't think I was meant to.'

'Of course you were meant to, Nan,' Ray said. 'You've never stopped going on about it. It's what you want more than anything in the world. You said so yourself.'

'Of all the contrary old women . . .' Vi said. 'You go on about it for years and now you can afford it you decide it's not what you want after all. What's the matter with you, Mother?'

'It just seems –' Nanny said.

'What?' Vi asked.

'Selfish. It seems selfish somehow when we've got so little.'

'Well, it isn't,' Ray said. 'Course it isn't. You said yourself you'd never get another chance to go and see Steve and Marion.'

'. . . and little Gary,' she added.

'That's right. Gary as well. All we've got to do is arrange it with Steve.'

And Vi said, 'Yes, Mother. It's obvious. It's what you've been wanting.'

'I suppose you're right,' she said at last. 'Thank you.' She was thanking us for telling her it was all right – for giving her permission. A new vista opened up for her – full of smartly painted ships, their flags fluttering and smoke pouring from their funnels, of being met by a long-lost son on a New York quayside. She beamed at us.

'Thank God for that,' Ray said.

The following day Julia caught me at the bottom of the stairs. 'Where's Ray?' She came up close and held me by the arm, surprising me with her flowery scent.

'Ray?' My mind was still full of ten-pound notes. We'd decided not to mention the money to anyone and the knowledge was worming away inside me.

'Your cousin – Ray. Where is he?'

'He's at work. Didn't you know? He started a new job this morning on the post.'

'What? Delivering letters? Ray?' She cupped her hand round her nose and laughed.

'It's not that funny,' I said, though obviously it was.

'He was going to take me out tonight. I thought I hadn't seen him around.'

She was oblivious to pain, to how she eased rapiers through a cabinet with me inside. I'd noticed the two of them together since that time I'd seen them chatting at the Palace – Ray pretending to be cool, Julia pretending to be grown-up. I'd seen them leaning next to one another in the house, moving closer when people needed to get past.

'Have you forgotten, Julia?' I asked.

'Forgotten what?'

'That you kissed me.' A couple of weeks earlier I wouldn't have dared ask her that. Now it seemed better than not knowing.

'Course I haven't,' she said. 'It was only last Friday.'

'And is that the end of it?'

'Nothing's been started, Ed. Come on. It was just a kiss. It was fun.' I was bewildered. She kissed me, she wanted to be with Ray, she thought she still loved Dave. She was misunderstanding me on purpose. 'I'm glad you were there, if that's what you mean.'

'Glad? Is that all? You'd have drowned without me. And if we hadn't nearly drowned we might never have kissed,' I said.

'Maybe. But if I hadn't met you on the seafront I wouldn't have been there in the first place, would I?'

'You're twisting my words round,' I said. 'Why did you kiss me if you didn't like me?'

'I do like you, Ed, but it was fun. There's nothing more to it than that.'

'But you must like having more than just fun, as well. Look at you and Dave. You were mad for him. You said it was love.'

'That was different. He gave me confidence and for a while he treated me like an adult. But you know what happened between him and me. Life's too short for getting into intense relationships, Ed. Life's for enjoying yourself. Being with Dave made me realize that.'

Maybe she was right. Everybody assumed that love was for life. But what if it was just a kiss-me-quick hat, worn for a week on the fairground rides and then chucked away when it was time to go home?

'Me and Ray are free spirits,' she went on. 'We've got that in common. Tell him I was looking for him if you see him, won't you?'

So it wasn't about Ray or me or Dave. She didn't have to choose because she knew she could have any or all of us. She kissed me on the cheek, quick as lightning. Then I was watching her sprint away, back upstairs to her room.

I wanted to show Julia that I could make things happen. She thought I was just a kid, that I didn't know much, but I did have my friends after all. Some of them had influence. Pete McCluggage understood the world and how it operated. He had contacts in the town. He knew all sorts of powerful people from his time on board ship and he'd talked about modelling. I decided to call in at the Box of Tricks.

'I'd like some advice,' I explained. 'It's about a friend of mine. Her name's Julia.'

'A friend, eh? Is she in trouble?'

'No,' I said. 'Nothing like that. She wants to be a model and you said you knew about models in Paris and Rome. You said you'd helped them.'

'I did? Of course. So?'

'I was hoping you might be able to point her in the right direction.'

'They all want to be models,' he said, adjusting his cuffs to show off thin wrists. 'I've never met a pretty girl who didn't fancy herself on a catwalk with everyone looking at her. Some not so pretty, too. Money for old rope. They all want to do it and who could blame them? It's natural for a girl to want to be the centre of attention.'

'She's pretty determined about it,' I said. 'And I thought you could help – seeing as you know people.'

'Being determined isn't enough, take it from me. A girl needs more than that. A girl's got to have . . .' He was searching for the word. 'Charisma, Eddie. Not just a pretty face and a nice pair of legs.'

'She's got that,' I said, thinking of the way she'd sung 'Fever' on the beach.

He took his round glasses off, polished them on a handkerchief. 'I suspect you've got the hots for this friend of yours, Eddie. Would I be right?'

'I don't know.' He wrong-footed me every time with his predictions and mind-reading tricks. 'Maybe. But that's not the point. I want to help her.'

'Why would you want to do that?'

'Because she's a friend.'

'Oh, yes, of course. Always the best reason. I don't expect you'd be doing it in order for her to like you more? Maybe give you something in return?'

'I think she's going out with my cousin.'

'Ah. And this would be a great favour I dare say?'

'So what do you think? What would you recommend?'

He was considering it, working out the possibilities. I thought he might give me a contact number. 'Well, I could help perhaps. I've got an idea I could. There's always someone on the lookout, and I do know people in the business. Bring her up to the shop. We'll have a chat.'

Suddenly I wasn't sure. I remembered the way he talked to his male customers, how he'd tried to coax them to buy his under-the-counter goods. I could see the brown paper bags spiked on a cup hook. 'Thank you,' I said.

'No need to sound so enthusiastic, Eddie. Nothing to lose by it, is there? That's how business works.' While we'd been talking he'd slipped his jacket on. 'Now, will you do me a favour? I'd like you to keep an eye on the shop for me while I pop out. Will you do that?'

'Now?'

'Why not? I'm very pleased you happened to turn up, Eddie.'

'I've never looked after a shop before.'

'It won't get busy. You'll be all right.'

'What if someone comes in?'

'Use your initiative. Let them buy whatever they want – then sell them something extra. You've seen how I do it.' He locked the till and left a pile of silver as a float. 'But remember – don't trust anybody.' Not even you, I thought. 'I've got important business to attend to. I'll be about . . .' he said, calculating how long he'd be, looking at his watch, but he didn't finish his sentence.

After he'd gone the shop was eerily quiet – the masks hanging dark and heavy from the ceiling. I thought of him filling the place with his magician's banter and understood now why he did.

A couple of kids came in and browsed through the racks. They flicked through the comics and smiled, sharing the jokes the way Ray and me must have done a couple of summers ago. It made me feel as if I owned the place now. I went behind the counter and leaned on it and looked down the shop at them. They glanced up at me, then finally left without a word.

Nobody else called. Pete seemed to have been gone for ever. I thought about Vi preparing food or making beds and wondered how I'd managed to end up here in the Box of Tricks where Ma Feeney had sat so often in earlier years. I needed the toilet.

I remembered Pete going through the door behind the counter to use the toilet. It was open so I went through and up the narrow stairs. The bathroom was at the end of the corridor – a white room with vein-patterned wall tiles and a musty smell. On my way back I couldn't resist peeping into the living room. The curtains were open a slit, a blanket neatly folded on the settee where Pete perhaps slept. It was almost ordinary, with a TV in a cabinet and at the far end some kitchen units with a Baby Belling cooker on top. Hard to imagine him living up here, above all the jokes and cheap plastic tricks, practising his illusions in a dusty mirror. The second room must have overlooked the yard at the back. I tried the door, but it was locked. That would be where he kept his best tricks, I thought, his Magic Circle secrets.

Against the wall in the third room was a single bed with a pink quilted cover. Next to it was a low cupboard with a table lamp, the shade trimmed with lace. Sticking out from under the bed was a pair of women's shoes, neatly pushed together. They made me shiver. Just ordinary, flat-heeled black shoes, but they made me feel as if Ma Feeney had left them for a reason. Her ghost would be close by, watching me. I bent down to touch the cold, hard leather.

So this had been Ma Feeney's room. There was no clue she'd ever been here, except the shoes. It was silent. No wonder lads didn't stay in the shop the way Ray and me had done in other years. The weight of all this was too heavy. Pete's presence had changed how it felt. I ran downstairs.

At the bottom, between the shop and Pete's flat, a door was open. I'd never noticed it before. There was a set of narrow wooden stairs. I put a light on, followed the stairs down and found myself in a cellar. It stank of wet coal and damp. The light came from a single bulb. There in the corner was a spade, a little pile of bricks and earth, a tin bucket, some boxes from the shop, a pile of magazines. I picked one up and it fell apart in my fingers, rotten with damp, a naked mildewed girl on the cover.

I heard something move, rattling amid the rubbish. Rats, I thought. I shivered. Then, in the corner, I saw a shallow box. It was like a large orange box or a luggage trunk, covered with sheets of newspaper, raised in places by an uneven shape beneath. I knew it had something to do with her, with Ma Feeney. I went across to the box and took a deep breath. It was time to be brave.

That was when I heard the electric werewolf go off upstairs. Someone had come into the shop. For a moment I stood looking down at the box, but there wasn't time now. Perhaps it was better not to see, after all. I rushed upstairs.

Pete was standing there. 'Where've you been, Eddie?' he asked evenly.

'Upstairs. Needed the toilet,' I managed to gasp. I realized I was shaking.

'I thought I heard you come up the stairs – not down.'

'No.' I tried to edge past him towards the door. He moved to keep me there, his hand on the racks of jokes to stop me.

'You shouldn't be anywhere except in the shop. That's what I asked you to do. I thought I could trust you, Eddie.'

'You can trust me. But you were gone ages. I needed the toilet.'

'You didn't touch anything, did you?' I shook my head. He could read my mind. Those glinting glasses were X-ray specs that could see through me so he'd know where I'd been and what I'd seen. He'd know I'd been snooping in bedrooms and places I wasn't meant to be.

'No, of course I didn't. Look, I need to go now. I'm late.' I realized I'd left the light on in the cellar.

'I really didn't intend to be so long.' He reached into the inside pocket of his jacket, pulled out his wallet, took out a ten-bob note and held it out to me.

'What's this?' I said.

'For looking after the shop. You didn't think I expected you to do it for nothing, did you?'

He could cut the note in half and put it back together again or turn it into a bunch of flowers. He could make it disappear from my hand if he wanted. 'Are you sure?'

'It's business.' I took it and thanked him, headed for the door. 'Come back soon,' he said carefully. 'Don't forget to bring that girlfriend of yours.'

13

The next day Vi was on the phone. At first, when I heard the quiver in her voice, I thought something bad had happened, but it was speaking to Steve in New Jersey that was making her sound different. She had to get the operator to connect her and even though she'd pulled the door of the cupboard under the stairs closed behind her I could still hear because she was talking louder than usual.

'Steven?' I heard her shout. 'Steve, it's me, Vi. Vi – your sister, you soft sod. Can you hear me? No nothing's wrong . . . Why? What time is it there? Oh, sorry – did I get you out of bed?'

Then she was telling him about how Nanny had finally decided to travel over and stay with him and Marion. There was a long silence while Steve was saying something back and Vi went on, 'Yeah . . . Yes . . . Yes.' The pauses between 'yeses' got longer. Then she said, 'Steve, I know, but . . .' and eventually she said, 'Your Marion's invited her lots of times and now Mother's got her heart set on it and it might be her last chance to see you. No, I'm not being funny; it's the God's honest truth. She won't be around for ever. She talks about you all the time. I mean *all* the time, Steve.'

There was another long silence and finally she said, 'So is it all right or isn't it? This call's costing me money.' And they must have agreed something because Vi said, 'Good.

We'll get the tickets then, shall we – before one of us changes our minds.'

And that was the end of the conversation except I heard her say, 'God bless, Steve,' which I'd never heard her say to anyone before and she opened the door onto the hall and caught me standing there listening. She was a bit flushed, which wasn't surprising because it was hot under there, stuffed in with the coats. 'What d'you want, Eddie? Get from under my feet.'

'My jacket,' I said, 'from under the stairs. I was just going out.' I was getting to be as good a liar as Ray.

'Where you off to? There's work to be done.'

'Just the shop. Won't be a minute.' I had to pick up my windcheater and put it on even though it was a sweltering mid-August day. Then I had to go out, pretending I was buying something. I walked a little way up toward Vicky Road and sat on a wall and tried to decide what I was going to say to Julia. The easiest thing was not to say anything about Pete and the Box of Tricks, to pretend it had never happened.

Plus, the more I did for Julia the less she appreciated it. I'd even checked to see what Myron Bloomfield had to say about what a man could expect in return for favours, but the only reference I could find was in Chapter Seven, 'The Road to Wooing', in which he revealed that girls liked presents and that flowers tended to make them sentimental and pliable. That wasn't much of a revelation. Everybody liked presents. He described the route to a girl's heart as a boulder-strewn highway and claimed that one of the ways a man could move those boulders was with gifts – not expensive ones, necessarily, but thoughtful ones. It sounded like hard work and pretty unromantic. More like a business transaction, in fact.

So I sat on the wall and decided not to say anything to Julia about Pete's offer. For all I knew Pete had something very different from modelling in mind. That joke shop, I thought – I wished I'd never been there. And what I really wished for was some other girl to come along and talk to me – someone uncomplicated but beautiful, like Lulu. But of course nobody did and in the end I went back to the house and was in time to help Vi make the beds.

In Charles's downstairs room everything was neat – his clothes were all out of sight except for a cravat folded over the back of a chair. On top of the drawers were his medicines placed in order of size – Andrews Liver Salts, Owbridge's cough medicine, white pills in a brown bottle, Enos and Beechams powders. I remembered how much Nanny had enjoyed how the light from the french window filled the room when it had been hers. I emptied the bin while Vi threw the sheets and blankets back into place, pocketing air and making hospital tucks at the foot, covering it all with a candlewick bedspread.

'Nan's definitely going to America, then?' I said.

'Looks like it,' Vi said. 'I was on the phone to Steven earlier to arrange it. Do you know I hardly recognized him?'

'Oh,' I said, pretending I didn't know she'd been talking to him.

'He's got an American accent.' She sounded sad about it, as if she was trying to remember who he used to be. 'Now all we've got to do is get the tickets. Doesn't seem possible, does it – an old lady like Nan going all that way on her own?'

'It's not that unusual. Women used to go round the world in the old days – travelling and exploring.'

'Yeah, I suppose so – and they probably had a bunch of servants with them, too. Trust you to think of that, Eddie.'

In the bigger rooms, where there was space to stand on either side, we shared the bed-making. It felt good to be precise about something for once. The rules were simple and we understood them, like a dance we both knew the steps of –

sheets, blankets and pillow-plumping. 'We'll make a hotelier of you yet, Eddie,' Vi said, smoothing the last bedspread out with the back of her hand. And I thought of what it would be like to spend the rest of my life making beds for people I didn't know, watching travellers come and go but staying in the same place myself. Vi's words sounded like a terrible threat – one that made me want to chop and change at my jobs like Ray or to travel the world like Steve.

Ray wasn't coping too well with his postman's job. The early mornings were beginning to affect him already – forcing him into bed before nine o'clock, causing him to fall asleep on top of the covers listening to Luxembourg, not bothering to get undressed and forgetting to set the alarm. He told me he wasn't sure the alarm clock *could* be set that early.

When I went up to our room after helping Vi with the beds he stirred. 'Man – is that the time?'

'Aren't you at work today?' I asked. He groaned.

'I don't think I can keep this up much longer, Eddie. I wasn't made to see the dawn. I'm not a morning person.' He stumbled out of bed and rubbed his eyes. It was eleven o'clock. 'They won't mind me being a bit late.'

He went to the bathroom and came back again. I sat on my bed while he struggled into his dark trousers and postman's shirt.

'No problem,' he said, as if he was trying to convince himself everything was fine, then he pulled his boots on and started searching for his jacket. 'If anyone asks, Eddie, right, I was delayed – unavoidably – OK? Tell 'em it was a family matter – someone was ill.'

'No one's gonna ask me, are they?'

He stood up and a couple of crumpled letters fell out of his back pocket onto the floor next to me. I picked them up. 'Give us those,' he said.

'What are they?'

'Letters. What do you think?'

I straightened them out – brown envelopes with little windows for the names and addresses. 'Aren't you supposed to be delivering these?'

'Course I'm supposed to deliver them,' he said. 'What did you think I was gonna do? They're just a couple of addresses I couldn't find, that's all. I'll stick 'em in today. It won't make any difference.' He snatched them off me and crammed them back in his pocket.

'Vi's spoken to Uncle Steve,' I said, hoping to get him out of his tetchy mood. 'It's arranged. Nan's going to New York.'

'Good,' he said, tucking his shirt in and heading out the door. 'See you later.'

I came across Maisie sitting on a bench near Vale Park looking out over the river. It was that early evening time after dinner that Vi didn't like – when guests would sometimes hang around the house because they hadn't made any plans or would drag their tired children out again, determined to make the most of their holiday.

Maisie had made an effort. She wore a dress that hugged her figure, made her chest look pointy, and a short-sleeved jacket in the same material. 'You look nice, Maisie,' I said. 'I like the dress. Mind if I sit down?'

It was strange how easy it was to say things like that to Maisie because I didn't fancy her. It didn't make sense: if you fancied someone it made you tongue-tied and awkward; if you didn't it made you chatty and relaxed. We'd been designed the wrong way round. She nudged up and made room for me.

'Thanks,' she said. 'I made it myself out of a skirt. Turned it sideways and sewed the jacket out of what was left.' I nodded. 'I'm waiting for Irene. We've got the night off. We're going to the Ship and maybe dancing after. On a nice night like this you can sit outside the Ship and watch the world go by. Come with us if you want, Ed.'

She was flirting, pouting her pretty mouth, raising her drawn-on eyebrows. Not how Julia would have done it – provoking and encouraging you to behave rashly. Maisie's flirting was funny and warm. *Dream Dating* had a section on flirting in Chapter Five. It advised the man to 'lean in' and 'move your eyes in a triangular motion between eyes, mouth and body'. It made it sound like a football strategy. Whenever I opened *Dream Dating* these days I'd find more pages coming loose. The flirting section fell out in a single, glued clump.

But I wanted some advice about Julia. Maisie might be able to explain why Julia seemed so contrary, why I found her so irresistible. In a way, Maisie was on the sidelines. She didn't talk about men in the way that Irene did either, which made me think she might be more objective and better at giving advice.

Tonight she'd thrown me off-balance with her crisp dress and her makeup, which made her look older and more attractive, almost as if she was a different person. I wondered how women learned about dresses and lipstick, and then kept what they knew from men. Was it a conspiracy? 'No knitting tonight, Maisie?' I asked.

She smiled. 'I don't take it everywhere, you know.'

'Can I ask you a question?' She nodded. 'What do you think about Julia – really, I mean?'

She glanced across at me. 'Oh, Eddie. I've seen the way you look at her, you know.'

'I can't help it. She's just so . . .'

'I know. It's the same with all the men. She's got a lovely complexion, hasn't she?'

'Well, there's more to it than that, Maisie.'

'She's gorgeous, yes. To look at, at least.'

'So,' I ventured, 'you can see that?'

'Of course. I'm not stupid.'

'I didn't know whether women could tell whether other women were beautiful.'

'How do you think we size up the opposition, Ed? In our business it's something we do all the time – judge one another, and on the silliest things. You know – legs and necks and hair, the size of ears, shape of a nose, curve of a waist. That kind of thing.'

'And do you think it's OK?'

'Do I think what's OK?'

'Me and Julia,' I stumbled.

'You mean, have you got a chance with her?' I wished she wouldn't be quite so direct, but it was what I meant. I nodded.

'No.' She must have seen my crestfallen look, because she went on, 'I don't really think she's for you. You're too –'

'What? Too young?'

'Oh, I don't think that. Age isn't important to most women. I was going to say down-to-earth. You're down-to-earth. Julia lives in the clouds.'

'Contrast is good,' I said. 'Opposites can attract.'

'Who told you that?'

'Nobody.' But it was Myron Bloomfield again. Chapter Six, 'Are You Compatible?' Or maybe Chapter Ten.

'Have you ever thought what it must be like to be her?' Maisie asked. 'What it must be like for people to admire you everywhere you go?'

'Sounds all right to me,' I said. Why should I try to imagine being her? It was hard enough being me.

'Being admired makes people think they're invincible. Julia probably feels as if she's the centre of the universe, walking around in a cloud of beauty. That's not the real world, Ed.'

I said, 'It doesn't always work like that. Julia told me the girls at school hated her for her looks.'

'I doubt it. If they hated her it was because she was spoiled and promiscuous, like she is now . . .'

Probably Maisie resented Julia for the way she attracted attention without even trying. I wouldn't have blamed her if she did.

'Let me guess . . .' Irene had come up behind us and was leaning across the back of the seat. 'The lovely Julia? The girl everyone wants to talk about – and no one wants to know.' She bent over me, her mouth in my hair. 'Poor Eddie. Take my advice and stay away. She's too crazy for a level-headed boy like you.'

But how could I stay away from her? We were living in the same house and kept coming across one another. I could treat her cool which, according to Ray, would be a good approach. Then she'd come running, apparently, because she'd miss the attention. More likely she wouldn't even notice, or she'd turn to Ray or someone else to flatter her. I don't think she was that bothered who charmed her, as long as someone did.

Maisie laughed. 'That's exactly what I said. I've asked Eddie if he wants to come with us. We'll show him a good time, won't we?'

'Of course we will. What a great idea.'

So we walked up towards the Ship, arm in arm the three of us, me in the middle thinking that this still didn't make sense and that I still understood nothing about women. But I was surrounded by their laughter and their perfume and I thought that perhaps, after all, this was it – the beginning and end of it, being engulfed in happiness.

'And as for Alastair,' Irene said. 'Did you see *him* today when Charles did his little stunt? He was stunned. He did laugh, though – in the end when he worked out what he'd done.'

Their laughter rang out on either side of me. 'What happened?' I wanted to know. We were going uphill, our breath getting shorter, striding out together.

'That stupid feud of theirs again. It's getting completely out of hand. Every joke's been more bizarre than the last. You've got to give Charles credit, though – he knows how to choose his moment,' Irene almost shouted and they both giggled again. I could feel the warm pulse of their bodies passing through mine.

Maisie said, 'He got Alastair's best tie – you know the blue striped one. Alastair left it on the back of a chair so Charles cut it right off with a pair of scissors. Then he Sellotaped it onto the bottom of that painting in the dining room so everyone could see. You should have seen Alastair's face.'

Irene said, 'That's cruel. Poor Alastair. His best tie as well.'

'He was furious. He pretended not to be, but he was,' Maisie said. She'd grown quieter, her voice back to its chiming tone. 'Do you know what he told me? That he was going to give Charles something to remember him by. He was talking about doing it during a show.'

We'd reached the Ship now. There was a tiny garden overlooking the river, high up. 'What? In the middle of a show? In front of an audience? He'd better not do that.' Irene had gone solemn.

'Perhaps he was just saying it. You know what Alastair's like. Full of talk.'

'That's taking it too far,' Irene said. 'Honestly, some people don't know when to stop. Charles has got responsibilities for the show – and he's not as young as he was. Did you hear the way he bawled out that sparkie when he heard him whistling backstage?'

'It's a superstition,' Maisie explained. 'Bad luck to whistle backstage.'

'Why?'

'In the old days they used to whistle orders on board ships – raising and lowering the sails and suchlike. So if there's whistling backstage someone might think it's an order and untie a rope – then a piece of flying scenery could come tumbling down where it's not supposed to.'

'I never knew that,' Irene said.

'It's bad luck to knit backstage, too,' Maisie said. 'That's why I haven't finished that last matinée jacket yet. My niece's baby's due in a couple of weeks.'

There were seats outside and Maisie and me sat down while Irene went for the drinks. She brought them back on a tin tray – a shandy for me.

'Now, Eddie, when I've had a few drinks I'll tell you anything you want to know about women,' Irene said, sitting beside me and tucking her hand under my arm.

'Tell me, then. What do I need to know?' They were actresses, Maisie and Irene, and knew how to tell stories, have a few drinks, have fun.

'Faint heart,' Irene was saying, 'never won fair . . . is it maiden or lady?'

Maisie tittered. 'Lady, I think.'

'Why does the man always have to do the winning?' I said. 'Why should the man do all the work?'

'It's his job, Eddie, that's why. It's what he's supposed to do – and he gets all the fun too,' Irene said. 'Then he just clears off leaving the lady holding the baby. Do you know how Neville won me over?'

'You never told me,' Maisie said, swigging her drink. She put her chin in her hand expectantly and turned her big eyes on Irene.

'Flowers,' Irene said.

'That's not so imaginative – flowers.'

'I'm a sucker for them. Easy,' Irene said. 'Just the look and smell of them gets me going – a big bunch of roses, oh, or a mixed bouquet with ribbons and carnations and ferns and a card that says "Missing you" or "With love", or some such lovey-dovey message. Plus . . .' she paused, 'there's a place only Neville knows.'

'Where? Morecambe?' Maisie asked and giggled.

'No – a place he knows to touch me, and I sort of melt.'

'Oh, tell us.'

'It's inside my elbow. There – now that's a secret.'

She showed us where the spot was in the bend of her elbow, and shivered when she touched it herself. I guessed she was thinking of Neville. It wasn't much of a secret, though. Maisie and I looked at one another and smiled. Flowers and the inside of an elbow, that's all it took. Irene was uncomplicated, after all, and beautiful in her own way, too. When I'd seen her in *The Pirates* the stage had been bathed in her glow. She'd stood out from the chorus as if there was a spotlight on her.

'It's brilliant to be out with you both,' I said, meaning it. 'Thanks for inviting me.'

'Good ol' Eddie,' Maisie said. 'It's the drink talking already. Let's get another one in.'

While Maisie was at the bar Irene said, 'Forget about Julia, that's my advice. There are plenty more fish in the sea.'

I knew she was right. Julia wasn't interested in me. She was taking advantage, that was all, and even if I did help her she'd do the same as she always did – walk off in a different direction without so much as a backward glance or a thank you.

After my second shandy I left them to it and walked home in the dark, promising myself not to expect anything of Julia. Maisie and Irene were right. They understood life.

Julia caught me in the dining room after breakfast the next day. 'Eddie,' she called across in a stage whisper. 'Eddie. Where've you been? Have you been avoiding me?'

I was collecting the last few plates to wash up and she was sitting at the table she usually shared with her mother, looking out at the road.

'Why would I avoid you?'

'I don't know. Because you're an idiot I suppose. Have you thought about what I asked you yet? You're my last hope, Ed.'

'Thanks.'

'No, I didn't mean that. I meant I've been exploring all the avenues. I've been scanning the papers, writing letters. I've sent off eight in the last week. I've asked Ray. I've even asked bloody Charles and Alastair. That's how desperate I am. But none of them are any good. Not one of them is willing to help. Only you, Ed.'

A couple sat on in the dining room, chatting, ignoring their toddler who cannoned between the chairs and tables like a pinball. I sat next to Julia; put my collected plates down in a pile. The kid tottered over and hung from the tablecloth and looked up at us with watery blue eyes. Julia smiled at him. 'Sod off,' she hissed through her teeth and the kid toppled backwards and sat down hard. 'Little brat. I hate kids. Bloody sickly things.' Then she looked at me. 'So have you managed to find anything out? Ed, you must know someone here who can help me get a modelling job.'

'No, I don't know anyone. I told you that.' I'd decided I wasn't going to mention what Pete had said. The Box of Tricks was too seedy with its unspeakable rooms and Pete always hovering with his magic. I shook my head. She stared at me again.

'You have found someone, haven't you? I can tell. It's written all over your face. Ed, you're a hopeless liar.' She started jigging in anticipation. 'Good old Eddie. I just knew you'd come up with something.'

'I haven't come up with anything. It was just a possibility but I've decided against it.'

'Why?'

'Cos I don't think it's safe. It's a bad idea.'

'I'll be the judge of that. What's "safe" anyway? Risks are part of my business. When you're in my position, Eddie, you have to take every opportunity. I know that modelling is my destiny – and I can't pursue it unless I take my chances.' Suddenly she was gentle, put her hand out – delicate with perfect pale fingers – and brushed the back of my hand. 'Come on, Ed. You can tell me.'

'It's just someone I know,' I said. 'He's been all round the world, so he's got lots of contacts. He's in business, that's all.'

'Who is he, this friend?'

'His name's Pete.'

'And what did you tell him about me?'

'Enough,' I said. 'Enough to get him interested. I wish I hadn't now.'

'I hope you said I was glamorous and gorgeous.'

'Course I did. As a matter of fact, I said you had charisma.'

She smiled. 'That's a big word, Ed. Thanks. You understand, don't you, that I've got to make the most of every day? Looks don't last long, I know that. But not everybody's wise enough to understand the fragility of their gift. I read that in a magazine once. So where do I find this Pete?'

'He runs the joke shop,' I told her.

She looked at me in disgust. 'A bloody joke shop? What does he take me for – some kind of freak circus sideshow? Like the bearded lady or something?'

'Don't be stupid,' I said. 'The joke shop's only part of what he does. He's a businessman. When he was working the liners he met loads of useful people including models. He's got contacts in Paris. Look, it was you who asked me about this, Julia. I wasn't going to say anything. Remember?'

She looked out of the window. Families were going past on their way to the seafront. 'Why didn't you want to tell me? Don't you trust me?' she asked sulkily.

'Of course I do. But there are rumours about him. When he took over the shop the previous owner disappeared. People say he did away with her.'

'And you think he did.'

'All I know is he can be really creepy sometimes. When he wasn't in the shop I went upstairs and there was a locked room. Then I went down into the cellar and . . .'

'And what?'

'There was stuff down there, but he came back before I could see what it was. I thought he was going to kill me.'

'Evidently he didn't,' she said. 'Is that all?'

'I think so.'

'It sounds like a load of nonsense to me,' she said. 'I'm not put off that easily.'

I looked around the dining room. The toddler had retreated to the other side of the room. He was sitting on the floor looking across at us. Julia had probably frightened him half to death while his mum and dad sat and chatted about the day to come, whether to go for a sea trip on the *Royal Iris* or sit in Vale Park for Joytime.

'What the hell,' Julia said. 'It's worth the risk. What's the worst that could happen?'

'You could end up cut into pieces, I suppose.'

'Come on, Eddie. Stop being so dramatic. I haven't any other options. I'm not going to pass this one by.'

'Well, I'm not taking you there,' I said.

'I'll find my own bloody way then. With or without you, Eddie. How many joke shops can there be in this godforsaken place?'

I couldn't help admiring her single-minded determination. People like her got things done. She pulled me into her force field. I didn't even care that she'd probably been with Ray and before that with Dave, who would have married her. I expected it to hurt, all this, and it did.

'Listen, Julia,' I said. 'I'll go with you, but only because I can't let you go there on your own.'

'Thanks, Ed. You're sweet.' She smiled at me as if she meant it, her hand on my arm. She emphasized the bow of her lips on the word 'sweet', like another kiss. 'I'll be eternally grateful for this, Ed,' she said. 'Eternally.'

14

Ray was out of work again. He told me he'd given in his postman's jacket, trousers and boots and told the post office where it could stick its job and its five a.m. starts. Vi got a different version of events. When she heard the story it was embellished with heroic sacrifice and layoffs. She didn't believe it. She told Ray she was past caring these days. Her bamboo stick had never been the same since they had fought over it, though it still stood forlornly in the corner next to the Baxi, twisted and split.

So for a day or two Ray had time at home. The three of us went out together – Ray and Julia and me. Julia loved being surrounded by lads. It was her idea of heaven, and I loved it when we were all together because people couldn't help looking at us, wondering what our relationship was. Ray could be funny and friendly with her, or he could be distant. Then Julia would come close, put her arm round me, whisper in my ear and make me laugh. We were friends and maybe we were cousins. It felt dangerous to be with Julia and Ray, as if the world was revolving around us just like Maisie described. It felt as though we could make anything happen. Anything we wanted.

We went to Fairlanes. Ray was telling Julia about how he'd left his job – a different story again. In this version they'd begged him to stay, even offered him a pay rise, but he'd refused because he had plans for a business venture that couldn't fail. The details were secret, but it was something to do with opening a fishing tackle shop and organizing fishing trips. I wondered how he managed to remember all his different stories. Probably he didn't bother any more. They floated like separate clouds in the sky, never quite connecting.

Ray swaggered up to the cash desk and paid for us all. He didn't need to, but he had money in his pocket. Then we hired bowling shoes – damp and smelling of other people's feet.

Ray was the only one who understood spares and strikes, or at least said he did, and, as he'd paid for us, he got to sit in the seat with the score card. It was him against me and Julia, which meant he got twice as many goes as us.

I watched him show Julia how to choose a bowling ball. She already knew, but cracked on to be stupid so she could feel his hand on hers. He said, 'Pick one up and weigh it, like – see how it feels for size.'

'I already know how it feels for size,' she said, laughing and fluttering her eyelashes at him.

'This is how you hold it,' Ray went on. 'Your two fingers go in these holes.' She laughed again. 'Don't want to get your fingers stuck in there, do you?' He held the ball and sort of guided her fingers into the right places.

'Leave me now, Ray. I know what I'm doing,' she said when it was our turn, and she picked up the nearest ball from the rack – a black one. She was fierce and wonderful, with that look of determination on her face, those almost clumsy steps – two, three – and the irresistible force of an overweight ball. The pins practically fell over in fright. I was glad she was on my side. She knocked eight down and cleared the last two with a lucky, swerving second ball.

'Brilliant!' I shouted.

She ran across and hugged me, the way I'd seen the

Rodcoopers do when something slightly good happened. I felt the solid resistance of her bra between us.

Then it was Ray's turn, then mine. I still hadn't decided which was the right ball for me. The mottled green one felt good, but someone kept taking it off the rack. I knocked eight pins over, which left a couple standing in the middle. 'Go on, Eddie,' Julia said. 'You can get 'em both. Aim straight – keep your eye on the pins – nice and fast this time. Give it all you've got.'

She annoyed me, the way she started lecturing. She wasn't perfect when it came to bowling – just a run of beginner's luck and a lot of big-mouthing. 'Shut up, Julia, for God's sake. Let me do it.'

'Get him,' she said, and sat down, sharing an ashtray with Ray and chewing gum at the same time.

I bowled at the two pins with all my strength, rattling the mottled green ball down the lane. I could feel her eyes burning into my back, watching me. There was an unintended curve on it and, although I jumped around and tried to change its course by shouting at it, the ball dropped into the gutter just short of the pins. It rolled out of sight and the machine came down to clear the lane.

Then she was up and behind me, shouting. 'Bloody hopeless, Ed. You should've done what I said. Why don't you listen?' Her eyes were blazing, like it really mattered, as if she was about to cry. She made me laugh, behaving like such a spoiled little girl.

'Hey!' Ray shouted. 'Sit down, you two. It's my turn now.'

So we sat side by side while Ray took his turn. I said to her, 'Every time I do what you want, Julia, it all goes wrong. Haven't you noticed?'

She looked across ready to say something and I smiled at her to show no hard feelings. But she knew it had been true so far – getting caught in her room, getting cut off by the tide. She picked up her ciggie from the tin ashtray. 'Your bowling's rubbish as well.'

'At least it's my own rubbish. Not yours,' I said. Then it was her turn again. I watched her bend to pick up the black ball.

Later, when we looked at the score, Ray was in the lead. It wasn't a surprise considering he was in charge of the card. Julia leaned over him and tried to tot up. 'That's not right,' she said, pointing to one of his figures. 'You counted that ball twice.'

'You're meant to,' Ray said. 'When you get a spare you count the next ball as well.'

She stared at it again. 'Why've you missed that spare of mine off, then? You haven't counted that one at all.'

'Oh, yeah.' He scribbled out the number and she watched while he added it up again and pencilled a different number in.

She marched off to pick up the ball for her next go. She had no technique, but some kind of willpower gave her an edge. She shouted at the ball mercilessly, as if her life depended on it. 'Go. Go.' She didn't care that people stopped in the other lanes and watched her. She yelled when she got another spare, dancing and whirling round. 'What are you bloody looking at?' she yelled at a man who'd stopped mid-bowl to gawp at her.

By the end Ray had managed to get in the lead again even though Julia had really got the hang of it. Perhaps he thought he had to win because he'd paid for us to play. Julia was looking over his shoulder, staring at the scores. 'You never had a strike there, Ray.'

'I did,' he said.

'Or there.' She jabbed her finger at the score sheet. 'You've been changing the numbers. I can see where you changed them. That seven used to be a one. You cheating . . .'

Ray started laughing. 'It's not funny,' Julia shouted, suddenly furious. Her mouth was tight and small. 'You were cheating. Why couldn't you let Ed and me win fair and square?'

'It's only a game,' he said.

'Only a game when you win,' she shouted.

'Come on, Julia,' I said.

'Shut up, Ed, I've had enough,' she said and started walking out. 'You've got no bloody principles, Ray, that's your problem.'

Ray was still sitting there laughing. 'Leave her,' he said, when he saw me watching her. She was already out and away. 'She'll come back.'

He was right. She'd forgotten to return her bowling shoes and didn't realize until she reached the front door. She glared across at us when she had to go back to the desk, slapped the shoes noisily on the counter and waited while they found hers. She left again, properly this time. 'She'll come back again – or she won't. Don't take it so serious,' he said. 'That's her problem – she takes everything too serious. It's not life or death – it's just a game, that's all.'

'That's what she's told me before,' I said. 'She told me not to take things too seriously.'

'Just shows what she's like, then, doesn't it? Says one thing and does another.'

Later that afternoon I saw them on the beach by the sandstone wall. She'd come back, like Ray said. She was running her fingers through Ray's spiky hair, which was getting longer now – almost Mick Jagger length. They were lying on the sand facing the Mersey and she stretched across and pulled Ray's head towards her and kissed him hard on the lips.

I hated both of them then. They were destructive and thoughtless and shouldn't have been together. They set sparks off one another, causing mayhem and damaging the people around them. Worst of all, neither of them had any idea of the pain they were causing.

I was tempted to pull out of my agreement to introduce Julia to Pete, but that would have been pointless, I thought, and childish. I still wanted to help her if only to prove I could do it.

The morning I took her to the joke shop she came downstairs in a yellow skirt and a sleeveless sweater that showed off her arms and shoulders. Her hair was sleek as though she'd spent hours getting that flicked-up style just right before spraying it into place. My heart leapt when I saw her.

'You look fantastic,' I said.

She smiled. 'Thanks. Come on – let's get it over with.' We walked out the front door and turned left up the hill away from the sea. A man sweeping the gutter stopped and leaned on his broom to watch us pass. 'I have this effect on people,' Julia said.

'I know. I've seen it.'

'I can tell you it wears a bit thin after a while.'

'You love it really.'

She laughed. 'Maybe. Sometimes I wish blokes wouldn't be so obvious, but if I want to be a model I've got to get used to people looking at me.'

'God, is this it?' Julia asked when we got to the joke shop. It looked particularly tacky this sunny morning with paint peeling off the window frames and the door closed. The bottom of the window had orange Lucozade paper stuck inside to keep the sun off. I'd never noticed before how jaded everything looked.

I thought she might change her mind and want to go back, which would have suited me, but she didn't say anything, just pushed the door open. There was the usual howl from the electric werewolf. She pretended not to notice it.

She was in front and smiled back at me. I admired her for that. Nothing terrified her.

Pete had a magazine open on the counter and as we walked down the shop he slid a newspaper over it. His eyes followed Julia. 'Good morning,' he said in an oily way, but more to her than to me.

'This is the young lady I was telling you about. Mr McCluggage, this is Julia. Julia this is –'

'Pete,' he said and held his hand out to her. 'Call me Pete. No need for formalities.'

'This is Julia, the girl I was telling you about.'

'Of course,' he said. 'Wants to be a model. How could I forget?' He put his chin in his hand and looked her up and down.

'Eddie says you can help me.' She stared right back as if she was challenging him. His glasses glinted.

'I know people. Yes, I imagine I could help,' he said. 'Surely you've been in beauty contests? Miss New Brighton?'

'No.'

'I'm surprised. Pretty girl like you. What about catalogue work? Littlewoods? Freemans? Does that interest you?'

'I'm thinking of fashion modelling.' The shop was cold and she stood there under the dusty rubber masks in her dazzling clothes, posing as if she was on a catwalk.

'Let's go,' I whispered to Julia. 'I've done what I said.'

'Not now. Not when I've come this far.'

'You're edgy this morning, Eddie,' Pete said. He'd have found the light on in his cellar. He'd know I'd been down there.

'I should be somewhere else,' I said.

'Don't let me keep you, then,' Pete said. 'Oh, London fashion houses. Yes, as I said I do have a passing acquaintance with Christian Dior. You could start in Liverpool or Manchester. I have contacts there, too. Maybe work your way up to Paris. Who knows?' He looked back at me. 'Eddie, why don't you go and choose a magazine for yourself – from the box at the end – as a gift? Any one. I'd like a word with your friend here.'

He smiled as if he'd pulled off a particularly clever sleight of hand, took off his glasses and polished them. 'No, thanks,' I said.

'Eddie, go on,' Julia said. 'I'm OK.'

I walked to the end of the shop near the hanging masks. It was horrible to think of them together. I chose a copy of *Mad*. It didn't take me long. Most of the magazines were rubbish. I knew he kept the best ones on racks out of the reach of kids and his special ones were locked up under the counter. The *Mad* magazine had one of those broad, stupid, smiling faces of a vacant-looking youth drawn on the front. Pete had ironed it flat to make it look new.

When I got back they were close together – on opposite sides of the counter, but with their heads almost touching. I could tell they'd made an agreement while I was out of earshot. Pete was whispering to her and they looked up as I came back clutching my magazine.

'Is that all, Eddie?' Pete said when he saw it and he smiled at Julia. 'You're easy pleased.' That front cover grinned at me – Alfred E. Neuman – as if everything was such a joke.

Pete had opened a little box. 'Mexican jumping beans. New in. Watch these.' He poured two or three of the cocoa-bean-sized objects into the palm of his hand. 'They're alive in there. The heat of my hand wakes them up. Little creatures. Try.' He held Julia's fingers and dropped the beans into her palm and they started to wriggle and roll about.

'That's horrible,' she said. 'You should let them out.'

'They're just little creatures, like caterpillars.'

'What happens to them in the end?' Julia asked.

'I don't know. They stop moving eventually. They die.' She put them back on the counter. The place smelled of damp, coming up from the cellar.

'We should go,' I said.

'Thanks, Pete,' Julia said and smiled at him as we left. I intercepted that look from her and Pete's knowing nod by way of reply, but all the way back home, beautiful as she was, Julia pretended she hadn't come to an agreement with him, refused to discuss their conversation however much I asked.

When we got back, Vi told me how she and Nanny had gone to get tickets for her trip to New York. The girl in Thomas Cook had a badge with her name on it: Sue. The way Vi talked about her I think she hoped Ray would end up with someone like Sue in her Thomas Cook uniform, who seemed to know where everything in the office was and who understood the modern world. Vi said she had something of Audrey Hepburn about her, like in *Breakfast at Tiffany's*.

'Everybody's flying these days,' Sue told them. 'We're living in the space age.'

Nanny said, 'You ought to be encouraging people to go by sea, love. Ships are what made this place what it is today. Besides, planes crash and nobody gets out alive.'

Sue showed Nanny a shiny plastic model of a Boeing 707 to demonstrate the safety features, but Nanny wanted to know how a model was supposed to make her feel better, when it was glued to a stand. If it was that good perhaps she could make it fly. 'Even the thought of them closing those metal doors behind me makes me feel sick,' Nanny went on. 'There's no proper air up there.'

Sue smiled and said they could put men into space nowadays and bring them home again, so it was dead easy flying people across the Atlantic. In fact, they were doing it every day. Sue had relatives in Australia and had flown there herself so she was a walking advertisement for air travel. She pulled a leaflet out of a folder to explain the route to America, but Nanny wouldn't even look at it.

What Nanny wanted was a sea voyage – one that lasted nine days. She expected to meet people and be able to walk about and talk to them over dinner, tell stories about her family and what she planned to do in New Jersey. She wanted to lean on a rail and watch the sea pass by at a respectable rate. Most of all she wanted to sail into New York harbour under the Statue of Liberty and see it for herself exactly as Steve had described it. 'Now I know I'm in America,' he had written. 'The land of freedom and opportunity.' The letter, one of the ones she kept in the tin, and one of the few she'd let us look at, was thin along the creases from folding and unfolding.

The other thing about the trip to New York was that Nanny wanted dinner with the captain before the ship left Liverpool. She was insistent, because Mrs Morris next door but one had told her you could do that, and that you could invite everyone who was seeing you off. 'You've all got to be there,' Nanny said to Vi. 'Lobster thermidor's always on the menu. I've always wanted to try lobster thermidor.'

But Sue in Thomas Cook wasn't so sure. 'There aren't enough seats at dinner for everyone – and the captain's always occupied at embarkation. It's one of the busiest times.'

Nanny couldn't get it out of her head. 'I'll check for you, shall I?' Sue asked, and she phoned Cunard. She put her hand over the mouthpiece. 'We can get you on the *Sylvania* – but no dinner with the captain, I'm afraid. Shall I book it for you?'

It was leaving in nine days so Nanny and Vi agreed. Nanny paid the money and that was that. 'I'm disappointed, though,' Nanny said, 'about her not organizing me dinner with the captain.'

Vi said, 'I suppose I'll have to phone our Steven up and tell him when you're coming. This is costing me a fortune, this is.'

Ray was keeping regular hours again, but starting and coming home late. I guessed he'd found yet another job. He wore a pale blue shirt, like the one he'd thrown back at the Post Office, gabardine trousers and heavy brown shoes. When he came home he'd toss the shirt into the corner of the bedroom and pull off the shoes. Their soles were ingrained with oily dirt. I asked him about the job. 'Can't tell you at the moment,' he said.

'Why? What's so top secret?'

He lay on his bed and looked at the ceiling. 'Nothing. Things are difficult, that's all. It's business. You have to keep your cards close to your chest in business. I don't want everybody knowing what my next move is gonna be, and what I'm gonna do.'

'Specially when you're doing nothing,' I said. He reached under the bed for his supply of magazines and began flicking through them. There was an Italian girly mag like the one he'd tried to nick off Pete. I could see it looking dog-eared among the others. 'Did you know I fixed Julia up with a modelling contact?' I asked.

'She told me.'

'It could be her big chance.' Ray seemed to have lost interest. 'You don't look that bothered.'

'Maybe I am. She'll do whatever she wants, won't she? Nothing I say'll make any difference. Far as I'm concerned she's just another judy.'

I was shocked. 'But you think she's gorgeous, don't you?'

He shrugged. 'So? There's lots of gorgeous women around and some of them've got more about them than Julia.'

I tried to make a joke of it. 'Come on, Ray. I've seen you with her. She looked like more than just another judy to me.'

He gave an embarrassed laugh. 'Life's too short for getting serious with women. Christ, Ed, I'm too young to die. I'm still a teenager.'

I wondered if he was worried about Nanny going to New York. Recently he'd been buying bars of fruit and nut for her. 'They're for the ship – in case you get peckish on the journey,' he'd say when he brought them home.

Vi had laughed. 'Ray, there's more food on those ships than you could shake a stick at. You can fill your boots all day if you want. Nan won't go hungry.'

'She can give them to the kid, then – in America. What's-his-name? Gary.'

'Is it Nan you're thinking about?' I asked.

Ray looked lazily across at me and turned to face the wall. 'Give it a rest now, Ed. I wanna sleep.'

It was a cloudless blue Tuesday, with only a slight breeze off the river, when the three of us – Ray, Julia and me – went to the outdoor baths. The concrete walls of the baths were painted white outside with a line of green tiles at the top and a black band at the bottom so it looked like a long sleek liner. Inside was a vast pool with raked seating all round with a circular tiled fountain at the shallow end which emptied onto a painted concrete beach where you could sunbathe. At the deep end were springboards and water chutes and a set of diving boards which were so tall that, standing on the top, you could easily see past Marine Lake and over to Liverpool. I'd never jumped off the top but Ray had. He said it was like leaping out of a plane. The baths were like the biggest, fullest beach you could imagine, the air full of shouts and screams and laughter.

Locals like us didn't bother using the changing rooms. They were underground and smelled dank, as if sea water was seeping through the walls. Ray and me had our trunks on under our clothes. We sat and waited while Julia got changed. Ray was looking around, surveying the hundreds of seats for his mates. Then he sat up on his towel and took his sunglasses off.

Julia came back wearing her Italian sunglasses, a bikini top and a skirt made of towelling material over her shorts. She squeezed onto the benches between us and rubbed coconut oil onto her face and body, Ray and me watching her open-mouthed.

Ray waited until she'd oiled every last part of her body including between her toes, then said, 'Anyone coming for a swim?'

She looked up at him. 'You've just watched me put all this on, Ray. What's the matter with you? Anyway, I'm not dressed for swimming.'

'It's a bloody swimming pool,' Ray said.

'It's not compulsory, though, is it?' She sat on a bench and adjusted her sunglasses.

Without another word Ray ran down the steps, through the crowds, out across the concrete and dived in with a sleek racing dive. He didn't resurface for ages. Then I caught sight of him, almost lost in the dazzle off the water, shaking his head to clear his eyes. 'Bloody show-off,' Julia said and turned her body up to the sun.

Ray was a strong swimmer. Everyone who lived here swam. The river was in their blood. Most of them had dreamed at one time or another of going to sea. They wanted to be river pilots or tug captains or lifeboat men or, at the very least, lifeguards.

I could have gone with Ray, but the thought of Julia, the heat of her body next to me on the benches, made me stay. It felt as if the sun had already got into her and I was absorbing its reflected strength. 'What have you agreed with Pete – about the modelling?' I asked casually.

'Nothing,' she said.

'I thought you'd made an arrangement with him.'

'Leave it, Ed,' she said fiercely. 'It's nothing to do with you.'

I was going to say that it had everything to do with me, but I saw Ray coming back up the steps, leaving damp footmarks behind him. 'Swim?' he asked, but Julia murmured something about having already told him. He showered her with water from his hair.

'Bloody idiot!' she shouted. 'You've got me soaked.' She sprung up and started wrestling with him, her hands locked with his, pulling and twisting, shouting, 'Leave me alone now, Ray. Leave me.' Then suddenly she was off and running towards the pool. The towel she'd worn as a skirt was left crumpled on the concrete but she was still wearing shorts and her hair was loose. She yelled and whooped as she ran down the steps, her body slippy as a fish, people standing aside to let her pass.

'Mad,' Ray said and ran down after her, his hair sticking up.

By the time I got there they were in the water near the deep end, entwined together, fighting to get the upper hand, though Ray was stronger and a better swimmer. He laughed and she struggled, and in the end she put her arms on his shoulders and kissed him to stop him. One of the pool attendants blew his whistle and pointed at them and Julia laughed back, not caring.

I dived into the deepest, coldest part where there were fewer swimmers. The shock hit me in the chest and, underwater, I opened my eyes to a blurry, salty world of blue. I swam towards the middle holding my breath as long as I could until I had to come up. I could see Julia's and Ray's heads bobbing amid the crowds. The noise of the place was distant and jumbled. Far away, at the shallow end, people splashed and ran around. I trod water and looked up at the sun and wondered if the three of us would always be in love.

Afterwards, we spread our towels out. Julia stretched herself across the benches and Ray sat with his sunglasses on and his feet on the seat in front, trying to look cool. 'In America,' he said, 'people have full-size pools in their gardens.'

'You can have that in this country as well,' Julia said. She was lying on her back so the words just went up in the air as if she wasn't talking to anyone in particular. 'When I'm a famous model I'm going to have a pool, maybe two – one indoor and one out.'

'How'd you know that?' Ray asked.

'Because I do. I'll have a huge house, too.' She squeezed water down her hair until it dripped onto the floor. 'You two can come and live there if you want.'

'Thanks,' Ray said.

'I'm going to have stables for the horses, so there'd be room for you. No problem.'

Ray said, 'I might be somewhere else by that time. You know – business and all that.'

'Oh, yeah?' she said. 'Here, Eddie, put some of this on my back, will you?' She handed me the bottle of coconut oil, turned over and unclipped her bikini top.

Ray pretended not to notice. He took a packet of Embassy from his jeans pocket and offered them round, but there were no takers. I was busy slathering the oil, watching it run into the furrow in the middle of her back, catching the rivulets and pushing them into her skin. 'Go easy with that stuff,' she said. 'It's nearly a quid a bottle.'

She was doing it on purpose, of course, tantalizing me, teasing Ray. 'Legs as well,' she said. 'You've got dead soft hands, Eddie.'

'Thanks,' I said. 'I shouldn't have – with all the hard work I do.' She laughed and dipped her head into her hands.

After a while I went to fetch ice creams from one of the shops that were dotted around the pool. Its tiled floor was cool out of the sun, but there was still a faint damp smell and the ever-present taste of salt drying on my lips. A girl served Eldorado tubs from behind a Formica counter. When I got back Ray had disappeared. 'What happened to him?'

Julia looked round. 'Dunno. One minute he was sitting there – the next he was gone.'

'Didn't he say anything?'

'No. He mentioned something about business again.'

'I got ice creams for all of us.'

'We'll just have to share them, then, won't we? Here, do me up, will you, Eddie?' I clipped her top back into place, making it look as if I knew what I was doing. I pretended it was an everyday thing like peeling spuds in Vi's kitchen or collecting dishes on a tray. We dipped our flat wooden spoons into the tubs, gouging out chunks of ice cream.

'It tastes of suntan oil,' Julia grumbled. 'Did you put your fingers in it or something?' It didn't stop her eating her tub and most of Ray's as well. 'Who's that big kid with ginger hair?' she said when she'd finished.

'Who? Do you mean Codge – the one who works at the amusements?'

'Yeah, him. He was here earlier.'

'Did Ray go off with him?'

'I didn't see. I was sunbathing.'

Then I remembered Codge calling at the house a couple of days before, asking to speak to Ray. I told Julia about it.

'What did he want?' she asked.

'Dunno. I answered the door and he just stood there, said he wanted to speak to Ray. When I told him he was out Codge said he'd wait. He sat out the front for ages, but Ray didn't turn up. It was dark by the time he left.'

'Perhaps it's something to do with Ray's new job,' Julia said.

'Did Ray tell you anything about it?'

She shook her head. 'He wouldn't say. I thought I could smell oil on him, though – or petrol. You can never tell what he's going to come up with next. Do you think he's in trouble, Ed?'

'Probably,' I said. 'He usually is.'

'I wouldn't want to see him get hurt.'

'You really like him.'

'Yeah,' she said. 'I can't help being attracted to lads who're a bit mad, if you know what I mean. I like the unpredictability of them.'

I don't know what made me say it, perhaps a sense of being left out. It felt mean even before I'd finished, but it was true. 'He told me you were just another judy.'

'He said that?'

The damage was done. I could tell by her reaction. I'd lit the fuse on a firework. 'In so many words. He didn't mean it.'

'Why did he say it if he didn't mean it, then? Tell me that, Ed.'

'I don't know. Honest, Julia. You better ask him yourself if it bothers you that much.'

'Course it bothers me. Is there something the matter with me? Look at me. I'm gorgeous and still people treat me like I'm a bloody beach ball or something to be picked up and dropped again whenever they feel like it.'

'I shouldn't have said anything. I'm sorry. I don't want you to get hurt.'

'Expect me to believe that?' She pulled her hair round her face and put a strand into the corner of her mouth. 'Bloody hell,' she said. 'Maybe I am just a judy.'

'No you're not,' I said.

'You don't think so, do you, Ed? I know you don't think I'm just a trollop.'

'No, Julia, you're not just another judy. You're amazing.'

'Thanks, Eddie – you're a mate. Well, you're more than

a mate really.' She turned and kissed me on the mouth with her salty lips. I shuddered. It was as intoxicating as a glass of whisky, sharp and fiery and potent. For a moment I thought about how rash and spiteful my words had been; how easy it was to betray people for the sake of a kiss.

Julia took her lips from mine and looked at me. She had caught the sun. Her skin had reddened, but then gone straight to a glow, like gold. She picked up her towel and bag, her hair down over her eyes again. 'I'm off,' she said and put the towel back round her waist and tied it.

'Look, Julia,' I said. 'I'm sorry.'

'It's not your fault, is it?'

So I pretended not to be bothered. I slouched back on the seats and closed my eyes. God, I was getting as bad as Ray for lying and acting up. I couldn't stop myself from peeping, though – watching Julia pick her way through the sunbathing crowds as the lads' heads turned on their towels.

15

The first thing we knew about it was when the phone went at about quarter to eleven on that same humid Tuesday evening. Vi answered it. I was watching TV and Ray was nowhere to be seen, as usual. When she came out from under the stairs she was already taking her pinny off and folding it absent-mindedly.

I said, 'What's the matter?' The little colour she usually had had drained from her face. 'Vi?'

She looked at me. 'Auntie Vi to you. It's Charles. He's had a ruddy heart attack – or something. He's in hospital.'

'Is it serious?'

'I don't know. It's a ruddy heart attack.'

'What happened?'

'They didn't say – only that he was in his dressing room after the show. Now he's asking for me.'

It made me feel queasy, thinking of Charles having a heart attack in the very dressing room where we'd so recently been. 'Blimey,' I said. 'Have you got to go in the morning?'

'No. He wants me there now. I'd better phone a taxi.'

'I'm coming with you,' I said, and she didn't disagree, which was odd for her.

That's how I came to be sitting under a painting of sunflowers in a corridor outside ward E7. Vi had gone in to see Charles and there was nothing to do except sit and listen to the hospital noises, the clacking of feet on lino, a trolley rattling along somewhere, the sigh of a lift. There wasn't even anything to read. They hadn't let me in because it was intensive care and it was past the proper visiting time. It felt as if I'd been there for hours while Vi sat with him.

A nurse walked past, stopped and came back and asked if she could get me anything. She reminded me of Julia. She had the same sassy walk. A little silver watch hung from her blouse, which tilted as she moved. 'I'm all right, thanks,' I told her.

She smiled. She looked about my age, maybe younger. I said, 'What are you doing after work?'

'You're a bit quick off the mark, aren't you? I'm working, you know.' She had a twangy Liverpool accent.

'I'm not usually,' I said, spoiling everything. 'Must be this place.'

'I know,' she said. 'Mortality, they call it.'

'Something like that.'

'You get used to it. So . . .' she hesitated.

'So what time d'you finish?'

'Not till eight in the morning. It's the night shift.'

'I can wait.'

'I don't think so.'

'Maybe some other time then?'

'Yeah, maybe.' She smiled again. 'Better go. That's the matron.' There were footsteps coming up the stairs. She must have recognized them. Trained ear.

It broke up the hour, that chat with the nurse whose name I never got round to asking. Ray would have been proud of me, the way I did that. Maisie, too. Easy. Nothing to lose. It almost made me forget about Charles.

By the time Vi reappeared it was well past midnight. She didn't stop to talk. 'Let's go,' she said.

'How is he?'

'Touch and go. I'll tell you in the taxi.'

It wasn't until we were sitting in the back of the second black cab of the night that she started sobbing. She pulled a hanky from her handbag and dabbed at her eyes. She said, 'He was lying there all wired up, tubes everywhere, and crying like a baby. There was that stupid makeup still on his face so he looked like I dunno what – a clown or something – and tears rolling down his face and he said, "Vi, Vi, I want to tell you something before I die," and I told him not to be such a dramatic old so-and-so. "You're not gonna die. Not for a while anyway." I made that up, but it cheered him up. He's still in pain and he doesn't like suffering. He always said it was undignified to be in bed while everyone else was dressed.'

'What was the big secret?' I asked.

She hesitated. 'That he loves me.'

'Blimey,' I said.

'And what's wrong with that?'

'Nothing. Nothing.' It was hard to imagine, that was all.

'It was probably the drugs they'd given him, but he said, "Vi, I want you to know I've never loved a woman like I love you. Except," he said, "my old mum, God rest her soul. When Mum passed over a part of me went with her."'

Vi went silent there in the back of the taxi. We were in the Mersey tunnel again. There was almost no traffic on the road except for us and we dipped down into the orange light, going deeper. Vi's voice came out of nowhere, 'He asked me to go and look after him. "If I should get out of this alive, Vi," he said, "I'd like you to come and live with me. Would you do that? I'd pay you of course."'

I asked her what she'd told him. I was afraid of what might happen, because it was exactly like Ray said it'd be and none of us had believed him.

'I said I wouldn't want ruddy paying for a start,' Vi went on. 'And I said not to be so morbid. But he's got a lovely house off Cheyne Walk in Chelsea. He invited me to

London for a weekend once and we did the shows. His house is just like you'd imagine, Eddie, with three steps up to the front door and lovely tall ceilings. There are paintings in every room and the most beautiful leather furniture. Not like we get – not out of the saleroom. And he said, "I know what you're thinking, Vi," and I wondered if he did. "There's plenty of space," he said. "You know you could have a room of your own. I mean, there'd be nothing between us – you know, nothing sexual." I wanted to say, "Why not? Why not?" I wanted to say, "There could be. You don't know," but I didn't.'

It was too embarrassing to hear her going on about personal stuff like that, painful almost. I looked out of the window at the lights flashing past and she went quiet. 'Does that mean you'll be going?' I asked at last.

'I don't know. We don't even know if he'll survive this. The doctor said it was touch and go. And what would Ray do if I went to live in London? He'd say "That's exactly what I said would happen, isn't it?" He'd say he told me so. I couldn't bear Ray to be like that – all self-righteous and furious – but Eddie, I love Ray, too, God help me. I don't know why cos he's the biggest load of trouble, but I'd never forgive myself if anything happened to him back here.'

I said, 'You could take Ray with you. He'd like London.'

'He wouldn't. I know him. He probably wouldn't stay and even if he did he'd be off the rails in no time. Anyway I don't know if Charles is going to get better, and there's Nanny to think of and the boarding house. I couldn't . . .' And she started sobbing again, taking fast little gulps of air.

I tried putting my arm round her, but she shrugged it off. I didn't much like the thought of trying to persuade her to go and live with Charles. I'd be letting Ray and Nanny down again. But I didn't like to see her so upset either. 'You deserve to be happy, too. Don't you think so, Vi?'

'I don't know. You sound just like your mother. Always ruddy preaching but without an ounce of sense in her. And it's *Auntie* Vi to you.'

'You told him you wouldn't go, then?'

'I didn't want to give him another bloody heart attack, did I? I said I'd think about it. That should keep him happy for a bit anyway.'

I didn't find out what had happened until afterwards. Vi's version of events was light on detail because she hadn't been there and she was too practical to spin a story out of nothing. I don't know where Julia's version came from because she wasn't there when it happened either, but I could tell it was full of fancy and speculation. It was only when I asked Irene, who *was* there that evening, that I was finally able to piece the whole thing together and it went like this:

Charles hated matinées even when they were sold out. He'd grown weary of the kids who didn't want to be there and laughed at the wrong moments, the OAPs with weak bladders shuffling to the toilet in the middle of his most difficult patter songs, the rustling of sweet wrappers and the coughs that broke his concentration while he was trying to remember the confounding, twisting words. And that day had been so hot and sticky.

After the matinée the Rodcoopers went to the Buck's Head. It was a place they frequented between the matinée and the evening performance. Charles often needed at least one large brandy and sometimes a small Sanatogen as well these days to keep him going. He was holding forth as usual about how unappreciative the audience had been. The brandy was finding its way into his system and Brenda was nodding and agreeing with him. Anyone would think agreeing with Charles was part of her contract.

'The wretched costume's so claustrophobic,' he was

saying. 'I can't bear it in this weather. It's like being shut in. I've suffered with claustrophobia for years.'

'Are you sure you don't mean hypochondria, Charles?' Alastair said. He was in the corner reading *Variety* – looking for his next career move, according to Irene. Maisie was there, too, smiling behind her knitting – her last matinée jacket, an especially gorgeous one in green and white. Three girls from the chorus were standing at the bar, together with some of the crew who called in for pints of bitter and a sandwich between performances.

'Ha-ha,' Charles replied, drily.

The problem with practical jokes was that you could never tell who was going to come off worse. It might be the person the trick was played on, but it could just as easily be the one who'd laid the joke in the first place. That was the thrill of them, too – they were unpredictable and could go off in any direction.

Charles had bought some of those annoying little explosive pellets you put in the end of cigarettes. They were about the size of a matchstick broken in half and you inserted them in the tobacco when nobody was looking and then, when the cigarette was lit, they were supposed to go off with a bang and blow the end of the cigarette to bits. Alastair opened a packet and lit up. The pub between performances was the only place he smoked. Charles must have spiked the cigarettes a couple of days earlier. He'd probably forgotten he'd done it.

Alastair drew on the cigarette, long and leisurely. Nothing happened. Then he put the cigarette down in an ashtray while he took a drink and at that moment it went off. It didn't make a bang. It was more of a loud fizzle like a sparkler and suddenly there was a flame in the ashtray, about a foot high.

Charles laughed. Alastair panicked, trying to put the fire out with his copy of *Variety*, but he only succeeded in fanning it more. Then the newspaper caught fire. The flames were licking everywhere. 'Help!' Alastair shouted, flapping at the fire which was alarmingly close to the upholstered seats and benches.

'Call the fire brigade,' someone shouted. But before they could the landlord rushed across and threw an ice bucket over the flames. One of the barmen squirted a soda siphon. They were like a couple of clowns at the circus.

It was Irene of all people who finally picked up a heavy seat cover and dropped it calmly over the flaming ashtray. 'There,' she said. Alastair was soaked with water and soda. He glared at Charles. 'This is too much, Charles. Look at me. I could have got burned to a cinder.'

Charles only laughed. 'You've been plaguing me with your childish humour ever since we came here.'

'Yes, and you've been plaguing me back – and your jokes are downright dangerous. Can't you see the difference?'

'You deserve it. You've sneered and tried to undermine me all season.'

'Don't be absurd,' said Alastair.

There was a smoky smell in the air. The landlord would certainly have barred them on the spot if it hadn't been for the regular trade they brought in. A scorched piece of newspaper floated off the table and landed on the floor. The girls were fussing over Alastair, wiping him down with their hankies, wringing out his sweater. That was what really infuriated Charles – that Alastair ended up getting sympathy and attention when what he should have got was humiliation. Alastair was supposed to be the laughing stock, but now he was almost enjoying himself.

Charles's face turned red with fury. 'Is this how you repay me for my guidance and instruction, Alastair?' he blurted out. 'You knew nothing when you came here.'

'Grow up,' Alastair shouted, which was rich coming from someone who liked black face soap and wind-up mice.

The pub had gone quiet. Brenda tried to smooth things over. 'Perhaps we've all been in one another's pockets too long. It's not healthy to be so close, and it's been a difficult season for us all.' She was referring to Julia, of course. As if she was to blame for everything.

Alastair looked across at Charles in a way that suggested he'd got the measure of him. Peace in the practical joke war had not yet been negotiated, not by a long way. Surprise was still the weapon of choice.

Charles said, 'You were unbearable while we shared that room – and you're unbearable now.'

'Ssh,' Brenda said.

Alastair said, 'And if it wasn't for Gilbert and Sullivan, Charles, you would be nothing. You would have nothing to say. You would simply disappear.'

'How dare you . . .' Charles started. 'I'd have you dismissed on the spot if there weren't a show this evening.'

'Oh, please,' Brenda said. 'This is terribly childish and entirely out of proportion. Be nice to one another. Shake hands.'

They reluctantly shook hands and Alastair bought a round of drinks, including one for Charles. He drank a silent toast to Charles, trying to spook him over the top of his whisky and soda, then chuckled and pretended the matter was closed.

So when Charles struggled onto the stage two thirds of the way through Act One of *The Pirates* that stifling evening, he wasn't quite wearing his Major-General's jacket with the elaborate epaulettes. That was because he was still trying to push his left hand out of the end of the sleeve that Alastair had tacked up. Charles, the old pro, managed to make it look as if it was part of the show. Finally he gave the audience one of his *Mikado* smiles, threw the coat on the floor and carried on in his braces. The audience, laughing, couldn't see the frustration and rage on his face that night as he sang something amusing about a '*washing bill in Babylonic cuneiform*'.

But by Act Two he'd turned pale and clammy. He was pulling at his collar and sweating like a pig. His clothes suddenly seemed too small for him. One version of events was that Alastair had put itching powder into his trousers, too. But I wasn't sure even Alastair was that irresponsible. How hard it must have been for Charles, the Major-General, to look Alastair, the Pirate King, in the eye and forgive him – which was, if I remembered it right, what happened at the end of *The Pirates*. The couples waltzed happily round the stage, they bowed, the curtain came down and Charles went straight to his dressing room.

That was where, an hour later, the stage manager found him. Charles was stretched out on the floor in his underwear, his feet half under a chair that he'd kicked over. It was hard to know if the episode was funny or sad. It was a fine line. Itching powder was funny, but lying alone on the floor in your underwear definitely wasn't.

The house was a different place after Charles's heart attack. During the hours when Charles hung between life and death the Rodcoopers went around more quietly as if they'd suddenly found their slippers in the bottom of their suitcases. Before, you could have heard them from one end of the house to the other, clumping down the stairs to fetch a magazine or rattling around in the bathrooms. But now they tended to come up on me by surprise and make me jump.

The morning after Charles went into hospital there was an emergency meeting at the theatre. They were thinking of calling the rest of the season off but Brenda came back and told us that in the best theatrical tradition they'd decided the show must go on. Alastair, as Charles's understudy, would step into the role of Major-General Stanley 'until such time'. She raised her eyebrows dramatically when she said this, and didn't elaborate on what 'until such time' might mean. A promising singer from the chorus would replace Alastair as the Pirate King.

'Does Charles know?' Vi asked.

'He'd want us to carry on, of course. I'm sure about that. But he's not well enough to discuss it.' That was probably sensible, I thought. The idea of Alastair stepping into his shoes would have caused Charles to relapse.

'But someone's got to tell him sooner or later,' Vi insisted. 'It's only fair.'

It was understood in theatrical circles that the understudy would take over the main role in event of illness, Brenda said. 'If he asks we'll explain, but we think it's best we make sure he's strong enough first. We don't want to distress him further.'

Vi and me looked at one another, because we both knew they were afraid of Charles. Suddenly I had a picture of Vi and Charles together, walking under the trees in a London park. They'd be on their way to the premier of a musical comedy in Drury Lane. Together they'd be invincible. Nobody would ever dare contradict them.

To tell the truth, I couldn't see what was wrong with Alastair. I liked him. He was much nearer my age than Charles's. He wouldn't get obsessed with the Rodcoopers because they weren't his life's work. I couldn't imagine him giving himself a heart attack. He wouldn't forget that the show was meant to be fun. Fun was the idea of them being here, I thought. How had life with the Rodcoopers ever got this heavy? I wondered.

They cancelled the afternoon matinée out of respect, then Alastair stepped in for the evening show. They had to do a bit of emergency needlework on the Major-General's costume, but nobody noticed and Alastair carried it off with great assurance. He had a surprisingly natural rapport with the audience and there was a mention of his performance in the *Liverpool Echo* which everyone hoped Charles hadn't seen.

My exam results arrived in the Thursday morning post. I'd passed everything except Latin, which made me smile when I remembered what Ray had said about writing prescriptions. I'd be going back to school. I called Mum at Grandad's to give her the news and tell her about Nan's trip to America.

And then I began to notice that Ray's bed hadn't been slept in for a while. I tried to work out if he'd actually moved out. I mentioned it to Vi, but she'd run out of sympathy. 'I don't know, Eddie. He's staying with his mates, I expect. He'll come back like a bad penny. He always does. He's still leaving his washing, so he can't be too far away.'

I hadn't seen him since the outdoor baths, but Nanny said he'd been in and out of the house. Some nights when she hadn't been able to sleep and she'd been wandering around the house she'd seen him. 'Are you sure, Nan?' I asked.

'Oh, yes, love.'

'You're not getting him mixed up with me, are you?'

She looked at me suspiciously. 'I'm not that daft.'

Preparations for the trip to America were well under way. Nanny had got a suitcase from the saleroom – a brown contraption covered in shipping stickers and with locks that expanded with a ratcheting sound. The well-used look had attracted her. 'You need a case you can trust,' she told me as she packed and unpacked it for the tenth time.

Now it lay open on her bedroom floor, piles of clothes and papers around it. There was a collection of the fruit and nut bars Ray had given her, an envelope with her passport, US visa and some traveller's cheques, and a present wrapped in blue striped paper for Gary, the grandson she'd never seen. I'd been there when she'd brought it home – a little sailing yacht like they used on the model boat pond, with cloth sails and strings to pull them up and cleats along the deck. It was better than anything Ray or me had ever had. I hoped Gary would appreciate it and that there'd be a park with a pond to sail it.

Nanny checked her list and made me point out where everything was – even the disgusting Granny things, the hideous flesh-coloured girdles and tins of Euthymol – so she'd know where they were when the final packing time came. 'Are you sure you're gonna need all this stuff?' I asked.

'I'm going to the other side of the world, aren't I? You can't buy the same things there.'

I was pretty sure you could get toothpaste in New York, but I didn't say anything. I couldn't imagine what picture of America she had in mind; one created from Marion's letters, I supposed, the recipes she'd sent for mint julep and pumpkin pie, from old films and faded photographs.

When she was satisfied everything would fit and that she knew where it would be, Nanny sat down. 'Have you heard how Charles is?' she asked.

I told her Charles had rallied and was out of intensive care. 'He'll be OK,' I said. 'Vi says he's recovering nicely.'

'Do they think he'll come back here?'

'I don't know. Vi thinks he'll probably go to London or to a convalescent home.'

'They'll miss him – the Rodcoopers.'

'But they'll survive,' I said. 'People like that always do.'

'Vi's fond of him,' Nanny said and sighed. 'By the time I get back she'll probably have moved to London. He asked her, you know.'

'I don't think she'd go – not while you're away, Nan.'

'She moved me out of my room to suit him, didn't she? So she might. I wouldn't blame her.'

I supposed it was possible. Anything could happen while she was in America. It wouldn't be too difficult to imagine her staying for the rest of her life, becoming an American. 'Here,' she said, starting to pack her case again. 'Check these through with me again, will you, Ed?'

Even Julia was subdued since Charles's heart attack. It had affected all the Rodcoopers in different ways. She hadn't seen Ray either. 'It's me. I'm sure it is,' she said when I mentioned him. 'Something about me drives lads away. It's the story of my life. I say something or I do something and it's like a green traffic light – they're off.'

'It's not you, Julia,' I said. 'Ray's always been the sort to disappear without saying anything. He's done it as long as I've known him. If he's gone anywhere it won't have been to get away from you.'

'I want to go and look for him,' she said. 'Will you come?'

We went to the Palace Amusements and spoke to one of the attendants. He was sitting on the rail of the waltzers counting tokens. Behind him screaming girls whizzed past, clinging onto the safety bars of their waltzers, hair flying.

He looked Julia up and down in a way that made me want to punch him. 'Doesn't come in here these days,' the attendant said when we asked about Ray. It seemed an age since I'd seen Ray wearing that maroon jacket and jangling his keys, though it couldn't have been more than three weeks. It almost made me feel nostalgic. 'He's not welcome, like.'

Julia asked why.

'The usual thing. He had a falling out, if you know what I mean.' He could tell we didn't, so he went on. 'Robbing out of the machines. He spoiled it for the rest of us. Everyone has a couple of bob now and then, but Raymondo – well, he had to overdo it, didn't he? Practically emptied the sodding cherry fruit special jackpot machine one Tuesday. I don't know how he managed to walk with all that silver in his pocket, but he did. Silly sod.'

'He told us he left to get a better job,' I said.

'Maybe. You can believe that if you want.' He laughed. 'People like Raymondo usually jump before they're pushed. It's best they do – let the rest of us get back to normal. Where'd he go anyway?'

'We were hoping you'd tell us,' Julia said. 'Last I heard he was working on the post.'

It was the same reaction as always. The attendant burst out laughing. 'Raymondo a postie? You're having me on.'

I didn't want Ray to be a joke, but Julia and I laughed anyway, to humour him. She said, 'We haven't seen him for a while.'

'Shame,' the attendant said. 'I haven't seen him either. If you catch up with him before I do tell him from me not to come back here. He's not welcome.'

The Palace seemed different that day – unused and neglected without Ray. We walked past the ghost train with its empty carriages queued up and its dark-coloured front, painted with spooks and skeletons. They looked like something out of a comic – flat and garish and not at all scary. The woman on the shooting range leaned on her stall and called out to us. Three shots for a bob, give it a go, love, but she knew we weren't visitors, and her heart wasn't in it.

Next to the ghost train was the mirror maze. 'I've always wanted to go in here,' Julia said. 'Come on, Ed.' She got tokens from the ticket desk. A man who looked like he hadn't slept opened the door for us. Nobody else was in.

At the start was a wall of different curved mirrors. One made us look squat with deformed heads; another made us look impossibly tall and skinny. I hated them, but Julia couldn't take her eyes off them. She kept turning on her heels to get new grotesque views. She understood mirrors, the way they told a different story every time you looked in them. I'd seen the way she glanced at her reflection when she passed a shop window.

When she got bored with that we went into the maze itself which was made of full-height mirrors set at angles. We got lost straight away. It seemed we were looking down endless corridors of prisms, but when we put our hands out there was either a reflection or a piece of plain glass or nothing at all in front of us. Everywhere we looked there were images of us looking bewildered and lost. Julia thought it was wonderful. She smiled and adjusted her hair in a thousand different directions.

At first I'd thought she might have come here to stop herself thinking about Ray, but now I could see that she wasn't that complicated. She was interested in the reflections, that was all.

She said, 'Why don't we stay and see what happens? We could live here and nobody'd ever find us. What do you think, Ed?' She pretended to panic. 'Help!' she shouted. 'We're never going to get out of here alive.'

The place was even more unsettling than the ghost train, to tell the truth, precisely because it didn't have any phoney ghosts or coffins or loud noises. All it had were endless reflections you couldn't get away from. The thought of living with that made me grimace.

'Come on then,' I said, putting one hand up so as not to collide with the glass. Touching was the only way to know what was around you, and Julia gripped my free hand to follow me, the way she had when I helped her off the sands away from the incoming tide.

We could see the way out, but at first we couldn't get to it. We had to navigate through glass triangles, bumping and feeling our way down reflecting corridors. Finally we emerged by the shooting range in the familiar Palace Amusements. 'Crap,' Julia said when we did. 'What a load of rubbish that was.'

After that we walked along the seafront. I said, 'Someone's always running away – have you noticed? First you, then Ray. It's this place. People want to get away from it. They always have.'

'I'd never thought of it. Now it's your nan. Before that it was your uncle – to America. Maybe seeing all those ships on the river is what does it. Do you think Ray could have stowed away?'

I said I didn't think he was the travelling sort. He was restless, but anchored here. As we passed the Ship I craned my neck to look over the net curtains covering the bottom half of the window. He wasn't there. A couple of blokes stopped with their pints halfway to their lips and our eyes met. They were looking at Julia.

'What about the modelling?' I asked. 'Have you gone off the idea yet?'

'Course not,' she said. 'I'm not that fickle, Ed. I'm working on it, as a matter of fact.'

'You're not thinking of seeing Pete again, are you?'

She looked across at me then. 'Someone like him couldn't help me, could he? Not really. Thanks for trying though, Ed.'

I knew she was lying.

The house was quiet when we got back. I opened the door to the kitchen and Vi was fast asleep, snoring in her chair by the Baxi. The wireless was on. It sounded like 'Music While You Work' on the Light Programme. Julia, behind me, said, 'Can I take a look?'

'Why?'

'I've never looked in, that's all. The door's always shut. I wondered what it was like.'

So Julia leaned past me and stuck her head round the door. She spent a long time in that position. 'What's so interesting?' I asked. 'Come on, Julia, she might wake up,' and I tugged at the back of her dress.

We closed the door, but she didn't say anything at first. Finally she said, 'I can't remember the last time I was in an ordinary room. It's untidy, isn't it?'

'Course it is. We're always busy. Don't have time for clearing up. Your part of the house is kept clean and neat, but ours is a mess.'

'It's like behind the scenes.'

'I suppose so. I bet you live in a mansion with servants and everything?'

'Yeah,' she said, but I knew she was being sarcastic. 'As a matter of fact we live in a flat in Sussex. Two bedrooms and a piano. We have to be near London, you know, in case Mother Brenda gets a call. I've got a photo upstairs. D'you want to see it?'

We were that close in the hall, our faces all but touching. Ray was no longer around. Dave was just a memory. Now there was only me. She reached out as if she was going to brush something off my shoulder – a hair or a speck of dust – but instead she held me there and pulled us together. The kiss took me by surprise, the aching heat of it. I didn't want it to stop, but she pulled away. 'D'you want to see?' she asked again and I nodded.

'What about Brenda?'

'She's out.'

So I followed her up to the room she shared with her mother. This was it – the Clincher, the Moment. I shook with anticipation. We closed the door behind us. I went to kiss her, but she pulled away again. 'Drink?' she asked. I didn't want a drink. I wanted her.

She'd turned as suddenly as the wind, pretending and acting again. She talked as if we were old friends meeting up for a gossip. 'It's OK. Brenda's got a little supply she doesn't tell anyone about. Whisky?'

'Please, Julia. Stop it now.' She spun away from me as neatly as the girls in the waltzer.

'I think there's a drop of gin. Can't stand it myself. Tastes like perfume.' She poured a good measure of Johnnie Walker into two glasses and topped them up with water from the wash basin. 'She won't know,' she said and refilled the bottle from the tap, then slid it back into Brenda's wardrobe. 'She drinks all the time. She's got no idea how much she's had.'

'Julia,' I said, reaching for her. But she'd moved again. She took a swig from her glass and grimaced.

'I bloody hate that stuff. Come on, Ed, drink up.' It tasted of lukewarm tap water, but burned its way down my throat and chest. Julia sat at the end of one of the beds. 'Now then, come and kiss me again.'

At last. We sat on the bed and grappled, our shifting limbs unused to one another's shape, kissing badly and desperately.

Then we heard the front door close and someone come in. Brenda's voice called out. 'Oh, sod,' Julia said, pulling away. She smoothed her dress down over her knees.

'I'm desperate for you,' I said. 'Julia. Please.' I reached for her again as if she belonged to me. 'We can't stop now,' I said. 'I'll stay here. I don't care if she finds out about us.'

'There's nothing to find out about us, is there?' Julia said. She'd got up and was brushing her hair, looking in the mirror on the wardrobe door. 'Don't go getting all heavy on me now, Ed. I happen to like you, that's all.'

It didn't begin to describe it for me, but I said it anyway. 'I like you too. A lot.'

'That's all right then, isn't it? We can . . . you know, another time.'

'Promise?'

'I don't make promises. I'd only go and break them.'

She was rinsing out the glasses in the basin. She opened the bedroom door for me to leave, kissed me on the cheek as she pushed me out. 'Some time soon, Ed,' she said, and giggled as if it was a joke. She left me standing outside her door, helpless with wanting her.

16

Suitcases constantly packed and unpacked themselves. Clothes gathered like birds on wire hangers, waterproofs massed threateningly in corners, coded notes appeared: *Check taxi booked? Mrs Morris. Collect shoes.*

Vi struggled to run the boarding house at the same time. 'You'd have thought we were moving house, not just one old girl going away for a couple of months.' She prodded a pile of Nan's stockings and Germolene-pink corsetry. 'I'll be glad when the place gets back to normal again – whatever that means.'

'Don't touch those,' Nanny said, coming in. 'Wanted on voyage.' The underwear looked as though it could fill a suitcase on its own.

'Sit down a minute, Mother,' Vi said. 'You're not going for three days yet.'

'I'm looking for my glasses.'

'There are four pairs on the sideboard,' I said.

'Not those. They're the cheap ones from the salerooms. I want the nice reading glasses.'

'On top of your head, Mother,' Vi said. Nanny made a phoo-ing noise when she felt for them, as if they'd been hidden from her intentionally. She left the room again.

On top of everything Charles was expected out of hospital in a couple of days. Vi had made his room dazzle, cleaned the windows, vacuumed the carpet and arranged freesias in a vase.

'It's all happening at the same time,' Vi said and plonked herself down on the settee. 'As bloody usual, and your nan's not helping matters.'

'She's excited about her trip,' I said.

'I know, but she's getting on my nerves with her packing and goings-on.'

Nanny had been telling me about Steve and Marion's place in New Jersey – neighbours who called round to offer homemade apple jelly, Halloween parties, fitted carpets and central heating, a phone in the kitchen. It was like *The Dick Van Dyke Show*, Nanny said. She didn't have any photos, though, only Marion's word for it.

'She thinks it's going to be the ruddy Sunset Strip,' Vi said, 'but I've got a feeling they live in a flat – or whatever they call them in America.'

'New Jersey sounds fantastic,' I said. 'It makes me think of fields full of cows.'

'I wonder if it was ever like that,' Vi said. 'Do you know where he works, our Steven?' I didn't. 'A bloody tyre factory. They take old tyres and break them down and turn them into new ones. If he'd wanted to work in a tyre factory he could have stayed here, got a job in Birkenhead or Stockport. I don't know why he ever emigrated, Ed.'

To make a better life, I thought, to be rich. He'd found a wife, had a kid. He was still a hero to Ray and me. People had watched ships sliding down the river with the tide for generations, so why should anyone be surprised when they got on board?

Vi said, 'I hope your nan won't be disappointed when she gets there. That's what I hope.' She stood up again, switched the iron on and started on the underwear. 'They'll make her welcome. That's the important thing. She thought she'd never see them, you know.

'When I last spoke to Steve on the phone they were making all sorts of plans for her. Steve's taking a fortnight off work and they're taking her to see all the sights and meet Marion's family. They'll make such a fuss of her. I even spoke to Marion and little Gary.

'So it's a blessing and it's nothing to do with where she's going, Ed. In the end what matters are the people she finds when she gets there.'

The next afternoon Nanny asked me to collect a pair of her shoes from the cobbler's. She wanted to pack them. I was on my way back when I turned into a street near the Tower Grounds, looked up and saw Julia. She was wearing a pale blue dress, walking quickly away from me. She was unmistakable. She brought that dull street to life. I stopped. What was she doing here? I was about to call out to her when she took a left turn down the road that the Box of Tricks was on. I knew at once she was going to meet Pete. It made me feel sick to think of her in there on her own with him.

I was about to run after her and insist on taking her home, but it was too late; she was already knocking on the door. She stood there waiting for an answer. I could see the place was closed and locked up, but after a moment someone let her in. I couldn't be sure from this distance, but I thought it was Pete. She didn't look back or say anything to him. She just disappeared – my single-minded, beautiful and mad Julia – inside the Box of Tricks.

I walked up to the door. There was a 'Closed' sign and a blind pulled down. Silence. Almost as if I'd imagined it, like that time when Dave drove off into the night with Julia. She'd been swallowed up in the same way then.

I caught a movement inside the shop – perhaps a flash of her pale blue dress between the racks of tricks, a door closing as Pete led her upstairs. What was it about her? Why did I always get into impossible situations because of her?

I tried to tell myself there'd be an explanation. She had business to discuss. She was old enough to look after herself. But I didn't believe it. I decided that if she didn't come out in fifteen minutes I'd knock on the door and demand to see her. That was my plan.

So I walked away to wait. I was nearly at the end of the road when I heard the shop door open again. It was Pete. He wore a crumpled navy blue suit. He looked both ways and carefully turned the key behind him. He walked off in the opposite direction.

He'd locked her in, left her trapped inside. I walked back up and tried the door, then banged on it. I shouted her name. 'Julia! Are you all right? Can you hear me?' But there was nothing. Just silence.

I decided I had to do something before it was too late. Like the war heroes in Ray's comics I had to act. This was no time to consider personal risk. Valiant wins the day. Faint heart never won, I heard Irene saying, is it maiden or lady? Never mind.

I sprinted down the back alley and stood at the end of the yards which ran along the backs of the houses. The Box of Tricks had the same crumbling walls and wooden gates as most of the others, but it had been the corner house and the dustbin had the words 'Joke Shop' painted on its side so I knew it was the right place. I stood on the bin and levered myself up to the height of the wall.

I saw a movement in the upstairs window. It could only be Julia – the room must've been the one I tried to get into that day I went up into Pete's flat. Its door had been locked then, too. I guessed it was where he kept his prisoners before practising his terrible, bone-crushing magic. Julia had been foolish – stupid, more like – but I had to try to help her.

Then I saw her stand in front of the window for a moment. From where I was, supported by my elbows on the wall, she looked as if she'd been crying. The expression on her face was one I'd never seen before. She looked into the room, stopped then moved again. I levered myself onto the wall, scrambled up and sat on the top. I swivelled round and lowered myself into Pete's back yard.

As I looked up, Julia passed the window again, dreamily as if she was half asleep. She could have been drugged – or hypnotized. Pete would know how to put her into a trance. I called out to her as loudly as I dared, but she didn't respond.

There was a single-storey outhouse attached to the back of the joke shop. I put one foot on a pile of bricks and hauled myself up the iron drainpipe, scuffing my shoes and scraping my knuckles on the way. Then I pulled myself over the gutter and onto the low roof. The slates were slippery but I managed to grab hold of the windowsill and scramble and slide up to the window.

Thank God. I could rescue her. We could escape together down the roof or out through the shop and for once she'd be grateful. We'd pause to call the police. Then I looked into the room, pressing my face up to the glass, and saw her. She moved in front of the window, not more than a foot away. I could have reached out and touched her. She was naked apart from a pair of lace-trimmed pants. She was posing, holding the skimpy end of a sheet in front of her. She reminded me of that woman on the pen in Pete's shop, her dress sliding away.

Facing her and me were three blokes with cameras in their hands. Off to one side was Pete. He looked as if he'd just walked into the room. He'd been to the off-licence to buy beer and was in the middle of handing bottles round. The photographers dropped the cameras from their eyes and stood with their mouths open, staring at me.

Then Julia turned round, too. For a moment I caught a glimpse of her whole body – the curve of hips, belly button like a little smiling mouth, her pale breasts. She pulled the sheet up over herself. As if her body was forbidden to me, but available to those blokes she didn't even know. Her face had lost the look I'd seen as she'd glanced out of the window. Panic, I'd thought it was, but now I recognized it as a model's face – teasing, artificial, available. I realized where I'd seen it before – in the Italian magazine Ray had tried to nick. It belonged under the counter in the Box of Tricks.

Her expression switched to one of pure fury. She came across to the window and flung it open, still managing to hold the sheet in place. I slid down two or three rows of slates, friction burning my hands and bruising my toes. The photographers were crowding behind her. 'Just what the hell do you think you're doing?' she yelled.

'I thought he'd locked you in. You shouldn't have lied to me, Julia.'

'You stupid little sod. What makes you think you have to look after me? What makes you think you need to come running around every five minutes to make sure I'm all right?'

'I saw you through the window. I thought you were in trouble, or . . . something.'

'Haven't you ever heard of acting?'

Pete put his head out of the window. It was unnecessarily close to hers. 'Who's this?' he started, then he saw me. 'Oh, it's you again. What the hell d'you want?' I'd never seen him even near to angry before, but now his forehead was red and his mouth contorted with rage.

'Eh, Pete, what's going on?' one of the photographers grumbled. 'Is this all part of the service, or what?'

'Is he your boyfriend, love? Cos you better get your clothes on and get off home if he is.'

'No,' Julia said. 'Just someone I know. Some weirdo.' She slammed the window down so hard it rattled the slates. One of the men drew the curtains.

I slid back down the roof like a clumsy skier, dropped into Pete's yard and opened the gate from the inside. I was halfway to Vi's before I remembered I'd left Nanny's best shoes at the end of the yard and had to run all the way back for them.

I was at Pete's gate again when I saw a woman coming down the alley. She wore a raincoat and was carrying a suitcase. I stopped. She seemed familiar – someone from earlier years perhaps – I recognized her face, but couldn't place her. The clothes were wrong. I'd seen her in another setting but couldn't pick out anything to make the connection.

She stopped outside the gate and we looked at each other. 'What d'you think's going on here, now?' she said. 'I've just come in off the Irish ferry and this is what I'm confronted with. Can't even get back into my own place.'

That was when I knew who she was. All I had to do was transfer that broad face to the end of a counter, immersed in a crossword, fogged with concentration.

'Ma Feeney,' I said, without meaning to.

'Mrs Feeney to you,' she said, 'and yes, here I am back again. That rotten brother-in-law of mine's changed the lock in the front door but it's still my shop and he'll have me to reckon with soon as I get in. Box of Tricks, indeed.'

I was relieved to see that her bones and limbs were all intact, all the parts of her body in place.

'And what are you staring at, son?'

'Nothing,' I said. 'I thought you were . . .'

'I was away on family business, that's all. And here I am back and finding the place looking like it is with the windows not cleaned and everything changed. I'm cut up about it.'

'I thought you were,' I said, standing in front of the gate.

'Stand out of the way now, son.'

'You shouldn't go in there,' I said.

She looked at me curiously, then pushed me aside. The gate was still open from when I'd last walked through it. 'Watch me,' she said and disappeared inside.

Nanny's shoes were still in the cobbler's brown bag where I'd left them. I picked them up and ran all the way back to Vi's without stopping.

I went straight to our room. Ray still hadn't turned up. His bed hadn't been slept in. When it was late enough for Luxembourg I lay on my bed and listened to it fading in and out, mixing with some French bloke burbling on. It sounded ominous and faraway, like wartime messages from occupied Europe.

Eventually there was a knock on the door. It was Julia, still wearing the blue dress. She looked flushed. She'd never been in our room before. She came in and looked around, leaned against the door. 'I don't want to talk to you, Julia,' I said.

'I'm sorry I lost it with you, Ed.'

'I don't care any more,' I told her.

'I know you were looking out for me.'

'Look, Julia, just go away now, will you?' I said. 'I've had enough of you. You've caused enough damage for one day.'

'Yeah, you're right. I'm sorry. I've been a complete cow.'

'You bloody have. Everybody lies to me. I suppose you thought you'd got some kind of modelling deal – but those blokes were a load of pervs. I bet no magazines have ever heard of them. They just wanted a gawp at your tits. And it was me introduced you to Pete in the first place. I'm always trying to help you. That's why I climbed up that roof.'

'I know. Wanting to rescue me, I suppose.'

'Something like that.'

'Fat chance. Anyway, we got interrupted a second time.

Some mad woman banging on the back door – said she was the owner. I thought you said she was dead.'

'Apparently not,' I said. 'What happened then?'

'Pete had to let her in and we all had to leave double quick. He just chucked us out on the street. "I'll be in touch," he said. The blokes were asking for their money back as he was pushing them out of the door. Anyway, Ed, just because you didn't know what their game was doesn't mean I didn't.'

'You mean you knew they'd make you take your clothes off?'

Julia looked weary. 'Not for certain. But I had a fair idea. That place isn't exactly bloody Pinewood Studios, is it?'

'So why'd you do it, if you knew?'

'It's the business, that's why. It's what you have to do sometimes to get known. Shit, Ed, even you must recognize that.'

I picked up one of Ray's comics and began flicking through it. I missed him.

She went on, 'So I came to say thanks – for introducing me to Pete and getting me a break – or a bit of one anyway. I know it was a disaster, but something might still come of it.' I carried on ignoring her. 'And to say sorry.'

'You've said it now,' I replied, 'so sod off, Julia.' Talking to her like that made me feel bad – especially as I could just as easily have loved her. It could have gone either way – as quickly as me sliding down that slate roof after that glimpse of her body.

I realized there were no rewards for noble intentions or even for being brave. I'd taken my life in my hands when I'd climbed up that drainpipe to rescue Julia and it hadn't done any good. All it had brought me was more trouble. People were never the way they seemed on the surface. Were Pete and Julia really so erratic and unpredictable that I'd always be misunderstanding them so badly?

I lay on the bed listening to Luxembourg and looking through *Dream Dating*. Another batch of pages came away in my hand. You can't get it all from books, Ray had told me, and he was right. Myron Bloomfield had taught me nothing. It was time for us to part. I folded *Dream Dating* in half and crammed it in the pocket of my jeans.

It was well past midnight, but I couldn't sleep for thinking about Julia and about how much my life had changed this summer. Seeing her body made me want her all the more. Things would never go back to how they were, and I was glad. But the summer was coming to an end and soon I'd be going home the same as the rest of the holidaymakers. I couldn't stay here for ever.

I went downstairs. The house was silent but I saw a light in Nanny's room as I passed, so I knocked gently.

'Come in,' she said. She was sitting in her chair wearing a beige coat and maroon hat. The suitcase, all packed and strapped up, was waiting. There was a new sticky label and a luggage tag tied with brown string to the handle, and the words 'Stateroom' in Vi's spidery handwriting. Everything was ready.

'Oh, Nan,' I said, 'it's way past midnight. You should be in bed.'

'I don't want to miss the taxi,' she said.

'You won't miss the taxi. You're not going till Monday.'

'That's what Vi keeps telling me, but I'm sure she's got it wrong.'

'No, Nan, she hasn't. Vi doesn't get stuff like that wrong, does she?'

'I must be getting my days mixed up then,' she said. So I helped her off with her coat and she made me drape it over the case so she couldn't possibly forget it. She wouldn't take her hat off, though, until I convinced her that if she fell asleep wearing it she might get stabbed with the hatpins and end up in hospital instead of America. Only then did she let me untangle it from her sharp old hair and lay it like a bird's nest next to her coat.

'Ray kept reminding me about the date. He didn't want me to forget. Every evening he'd come and cross off the day on my calendar. That's how I knew where I was. But he hasn't been for a while now. Typical of him to disappear at the last minute. Where's he gone?'

I said I didn't know.

'So that's how I must have got mixed up. I tried to cross one day off every time I woke up in the morning but, well, with these afternoon naps I expect I lost count. I thought it was tomorrow. It's a good job you came along to set me right.'

I asked her if she was looking forward to seeing Steven again.

'Oh, yes, love,' she said. 'Only sometimes it seems like a dream. Then I'm afraid I might wake up and find I'm not going after all. Sometimes I think I don't deserve to go.'

'Course you deserve to go,' I said.

'It's my last chance. I'll never see them again after this, so it's not *that* selfish, is it?'

'It's not selfish at all.' The prospect of America had brightened her up, made her look ahead to the future. I wondered what she'd think of her long-lost son when she got there, and the daughter-in-law she'd never met, and their American boy; the plans they'd made to make her happy.

'By the way,' she said in a confidential voice, 'there's no farewell dinner with the captain. That's disappointing, isn't it?'

'It won't spoil the trip, though. You'll get to see the captain during the voyage – maybe even have dinner with him. Or how about cocktails?'

'I thought the farewell dinner was a tradition like

breaking a bottle of champagne when a ship's launched. We're thinking of having something ourselves anyway – to mark the occasion. I want you and Ray to be there.'

'What? A dinner?'

'Yes. And you and Ray'll come and see me off, won't you? He's a bugger, that Ray, but he's good to me. I know that.'

'Get some sleep first, eh?'

'Yes, but make sure Ray comes, won't you?' She'd forgotten we didn't have a clue where he was.

'I'll remind him when I see him,' I said.

'You do that, Eddie.' She started unbuttoning her dress to get ready for bed, as if she'd forgotten I was there. I shut the door quietly behind me and went downstairs. Then I went out of the back door and into the yard. I dropped the dog-eared remains of *Dream Dating* into Vi's bin as I passed. Then I carried on walking.

The late-night streets were never completely silent. In the early hours you usually came across people staggering home from parties, friends shouting their goodnights to one another, tipsy women climbing out of taxis.

Those sorts of noises filled my nights here; they were part of the fabric of the place. Sometimes the sound of arguments and violent shouting in the street woke me. Other times when I looked out of our top bedroom window there'd be a lone drunk singing his way home.

Now I walked by the seafront, my head full of Julia and Ray. Everything was a mess. Ray was missing, Julia only cared about herself. There was no making sense of her.

I walked past the model boat lake, dark as oil in its concrete container. A couple of gulls who seemed to think it was daytime stood expectantly on the edge. Near the pitch and putt a man came round the corner of one of the shelters and cannoned into me, his head down in the collar of his jacket. 'Oi,' I shouted as he hurried past.

He muttered something that might have been an apology, and carried on. It was a moment before I realized it was Ray. I turned around but he was already a good way past me and walking quickly, his grubby baseball boots flashing in the dark and his hair sticking up at the back, same as always. 'Ray!' I shouted. 'Ray! It's me.'

I started after him but he broke into a trot, heading towards the town. 'Stop,' I shouted, but he kept going. I was sure it was him so I ran too, watching as his shape dipped in and out of the shadows cast by the streetlights. By the tennis courts he turned right. I was gaining on him. 'Ray!' I shouted. 'Stop. I need to talk to you.'

But by the time I turned the corner he'd disappeared. Everything had gone quiet again. I couldn't even hear the sea from here. I stopped and listened. There was only the sound of a car fading in the distance. Ray couldn't have disappeared. On one side of the road were a seedy hotel entrance and a row of shops, all shut up for the night. Opposite were the tennis courts with their tall wrought-iron gates and railings. He could have climbed them, but I didn't think he was that fit. All those fags slowed him down. If I waited he'd show himself eventually. He'd be breathing heavily and I'd be able to hear him. I stood still in the middle of the road.

A car came down the hill and I had to move out of the way. Its headlights lit up a figure standing in the recessed doorway of the hotel. And I remembered that moment in *The Third Man* when Orson Welles gets spotted in the shadows of the doorway by Joseph Cotten when he's supposed to be dead, and he smiles and steps out and says, 'Hello, old boy.'

But Ray wasn't Orson Welles and this wasn't Vienna. Ray hoped I hadn't seen him. He stood there until eventually

I said, 'I know you're there, Ray,' and he kind of shuffled onto the pavement looking all round him and said, 'So . . . what d'you want?'

'I was wondering where you were, that's all. Couldn't help noticing you haven't been home for a week.'

'I got another job.'

'You had another job before you went. It doesn't explain anything.'

'I don't have to explain. Anyway it's late. What you doing out at this time?' He lit an Embassy and flicked the match into the gutter. Still an expert, I was pleased to see. But he was out of breath, too. The running had done him in.

'I couldn't sleep,' I said. 'I'm glad I've seen you, though.'

'Why's that?'

'Nanny's been missing you for one thing.'

He sighed. 'Don't try and make me feel guilty. She's not poorly again, is she?'

'No,' I said, 'but she's going to America on Monday.'

'God,' he said as if he'd lost track of time. 'That's come round quick. Where's she sailing from?'

'Liverpool. Prince's Landing Stage.'

'I'll see her when she comes back. She's only going for a month or two, isn't she?'

'Eight weeks. Will you be there – to see her off?'

He shook his head. 'I can't.'

'She'll be disappointed.'

'I know, but I can't. Give her, you know . . . a hug or something from me. Give her a kiss from me if you want.' Two people appeared at the top of the hill in the light between shadows, near the Maris Stella convent. It was difficult at this distance to tell if they were men or women, but Ray dodged back into the doorway. 'You haven't seen me – right?' I nodded. 'Don't sodding well hang round here then, making it look obvious. Clear off a minute,' he whispered.

It was two middle-aged blokes on their way home after a night out. They chatted as they approached, and one of them glanced at me because I was hovering and acting suspiciously. 'All right, mate?' he said as they passed – the greeting of people who only had one thing in common, the fact they were out on the streets at the same time. I grunted and carried on.

Afterwards I went back to the hotel doorway, half expecting Ray to be gone. He was still there. 'What's going on, Ray?'

He shrugged. 'Nothing. I've got myself into a bit of difficulty, that's all.' He smirked at the phrase. 'It'll all be forgotten in a week or two, then I'll come home.'

'Is it that thing with the amusements? Julia and me went back there and they told us you'd emptied one of the machines. That's why you had to leave, wasn't it? Nothing to do with getting a better job on the post. What you do it for?'

'It's not that,' he interrupted. 'I can't say much, but I couldn't stay at home with things as they are. I've got to lie low for a bit.'

'And that's why you can't come and see Nan off?'

'Make some excuse for me, will you, Ed? Nanny doesn't have to know this has happened. Tell her I had to go away for a while.'

She'd already worked out for herself he was in trouble. With Ray it was the obvious conclusion. 'What've you done this time, Ray?' I asked. I didn't see why I should lie for him.

'I can't say.'

'Is it the police?'

'Still asking questions,' he said, 'still sodding questions – and does it do you any good even when you get an answer? No.' There he was, sliding away from the truth again. That's what upset Vi – he'd get himself into these stupid messes when anyone could have told him where he was heading. His life was like those fairy stories you hear over and over, where the ending is always the same.

'You're Nan's golden boy,' I said. 'God only knows why. She wants you to see her off. You ought to do that for her if nothing else. It's not much to ask, is it?'

He sighed. 'No. She probably thinks she'll never see me again. Silly old woman. Look – I'll get there if I can. Will that do?' I nodded. 'And have you slept with Julia yet?'

'Well, nearly.'

'What kind of a screw is "nearly"? Man, you better do it soon before one of you changes your mind or winter sets in. There's no such thing as "nearly". You either have or you haven't. You do or you don't.'

'I'm not sure she wants to.'

Ray laughed – an eerie noise like an owl coming out of the darkness. 'Shit. Of course she wants to.'

'How d'you know?'

He might have said because she'd told him, but nothing was ever that simple. Instead he said, 'You only have to watch. She fancies you like hell. She's looking at you all the time.'

'I know that,' I began, 'but it could mean anything. It could mean she wants to borrow some money or ask me for a sodding bus timetable. How do I know?'

'Take it from me,' Ray said.

'But . . .'

'Look, I haven't got time for this now. I gotta go. The longer I stay here the more chance someone'll see me.'

'Where are you staying, Ray?' I asked.

'With friends. That's all you need to know. And listen – don't tell anyone you've seen me.'

'What about Nanny?'

'No one.'

'What about Julia?'

'For God's sake – *no one*. You haven't seen me. Now you go that way, cos I'm going this way. See you around, Ed.' And he walked out of the doorway and on up the hill, his head still in his collar, trying to be inconspicuous, but glancing round from time to time, checking out the territory as he went.

17

The following day was the last Sunday in August, the day before Nan's trip to New York. The Rodcoopers decided to have a picnic. I went with them, along the seafront and out towards the end of the peninsula where there were dunes, outcrops of wind-worn sandstone and a spit of soft sand. That part of the beach was a long way from the amusements and slot machines. Holidaymakers seldom ventured there.

There were six of us – Maisie and Irene, Brenda, Alastair, Julia and me – sitting on mats and towels borrowed from the guest bedrooms. A warm wind blew off the Irish Sea. We looked out to where the ships balanced on the horizon.

'I never dreamed we'd be in this situation . . . with Charles, I mean,' Brenda said. She was due to collect him from hospital that afternoon. 'I can't see him adjusting to not being in charge. It's not in his nature.'

Alastair lay back on the sand and bit into one of the sandwiches Vi had packed for us. It was her speciality – cheese, onion and tomato. Alastair was wearing a pair of trousers that must once have been cream, like a cricketer's, but they'd been washed almost colourless. 'He'll get over it,' he said. 'The Rodcoopers are bigger than any one of us – even Charles. That's what's so good about them.'

Brenda sighed. 'I just can't imagine it without him.'

Julia was keeping quiet about modelling, saying nothing about her photos. Behaving herself for once. Maybe she was finally accepting being here. Perhaps she realized there weren't that many days left of the season. I noticed that it was true what Ray had told me. She did look my way quite often, asking me to pass the salt and pour her a drink. It made me realize how wonderful she was yet at the same time how selfish.

After the sandwiches Alastair started juggling with apples, laughing when he dropped them in the sand, rolling, gathering grains.

'You're hopeless,' Irene said. She lay back and tucked her skirt between her knees and smoked a cigarette.

'But I'm improving,' Alastair said. 'Practice makes perfect.' He started playing with a ball that Maisie had brought, throwing it in the air and diving in the sand to catch it, even though he could easily have reached it, then chasing it along the beach, pretending it had gone out of control, tumbling in a comic attempt to stop it.

Then we all had to join in – even Brenda and Julia who would have preferred to stay sitting on their towels. We spread ourselves out and played piggy-in-the-middle. First it was Irene in the middle, who played rough and thought nothing of pushing anyone off the ball so she could get it; then it was Maisie who ran hopelessly from person to person, always too late to catch the ball, always too short to be under its arc, or mistiming the bounce until I felt sorry for her and let her have it instead of catching it myself. She was triumphant, as if she'd won an Olympic medal.

I was Piggy then and stood facing Julia who had the ball, waving my arms, trying to intercept it, conscious of Alastair dodging behind me. Julia's eyes shone as she moved one way then the other, pretending to throw, but reluctant to let it go. In the end she chucked it to Maisie, who caught it badly with a shriek and lobbed it straight back towards Julia. But it was a poor attempt – Julia and me were running towards the same spot, kicking up soft sand. She got there first, but couldn't collect the ball. Then we were holding one another off it – arms and legs – and the ball just out of our reach. She kicked it further away and again we tussled. She got it in the end and held it up and laughed and everyone clapped. I sat on the sand, flushed and happy, and Julia sat down next to me. I could feel the heat of her arms and legs.

I loved the Rodcoopers that day. I would have run away and joined them if they'd asked me. I wanted to listen to their voices for ever – even their laughing, shouting, juggling voices. After a while the wind got up and we packed everything away. Maisie hummed and rinsed sand off her feet with sea water.

Irene said, 'That was a lovely picnic. Doesn't it show you can have fun with nothing but a few friends?'

Alastair said in a Goons voice, 'Just like in the war, Mother.'

'Being here makes me feel alive,' Brenda said and ran her hands through her bleached hair. She tied a scarf in it for the walk home. 'Better than the dusty old theatre.' I wasn't so sure. The theatre seemed fine to me – alive in a different way, that was all.

I felt so confident that on the way back as we were passing the sand dunes I whispered to Julia, 'Come over here with me, Julia. I want to talk to you.'

'What about?'

'About what happened at Pete's.'

She smiled and said, 'All right,' and didn't even ask what I meant by it, just called to her mother, 'We'll catch you up.'

'Ooh,' Irene shouted after us, 'Be careful!' What I was doing was against all the advice she'd given me.

'Don't be long,' Brenda said. 'We've got a show tonight, don't forget.'

The bulk of the dunes cut out any sound from the sea and we sat in a concave hollow with clumps of marram grass above us. I said, 'I don't care you did those glamour photos, Julia. I don't care those blokes saw everything you've got.'

'Not quite everything,' she said. 'Even I've got my limits. It shook me up a bit, though. Those blokes just staring at me. I expect I'll have to get used to it.'

'I was only looking out for you – that's why I turned up outside the window.'

'Let's not talk about it,' she said. She picked at the stalks that poked through the sand and wound them around her fingers. 'I might have made a mess of everything. I don't know. I'm not very good at being good, that's all.'

'I just wish you'd told me the truth. I'd have understood. But it doesn't make any difference.'

She leaned back on her elbows and blinked into the sun. 'I'm not sorry I did the photos. They make me feel cheap, but I'm still not sorry. Is that terrible?'

'No,' I said. I leaned in and felt her pressing against me. I kissed her neck.

'Don't bite me.' She laughed. 'There's my image to think of.' Her fingers were in my hair and we kissed and lay back under the hill of the dunes.

'Shall we?' I breathed and we kissed again, deeper this time and I slid my hand under her blouse. Suddenly she rolled over and sat up.

'What's the matter now? Stop doing this to me, Julia.'

'I'm sorry, Ed. We've got company.' There was a girl – about ten years old, with red plastic sandals and a floppy fringe – standing on the crest of the dune, looking down at us.

'How long have you been there?' Julia demanded, straightening her blouse, shaking sand out from inside. The girl shifted expectantly, as if she was about to say something.

'What do you want?' I asked.

'Can you come and look?' the girl said. 'We found something – something that might be important.' She slid down the slope and stood in front of us.

'Bloody hell,' Julia said. 'Kids again.'

The girl led us to where her two friends were waiting in the shelter of another dune. They looked up when they saw us coming. 'What have you found?' I asked. 'This better be good.' One of them showed us where they'd been digging.

'These,' the first girl said, scrabbling around in the sand. She dug something up and put it in my hand. It was an envelope with a window for the address. It was empty. 'And these . . .' She pulled more out, brushed the sand off and passed them across. Some were addressed and unopened but crumpled. Others had been torn open.

'There's loads,' the boy said. He stood with his tin spade as if he'd unearthed a treasure trove, then poked again at the base of the dune. The letters had been barely covered. A breeze flapped their damp edges. 'Hundreds probably! When we saw them we thought we'd better tell someone. That's why we came and found you.'

Julia kneeled down and dug around. The boy was right; there were letters crammed into the bottom of the dune. She pulled them out one after another and piled them up until the wind started carrying them away.

'Best leave them,' the boy said. 'Do you think? Someone might have buried them here. They might be coming back for them – like treasure.'

'Do you think it could be spies?' the girl asked us.

'Or smugglers?' the boy added.

Julia and me looked at one another. 'No,' she said quietly, 'it'll be Ray,' which was exactly what I'd been thinking. I picked up one of the stray envelopes, addressed locally. It had been opened – a birthday card with a message about money, but no money in it. It made me feel sick.

'We're gonna tell our mums,' the girl said. She must have sensed our uncertainty. 'That's what we should do, isn't it?'

'Yeah,' Julia said. She gathered the letters and envelopes and put them carefully back in the sand. It was almost as if she cared. 'That's the right thing.'

That evening Charles came home. I watched through the open front door as he struggled up the steps. There was a frown on his face from the effort and he was leaning on Brenda's arm. She'd collected him from hospital in a taxi. By the time he'd made it into the hall there was sweat on his forehead. 'Hello?' he called out, a bit feebly. 'Anyone at home?'

The rest of the Rodcoopers were in their various hiding places, pretending to have gone out and forgotten about Charles – Maisie and Irene in the dining room watching through the window, Julia under the stairs. Trust her. I wanted to be in there with her, grappling among the coats. On the way back from the picnic we'd decided on silence about the envelopes. There was no point in saying anything – the kids would tell their parents soon enough, and we couldn't be certain Ray was involved, though both of us were pretty sure he was.

Vi was waiting in the little place where the hall widened next to Nan's old room – not much of a hiding place, but she was only small. Alastair was just hovering, probably hoping Charles had forgiven the practical jokes, or at least put them to the back of his mind. This wasn't the day to revive old grudges.

Then they came out of their hiding places all at once and shouted, 'Surprise!' In fact, Brenda had stopped him in the hall and made a little gesture with her hand so they knew when to appear. This, and the look on Brenda's face, allowed Charles to guess what was about to happen. There was no point making it too much of a surprise, anyway, or in shouting too loud and risking another heart attack. The results could have been fatal. Timing. That's what it was all about.

Alastair told me once that when the Rodcoopers were on stage it sometimes felt as if they were one living organism. That's how well they knew one another – too well, sometimes, Alastair joked. They knew that someone had forgotten their lines almost before the person himself and they understood that if an inexperienced or preoccupied actor was on stage then they might have to ad lib to cover for them. Alastair said they were like liquid, the way they filled up holes in one another's performances. They did it so well that most people in the audience never knew.

So, with Charles, when he came in he realized there was something happening even though he pretended he didn't. And for a moment I was envious and wished I could have been part of that closeness. I wondered if I could learn it, or if it might rub off on me if I got close enough to Julia, because I was sure she had that knowledge, too. It was to do with how she'd been brought up. Not like Ray and me. I thought how good it would be to know what the other person was thinking almost before they did themselves.

Meanwhile Charles was playing at being shocked. 'Oh!' he said. 'I'm so pleased to see you all. Thank you. Thank you so much.' He put his hand up to his heart like they did on stage before they took the final bow. But then when he got into the dining room and saw the cakes and sandwiches they'd set out for him and the flowers Brenda had brought back from the theatre and the banner hanging over the mantelpiece with 'Welcome Home, Charles!' on it, his eyes filled with tears. I could tell it wasn't pretend this time because he had to sit down on one of the dining-room chairs and he put his elbows on the table next to the cruet and the jug of water left over from lunch and fumbled around in his many pockets for a handkerchief.

But of course he couldn't find one. 'Sorry,' he mumbled. 'Sorry, everyone. It was the sight of you all – and these lovely things. I was all right till then.'

'You're fine,' Brenda said, and squeezed next to him on the edge of his chair and put her arm round him.

'I don't deserve you. I'm just a little emotional – and it's so bright and cheerful in here, compared to the hospital, I mean. It's delightful. I never expected any of this.'

So they spoiled him a bit and Vi said, 'No, no, Charles, don't you move. What can I pass you?'

'Vi,' he said, 'you're a treasure. I love you.' Brenda and Alastair were drinking gin again and there were a couple of bottles of beer, but Charles refused it all. 'Tea,' he said bravely. 'That's all I want. I'm a man of simple tastes.'

Brenda said, 'Well, I've never heard you described as that before,' and everybody laughed.

'Since I've been in that hospital what I've missed is a decent cup of tea like Vi makes. It's worth at least ten bottles of cognac.'

Alastair stood and leaned against the mantelpiece with his glass in his hand and looked around the room. He never would have done that before all this happened to Charles. Before, he would have sat in one of the armchairs and made a joke or tried to interest them in a puzzle involving matchsticks, but in a strange way Charles had cured him of his practical jokes. It seemed to me that, until Charles got ill, Alastair might have thought he was just passing through, but he'd got snagged on some rock or other and now he was caught here with the rest of us, like some colourful fish left behind in a rock pool after the tide has gone out.

He cleared his throat loudly and Brenda called out, 'Speech!' He acted surprised, though everyone knew he'd been preparing it for days.

'Unaccustomed as I am . . .' Alastair began and everyone laughed again. He said how delighted he was that

Charles was 'back among us' and how distraught that he wouldn't be staying. He wished him a safe return to London and a speedy recovery. He was certain, he said, that Charles's indisposition would only be a temporary setback and that soon – in no time at all, as a matter of fact – he would be treading the boards with the rest of the Rodcoopers again. Though everyone cheered at this, Charles looked down into his cup as if he was thinking something else entirely, probably about the words he and Alastair had exchanged over the summer. Vi smiled and put her arm round his shoulder. Alastair said how he'd felt sincerely humbled to have stepped into the shoes of the great man and how he hoped he'd done justice to such esteemed footwear. The way he saw it, he said, he wasn't doing anything more than keeping the limelight in working order in readiness for Charles's return to his rightful place under it.

What a speech it was. I believed every word of it despite what I knew about them. It was one of the things Alastair had learned this summer – to hold forth with such sincerity, to tell pleasant little lies as if they were the absolute truth and to know that if he did it with enough assurance nobody would ever disagree. They all clapped and Brenda pulled a long box out from under the table and gave it to Charles. 'No, don't get up,' she said.

So he unwrapped it, sitting there in the chair. It was a dressing gown in deep green – silk or a good imitation – which rippled in rich colour when he opened it out. 'Thank you,' he breathed. 'Thank you so much. I love you all,' and he beamed around the whole room, taking them in one by one, even Alastair, and he managed a comical eyebrow lift and a brief *Mikado* smile. He seemed to think the world of them at that moment. 'This will be perfect for my comeback – for the dressing room.'

Julia crept next to me by the door and whispered, 'But it'll still do for him at home as well – when he retires.' She was right, of course. Everybody was thinking that, but trust her to say it. She put her lips close to my ear. 'Would you do something for me, Eddie?'

I was tired of doing stuff for her, of giving in. 'What?'

'Will you let me show you those photos tomorrow? The ones of my house – you know. They're in my room. Have you forgotten?'

I was suspicious. She didn't offer to do things without a reason. 'Why?'

'Come on, Ed. I know you want me. Everyone does. I just want to know how much.'

'What do you mean?'

'It might be our last chance. Brenda and the others will be seeing Charles off at the station. The house'll be empty.'

Tomorrow, I thought. Then I remembered. 'Oh, no. Nan's going off tomorrow. I can't. I'm going over to Liverpool to see her off. I can't miss that.'

She looked at me again, widened her dark eyes. 'Shame. I thought we could have some fun together.'

'Don't, Julia,' I said.

'Some men would give their eye teeth for an hour with me.'

'I know that.'

'Isn't there any way you can . . . ? You know – find an excuse?' She touched me then, put her hand round my arm, put her chin on my shoulder so I could feel the weight of it, and I melted. I didn't want to. I was thinking of Nan and Vi. I was even thinking of Ray. But the thought of Julia was stronger. I was ashamed, but it was true: even now I'd have done almost anything to sleep with her.

'No,' I said. 'Julia, I can't. It wouldn't be right.'

'Lots of things aren't right, but it doesn't stop them happening, Ed. Some men know what they want. They'd find a way.'

She was playing with me, testing how far she could push

me. I knew it. I still couldn't trust her. 'How do I know you'll be there?'

'Have I ever let you down, Ed?'

'You know you have, Julia. Loads of times.'

'I'll wait for you,' she said. 'Come if you want – as soon as there's no one about.'

'Listen . . . Julia.'

Vi interrupted. She'd seen us talking. 'Help me clear this stuff up, Eddie, will yer?'

I started to help her move the plates and cups into the back kitchen and Julia smiled. 'Don't forget,' she said.

I could hear the noise of the Rodcoopers all the way in the back kitchen, the rattle of the piano. They were singing the old music hall songs – 'The Lambeth Walk' and 'Honey, Honeysuckle'. It was going to be another long night for Vi – keeping the guests happy, making sure Nanny had packed everything.

Mrs Morris from next door but one would be coming in the afternoon to serve up a salad for the guests while Vi was seeing Nanny off. The house was a ship that just kept on going under its own momentum; it would take days if it ever needed to change course. 'It's never-bloody-ending,' Vi said, pulling on her rubber gloves for the dishes.

'Have a rest,' I told her. I couldn't understand what drove her, how she kept on absorbing all this work.

'How can I rest with all this still to do?'

'Try. The world won't end.'

'Cheeky young bugger.' But after the dishes she gave in and sat in the armchair and put her feet up on the pouffe. The Rodcoopers had gone quiet, though I could still hear them laughing occasionally, gossiping.

'What are they up to?' I called through to Vi.

'Probably playing charades. They love their party games.'

There was a knock on the kitchen door and Vi and I

looked at one another. The door opened and a face appeared. 'Come in, Charles,' Vi said.

He came in and sat down looking frail. I could tell he was nervous, because he was messing about with his fingers. 'Vi,' he said at last, 'I've come to understand my mortality.'

'How's that?'

'In the hospital it came to me. Lying there with tubes and wires all over my chest and the daylight coming in through the window opposite, well, it made me realize I wasn't going to go on for ever.'

'Did you think that before, then?'

'Yes,' he said. 'As a matter of fact I believe I did. That's vanity for you. And now I'm ill.'

Vi said, 'You were always ill. Don't you remember? Dyspepsia, neuralgia, claustrophobia. Nothing less than nine letters for you.'

'I mean really ill. The doc said another do like that'd kill me.'

'Don't say that, Charles.'

'It's true, though. It's really true this time.' His face flushed and I thought he might be about to start sobbing.

Vi said, 'You don't have to dwell on it. You just need to get back to work and you'll be right as rain.'

'No,' he said. 'I won't work again. I'll be leaving it to the younger members of the company from now on. How old do you think I am, Vi?'

She shrugged. 'Fifty-eight?' She was being kind.

'Sixty-three,' he said. 'My singing days are over. And Vi, I'd really . . .' He got up stiffly and put his face close to Vi's so I couldn't hear. He glanced across at me as he whispered.

'Oh, Charles,' Vi said, 'please don't . . .' and then she seemed to remember me, because she said, 'Eddie, find something to do, will you?'

'I've got something to do.'

'In another room – or outside. Just give us ten minutes, will you?'

So I left them to it and wandered out of the back door. Before I did Charles made a gesture, a move towards her hand, which he held between his.

For what seemed like ages I hung around in the back yard like a kid, messing with the rusted wheel of the mangle, clicking it to and fro. There was a light on in Nanny's room. She'd be sitting there guarding her luggage, afraid to go to sleep in case she missed her precious ship.

I looked in the kitchen window a couple of times, but as far as I could tell Charles was still there. He'd give himself another heart attack with all this emotion, I thought. Perhaps I should hang around in case I had to phone the hospital – but I knew Vi was more than capable of that.

In the end it seemed better to go out properly and leave them to it – perhaps a stroll to see if I could find Ray again, a check on the amusements or in Fairlanes. I unbolted the back gate, walked down the alley and onto the bombsite. It was a warm night but there was no moon and the bomb-site was dense with shadows. The old chimney breasts and pillars always made hiding places, even during the day. Now they seemed threatening. Broken glass crunched under-foot, like frost.

Suddenly I heard footsteps coming towards me – not quite running, but fast and heavy. There was more than one person. I walked quicker, kicking up glass as I went, tripping over brick ends, but the footsteps were getting nearer. It was like waiting for an avalanche in the dark, hoping it would go on past.

'There he is – the sod,' a voice said. 'Get him!'

I started running, clumsy and blind over the bricks and broken glass. The footsteps were right behind me now. I was close to the brick wall. I tried to shout, to get to the light of the street before they reached me. Suddenly I was grabbed from the back, bundled hard against the wall so all the breath left my body in an 'oof!' that sounded as if someone else had made it.

I was roughly turned round to face them. I screwed my eyes up, waiting for the first punch, trying to anticipate if it would be to the body or the face. 'Leave me alone,' I shouted. 'What do you want?'

But there were no blows. Instead a voice said, 'Raymond Bartlett, I'm arresting you on suspicion of –'

'No. Wait. You got it wrong,' I heard myself saying. They were panting, trying to catch their breath. Their bodies blocked out what little light there was.

'Save it,' the voice said. 'We're the police.' That should have made me feel relieved but it didn't. I was alone and vulnerable. Besides, they weren't wearing uniforms, only dark sweaters and coats in the middle of a warm summer evening. They could have done whatever they wanted and left me for dead. The voice started on the arrest routine again.

'But I'm not Raymond,' I managed. My eyes were getting more used to the dark. I could see their faces now. They looked angry at having been made to chase after me.

'I don't think it's him,' a second voice said. He found a torch and shone it in my face. 'Who *are* you, then?'

I told them my name.

'So what were you doing coming out of that yard gate at this time of night?'

'I live there,' I said. 'Well, I'm staying there – helping out. Vi's my auntie.'

'That makes Raymond Bartlett your . . . cousin?'

I nodded. I shouldn't have been surprised it was the police. I didn't see why I should help them, though, after the way they'd chased me without explanation. 'What's he done now?'

'We need to ask him a few questions, that's all.' That's what the police always said – that they needed 'to ask a few questions'. Even I knew that. I was shaking. Was it fear? Anger? 'When did you last see him?' they asked.

'I dunno. About a week ago.' I didn't mention coming across him in the street at night or about the letters in the sand dunes.

'And he hasn't been home?'

'I don't think so.'

The policeman let go of the front of my sweater and I felt the weight ease. They started chatting to one another as if I wasn't there. 'Look, we can't waste any more time on this. It's a dead loss.' Then, to me, 'We've already spoken to your auntie, so we know what's going on. Listen – if you see him . . .'

'I haven't seen him,' I said.

'But if you do – tell him you've met us and he needs to stop being stupid and just pop into a police station as soon as he can. All right? It'll be easier for him that way.'

'All right,' I said.

'If we don't get him tomorrow it'll be soon.'

'Tomorrow? Why tomorrow?'

'It's a figure of speech, that's all.' They stood back to let me go and I stumbled my way back to Vi's. Behind me I heard them crunch off across the bombsite into the darkness as if nothing had happened.

By the time I got back to the house I was trembling and breathless. When I went into the kitchen Charles had gone and Vi was sitting in her chair under the clothes airer. For once the television wasn't on. The shock must have been obvious on my face.

'What's up with you?' she asked.

'The police were outside. They jumped on me. They thought I was Ray.'

She blew her nose noisily in a matter-of-fact way, but I could tell she was holding back tears. 'I'm sorry, Eddie, I should have told you – but what with Charles coming home and everything I forgot. They came here looking for him at dinnertime.'

'What's he done, Vi?'

'They wouldn't say. They wanted to know if he was here. I told them I hadn't seen him for weeks.'

'Did they believe you?' She shrugged. 'Did they say why they were looking for him?'

'Questions,' she said. 'It's always questions with you. Don't you ever shut up?'

That upset me, because I was only trying to help, trying to understand. I couldn't help not being very good at it. And Vi could probably see the sulky droop to my mouth because she said, 'Sorry. No, they didn't say.'

'Perhaps they want to give him a reward – you know, for rescuing someone or something,' I said.

'Yeah.' She smiled. 'Course they do.' She pushed her hanky up the sleeve of her dress, then immediately pulled it back down again and dabbed at her eyes.

'Charles is gone,' I said, trying not to make it sound like another question.

'Make us a cup of tea, Eddie, will yer?' she said without looking up. 'If it's not one thing it's a bloody other.'

I went into the back kitchen and made a pot of tea and brought it in on one of the guest trays complete with cups and saucers and the milk bottle and a load of Marie biscuits on a plate. 'You're making more washing-up,' she grumbled. 'I'll be up all night as it is.' But she was grateful for the tea and started sipping it straight away and dipped one of the biscuits and sucked at it. The spoon in the saucer rattled with her nerves.

'Charles wanted to know if I'd made up my mind about going down to London. Says he'll need someone to look after him even more now. He said he . . . loves me, but I don't know what he means by that, Eddie, and I don't think he does either.'

'What did you tell him?'

'I said I was still thinking about it. But how the hell could I go? At my time of life – and with Nanny to think about and Ray in all sorts of trouble.'

'Some people would,' I told her. 'Some people would go without any hesitation. They'd jump at the chance.'

'Well, I'm not "some people", am I? I've got a bit of common sense – a bit of dignity.'

I said, 'Is that what you call it? Dignity and common sense?'

'What do you call it then, Eddie, if you're so clever?' Her voice went angry, but I didn't care much what she thought about me at that moment. She'd been making sacrifices all her life and I didn't want her to make any more.

'I'd probably call it – being afraid.'

She snorted. 'Yeah, I'd call it that, too. But not afraid for me. It's Nan and Ray I'm afraid for. And do you know what? I'd really love to go down to London. You wouldn't believe what he promised me. Ray says he doesn't mean it, but he does. I know. I can tell by the way he says it. Tickets to the shows, nice clothes, holidays and stuff. Sometimes he goes to Japan and Buenos Aires. He told me all about those places. I tell you, Eddie, they're places I wouldn't even dare to dream about normally.'

She paused for a moment. 'He told me about his friends as well. He said he had some close friends – men, you know. "Vi," he said, "it's the way I am." And I said I'd kind of wondered and he said did I mind and I said no, I didn't, because to tell the truth I don't. He's well-off, Eddie, and all he wants is a bit of company and someone to look after him. I'd be happy doing that.'

'You deserve something good for yourself, Vi.'

'I know. I've worked for all these years and never had a break. Nothing lucky has ever happened to me before except Ray. God, I loved him when he was a baby. He was beautiful. He had his dad's handsome dark eyes. But look what he's turned out like.' I'd never heard her even mention Ray's father before.

'Go,' I said. 'You ought to go to London. Nanny could go as well – after she comes back from America. There'd be room, wouldn't there?'

She seemed to be wavering. 'What about Ray?'

'He could go as well. Anyway, he's old enough to look after himself.'

'Charles said he'd let me think about it a bit longer.'

'Where is he now?'

'Packing. He's catching the train in the morning. He said he'd go back to London and wait to hear from me. God, he's so considerate. He's such a bloody gentleman.'

'Don't think about it too long,' I said.

She shook her head. 'There's no need to think any more. My mind's made up.'

'Are you going?'

'Course I'm ruddy well not. Can you imagine anything as ridiculous as me in London? I'd be a fish out of water. I don't know what I was thinking of to even consider it. Who am I kidding?'

'I could imagine you there.'

'Well, you've got more imagination than sense. I belong here, Ed. London's OK for visiting, but nobody in their right mind would want to live there. I'll send him a letter telling him my decision.'

I realized how hard she was in a lot of ways – how practical and realistic. All the years here had done it. I couldn't imagine her writing that letter, but I was sure she would. One quiet afternoon, the season finished, she'd sit down and write it. Vi didn't like loose ends.

'Will you ever see him again?'

'I'm sure he'll let me visit once in a while. He can take me to the shows and the posh restaurants and in between times he can get on with his life. That way we'll all be happy.' She sighed. 'I'm not sure about the others, though. With Charles retired they might find somewhere else to stay. I wouldn't blame them after this year.'

'Has it been that bad?' I wondered if my being here was the problem, or maybe it was Julia.

'I don't know. But we'll get over it.'

At that moment the kitchen door opened again. It was Nanny. 'Get over what?' she wanted to know.

'Nothing you need to worry about, Mother,' Vi said.

'Nothing can be that terrible,' Nanny said. 'Worse things happened in the war.'

We laughed. 'That's right, Mother,' Vi said. 'They did.' Nanny had her hat and coat on. Vi sighed. 'It's not time, Mother. Go back to bed. You've got to have another sleep yet.'

Nanny looked crestfallen. The day wouldn't come quickly enough for her. 'Has anyone seen Ray?' she asked.

'No,' Vi said.

'Don't forget he promised to come and see me off.'

'He will if he can, Mother, you know that.' Vi glanced across at me. 'He's . . . busy at the moment.'

'It won't be the same without him. He's my favourite. I want him there to see me off.'

I said, 'He'll be there.'

They both turned to me in that accusing way. 'How can you be so sure?' Vi asked.

'If I know him . . .' I began. 'I dunno. I've just got a feeling.' They snorted together like they'd rehearsed it.

'He'll be in trouble again,' Nan said. 'That's why we haven't seen him. He always was one to disappear when the going got rough. The police were here today. I told them he was a good lad, but there's no point in him running away all the time. They catch up with you eventually. What's he done now?'

Vi shrugged. 'I don't know, Mother. They wouldn't say, would they?'

'We'll see,' Nanny said and turned to go but nearly tripped over something.

'You've never brought your suitcase down with you?' Vi asked.

Nan nodded. 'Yes, I'll need it in the morning.'

'Leave it here. We won't forget it.' But Nan didn't trust anyone any more. She started to lug it back out of the room, so I went to give her a hand and we heaved it back up the stairs together, one at a time.

It was time for bed, but when I came back down Vi said, 'I've got a couple more things to do.' I helped her in the back kitchen tidy away the unwashed supper dishes. She still wasn't ready for bed. 'I'm going to listen to Luxembourg for a bit,' she said. The television had long since shut down. It was going to be another night in the chair. She said, 'Don't wait up. We've got a busy day tomorrow. We're going over early so we can have something to eat first – instead of that dinner with the captain.'

'Good idea,' I said. Julia had been on my mind all this time, like a dark, urgent dream I couldn't shake off. I wanted her. All I had to do was find a reason not to go with them to Liverpool. 'I feel a bit sick,' I said suddenly.

Vi looked at me suspiciously. 'What's the matter? You're not usually ill.'

'It might have been the shock of those bobbies attacking me – or something I ate.'

'There's nothing wrong with my cooking,' Vi said.

'No. I had something off the seafront,' I lied.

'More fool you. Hope you're going to be all right for tomorrow.'

'Me too.' It would give me time to decide. I could be well in the morning. I didn't have to be wicked yet.

'At this rate it'll just be the two of us. Nan's going to be disappointed about her big send off.' She shook her head. 'Do you need a bucket?' Trust her, I thought. No one could accuse Vi of being sentimental.

I went to bed at last and lay thinking about Julia. My thoughts stopped me sleeping in that empty bedroom with Ray's bed made up next to mine. She didn't really want me. She was toying with me, that was all. She might not even be there in the morning and I wouldn't be too surprised to find she'd forgotten her promise – if that's what it was.

Then I was asking myself if Nan would care if I didn't go to Liverpool to see her off. Ray was the one she really wanted. In the end, even though I was her grandson too, I didn't live with her all the time.

Half-asleep, I dreamed of clothes – the sleeveless pull-over and bottle-green shirt I'd worn to the party. Vi had washed it for me and now it hung in the wardrobe waiting for just such an occasion as might present itself tomorrow. Then I woke up again. Ray kept his can of deodorant at the bottom of his bedside cabinet and I got out of bed to check it was there. It was tucked under a pile of magazines. At least he'd left it for me. I smiled. Perhaps he knew I'd need it.

I was being pulled by irresistible forces like the sudden undertow that washes away the ground you're standing on and sweeps you out to sea. All my thoughts were of Julia, sleeping in the room below, perhaps dreaming of the morning to come.

Then I was wondering what Ray would be doing now, whether he had a comfortable bed to sleep in, or if it was a settee in someone's living room. I could imagine his head on one cushion of the settee and his feet sticking out at the other end. His baseball boots would be kicked off onto the floor. From here he seemed romantic and reckless, like Billy the Kid or some other foolish outlaw driven by a sense of adventure. I couldn't believe he'd have done anything truly bad. Not Ray; he just wasn't like that.

It was starting to get light outside when I finally drifted off to sleep.

18

It wasn't all that surprising to find when I woke again, which seemed like only five minutes later and with Julia still on my mind, that I did feel sick. I had a headache, too, and it made me feel guilty, as if I'd brought it on myself.

So when Vi stuck her head round the door and said they were going in about half an hour I said, 'I don't think I can come after all, Auntie Vi. I feel so bad.' I tried to lay it on thick, the way Ray might have done if he'd been here, only I liked to think I was a bit subtler, without quite so many groans. I did put in one or two, but they were gentle and I was holding my stomach at the samc time for convincing detail.

Vi came into the room. She'd got her best grey suit on. 'Are you sure?' She put her hand on my forehead.

I groaned again, said I thought I might be sick. Vi was an expert at seeing through malingering. She'd watched Ray through the years, so knew a thing or two about how it was done. I wasn't sure she was completely taken in by my performance. She shook her head, resigned and slightly despairing. 'The taxi'll be here in about half an hour.'

All I had to do was wait until they'd gone, keep up the pretence that long. Somewhere in that half-hour Nanny came up to see me. That was the worst bit. When I heard her slow footsteps on the stairs I pretended to be asleep. She looked in – I could hear her breathing – and I couldn't resist opening my eyes. 'Have a nice time, Nan,' I said, sounding all pathetic again and hating myself.

'Course I will,' she said. 'Sorry you won't be there to see me off.'

'I know. I'm sorry, too. You're early, though, Nan.'

'I know. You can't be too careful. Vi says we can have our farewell dinner in Liverpool. Ray might turn up as well.'

'Yeah.' I closed my eyes again because I didn't want to have to start giving an account of myself. I wondered if I'd ever see her again.

'I'm really looking forward to seeing Steven and Marion,' she said.

'And little Gary.'

When she left I began to wonder which one of us was the dishonest one – Ray who couldn't help taking things, or me who deceived the people who cared for me. Perhaps I was turning bad like Julia. I'd hoped the good parts of her might rub off on me – the ability to know how people's minds were working, perhaps – but it was the slippery, wicked parts that seemed to be taking root.

Eventually I heard the taxi pull up. I got out of bed and peeped through the curtains. I heard the driver's brisk voice, then saw him hauling Nanny's huge suitcase into the back of the cab. Nan stood on the pavement a moment waiting for Vi. Then Vi appeared with more luggage, looking so smart in that grey suit with her tiny waist, cut in and with straight pockets – just as she must have looked when she went out dancing with Kamil all those years ago. And I knew I was supposed to be there with them, but there was a pain in my loins and no visit to any ship would be enough to ease it.

Half an hour after that the Rodcoopers left to see Charles off and the house was empty. I'd intended to have a bath, but there wasn't time, so I washed at once, shaved and doused myself with Ray's deodorant and got dressed. I put on a tie, then took it off again. I was trembling with anticipation. The house was absolutely silent. It felt desolate, like a Sunday. I took another look at myself in the mirror on the wardrobe door. I looked like a liar, a malingerer, a hostage to hormones. Hadn't that been one of Myron Bloomfield's phrases? 'Nobody wants to be a hostage to hormones.' I think it was in Chapter Eight – the one about 'Sex', or Nine, 'More Sex'. It was too late for me, anyway. I was already captured.

I ran down the stairs to Julia's room then stood outside regaining my breath, praying she'd be there and alone as she'd said. I knocked on the door.

'Come in,' Julia's voice said and at once I felt my heart racing. Her voice alone had done that. What could the whole of her do? Before I'd had chance to open the door she pulled it open herself, grabbed me, yanked me inside and began kissing me. We leaned against the door until it closed with a loud click and we lurched backwards. She laughed and pulled me onto the big bed and we slid fully clothed between the sheets, holding on to one another. She felt small, and flimsy, ready for me. The morning light through the drawn curtains made shapes of the bedclothes, which smelled of Auntie Vi's house. That put me off a bit, to tell the truth. But this was what I'd come for. After all, I told myself, being in bed with Julia was what it was all about. It was easy to forget about Nanny and Vi in the taxi, speeding towards the Pier Head. Julia's hands could make me forget that and everything else too, except, for some reason, what Myron Bloomfield had explained about the importance of foreplay.

'Stop messing about,' Julia said when I touched her thigh ever so gently. 'Kiss me properly.' She wasn't kind or thoughtful, but she was more than enough for me.

We didn't say anything at all while we struggled to take one another's clothes off. I was here with her finally, kissing in the morning light, her naked body cool and smooth against mine, our clothes strewn alongside the bed. 'I don't want to hurt you, Julia,' I said.

'As if,' she said. 'Come on, now, Ed. I've been waiting all summer for this. What took you so long?' She pulled me to her and gave a little laugh, which was quite unexpected, as if she really had been waiting.

'Me too,' I said and pushed against her until we bumped and slid together. 'Oh, Ed,' she said in my ear, so close it almost hurt. 'Please. Quick.' She let out a moan – as much to encourage me as anything. She said my name twice more and then I was holding on to her and it was over. What did I know, after all? Probably she was just acting like she always did, but I didn't care about that either. It was better than anyone had ever explained, fuller and more surprising and tender.

She sat up and pulled the eiderdown around her, coy again. 'That was good,' she said, as if we'd just shared an ice cream. 'That was your first time, wasn't it?'

'Course not,' I lied. 'Will you . . . you know, get into trouble?'

'Bit late to think of that,' she said. 'No. It's OK.' She reached down to pick her bag off the floor, lit a cigarette and took a deep drag and let it out again.

'It was good,' I said. A deep feeling of laziness came over me. I'd cracked it. That, actually, was it – the thing they talked about in pubs and secret places all over the world, the act that was referred to in jokes and on postcards and by winking comedians on the ends of piers. I'd joined their club, could look them in the eye. I understood.

'It was over with quick, though,' she said. 'Suppose I expected that.'

I tried to ignore her. It was a slight, of course.

'Wanna do it again, then?' I asked. She seemed to ponder the question.

'Would be nice.' She took another long drag, let the quilt slip a little lower, but nothing more than I'd seen at the outdoor baths. 'But let's save it for next time,' she said.

'There mightn't be a next time.'

'Why not?'

'It's finished, hasn't it – your season here? You'll all be going back soon to where you live – the real world.'

'Real world,' she said. 'Hah. That's a laugh.'

But this was our real world for now. Nothing was going to interrupt us. That was how it felt. No signs or sounds outside the windows, no threats of someone returning, fumbling around in the house downstairs. Nothing else mattered – apart from us – for that short time in the waxy light of the bedroom. It was going to be another hot day.

Julia sighed. 'I really like it in the morning.'

Now I was no longer a virgin I was permitted to make wisecracks about sex. 'You mean you like *it* – or you like it? I thought you were more of a night-time person. That's what I'd have thought about you.'

'No,' she said, staring off into a corner of the ceiling, high up where the plaster cornices met. She blew a perfect smoke ring and watched it bubble and break up.

'Who taught you to do that?'

'Dunno,' she said. 'Someone.'

I swung out of bed and pulled on my pants. I was restless and wanted to be on the move again. I sat on the stool near the dressing table and looked across at her, still propped on a pillow.

She said, 'You've got a good body.'

'Thanks,' I said. No one had ever told me that before. Not my mother or anyone else who was supposed to love me. It made me feel good to hear it from Julia. 'You have, too.'

'You don't need to give me the old crap. But thanks anyway. I like hearing it. I already know about my body, as it happens.'

'And you think I don't?'

She laughed again. 'It was Ray who taught me how to blow smoke rings. Right here, as a matter of fact.'

'I wish you hadn't told me that.'

I wondered if she missed Ray. Probably not. She only seemed to want someone to hold her and tell her how fabulous she was. It wasn't difficult – anyone could do it.

She said, 'Ray was good to be with. He'd do anything for me.'

She was lying. He liked her all right, but not in a deep or lasting way. She seemed to have forgotten he didn't always give her the attention she wanted and that they argued. She wrapped her arms round her knees, looked thoughtful.

I said, 'You've got things in common. I can see that.'

'Yeah. We've got the same sense of humour.'

'I was thinking how you both seem to live one day at a time.'

She said wistfully, 'That's the best way. Ray knew about life.'

It sounded like a criticism of me. I said, 'At least I'm a hard worker. Ray does nothing but skive.' I hadn't meant to badmouth Ray but I was annoyed at how she was singing his praises and wanted to stand up for myself.

'He was generous,' Julia went on. 'That was another good thing about him. Even when he only had a bit of money he'd share it with you. That's what I call generous. Did you know . . . ?' she hesitated.

'Did I know what?'

'Nothing.' But I could tell she'd been about to tell me something important.

'What, Julia?' She shook her head again.

I didn't know how to persuade Julia – or any woman for that matter – to do what I wanted. Another gap in my understanding. I considered bribery. Or perhaps it was a physical thing – like lovemaking.

So while she didn't expect it I walked across the room and pushed her back down on the bed. 'What are you doing?' But I didn't answer, just put all my weight on top of her, shoving her into the mattress. She tried to push me off, but I was heavier than her. I remembered the technique from those wrestling matches with Ray when we were younger. Spread your weight. She only had to say 'Submit', but she didn't know the game I was playing.

I meant it as horseplay, that was all. But she was thumping on my back in a desperate way, like she was trying to get out of a locked room. I rolled off her and she sat up. Her face was red. 'Twat,' she gasped. 'You could have killed me.'

And I realized that perhaps I could have. 'I'm sorry. God, Julia, I'm sorry. I didn't mean it.' I started to stroke her back and, surprisingly, she let me. But she didn't turn towards me.

'You aren't generous,' she said, 'that's for sure.'

'I know. What was it you were going to tell me?' My hand ran round her ribs and she shivered.

'Ray paid for your nan's trip to America.'

The room fell silent. Strange. No cars moving outside. No other noise in the house. I could have made love to her again then, at that very moment, in the shelter of the silence. 'No, he didn't,' I said. 'She found the money in the bottom of an ornament she got at the saleroom. That's how she paid for the trip. I was there when she found it. She wanted to give it back, but we persuaded her not to. She wouldn't have gone otherwise.'

'That's what Ray wanted you to think.'

'What are you talking about, Julia?'

'Ray broke the ornament, didn't he – not your nan?'

'It doesn't matter who broke it. I was there and I saw Nanny find the money.'

'Ed, you only saw her pick it out. It was Ray who put it

there. He took the cash and put it in among the broken bits. That's what he said – and for once I believe him. We were sitting right here when he told me.'

It was possible. I'd believed what I'd seen – but perhaps it was like one of Pete's cheap conjuring tricks, the sleight of hand, the mysterious disappearing matches, the game of Find the Lady. Watch my hands. Watch carefully. 'Why would he have done that?' I said. 'He could have given her the money if he was that bothered.'

'She wouldn't have taken it if she'd known it was borrowed, would she?'

'What? He borrowed three hundred quid to give to Nanny? Who'd be stupid enough to lend Ray that sort of money?'

'Who do you think? That big, ginger-haired lad at the slots – Codge. Apparently his great-uncle died and left him a load of money. Ray persuaded him to part with some of it.'

'Shit,' I said. 'And I suppose Ray couldn't pay him back.'

'Naturally.'

'So that's why Codge was round here looking for Ray. I thought it was something to do with business.'

Julia said, 'It was business in a way. Remember when Codge turned up at the baths and Ray disappeared?'

It was too obvious, inevitable. It angered me that I'd let it all pass me by and never thought to ask the right questions. 'Did Ray tell you all this?'

'Bit by bit. He was never good at keeping secrets, was he? Too generous to keep anything.' I didn't like the way she kept referring to Ray as if he was dead. She went on, 'I told him that would be his downfall. Codge was chasing him to get his money back. He's a big lad – he'd have killed Ray. Remember that tattoo on his knuckles?'

I nodded. 'But why are the police after him now?'

'I don't know, Ed. It's probably got something to do with those letters.'

'He didn't tell you?'

'I've only seen him once since that day at the baths.'

I felt sad at the thought of all these sacrifices. If it wasn't Vi, it was Ray. 'It shows how much he thinks of Nanny, doesn't it?' I said.

'Yeah.'

'He must have been listening all the time while she went on about Steven and New Jersey. I thought he wasn't taking any notice, but he was. We all knew how much it meant to her, but he was the only one who did anything.'

'Action's what counts, Ed,' she said. 'Not thinking about it.' She yawned, a delicious wide-mouthed yawn. 'Well, they'll catch up with him. They always do.'

'They might not,' I said, refusing to believe it. 'He could leave the country or something. He could stow away on a ship or get a job in the Merchant Navy. He might already have done that by now. No one'd know.'

'Maybe,' she said.

'You obviously don't care for him, Julia,' I said. 'Otherwise you wouldn't treat it so lightly. You'd do something about it.'

'Course I care about him. But there's nothing I can do now, is there? They'll catch him today.'

She sounded certain of it.

'Today? The police said that, too. What makes you so sure?'

'He'll want to see your nan off. They'll be there to catch him.'

I said, 'They don't know about nan, though. How could they?'

'Ed, they don't know for certain but they came here yesterday, didn't they? I was in and I could hear your nan blathering on about her trip to America and about how good Ray was and how she hoped he'd see her off. Your auntie tried to shush her up – the police were standing in the hall – but she just went on. Ray'll be there – if he knows about it, that is. He's soft enough.'

'Oh, God. He does know about it.'

'How?'

Then I told her how I'd met him and tried to persuade him to be there. She was right. Ray was too soft-hearted. He'd do anything for the people he cared about. I shivered despite the gathering heat of the day. It was the thought of Ray being arrested. They'd use handcuffs this time. He'd end up in Walton. Until this moment, even when the police had me pinned against a wall, I'd never thought of it as anything but an adventure. Ray was just a kid who got things wrong sometimes – sums and spelling and stealing. But now it was all out of control and there was no knowing where it would lead.

Julia yawned again, made a noise from the back of her throat, like a cat. She purred and lifted her arms as if she was stretching. She knew what she was doing. Her pink fingernails moved into little fists and the sheet she'd been so carefully holding in place dropped away to her waist, the way it had done for the so-called photographers. She said, 'Make love to me again now, Eddie. Come on.'

And, seeing her there all stretched out, it would have been as easy as anything. The word 'languid' came to mind, from where I don't know – it didn't sound like one of Myron Bloomfield's words. Perhaps it was in *Tit-Bits*. I thought of water flowing over a smooth stone, the tide drawing back from the lip of a rock pool to leave a stranded sea urchin. She said, 'Make love to me,' and I wanted to. I couldn't remember ever having wanted to do anything more, except for making love to her the first time, but now a bit of me was thinking about Ray and how he'd be wanting to see Nanny off. I could almost see him step out of the shadows of some warehouse on the Pier Head, like Harry Lime again, only this time the police would be putting him in handcuffs before he had chance to get anywhere near the ship.

'I can't,' I said. I was standing there in two minds, dawdling between choices, half-dressed and thinking of her. But there was another pull like the tide coming in, sucking at the mud under my feet and making it quake.

'That's what I thought,' she said.

'I don't mean I couldn't, Julia. I mean I won't,' I said.

I was trying to remember the ship's time of departure. I knew they'd said they were going to be early because Nanny was agitated and wanted to have a look round. But how early? I wasn't sure. Twelve-thirty came to mind, but was that when the ship was due to leave or when they could go on board?

I began putting my clothes back on. Because in the end none of it mattered – or else it all mattered equally – which meant that all I was left with was a sense of what I ought to do. It was clearer than anything had ever been before. Julia was right. It was action that counted, not words. It was simple.

'Where the hell are you going?' she said.

'The Pier Head. Sorry. I need to tell Ray.'

'You'll be too late.'

'I've got to try, though.'

'Come on, Eddie. They're gonna get him sooner or later. It's obvious. Grow up.'

I paused, mid-button. 'I think I have grown up. Maybe you're right and they will catch him.'

'Well, then . . .'

'But not if it's anything to do with me.'

'It's aiding and abetting.' She looked so tempting lying there. 'Anyway, he's got it coming to him. He'd probably say the same himself.'

She could say some cold, callous things. By now I was dressed and my heart was already outside. I'd loved her briefly and perhaps that was the best way. I said, 'Thanks, Julia, but I'm going. Do you wanna come with me?'

She shook her head and stood up, holding the rough blanket round her as she reached for her ciggies. She said, 'Just bloody well go, then.'

So I did.

19

I realized I had no plan, no idea of what I was going to do next. I ran back up to the bedroom and took the envelope from the zip-up compartment in my suitcase with the money my mum had been sending. I took out ten pounds in pound and ten-bob notes – the whole lot – and put it in my back pocket. It made me feel incredibly rich.

By the time I got downstairs I was already running, though I still didn't have any idea what I was going to do. The New Brighton ferries were unpredictable, especially when the tide was low. Then I remembered Ray's bike in the back yard and I went and pulled the tarpaulin off it in a shower of dirty rainwater. Nobody had used it for months. The chain was completely dried up, but it looked reasonable otherwise. I tried the brakes, pumped at the tyres a few times with the rusty pump and set off down the alley, across the glassy bombsite and along the seafront as fast as the bike would go. As I reached the pier the New Brighton ferry was just pulling out, overflowing with passengers. I'd have to go on to Seacombe. I steered along the seafront, swerving in and out of the knots of strolling holidaymakers – kids struggling to stay on their roller skates, women with annoying little dogs on leads. The bell on the handlebars made a dull, throttled noise.

At Seacombe I left the bike leaning against the railings, bought a ticket and dashed down the floating tunnel just before they pulled the gangplank away. Even from here, across the water, the liners could be seen on the landing stages and further back in the docks – decks dazzling white in the sun, lines of red and black funnels.

I sat outside on the ferry bench seats and felt the river move under me. There was the familiar stink of fuel and the churning noise of the engine. Seagulls sat on the rails and stared at me. They took off occasionally, fought over some scrap of food and landed again.

Once ashore in Liverpool I got a cold shiver of panic. I hadn't been here since the night of the Rodcoopers' show. I didn't know where anything was. It was a city – bewildering and bustling. There was the unmistakable Liver Building with the birds on top that looked as if they were tied in place to stop them taking flight. But the other buildings looked confusingly similar – huge glazed entrances, walls of massive stones with carved corners, statues, important-looking offices. This was how I'd always imagined New York. But, of course, that was the idea – two sea-going cities mirroring one another across the Atlantic, both built for welcome and departure.

All I could remember about Nanny's arrangements was the name of the ship – *Sylvania*. I spoke to one of the ferrymen and he directed me along the river front. 'Prince's Landing Stage,' he said. 'That's it – there,' and although it was still a good distance away the bulk of the ship was clear and beautiful, as if everything was drawn to that spot – every railway line, road and river. No wonder we'd looked at the liners from the other side of the river with such awe. No wonder Nanny thought it was the only way to get to America. Everything else was shabby by comparison. The hull, red near the water and black higher up, towered above the landing stage. Water poured from the anchor point. High up on the stern in white letters so there could be no mistake was the name SYLVANIA and under it

LIVERPOOL. Above that were dazzling white decks, a row of lifeboats and, highest of all, a single swept-back Cunard funnel, red with a black top. The *Sylvania* sat there, the centre of attention, waiting for the tide.

The salty smell of the sea was mixed with smoke and engines. This close to the ship I smelled paint and hot metal, too. Three tugs with single tall funnels were moored alongside. It was so thrilling that I didn't want to leave. Finally I asked an official in dark uniform what time passengers could go on board. 'Tourist or First Class?' I didn't know. 'Tourist, twelve-thirty till two; First Class two till four. Sailing at five.'

It was coming up to twelve-thirty. Travellers were already arriving with their bags, labelled suitcases and families to see them off. I was sure Nanny and Vi wouldn't be far behind. Nanny would want to be one of the first on board, if I knew her. Then Ray would appear and he'd be dragged away.

A couple of uniformed policemen stood conspicuously at the top of the walkways. They probably had a description of Ray in their minds or tucked in their pocket books. They strolled up and down and chatted. I didn't want to be afraid of them, but I was. I avoided their eyes, hoping I didn't appear too out of place.

At least it didn't look as if anybody had gone on board yet, though crowds were gathering as I stood waiting. If I stayed here I wouldn't be able to warn Ray, but I didn't know which direction he'd be coming from. I wasn't even sure he'd be coming at all. But the longer I stood the more likely it was that Ray would turn up. I realized I had to do something. There was nobody else who could.

The advice at times like this was to stay in one place and not move around. That was the most sensible course of action – the one with the best chance of finding the person you were searching for and it was true that if I waited long enough Vi and Nan and maybe even Ray would all turn up sooner or later. But that was what the police were banking on, too. That's why they were standing there.

So I started walking back the way I'd come from the ferry. I didn't know which direction Ray was going to come from, but I owed him my best effort. There was an access road at a higher level and I went up and stood there, looking down for him amid the crowds flocking towards the ships. It felt hopeless and rather stupid.

Then I saw him. He was in the middle of the crowd heading for the *Sylvania*. He had his head down and his hands in his pockets. He looked the same, though his hair had grown longer. I called out to him, but either he didn't hear or he chose not to.

I dashed back down the stone stairs to cut him off, but there were too many people with cases and trolleys trying to get the same way and Ray was walking quickly. I lost sight of him. Then he was there again. I dodged through the crowds, managed eventually to get in front and tried to bar his way. 'Ray.' But he was concentrating so hard and was so keen not to be noticed he stepped round me, head down. I grabbed his arm. 'Ray! It's me.' He stopped and blinked, as if he'd just woken up.

'Ed?'

'Yeah. It's me.'

'Where's Nan? Has something happened?'

'No, they're fine. But the police are there. They'll be waiting. There's been all sorts of trouble.'

He seemed resigned to the trouble, as if it was always going to find him. 'Why are you dressed like that?' I was still wearing my bottle-green shirt and sleeveless pullover.

'It's a long story.'

'I gotta get to the ship,' he said. 'Nan wanted me to see her off, didn't she?' His skin looked sallow, with an almost greenish tinge. 'I mightn't ever see her again.'

'Course you will. She'll be coming back. But you might not see her anyway. If you carry on you'll be arrested before you get anywhere near the ship.'

'You wanted me to come, Ed. Didn't you think of that, then?'

'I didn't know,' I said. 'Honest. That's why I've come over now – to warn you. Julia told me about the money. I wanted you to know. It was a good thing you did.'

'They'll let me say goodbye to her first anyway, won't they? After that I don't care what happens. I'm tired of hiding in people's front rooms and sheds and not being able to go out in the day.'

I said, 'Nan would love to see you before she goes. You're her favourite.'

'Don't know why. All I've ever done is hang around.'

'That's the point. You've taken her to the pictures and the wrestling and you've talked to her, which is a lot more than some people have ever done.'

'Well . . .' He seemed lost for words. 'Where are they anyway?'

That was the problem. I didn't know. There wasn't time to tell him the whole story and besides it wouldn't have made any difference. 'Vi mentioned something about them having dinner before they got on board. Nan had this fantasy about dinner with the captain.'

'Yeah. Lobster thermidor. I know.'

'But I've no idea where they'll be.' Crowds were surging past us. If the police were expecting him to be there it would only be a matter of time before one of them recognized him. I felt conspicuous there with him, his guilt as obvious as new paint. Maybe the police would expect him to be alone, so me being with him might help.

'They can't be far,' he said. 'They've got all the luggage with them, haven't they?' I nodded. He stopped. 'I bet I know –'

'Where?'

He was already walking. 'It's a restaurant place – not far. Nan and me came over to Liverpool on one of our days out and she saw it and said that's where she'd like to eat. They do posh stuff like lobster – they've even got tablecloths. This way, quick.'

It was the sort of place where I imagined sea captains and rich passengers would dine before the voyage, with a window overlooking the river. We walked round the terrace but couldn't see them, so I went in, leaving Ray outside. I didn't mind making myself look stupid.

'Can I help you, sir?' a waiter asked pointedly. There was a fish tank full of live lobsters in the entrance area. They climbed over one another and clawed at the sides, slow and desperate.

'I'm looking for someone,' I said.

'Anyone in particular, sir?' I didn't like the way he said 'sir'. I scanned the tables, hoping to see Nanny and Vi. They weren't there.

'It's fine,' I said. 'We'll take our custom elsewhere.'

Ray looked downcast and pushed his hands further into his pockets when I told him. 'Sorry, Ray,' I said.

'Let's go back to the ship. At least we know they'll be there some time.'

It wasn't like him to accept situations without a fight. Before, nothing would have made him give up. I said, 'Julia sends her love.'

He brightened. 'That's good, that is. And how far did you get with her? I hope you got her into bed finally.'

I shook my head. 'She wouldn't.' I wasn't sure whether he believed me or not, but it seemed a lie worth telling just now. 'She likes you too much,' I said, and he laughed. It was good to hear him laugh again.

We looked at one another, Ray and me, and I could see him scanning for police or for anyone in authority. I was sorry it'd turned out this way. 'What did you do, Ray – for them to be after you like this?' He shrugged. 'I mean, it wasn't for taking coppers out of the machines, was it?'

'Questions,' he said. 'It's still always questions with you. When are you gonna learn?'

Next to the posh restaurant was a much smaller, grimy tea room with steamed-up windows and plastic tables. 'Look,' I said. There were Nanny and Vi sitting at a table near the back. They looked sad, as if they'd nothing left to say to one another. 'Come on!'

'You go in first,' Ray said. 'It might be a trap.'

'God, you make everything sound so dramatic. They only do that in the films.'

'Don't you believe it. You can't be too careful, believe me. There could be a gun.'

So I went in. I could tell by Nanny's face when she saw me that she wished I was Ray. It didn't matter. I knew she loved him and I couldn't blame her.

Vi said, 'Eddie? What are you doing here? I thought you were poorly – but you're all poshed up.'

I looked around. The place was full – couples, families, people on the move, absorbed with their own stories. Nobody lurked suspiciously behind a newspaper. 'There's someone here to see you,' I said, and I waved at Ray outside the window and he lumbered in and stood there, not knowing what to do or say. Nanny got up and gave him a hug. She was wearing her best light blue coat and hat, with a big flower brooch.

'Oh, Ray, I knew you'd come if you could,' she said. 'Thanks for bringing him, Eddie.' She was crying.

'It's OK, Nan.'

I could tell Ray was glad to be here, but he pulled

himself away from her and said, 'It's all right, Nan. Don't make such a fuss. You'll only be gone a couple of months. You'll be back again before you know it.'

'But it's such a long way, love,' Nanny said. 'I'm glad you've come to see me off. I'm so pleased to see you.'

Vi said, 'God, Ray, where've you been? You look dreadful.'

'Thanks, Mum.' She was right, though. In this crowded space I could see him close up. His cheeks had got bonier. He looked like he hadn't eaten for days and he hadn't shaved properly.

'What the hell have you been up to? The police have been looking for you.'

'Nothing much,' he said. 'They probably want to ask me some questions, that's all.'

'About what?'

'I had a bit of trouble on the post job – so I left.'

'There's more to it than that. Come on, I wasn't born yesterday,' Vi said.

He shrugged. 'And I had a job at a petrol station. Some money went missing. They think I had something to do with it.'

'And I suppose you didn't?'

'Course not.' But I could tell she knew he was lying again.

'Oh, Ray. For God's sake. What's the matter with you? What did I do wrong?'

'Nothing,' he said. 'You never did anything wrong. Stop blaming yourself, Mother. It's me, not you.'

We were all quiet for a while then Vi looked at her watch. 'We should go. They'll be boarding now.'

'Come and wave me off,' Nanny said.

Ray and me looked at one another. 'I can't,' Ray said. 'You'll have to go without me.' Now that he'd seen Nan and I'd told him about Julia his will for survival had returned.

'I was looking forward to you being there,' Nanny said. 'This isn't a proper farewell in this grotty café. You'll be OK at the landing stage; the police might not be there.'

'They are,' I said.

'You should face the music,' Vi said. 'You'll have to at some point.'

I couldn't imagine Ray in prison. It didn't seem right. He was my older cousin, after all – funny and daring and kind – and not cut out to be a jailbird.

Nanny said, 'I want to spend some time with Ray. Let's stay here for a bit.'

'You'll miss the damn ship, Mother,' Vi said. 'This is what you've been building up to for years – now you'd rather stay in the caff a few more minutes.'

'There's time,' Nanny said. 'The ship's not going to sail till five.'

'But everybody's got to get on board, Mother.' There was a touch of panic in Vi's voice. But we stayed and Nan ordered more sandwiches and crisps. For me she ordered cream soda and for Ray, without asking him, a bottle of Worthington.

The sandwiches were dry, but we pretended they were just as good as any meal with the captain. 'All that fancy stuff is bad for the stomach,' Nanny said. 'Specially before a long voyage.'

'It'd all end up over the side,' Ray said.

'I don't like lobster thermidor anyway,' Nanny said.

'Mother, you've never had it. How do you know you don't like it?'

'They put them live into the boiling water. You can hear them scream, you know.'

Ray looked at his sandwich. 'I think I can hear this bread screaming.'

'Yeah, it's screaming out for some butter,' Vi said and

we all laughed. I noticed that through all this Nanny was holding Ray's hand. He didn't pull it away.

Then it really was time for us to go. 'Quarter to bloody two,' Vi said. 'It'll be too late. They'll be shutting the doors.'

'It's all right, Mother,' Ray said, then he got up and went to the toilet.

There was a man coming through the door. He walked across to us. He wasn't in uniform, but I knew straight away he was a bobby from his short hair and dark clothes. He stood over us and launched straight into the speech. 'Raymond Bartlett, I'm arresting you . . .' He was looking directly at me.

'I'm not Ray,' I started. 'I told those other blokes.'

Nan had gone blank again. It was sudden, like a blind being drawn down. 'Oh, Ray,' she said to me. 'What've you done now?'

'Nan! It's me. Eddie,' I protested, and off the bobby started again. He would have taken me away if Vi hadn't intervened and I wasn't sure whether Nanny had said that on purpose to give Ray a moment more freedom or whether she really had got us mixed up again.

Everybody in the café was staring now. It had gone completely silent apart from the steam machine rasping away behind the counter. 'This is my nephew,' Vi said. 'Now we've got a ship to catch. There really isn't time for all this.'

'Where's Raymond Bartlett, then?' the bobby demanded. Nanny looked straight ahead, but Vi and me both glanced at the toilet, because we really couldn't help it. The bobby rushed into the toilet and we expected him to come out dragging Ray by the scruff of the neck but he didn't. Instead he came out empty-handed. 'Gone!' he said. 'Somebody must have warned him. The window's open.'

'Well, it wasn't us,' Nanny said with a touch of triumph. And it was true. Instinct was what I put it down to – the same instinct Ray used to avoid Vi in the amusements and

Codge in the outdoor baths – either that or luck or split-second timing or trickery. It didn't matter what you called it.

'Which ship?' the bobby asked. He was annoyed that Ray had given him the slip.

'*Sylvania*,' Vi told him.

'Come on, then,' he said grudgingly. 'Or you're going to be late.'

The four of us – Nanny, Vi, the bobby and me – walked back to Prince's Landing Stage with Nanny's luggage shared between us. Even the bobby carried a little attaché case, very obliging because he thought he might still get hold of Ray. Nanny wasn't so fast on her feet, but time was getting on and we couldn't go slow enough for her. 'Don't dawdle on my account. You go ahead – don't let them go without me.'

'It's not the number six bus, Mother,' Vi said. 'They'll leave when they have to, whether you're on it or not.'

'The things I do . . .' the bobby muttered.

By the time we got back it was close to two o'clock when the First Class passengers were due on board. The waiting area was starting to fill again with travellers and luggage. These would be the film stars, I thought, the models and business people and politicians. Julia would have loved it. She'd have spoken to them, told them all about herself, made a deal.

'You're cutting it a bit fine,' the officer at the desk said, looking us over, checking Nan's passport. He put her luggage on a trolley. 'Stateroom' was labelled on the suitcase. It sounded grand and official. For a moment I envied her.

Behind us was the huge roof of Riverside train station. In front were the gangways and the ships. He nodded us through. Vi and me had passes to see Nanny off. The bobby hung around, hoping to catch Ray heading for the ship.

'He won't be that stupid,' Nanny said. I wasn't sure even now. Anything was possible with Ray.

'We'll catch up with him, you know,' the bobby said. He left us there.

Then we were clack-clacking down the wooden floor of a tunnel that led to the landing stage. We stared up at the *Sylvania*'s towering dark hull. 'That'll never float,' Vi said, trying to make light of it.

Nanny could only manage an 'Ooh!' She'd been working her way towards this moment. The *Sylvania* was beautiful, huge as a five-storey building, bristling with masts and rigging and rows of lifeboats. It was going to be Nan's home for the next nine days. A double door was open in the hull, a gangway leading direct from the landing stage deep inside the ship.

'This is it,' Nanny said and set off first because there was nothing else for it – the last of Liverpool. She was probably thinking about her beloved Steve who'd taken these same steps fourteen years earlier.

We followed the other passengers into an embarkation lobby deep inside the ship. The light from electric lights in the ceiling was dim. Families stood together waiting to be shown to their rooms. Youngsters dashed around exploring corridors or disappeared to find the best views. Parents kissed their children and men in neat white coats hurried between them all.

Eventually one of the stewards announced Nanny's name. 'This way, please, madam.'

We followed him down silent, panelled corridors. He often had to stop to allow Nanny to catch up. 'How will I ever find this again?' she asked.

He seemed busy and distracted. 'You'll soon get used to it. It is rather confusing at first.'

'I'll need a ruddy map.'

'There'll be instructions in your room, madam.'

At last he pushed open a door and ushered us inside. It had the same wooden panelling as the endless corridors and no windows, just dim, comfortable lighting. 'It's a bit ruddy small,' Vi said. 'Hardly room to swing a cat.'

Nanny didn't seem to mind. 'I won't be spending much time in here anyway,' she said. 'And look – there's a place for everything.' She folded down a desk flap, opened a neat wardrobe.

'It's nice,' I said. The tables had little lips to stop things falling off in rough weather. 'It's a proper cabin.'

'Not a cabin, Ed,' Nanny insisted. 'It's a Stateroom.'

'Oh, look, Mother,' Vi said. 'Writing paper with the ship's name and everything. Write to us, won't you – then I can show Mrs Morris.'

'Of course I will. I'll write when I get there as well.'

'Give our love to Steve.'

Nanny said, 'It doesn't seem possible, does it, being here? I never thought I'd see him again. If we hadn't found that money . . .'

'You mustn't think of it like that,' Vi said.

The luggage came. There was still a while before the ship was due to put to sea so I left them to it and found my way onto one of the outside decks. I leaned on the railing and looked out at Liverpool like a real voyager, but knowing it wasn't me who was travelling. I wondered where Ray would be now – halfway home on a ferry, with a mate in some Liverpool pub or waiting on the landing stage until he'd seen Nan's ship safely over the horizon.

By the time I found my way back they'd fallen into silence, just waiting, throwing out bits of conversation as if, in her heart, Nan had already left. Her mind was on the voyage now – on the encounters to come, the friends yet to be made, the nights at sea.

'Do you know where your tablets are?' Vi asked. She'd arranged them for her on the little bedside table where she wouldn't forget them and had written a note to remind her which ones to take.

At last there was a gonging in the corridor. It passed our door and faded away. Then there was a huge blast on the ship's whistle – so loud it shook the cabin.

'Time to go,' Nan said. There was a touch of relief in her voice.

The embarkation lobby was full now of families saying their goodbyes. Nan kissed me, then Vi. I could feel the pale bristles of her chin long after she'd finished hugging me. 'Have a wonderful time, Mother,' Vi was saying. 'Come home safe.'

'I will,' she said. She wanted us to go then, so Vi and me trudged back up the corridor and onto the gangway.

We stood on the pier with a few officials in uniform and families who'd been seeing their loved ones off. Everyone was quiet. We watched as the ship pulled out, slow and vast, dwarfing the tugs. The funnel started pouring out dark smoke, then there were two more enormous blasts on the whistle. They split the air and made me shake deep down. Vi felt it, too. I could tell.

Tonight the liner would be another of those sets of lights at sea – like the ones Nan had seen from the prom and pined over. I pictured the *Sylvania* entering New York harbour in a dash of ships and yachts and tugs, with Nanny on deck taking it all in.

The ship turned slowly in the river, pushed and pulled by the tugs to face the Atlantic. At first we could make out the faces. 'There she is,' Vi said, pointing to the upper deck, but I couldn't see her. We waved just in case. In the end the crowd on board was just a colourful blur. We stood until the ship looked quite thin, a dark ghost on the horizon with a smudge of smoke above it. Then there was only the smell of the sea and the space where the liner had been. We turned away.

'Thank God that's over,' Vi said. 'Now we can get back to normal.' But she didn't mean it. It was just her way of marking the end of something, of putting a full stop there, which allowed her to get on with other things.

On the way back on the ferry she didn't say anything. She sat and looked at the seagulls wheeling overhead and watched the brown-green-grey surge of the Mersey gurgling beneath us.

20

The following Wednesday Vi heard that Ray had been arrested. She shook her head when the bobby told her. They were sitting in the kitchen and it was as if they were just a couple of neighbours sharing gossip, because Vi had been expecting it. 'Police,' I'd heard him say when he came to the door, and Vi just let him straight in like they were old mates.

While they were talking I couldn't help noticing the bamboo stick still in the corner by the fireplace and I wondered if Vi would leave it there to gather dust. If it was up to Ray I knew what he'd do – shove it in the Baxi. He'd have broken it up with his bare hands or maybe chopped it up in the coal shed. I just couldn't help imagining Ray in front of the fire, unlatching the door with the poker and pushing the bits of broken stick inside. He would have watched it as it burned. He loved to mess around in the Baxi like that.

The bobby was telling Vi what had happened. Ray had left Palace Amusements under a cloud. Well, Julia and me already knew that, but Vi obviously didn't. Luckily for him, the bobby said, the manager at the Palace didn't want to press charges, so it wouldn't go any further. After that Ray worked on the post. There were no problems there as far as the bobby knew. He obviously hadn't heard about the missing post yet. Perhaps not enough people had reported their birthday cards missing for the authorities to make the connection; perhaps those kids hadn't told anyone about the letters in the sand, after all. Maybe they'd buried them again like secret treasure.

'The early hours were what defeated him there,' Vi said. 'He was never one for getting up early.'

'Kids of today,' the bobby said. 'I've got two lads myself. All they're interested in is pop music. There's a lot of temptation about. They should bring back conscription.'

Then, the bobby said, Ray had got a job at a garage. None of us knew about that, but I'd had my suspicions. It explained the oily shoes. 'Yeah, the Shell garage on Chester Road. He seemed to be doing well there – he got on with the customers. The bloke who owned it let Ray work the late shift on his own. That was a big mistake.'

The bobby shrugged and fiddled with the button of his top pocket. 'Temptation,' he said, 'and circumstances. Wicked combination.' Vi nodded as if she understood exactly what he was talking about. 'Seems he owed someone quite a bit of money – and that person wanted it back. In fact, that person was getting quite impatient if you know what I mean. So, it appears . . .'

He was telling it like something out of Vi's Sunday night *Armchair Theatre* presentation, like it was a story. But it wasn't. It was my cousin Ray he was talking about.

'So?' Vi said.

'So he had to find a way to get the money, and quick. He staged a robbery.'

'When?' Vi said. 'I never heard about that.'

'It was in the paper when it happened last week. His version of events wasn't too convincing, I can tell you.' Vi nodded because that wasn't difficult to imagine either.

The bobby described how Ray had phoned the police at about eleven o'clock telling them he'd been held up at knifepoint and had been forced to hand over cash from the till.

The police went straight out there. They were suspicious from the start. Although there were signs something had happened – a light fitting was damaged, a piece of glass in the kiosk door was broken and the floor was littered with sweets and cigarettes from the shelves – Ray was surprisingly calm. In addition, they couldn't work out how the robbers had forced their way in. Then Ray told them two lads had run off towards Birkenhead, but in the next breath he was talking about a car. 'What sort of car?' they asked. He didn't know. 'Well, what colour?' It was dark, he hadn't seen.

They asked him if he wanted a lift home; he declined. Something didn't add up. They should have taken him straight down the station, but they didn't. By the next day, when the garage owner got back from holiday and they'd had chance to talk to him, Ray's story was looking decidedly shaky. 'He had us fooled for about twenty minutes,' the bobby said.

'That'd be Ray,' Vi said.

'Then he went missing.'

'God,' Vi said. 'So that's why we haven't seen him.'

'It was a toss up between us and the garage owner as to who'd get to him first. Luckily it was us – otherwise we'd have had a GBH case on our hands.'

'How much did he take?' I asked.

'It's nothing to do with you,' Vi said. 'I always said he was a thieving little sod.'

'Around three hundred quid we think. Quite a lot was left in the till. That made us suspicious, too,' the bobby said. 'We don't know yet why he'd borrowed that much in the first place, though. Did he gamble?'

'A bit,' Vi said. 'But I didn't think it was anything to worry about.'

'Or drink? Did he have a problem there, do you think?'

It was awful to hear them running Ray down as easily as that. I couldn't let them get away with it. I took a deep breath and said, 'He gave the three hundred quid to Nan so she could go to America. That's why he borrowed it.' They both looked at me as if it was my fault. For a moment neither of them said anything.

'He couldn't have,' Vi said.

'Well, he did.' I told them about how Ray had borrowed the money off Codge and put it in the ornament for Nanny to find. I thought it would be good for Vi to appreciate there might be more to him than she realized. I knew he was her son and all that, but sometimes you could get too close to people and you didn't see them properly.

'Interesting,' the bobby said. 'That'll all come out in due course I dare say. It might be mitigation. But it's beside the point. The point is he took the money. He admitted it straight away once we confronted him with the facts.'

'Hmm,' Vi said. 'S'pose you're right. That is the point really.'

I was glad I'd said it, though, because it had made her think, and she'd need all those good thoughts for when she had to visit him in Walton or wherever he ended up. He might be a thieving little sod, but he wasn't rotten to the core. I wanted to make sure she understood that.

'And to think I never knew all this was going on,' Vi said.

'Why should you? He ran away from home of his own free will. In the end he's responsible for his own actions,' the bobby said.

'Not that responsible,' Vi said. 'He's a stupid bloody fool.'

'If he pleads guilty he could be back home in six months. Why don't you come down the station now?' the bobby said. 'He's probably got some explaining to do.'

'Yeah,' Vi said in a high, squeaky voice. She started crying. Not noisily, but her face kind of changed shape and her mouth went all wobbly around her chin. The bobby looked at me as if I should do something, so I went and sat on the edge of the settee and put my arm round her. She let me. Her dress smelled of ciggie smoke and cabbage.

The next day the Rodcoopers went home. They'd managed to last to the end of their season, but only just.

Brenda told me that Alastair had signed up with them for another year, though she'd never expected him to. She said, 'He'll be here for life now. That's the way it gets you, you know, Eddie.' I couldn't remember her ever calling me by my name before.

The bedrooms were cleared and the bags were in the hall once again and because there was nowhere else for us to go Julia and me sat on the wall outside. She let her leg rub against mine almost by accident and pretended she hadn't noticed.

'It's been all right this summer,' she said without looking at me. That was quite a concession from her, but I didn't press the point. 'Will you tell Ray I'm sorry about what happened?' I nodded. 'He's too good for this place, if you ask me. Tell him that as well. I really liked him. He's a good laugh. That's important as far as I'm concerned – that he's a laugh.'

'Yeah,' I said. 'Do you want my phone number, Julia? I could come down to Sussex to see you if you like.'

'I've already got it, haven't I?'

'No, not the number here. I don't live here, don't forget. I could give you my phone number at home in Derbyshire. Do you want my address?'

'I'm not much of a letter writer.'

We fell silent for a while.

'You're going to be a great model,' I told her.

'You're full of bull,' she said.

'No, I mean it. You know how to get what you want – and you're dead attractive. Honest. You've got what it takes. That's what I think.'

'You're just the same as the rest of them, Eddie. Say something nice and see what you can get.'

'Except I mean it. That's how I'm different.'

There was another pause and she was looking around as if she was bored, looking for something to fill the silence. She didn't like gaps and vacuums. She had to fill them up, just like all the other Rodcoopers, even Alastair.

'Come on,' she said. She led me to the little cupboard under the stairs, still full of coats and ironing. At the back was a shelf of biscuit tins which rattled as she leaned into me. She kissed me hard and took my hand and put it on the line of dimply skin above her knee. She stopped and looked at me. 'This is so you won't forget me,' she said.

'I won't do that. I won't forget you.'

I kissed her again and moved my hand gently, following the crease of her thigh like a contour line, and at that exact moment the phone rang next to her ear, a long rattle that made us jump. She picked it up before it went a second time. 'Wrong number,' she told it, and smiled at me. Tiny bits of light found their way into the cupboard. Her smell reminded me of a nature table at school – apples on the turn, acorns – but as well as that there was the scent of coats thrown in after a rain shower and of dried peas.

The cupboard had been her idea, but already she was looking for an excuse not to stay. The phone was one. Then we heard Brenda calling. 'Julia? Where are you now? Where is that girl? Julia – the taxi's here.'

'Better go,' she whispered. 'Wait here, Eddie, until the coast's clear.'

By the time I came out she was in the back of the taxi. She pretended not to look at me. Perhaps she preferred not to. She was squashed in between her mother and a pile of luggage. Alastair was in the front, Maisie and Irene were in the other taxi, waving. Julia had the same set look on her face that I remembered from when she'd first arrived –

as if life surrounded by these people might all be too much trouble.

'Everybody's leaving me,' Vi said desperately after the taxis had gone. Without the Rodcoopers the house was quiet. There were beds to be stripped and sheets to be washed. Neither of us felt like doing any work.

'I'll be here for a bit longer,' I said. 'You'll be glad to see the back of me when I go.'

'No. You've been a help. Your mum's the same – always being useful, always being put upon. You wanna watch that, Eddie. It's a bad habit to get into. You'll end up like me – not helping yourself.'

She didn't mention Julia. I wasn't sure whether she knew about us or whether she took it for granted, the things we young ones got up to, and thought it was just too vulgar to talk about. But the mention of my mother made me realize it was time I should be going after all.

I said, 'And before you know it Nanny'll be back. Do you think she'll bring presents home from America?'

'I expect so. Specially if there are any salerooms over there.' We laughed. I loved the way Vi laughed. It started wheezy in her chest and she held it there till she couldn't hold it any longer and her shoulders shook with it. Her face seemed surprised the rest of her had found anything amusing, then it couldn't help joining in. Her eyes were the best. They enjoyed it most because they were last in on the joke.

My mother phoned. She sounded confused. Someone had told her it was the wrong number so she'd thought there was something going on at Vi's. I said not to worry; it was probably just one of the guests messing around. High spirits at the end of the season.

It wasn't fair on Vi to leave me there any longer and there was school to think of, she said. They were on their way down from Scotland to collect me.

I said, 'There's a lot to tell you about.'

'Good,' she said. 'Did Nanny get away OK?'

'Yes – but Ray didn't.'

'What d'you mean?' I tried telling her that Vi would explain later, but she insisted on knowing, because it was obvious that something significant had happened. 'Put Vi on,' she said. 'Now, Ed.'

So I called Vi. 'She wants to know about Ray,' I said and handed her the phone.

Strange how, when they arrived, they looked as if they'd never been away. Mum wore the dress she'd made on the Singer from a tissue pattern, Dad had on his brown trousers and checked cap. They both had a confident air about them, as if now they'd managed to sort Grandad out nothing would be beyond them again, but I knew they just wanted life to get back to normal.

There was a lot of talk about Ray. Dad offered to pay for bail, but Vi didn't think it was possible. Mum and Vi had a little weep together in the kitchen when they thought nobody was looking. After that they were quite cheerful. Mum and Dad had found Grandad a place in a home outside Aberdeen. Apparently it had been built for a paint magnate and then converted into an old people's home with self-contained rooms. Grandad had been lucky to get a place because they tended to fill up so quickly. Foxlands, it was called.

Dad told me how that first evening when they'd taken Grandad for a look round, they'd seen a young fox in the grounds. It had stood watching them curiously and not in the least afraid. In the end it had turned and trotted away into the thicket at the boundary of Foxlands. Grandad decided that the fox was a good omen, even though in the past he'd pooh-poohed Mum for the way she touched wood and refused to walk under ladders. His room had its own door onto the garden. There was even a doctor on call if any of the residents needed it. The home wasn't perfect, Dad said. Grandad was still a long way away – but he was happy with how it was working out.

I'd expected them to have been changed by their difficulties with Grandad, but they seemed exactly the same, at least outwardly. I hoped the summer hadn't left me unchanged. A badge or a tattoo to mark me out as a man would have done it, a small medal perhaps. There ought to be some way to show that I'd experienced more than can be learned from the pages of a book.

Mum handed Vi an envelope with money in it – for looking after me – and Vi said, 'Thanks, Beryl. You shouldn't have.'

'Well, I couldn't let you struggle,' Mum said, 'and I expect you could do with it.'

Vi put the envelope on the mantelpiece. She probably thought that, what with Ray not being there now, it was safe to leave cash lying around in envelopes.

They stayed a couple of nights in the front bedroom where Brenda and Julia had been, while Vi got the house back into some semblance of order.

'She's a funny one,' I overheard Mum saying to Dad, meaning Vi, her own sister. I wondered how it happened, how they could have turned out so different from one another. When he wasn't given bail, the three of them went to see Ray, but I wasn't allowed to go. I was glad.

I left my packing until the Saturday morning we were due to leave. There wasn't much to do. In fact, I was surprised I'd managed to survive the summer with so little. I looked around the bedroom. Ray's Airfix models of Spitfires and Hurricanes were still hanging from the ceiling, and his piles of *Victor* comics and *Mad* magazines were on the floor between the beds. He was such a kid, no matter how hard he pretended to be cool and worldly-wise.

I crammed my clothes into my holdall, not bothering to fold anything. Then, while my dad was checking the car over and my mum was saying her endless goodbyes to Vi, I went for a last walk along the seafront. In a couple of days I'd be starting sixth form.

I sat in a shelter near the bottom of Vicky Road – the same one I'd left Julia in while I fetched her suitcase that night – and thought about her. By now she'd be at home with Brenda, still yearning to become a model. She'd do it some day. I'd come across a photo of her in the papers or in a glossy magazine. Miss Julia Vernon. She'd be on the arm of a professional footballer or a pop star, wearing something outrageous and I'd be able to say I knew her once. More than knew her.

New Brighton was quieter now summer was coming to an end. Dredgers clanked in the Mersey. A cargo ship edged past Fort Perch Rock and the lighthouse and on towards where the shelter of land ended and the sea turned stormy as it stretched out towards Ireland and the Atlantic.

The donkey man was reduced to just one donkey trudging back and forth next to the pier. The girls had taken to wearing sweaters. Most of them seemed to be in a hurry to get somewhere, though I couldn't imagine where.

I gulped the raw sea air. If only I could keep a salty trace of it in my lungs I'd be able to feel that this whole summer had worked its way into me. Then I'd know the memory of it would be lodged in my bones until I could come back.

A girl walking past caught my eye. She turned and smiled and I smiled back. It was there again – that sense of excitement and possibility. Lust. I recognized it now. She paused as if she might say something, but carried on along the seafront. I didn't regret it – there'd be other opportunities. Today there wasn't time for more than a glance and a smile.

I stood up and headed back to Vi's, ready for home.

About the Author

JEFF PHELPS was born in New Brighton. His stories and poetry have been widely published, notably in *London Magazine*, and he was the winner of the *Mail on Sunday* Novel Competition in 1991. He is married with two grown-up children. He lives in Bridgnorth, Shropshire and works as an architect in Wolverhampton. *Box of Tricks* is his second novel.

Acknowledgements

Many thanks to Tindal Street Press – Alan, Luke and Emma – for their support and belief in this book. I would also like to thank my writing groups in Birmingham and Bridgnorth for responding so well to extracts, often out of context, to Simon Fletcher for his advice and encouragement, to Jim Woods for helping me with research material and to Joy Hockey for so generously sharing her incomparable knowledge of New Brighton. Finally I would like to thank my wife, Maddy, for giving me space to write and a huge amount of quiet faith.

Also available from Tindal Street Press

PAINTER MAN

Jeff Phelps

'Who needs a printed Picasso anyway, when we can have an original Malcolm Eggart?'

Malcolm is the Painter Man, out of step with the art scene but determined to find his place in the landscape. He loves his family but unwittingly isolates himself from them. When his wife turns elsewhere for attention she takes their two children and leaves Malcolm, hanging by a thread, to his restless art and his demons.

Recognition by an enigmatic art buyer is some comfort; but it is only when Suzie, a breezy aromatherapist, enters Malcolm's life that recovery seems possible. Together they track down the mystery of her London ghosts, and Malcolm sees a chance to free himself from his own nightmare – a long-ago accident in a Black Country steel works.

'A thoughtful novel' *Independent on Sunday*

'A perceptive and sensitive study of the breakdown of a marriage. With understated clarity, it analyses the artist as outsider, as observer. Ultimately, this is an uplifting story of the reconstruction of a troubled man through love, set against the bleak and sinister beauty of the Black Country' Clare Morrall

'Astounding . . . [The story of an] obsessive man's attempts to capture and shape his life through his art' *What's On*

'The Black Country is itself as much a character as a setting. Having to develop a new identity, post heavy industry, to come to terms with ghosts from an overbearing past, its story runs parallel to that of all the main characters . . .' *Raw Edge*

ISBN: 978 0 954791 33 9